BOOK ONE OF
THE LAST RIVER SERIES

BY THE BREATH
OF THEIR PEOPLE

BOOK ONE OF
THE LAST RIVER SERIES

BY THE BREATH
OF THEIR PEOPLE

GIL BEAN

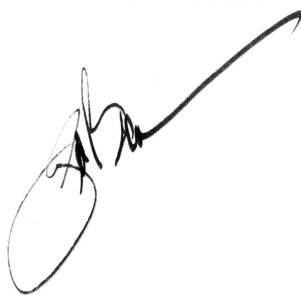

LANGDON STREET PRESS
MINNEAPOLIS, MN

ISBN-13: 978-1-62652-965-6
LCCN: 2014944264

Distributed by Itasca Books

Cover Design by Alan Pranke
Typeset by Jenni Wheeler
Edited by Robert Christian Schmidt

Printed in the United States of America

For Margaret Martin and Lillian Ralph,

with everlasting gratitude.

"Profound is the law of entrance into the production of connected causes."

— Rev. Dr. John F. Lundy,
July 27, 1886

PART ONE

"I have a little boy . . . if he is not dead, tell him that the last words of his father were that he must never go beyond the Father of Waters, but die in the land of his birth. It is sweet to die in one's native land and be buried by the margins of one's native stream."

—Tsali
Cherokee Medicine Man
(awaiting execution, 1838)

Prologue

APRIL 1738

Through the fire of his pain walked the understanding that if he lost consciousness he was going to die.

He looked up into the forest canopy, trying to focus on a portion of a cloud that drifted high above the emerging leaves, but the gathering fluid in his eyes made it impossible. He could hear the sound of the stream as it rushed by only a few yards away, and he knew that he had to reach it.

Pulling himself up onto his elbows, he flattened his palms against the ground, wanting desperately to push himself to a seated position, but the exertion caused the wound in his lower abdomen to gush blood. The front of his shirt and leggings were already black with it. Struggling to stay upright on his elbows and fighting the urge to drift into sleep, he began to talk to the light above the trees.

"Who will remember me?" he asked aloud. "Who will remember . . . ," he sucked in a huge gasp of air against the pain, ". . . that I walked this land?"

He could make out, twenty yards away, the motionless form of the young Iroquois who had attacked him—the Iroquois who had ignored his sign of peace and rushed at him, knife drawn; the Iroquois whom he had killed; the Iroquois who had killed him.

"Who will bury my body?" he asked in little more than a whisper, lifting his eyes toward the clouds once again. "Who will prepare it for its journey to the stars?"

As the words dissipated in the blood that was gathering in the back of his mouth, he managed to turn himself onto his left hip, grimacing from the pain that shot through the other side of his body. Now he could see the water beyond the trees.

"Remember me, Creator. Remember me and the Lenape people." The words echoed through his thoughts as if they were trapped in the current of the rushing stream. *Remember me. Remember my people.* They summoned a final thread of strength, momentarily drawing him away from the touch of death. As his blood seeped through his clothes and onto the ground, a quiet reassurance began to fill him. "Take care of them always." Images of countless weathered faces shot through his mind. "They *are* this land." He pushed himself up onto one knee. "They *are* its children."

Bracing against a tree, he tried to stand, but the crushing agony in his gut stopped him halfway. He stumbled toward the stream, hunched over, pressing a hand against the knife wound. With each pained step, he could feel the slippery wetness of the blood oozing onto the beads of the *wampum* belt at his side.

"They *are* this land," he repeated, blood now spraying in front of his words. "They *are* its people."

The stream, swollen with the spring rains, rushed by at his feet. He wanted to step down into the water—he wanted to wash his wound and slake his searing thirst—but he was too unsteady to try. He dropped to his knees, the impact jolting his midsection and forcing him to cry out in pain. Panting from the exertion, he reached toward the water with his left hand, but it was too far away. He nearly lost his balance, catching himself with both hands on the edge of the bank.

In the current beneath him, he could barely make out the distorted reflection of the crescent amulet that hung from his neck. Its mesmerizing motion filled him with a sense of peace that belied what was happening to him. He imagined that the water was speaking to him, quietly offering peaceful transport to a body no longer able to move on its own. His pain subsiding, but no longer able to stay awake, Walks Alone looked down into the water and silently mouthed the words for the last time: "Remember my people." Then he pitched forward into the timeless rush of the stream.

One

THANKSGIVING 2010

The woman stepped between chairs and took her place in the circle, her year-old daughter in her arms. She seated the child on her lap, bracing her with a forearm so that both of them could see the fire. For a few moments they both watched it quietly, one of them—and perhaps both of them—remembering.

As the woman recalled all too well, the fire pit in front of them had been designed with clear intent. Recessed two feet into the floor, it could accommodate a large, welcoming fire without obstructing the view of people gathered around it, and without impeding their conversation.

Eight feet above the flames, a massive copper hood matched the circumference of the fire pit. It tapered upward into a large cone, eventually feeding into the aluminum flue that rose through the rafters above. Reliefs of animals had been hammered into the copper by a man very skilled at his work, and the woman could picture the artisan's face as she thought about the morning when they had decided where each of the animals would be placed on the hood.

"Where the bear walks, there is wisdom," she could remember her father saying to the small group of people assembled around the table, sorting through cutouts of animals as workers hammered on the roof above them.

The fire danced among a dozen ash logs, the remnants of trees that had been cleared to make room for the house of the woman's sister. She and her husband sat on the other side of the circle, their own child, also a girl, sitting on the floor in front of them. The woman could see the orange reflection of the flames jumping in her niece's eyes.

Everyone was seated in the circle, at least everyone who would sit in it this time. Everyone was there except him.

As she looked at the faces around her, she understood clearly that this was his dream. It would have been easy for an outsider to look at everything beyond the fire pit, beyond this gathering barn, and conclude that all of it was her father's dream. He had envisioned a refuge from the world and had created it as he had seen it in his heart, and it stretched for acres in every direction around the barn. But she knew that all of it was nothing more than a place where his dream could live, and that this circle of people was the real dream that lived there.

As her daughter squirmed restlessly in her arms, the woman stared into the fire and spoke.

"Generations stand behind us as we sit here tonight. They cannot tell their stories, but we can tell their stories for them. We can tell the stories of those we remember, and we can tell ours so that the children among us will remember."

A burning log spit a cluster of sparks into the air. They rose in a flash of orange that exploded into nothingness.

The woman paused, looking into the fire, speaking to whoever might speak next.

"So who would like to begin?"

Two

April 2009
(twenty months earlier)

Jeff Phillips sat on a makeshift log stool by a circular foundation where the brick walks on each side of the main paddock converged. Within a few days, the foundation would support a stone wall that would hold a pool of water and a fountain. He had envisioned a rock sculpture over which water would cascade in all directions, but his vision had not been precise. To the contrary, it had been excitingly malleable, filled with creativity and possibility like everything else here on his land above the river. He knew that the final form of the fountain would reveal itself soon enough, so he felt content in this moment of incompletion. A few feet away, the pipe that would feed the fountain with water stood temporarily exposed, waiting silently to be entombed in darkness.

The morning was clear and cool, full of promise for the trees that were beginning to bud and the perennials that had only just begun to poke green fingers above the soil. Jeff knew that early

April was an unpredictable time in eastern Pennsylvania, and that weather like this could be preceded or followed by just about anything. The previous day had been a good day to work outside, and it looked as if this one would be as well. He smiled at the possibility.

Jeff loved mornings and all of their subtleties. The pre-dawn hours, the first hours of daylight, and even the hours that gave way to midday, each affirmed in their own way that the day was new and waiting eagerly for whatever life he chose to bring to it.

For him, mornings were quiet, meditative times, and this morning held more than its share of reflection. He thought about all that was going on around him, all the newness that was coming into being on his property, on his land. His life was so different than what it had been only a few years earlier. Fate had decreed that numbered Ping-Pong balls would fall into a plastic tube and make of him a wealthy man. He had done nothing to deserve it. He hadn't even meant to buy the lottery ticket. It had just happened. The money had just come to him, along with its blessings and responsibilities. Fate had also insisted that he decide how to use his wealth, just as each new morning waited for the life he would bring to the day, and he had decided to create a place that would belong to his family for all of time.

Off to his left, beyond the fence on the north side of the paddock, Jeff could hear the sound of a door closing, and he knew that Jill was on her way. A few seconds later, she emerged from behind the fence, walking briskly in his direction, her jacket collar turned up against the coolness of the morning.

In the nearby paddock, horses grazed quietly on wet grass, reminding Jeff of the currency he had used to bribe Jill and her husband to leave Florida and move to Pennsylvania. The horses had proven to be irresistible, but he was well aware of just how small a price it had been to pay. Since their arrival, Jill and Edward had overseen the creation of just about everything in the upper meadow, including their own house, the horse barn, and the large oval paddock. They were exactly the foremen he needed for the work that had taken place and all the work that remained. He smiled at the thought of them running things.

As Jill continued toward him, one of the horses, a spotted Saddlebred, caught sight of her and started toward the paddock fence.

"Hey, Bandit," Jeff heard her call out as she extended a closed fist toward the animal. "How are you this morning?" She rubbed her other hand down the length of his face as she opened her fist to reveal a halved apple. The horse took it from her flattened palm effortlessly.

As the other three horses moved toward the fence, she pulled pieces of apples and carrots from the pocket of her jacket, greeting and feeding them one by one. They bumped at each other, vying for her attention, but she was all too experienced at ensuring that each got its share.

Jeff watched his daughter from a distance. Her 5'3" frame supported a body that wasn't naturally fit—it had to forge fitness from exercise and hard work—but she had the presence of a woman who was born to be outside. She radiated the very elements to which she had become so accustomed. He remembered well that even as a very young child she had always balked at coming into the house. He could picture her standing in the yard protesting, her dirty hands and mussed blond hair in need of attention after an afternoon at play. In later times, when divorce had kept him from seeing her whenever he wanted to—whenever he *needed* to—he had often remembered her as that young child. Now she was about to have a child of her own. She had only just found out that she was expecting, and it would be months before her pregnancy was obvious, but as she walked toward him, he wondered if his grandchild would love the outdoors as much as its mother did.

"Hey, Dad," Jill said as she approached. "What are you doing up here? I thought you'd be down in the greenhouse getting stuff ready to move into the flowerbeds."

"I was down there earlier," he answered, "before sunup."

"You're allowed to sleep in, you know." But even as she said it, she knew that it was a wasted observation. He never slept in. Even if he went to bed late or got up in the middle of the night to write, he always woke up early.

"I want to build a barn," he said, almost as if he hadn't heard her comment, "over where the tractor shed sits."

"A barn? What for? There's plenty of room in the horse barn. There's extra room for hay and feed, and we can add at least five more stalls, if that's what you have in mind." She grinned at the thought. "Are you planning to buy more horses?"

"Not that kind of barn. I want a meeting place, a place for our family to gather . . ." He paused and looked over his shoulder toward the tractor shed. ". . . a place for people to gather. A place for birthday parties and wedding receptions, a place where we can dance."

She had no intention of challenging him. She knew that he had already seen it in a vision or dream, probably more than once, possibly before she was even born. That was how all of this had started. She remembered how he used to talk about the house that he saw in his dreams, how he used to describe each of its rooms, how he used to draw pictures of it. He was always so sure that he would build it, but he never had the money to do much more than dream about it. Now it stood two hundred yards to the east of them on the other side of the creek.

"Describe it for me," she said, looking across the field toward the tractor shed.

He looked at her and smiled. This was his oldest child, and she had grown to understand him perfectly, perhaps because she was so much like him.

"Big place," he began, "with a high pitched roof and open rafters. There are windows the entire length of each side, something like a church. A lot of open space inside, plenty of room for tables and chairs."

He paused, turning his face slightly, as if looking at a different part of the building he was describing.

"There's a kitchen at one end with an apartment above it. Guests can stay there, but I see it more as a place where the kids can stay when they're home from school."

"Guests?" she asked, gently poking at his vision. "What about the bedrooms in the main house, and what about the Creek House? And . . . ," she paused, as if processing something he had said, ". . . and what kids are you talking about? Valeria won't be four until next month. This one," she added, placing a hand on her abdomen, "isn't even born yet."

"There's a stage at the other end," he continued without answering her questions, describing it as if he had stood upon it many times.

"A stage?"

"I'm not sure what it's for. Maybe the band." His face broke into another smile. Then he paused and looked once again toward the tractor shed. "At first I saw a huge stone fireplace at that end, but over time I saw a stage." Turning to face her again, he added, "Nowadays, I see a stage."

"What happened to the fireplace?"

"I don't know. I just see a stage."

He paused for a few moments, as if looking for something, as if searching for it behind the door to an unseen room.

"The guys will be here soon to start laying the stones," he resumed, turning toward the pipe in the middle of the foundation. "Maybe you and I can take a walk over to the tractor shed after they get started."

In the paddock behind them, one of the horses startled and galloped toward the tree line at the back of the meadow. The other horses followed. They settled almost as quickly as they had jumped, finding new grass to graze on.

"I'll be back in a little while," Jill said, continuing on her way to meet the men who would work on the fountain. As she left, she continued silently to herself, "And I'll leave you alone to find the fireplace."

* * *

In the main house, up in the big front bedroom that overlooked what they called "the lower meadow," Dae Phillips had awakened from a dream. Her eyes fixed on the yellow line painted on the far wall by the sunlight that squeezed through a narrow opening in the curtains behind her. Rolling slowly onto her back, she re-traced the path of the light up the wall and across the ceiling toward its source, as if she were looking for an alternate route on some celestial map.

Her dreams had been troubling lately and this one had been no exception. Deep within it, she had been fully aware that she was dreaming and had tried to wake up, but the dream had held her, ensuring that she would remember it.

And she did remember it. First Jeff's mother had appeared to her, standing stoically a few feet away. The woman didn't look like Jeff's mother—and Dae had seen many photographs of her—but Dae knew it was her. She said nothing; she just stood there looking straight into Dae's eyes. Suddenly aware that she was dreaming and not knowing if she wanted to stay or leave, Dae closed her eyes. When she opened them, her own father was standing next to Jeff's mother and others were standing with them. Some were familiar to her; others were not.

Her father's presence made her want to stay, and she reached out to him. He smiled softly but said nothing.

This was a peaceful place, a reassuring place, so why did she feel such ambivalence? Why was she so compelled to both stay with these people and leave? She felt something brush across her face, awaking in the same moment to push the buttoned edge of the duvet away. She lay still, thinking that she might lapse back into her dream, but she knew that neither sleep nor dreams would return this morning.

"How did I know it was Jeff's mother?" she whispered to herself. The woman had died years before Dae and her husband had met. "How did I know?" she repeated to herself. "What about her did I recognize?"

The line of sunlight continued its slow descent down the wall.

"And what were my father and the others doing there?"

As Dae got out of bed, she reached for the robe thrown across the chair a few feet away. These were good mornings. The darkness of the short days of winter was gone, but it was still cool enough to need a robe. And April mornings could be bright, as this one was, alive with the promise that spring was about to return again.

She walked over to the huge window on the east side of the room and drew open the curtains, squinting at the sunlight that greeted her. The landscape sprawled before her in the brilliant greens of a manicured lawn and the rough browns and grays of the lower meadow, separated by a three-foot stone wall a hundred feet from the house. The meadow was only beginning to emerge from dormancy, its wildflowers and thistle still in hiding, but Dae knew that within the month the meadow would be alive with an ecosystem that had thrived on this land for thousands of years, an ecosystem created by the river that flowed off to the east.

The Delaware River was wide and imposing this far north, and in the spring it rushed impatiently, dangerously, toward a more tranquil destiny in the bay that waited for it more than a hundred miles to the south. Dae watched in awe as the sun began to push its way above the still-leafless trees on the far edge of the meadow. In her mind, she could see the terrain beyond. A long wooded hill rushed down to the river from the tree line. A road edged along the base of the hill, flanked by a canal that traced a nearly perfect path between the road and the river. Somewhere inside, she felt both the beauty that she could see and the beauty that lay far beyond her view. She didn't say, "beautiful;" she didn't even think it; she just felt it.

Almost forcing herself to turn away, Dae saw a tablet of paper lying on the chair where her robe had been. It hadn't been there when she and Jeff had gone to bed, so she knew immediately that he had been writing in the early hours of the morning. Reading glasses and a pen lay on the nightstand on the other side of the chair, confirming what she knew. She pulled back the two pages that had been turned over the top of the tablet. On the first, she found partial lines and half stanzas, words crossed out and other words inserted above them, and occasional hash marks noting meter. She knew immediately that this poem had not come easily. The idea had probably come to him in an instant, perhaps in a dream or in a vision from the netherworld of semi-consciousness, but the words had lagged behind the idea. She knew that he both loved and was frustrated by that place where words would not keep pace with inspiration, because for him it was the cradle of creation.

The second page was more of the same but less scattered, less confused. The maelstrom of edits had given way to increasing order. On the bottom half of the page lay sixteen lines of Jeff's poetry.

> When do they stop, these raw, unfinished things—
> These things that neither rest nor take a breath,
> That feel not the need to sleep or dream,
> And haunt each day of life, each night of death?

What dreams fulfilled will let me rise above
The stabbing at my soul these troubles bring?
What threshold must I cross to realize
Redemption from their sharp and constant sting?

The body finds its rest, the mind its peace,
When time is full and wandering complete,
But Spirit journeys on through space and time,
And takes along what it cannot defeat.

If being inside out and upside down
Is insufficient penance for this life,
May now the twisting and the shredding start—
The carving of this soul beneath the knife.

Dae breathed deeply, trying to take in the meaning of the words. Then she read them again. There was no one on earth that she knew better than she knew Jeff, and still she found herself capable of wondering, "Who is this man I love?"

Anyone who knew her husband probably believed that he had everything he could possibly want—everything that anyone could possibly want—but Dae understood that there are things that transcend wanting and having, things that cannot be achieved through hard work or clever politics, or even the generosity of fate. Some people compete in an internal game that cannot be won or lost because it never ends.

Dae flipped the two pages over, revealing the page that had caught her eye originally. On it were eight lines. The last stanza was written out in full, but the third line had been struck through.

The stanza was re-written immediately below with a new third line inserted.

> If being inside out and upside down
> Is insufficient penance for this life,
> Then let the cutting and the slicing start—
> The carving of this soul beneath the knife.

Dae had never pretended to fully grasp many of Jeff's poems, and she wasn't sure that she even wanted to grasp this one, but she knew that with this modification he wasn't allowing the dissection of his soul, he was inviting it. Life had given him everything a man could want, but some unconquered demon deep within him was still shaking its fist at heaven.

The sun crested above the trees that lined the distant river and pressed into the room.

* * *

Halfway between her father and the main house, Jill walked downhill to a footbridge that crossed a wide creek bed and a disproportionately narrow creek. There was a time, she imagined, that the upper and lower meadows were heavily wooded and the creek cut a more imposing path between them, but that was long ago and all that remained now was a peaceful country stream.

A few yards off to Jill's left sat the Creek House, a place that her father had added for special guests. A small, two-bedroom bungalow, it reminded Jill of something out of a Tolkien story, sitting close to the creek, protected in almost constant shade and coolness, even in the heart of summer. She and her husband had lived in it while they were building their house on the upper meadow, and she had always loved the wonderful perspectives it provided. She carried vivid memories of the sounds that came through the screens in the bedroom windows—the soft gurgling of water at night, the joyful music of songbirds in the morning.

As she climbed the short hill on the other side of the creek, Jill could see Dae standing at one of the screened windows of the sunroom, a mug of coffee clutched in her hand.

"Morning, Dae," she called, waving a hand above her head.

When Jill thought about the main house, she always pictured the view she was seeing now. It was quietly grand, blending into a gentle hillside that rose another thirty feet above the creek before leveling into the lower meadow. On the lowest level was a greenhouse that extended out from the foundation, its pitched roof of glass panes extending twelve feet up the wall. High above it were the screened windows of the sunroom that extended across most of the back of the house.

"Hi, Jill," came the response. "Want a cup of coffee?"

"No, thanks. Gotta meet the work crew. We're going to work on the fountain today."

"What's it like out this morning? Will I need a sweatshirt?"

"Nope, it's perfect. I'd take a whole year of mornings like this." Jill paused about halfway through the yard. "C'mon up later. We can talk about what kind of water plants to put in the fountain." Then she added, "And, besides, you'll want to hear about the new barn."

"What's wrong with the one we have?" Dae asked.

"Not that kind of barn," she answered, mimicking her father perfectly. She smiled and turned toward the drive that led down to the service road from the house.

Dae knew that no further explanation was required. She shook her head, smiled, and raised the coffee mug to her lips.

* * *

Still seated on the makeshift stool by the fountain, Jeff Phillips winced as his lungs involuntarily sucked in a huge gasp of air. It always began with his breath, and it didn't matter what he was doing—working in the greenhouse or somewhere on the grounds; writing or doing research in his office; exercising in the workout room; or just sitting quietly as he was now—it came when it was ready to come. It even came in the middle of dreams.

He would inhale violently, as if someone was standing behind him, reaching through his chest and drawing back into him more air than his lungs could possibly hold. It had been happening for years, thirty—maybe thirty-five—of them, and over time it had grown increasingly uncomfortable. Sometimes, like this time, it was painful.

The infusions of air were preambles to what Jeff had come to think of as transcendence. With each of them came an experience that few people would understand or care to understand. Jeff didn't know if even he understood them, but he had stopped fearing them. He had come to accept them as part of who he was, just as his heart and brain were parts of who he was.

As he rose from the stool, the temperature dropped dramatically. The air that had been filled with the coolness of a spring morning was suddenly consumed by the chill of a night that hung on the front edge of winter. It was dark in the upper meadow and the wind panted in gusts that made Jeff pull up the collar of his jacket.

The fountain was finished, but it looked different than the one he had envisioned, and he was surprised to see that the water had not been drained for the coming winter. Through the leafless trees, Jeff could see the lights of the Creek House below, as well as those of the main house on the hill beyond. Then, turning to his left, he saw it—the new barn, the gathering barn that he had seen so many times after a rush of air had transported him to this altered state.

Walking toward the barn, he recognized the unmistakable smell of hardwood smoke as it rose above the roof and into the late autumn drear. He knew that the flames below were high and well fed because the white plumes rose easily into a black humidity that would have repressed a lesser fire.

"Something like a church," he said to himself as he approached the windows on the meadow side of the building. "Something like a church." Inside, in the middle of the building, a group of people were gathered in a circle around a fire that seemed to rise out of the floor, its orange fingers straining toward the massive copper hood suspended above.

Jill sat with her back to him, her unmistakable silhouette framed by the firelight. She appeared preoccupied with something on her lap, and he knew instantly that his grandchild was the focus of her preoccupation. To Jill's right sat her husband, Edward, his own attention drawn toward someone to his right. Across the circle sat Hope, his second daughter, and Scott, her husband. Their daughter, Valeria, sat on the floor in front of them. On

Hope's right sat Jeff's youngest child, Harry, apparently home from school. *Thanksgiving*, Jeff thought to himself.

Between Harry and Jill sat a man and a woman whom Jeff did not recognize. He somehow knew that they were a couple, perhaps, he thought to himself, because of the quiet dignity they seemed to share. Across from them, their faces illuminated by the light of the fire, sat one of Jeff's nephews and his wife. Their two children sat in front of them, staring into the fire pit. Next to them sat Jeff's sister, Chick, and her husband, Wade. Chick's eyes were watching the fire, but they seemed transfixed on something far beyond, and she was talking.

To Wade's left, Dae sat quietly. He could barely see the back of her head, but when Edward leaned toward Jill to whisper something, Jeff saw Dae's profile clearly. Like the others, she was listening to Chick.

As he stood watching, Jeff understood that just about everything he loved was sitting around that fire. And he understood something else, something obvious that he had instinctively tried to repress. He was not with them. He was not there. The reality of it rose into the dark November air, unable to be held back, like the white smoke from the roaring fire in the center of the gathering barn.

* * *

Walks Alone was facedown in the water, his body moving on the swift current of the stream. He was confused. His lungs should have been filled with water, but instead he was breathing calmly.

Suddenly, two hands reached beneath his arms and lifted him to a standing position. The current under his feet felt solid and stable, as smooth as the face of a polished river stone. He opened his eyes and found himself face to face with another Lenape man, a man whose face was filled with kindness and love, a man whose eyes were filled with light. None of this made sense to Walks Alone but, for some reason that he could not grasp, it didn't seem to matter.

The man who stood before him, his hands now bracing Walks Alone's shoulders, was his age, maybe younger. He looked comfortably familiar to Walks Alone, like someone he had seen in a good dream.

"Who are you?" he asked.

"I am Black Turtle," the man said softly. "Your father."

Walks Alone jerked backward, not believing what he was hearing, yet knowing that it was true. He pulled away from the man, instinctively bracing himself against his inevitable fall into the water, but he didn't fall. He just stood there, the swollen stream rushing beneath his feet.

"You are with us now," Black Turtle said calmly, trying to reassure his son. His dark, soft eyes looked straight at Walks Alone as he reached out a hand to him.

"Us?"

"Yes. All of us."

Then, as if they had been there from the beginning, countless Lenape stood behind Black Turtle. Some of them stood upon the water, others on the banks of the stream, and still others in the trees beyond. They all shared the same stillness, the same obvious peace that surrounded Black Turtle.

"We are the answer to your questions," Black Turtle offered, "the questions you asked in your lifetime. You were raised by the others because your mother was not there . . ." He paused, taking his son's hand. ". . . because I was not there. But all of us are here now."

"I was afraid that there would be nothing here," Walks Alone said softly, surrendering to the truth that was overtaking him, "just as I often felt there was nothing back there."

"Both may be nothing," his father answered. "And both may be everything. It's not for us to know."

He drew Walks Alone closer and hugged him, holding his son as if a single embrace could make up for those that had never been given, for those that had never been felt. Safe in his father's arms, Walks Alone closed his eyes and took in a deep breath.

When he opened them, his attention was drawn to a young woman who stood farther downstream, apart from everyone else. No more than seventeen, she was dressed differently than the other women. She didn't seem to belong and yet he felt a strong connection to her. She held her arms out in front of her, the palms of her hands turned down as the body of a young Lenape man drifted past. The man was facedown in the current, his long, dark scalplock floating on the water behind his head. Walks Alone watched the scene with a strange detachment until the body disappeared from view.

Three

JULY 1727
(ELEVEN YEARS EARLIER)

Walks Alone stood quietly beside the entrance of the lodgehouse, his head tilted slightly, peeking in. It was a large building, higher than the *wigwams* in the village and more than a hundred feet in length. With skins hung across the openings in the bark walls, including a smaller entrance at the far end, the interior was cool and dark. On the wall to the right, a line of sunlight cut between the edges of two deerskins and stretched across the dirt floor toward the middle of the building.

The young Lenape, now in his ninth year, had been in the lodgehouse many times, and he had become increasingly fascinated with it. The other boys in the clan stayed away from this place, except when they came with their parents for meetings, or in times of festival and celebration. Walks Alone often wondered why they seemed so intimidated by it, since he felt as if he belonged here.

The boy squinted into the vastness of the lodgehouse, trying to see all the way to the other end, but what would have been easy if the skins had been drawn aside to let in the sunlight was impossible in the darkness they now secured. In the middle of the building, he could make out the stout wooden poles that stretched from floor to ceiling, and he knew that the face was carved in one of them, watching over the huge fire pit where the people of the village gathered to dance and sing. Neither the pit, with its black residue of countless fires, nor the stoic face on the pole ever changed, although it was easy for a young boy to imagine that they might; they just waited, fixed in time, while everything beyond the walls of the lodgehouse changed around them.

"What are you doing, Young One?" a voice asked from behind, startling Walks Alone. He jerked around to see the face of an old woman.

The boy looked up at her nervously. He tried to speak, but was unable to manage anything more than a quick burst of incoherent sounds.

"It's alright," she assured him. "I know why you're here."

Walks Alone had no idea what she meant. He didn't know why he was there, except that it felt good to him. So how could she know?

Placing a hand on the boy's shoulder, she gently turned him to face the open entrance to the lodgehouse. "What you seek is not out here," she said, leading him into the stillness of the building.

As they walked into the lodgehouse, Walks Alone's pulse quickened with the things that touched his senses. The interior was cool, as if it were immune to the effects of the summer sun beyond its walls. His eyes adjusting to being inside, the boy could now see the far end of the building. The space was at the same time welcoming and daunting, and he was confused by the ambivalence it inspired in him.

As they neared the fire pit, the lingering smell of long-burned-out fires rose up to meet them. It permeated everything—the wooden pole; the skins in the nearby openings; and the rocks in the pit. It hung in the air like an invisible sentry that would not be driven from its post.

"Do you feel the Great Spirit?" the woman asked the boy. "This place is filled with it."

Walks Alone looked at her quizzically. He knew what the Great Spirit was—for as far back as he could remember, stories about all of the spirits that watched over the Lenape had been a part of his life—but he wasn't sure how something unseen could fill a place as big as the lodgehouse.

"The Great Spirit is in everything . . . ," the woman continued, ". . . everything that is. It's in the ground we walk on; it's in the sky above us." She looked straight into the boy's eyes and was pleased that he did not look away. "When you breathe in, you take it into your lungs, and when you exhale, you send it back into the world.

"It's in your best friend, Young One, but it's also in your worst enemy. It's in your heart when it feels warm, as well as when it feels cold; when it loves and when it is less than loving."

She paused, giving the boy time to absorb what she had said. "It is with you always," she continued, "because it was here before you were here and it will be here long after you are not." She could see that the child was trying to grasp the meaning of the abstractions. "Do you understand?"

"I think so," the boy offered, feeling as if her gaze was passing straight through his head. The woman was talking as if they had been together like this before, but the only time he had ever been alone with her was when he was much younger and very sick with fever. He had seen her many times, but not every day like the way he saw his aunt and uncle. "Well no, not exactly," he added pensively. "Not exactly."

"What you feel when you come here," the woman said, "is the Great Spirit. It's very strong in a place like this." She paused before adding, "Or maybe we're just more aware of it in a place like this. Our people feel it here, even the children, but you feel it more than most."

"Me?" the boy asked. "Why?"

"Because, in some ways, it is all you have. It is all you have had for most of your life. For more than five winters now, you have been without your father. The others have taken you in, and that is as it should be. Looks Back and Talks For Us have become your parents, but you have still been alone in many ways, even with so many looking out for you."

"Is that why I am called Walks Alone?"

"In part." She wanted to tell him that the name described the journey of his heart as much as the journey of his body, but she let the impulse subside.

"And what was I called before that?"

"Something that suited you less." The words felt painful in her throat. She knew all too well that any name other than the one he had would have suited him less.

"You are like this lodgehouse," she said, her head moving slowly from side to side, "you are both full and empty at the same time. And any Lenape would struggle with that."

Although he didn't understand her words, Walks Alone felt reassured by the way in which she said them. He knew in his heart that she wanted to help him—that she was helping him—but he didn't know why. He knew that she was an important person, a woman who was respected by the people of his village and other villages along the river. Some even feared her. She didn't do the same things that the other women and the girls did. She didn't gather firewood or prepare skins, and he had never seen her cooking food—not even for herself. But when it was time to sing and dance and drum she was always in the middle of the celebration, she was always in a place of honor. The boy knew that her attention was a special gift, but he didn't know how to react to it.

"Come with me, Young One," she said, taking his hand. They walked a few steps to the edge of the fire pit, where she lowered herself onto the hard dirt floor, crossing her legs beneath her. She pulled on Walks Alone's hand, silently instructing him to do likewise. He sat down next to her, looking into the black pit.

"What do you think about when you come here?" the old woman asked. "What were you thinking about when I found you at the entrance?"

"The celebrations," came his reply. "I love it when everyone in the village and people from other villages are here together. I can never stay awake long enough. Sometimes I fall asleep during the drumming, and when I wake up the drumming is still going on."

"Me too," she said. "I love the celebrations, and these old eyes sometimes fall asleep too. But that will have to be our secret."

Walks Alone smiled at the thought.

"What else do you think about?"

"Him," the boy answered, looking up at the face carved into the pole. Half black and half red, it stared out above their heads toward the entrance to the lodgehouse.

"Do you know who he is?"

"He is Meesing." The boy paused before adding, "The provider for our people."

"And do you know how he became our provider?"

Walks Alone stared at the face but said nothing.

"One day," the woman began, "Meesing confronted the Great Spirit, claiming that they were equal in power. 'I see,' answered the Great Spirit. 'Would you like to have a contest to see if we are equal?' Eager to prove himself, Meesing agreed. 'Let's see who can move that mountain the farthest,' said the Great Spirit, pointing to a huge mountain on the horizon. Meesing tried to move the mountain, but it was too massive. He gave up after a few minutes, gasping for air and hanging his head in fatigue. When he looked up, the mountain hit him squarely in the face, tossed effortlessly by the Great Spirit.

"Realizing that he had been defeated, Meesing asked if could make up for his insolence through an act of service. The Great Spirit accepted his offer, suggesting that he become the provider for the Lenape. Since then, he has given the Lenape the animals, the birds, and the fish that are so important to our existence. He gives us the earth with its plants and the sky with its sun and rain. We are sustained by all that he gives us so we honor him and give him thanks. We celebrate his generosity."

"I have seen Talks For Us honor him," the boy said eagerly, "when he offers tobacco to the winds after he has killed a deer."

"Talks For Us is wise," the old woman said. "His gift makes Meesing smile and inspires him to provide even more."

An extended silence fell between them. The long-latent mother in the woman wanted to comfort the child and let him know that it was okay to say whatever he wanted to say, but the shaman in her knew that they were drifting toward that transcendent ether between this boy's unique need to understand and her singular ability to provide that understanding. She sat quietly, allowing it to envelop them.

"Why am I . . . ?" the boy started, before letting his question evaporate back into the silence.

"Why are you what?" she asked, knowing full well what he was about to ask, and knowing equally well that some questions must be carefully pondered, even by children, because once they are answered they can never be otherwise.

"Why am I here?"

"Here in the lodgehouse?" It was painful to test the boy, but she knew it was necessary.

"No. Why am I *here*? I remember my father's face, but each day I see it less clearly. I cannot remember my mother at all. Sometimes, after the others are asleep, I try to remember her but I cannot. I cannot see her face, even in my dreams."

"Looks Back is your mother now, and Talks For Us your father. And Quiet Bird, is she not your sister?"

"Yes, and I try to be a good son to them, and a good brother to Quiet Bird, but . . ."

"But what?"

"But I call Talks For Us 'Uncle.' And when the other children recite the names of their ancestors I say only that I am the adopted son of Looks Back."

The old woman took a deep breath, drawing the air down into her belly before exhaling it slowly. The human being sitting next to her was a child, and she knew that within the hour he would be outside playing with the other boys or asking Looks Back about this encounter in the lodgehouse, but the spirit within him was much older and far wiser, and it was beginning to stir with a restlessness that would not be quieted easily. She drew in another breath, letting the pungent smell of the fire pit penetrate deeply into her nose, and began to speak. "For as long as people have been here in this place, *our people* have been here in this place. . . ."

* * *

Jill Martin walked away from the main house on the road that ran along the east side of the creek. Less than a quarter of a mile up ahead, the road curved gently to cut straight across the creek before continuing up the hill and out to the highway.

Within a few minutes she could see the bridge up ahead on the right. It was a more imposing structure than the footbridge by the Creek House, having been built to support the construction equipment that had moved to and from the site of the main house. Heavy concrete pilings anchored the corners and supported the metal I-beams that, in turn, supported the bridge. Laid across the beams and secured on each end by huge bolts, thick rough-hewn planks formed the bridge's surface, the outside edges of which were bordered by low railings fashioned from four-by-fours. The bridge was much more than what was required to span the quiet creek that ran beneath it, but the banks of the creek were steeper here than they were down by the Creek House. Heavy construction equipment would never have made it back and forth to the site of the main house over a less-substantial structure. She heard the rumbling of the big truck a few seconds before it appeared at the fork of the service road above the opposite bank of the creek. As it turned toward her and down to the bridge, she could see the three-man crew seated in its cab. The man sitting on the passenger side of the truck raised his hand in greeting, a toothy grin spreading across his face. Jill paused as the truck rumbled across the bridge and jerked to a stop.

"*Buenos dias*," the man on the passenger side said as he opened the door. "*¿Es un hermoso dia, no?*"

"*Buenos dias*, Roberto," Jill answered. "Yes, a very beautiful day."

As the other two members of the crew jumped out of the truck, Roberto pointed at the first and said, "*Este es mi primo Hernando . . . ,*" and then at the driver, saying, "*. . . y este es mi primo Felix.*"

"*Buenos dias*," Jill nodded, acknowledging each of them in turn. "*Me llamo* Jill Martin." Then she laughed and added, "*Y tengo muchos primos, pero no tengo tantos primos como Roberto.*"

"Mees Jill," Roberto smiled, gently wagging an index finger at her, "your Spanish is still very good, and yes, I have many more cousins than you."

"*Gracias, Roberto pero solia hablar major.*"

"I do not know how good eet used to be, Mees Jill, but eet is very good now. So, are we headed down to the point?"

"Yes," Jill answered. "I'm going to walk. I'll meet you down there."

"I'll walk with you," he suggested, motioning to his cousins to take the truck on ahead. A few seconds later, it was rumbling through the field on the east side of the creek.

As they walked, the ground in front of Jill and Roberto began to narrow toward a point where the creek bed dropped through the tree line and down the hillside toward the river. The terrain grew increasingly rocky as they neared the tree line, a harbinger of the rugged path the creek had cut on its ancient journey across the land. When the creek was high in the spring, the water cascaded over the rocks and down toward the river in countless billows of white and blue. In drier months, it snaked its way between the rocks in quiet ribbons of green.

Up ahead, Roberto's cousins were waiting by the side of the truck. In front of them lay an area where different natural materials had been set aside after being excavated or cleared to make room for the buildings on the property and the paddock that occupied the upper meadow. Hundreds of trees, most of them no more than six or seven inches in diameter, had been shaved of their branches and piled in the field. They waited silently for whatever use they would be put to eventually, even if it was only as firewood. Huge mounds of soil were piled nearby, as were hundreds of big rocks that had been separated according to their general shapes. The area was neat and orderly, resembling the yard of a home improvement center more than the dump it could have easily become. Like her father, Jill knew that everything here had a purpose, even if that purpose had not yet been revealed.

Jill walked over to a large pile of flat rocks. "Most of this is shale," she said to Roberto, "but I think it would be good for the fountain."

"*Si*," Roberto answered, lifting one of the rocks from the front of the pile. "We can make these look very good." He motioned to Hernando and Felix, who started sifting through the pile. One by one, they lifted the rocks while Jill and Roberto examined them carefully. The ones that seemed best suited for the project at hand were loaded onto the open bed of the truck; the others were returned to the back of the pile.

It took about an hour to pick out the two hundred rocks that would be moved up to the site of the fountain. When they were finished, Roberto walked over to Felix and explained what he wanted the two men to do with the load of rocks. He spoke in very rapid Spanish, some of which Jill could not understand, but his hand motions were unmistakable. He was telling them to go back across the bridge and, once they reached the top of the far bank, take the right onto the portion of the service road that led to the upper meadow. Then he put his hand on Felix's shoulder and, making an exaggerated gesture with his left hand, said very slowly, "*Ten cuidado te acerques el puente. El angulo es muy fuerte.*" He said the last part slowly enough for Jill to understand him clearly—"The angle is very sharp."—and she knew that he was talking about the turn back across the bridge.

"*Si*," Jill confirmed, "*muy fuerte.*"

"*Si, si,*" Felix nodded as he jumped up into the cab of the truck.

Roberto and Jill started walking back toward the main house as the two men drove away. They were about halfway back to the bridge, talking about the design of the fountain, when they heard the crash.

* * *

In the pre-dawn hours, Walks Alone stirred in his sleep. He dreamt of his time in the lodgehouse with the old woman, listening to her talk about the things she seemed to know so much about: the Great Spirit, Meesing, the origins of the Lenape. She sat facing the fire pit; he sat on the floor by her side. He was transfixed by her words, even the ones he did not understand.

As they sat there, everything around them began to change. A fire began to rise in the fire pit as if it had been there all along, as if, through some will of its own, it had never burned out completely. It cast its flickering orange shadow on the carved face of Meesing. Sitting ten deep around the fire pit, hundreds of Lenape filled the center of the lodgehouse. There were more of them than Walks Alone had ever seen in the lodgehouse for any celebration, and they were listening to the words the old woman was saying. They were listening intently—even the children.

Then the woman stood, picked up a skin drum that lay at her feet, and began to tap it with one hand. The sound was barely audible. If people had been talking it wouldn't have been heard at all, but no one was talking. They were listening to the low staccato of the drumming. Thump, thump, thump—a simple repetitive beat like the sound of a strong and steady rain on the outside of a wigwam. Thump, thump, thump.

Men and women began to rise to their feet, clapping their hands and moving their feet to the beat of the drum. Two or three of the huge logs that had been stacked on end to form the fire collapsed inward, sending a bright cloud of crackling sparks into the air. A handful of voices whooped in response.

The woman increased her drumming—thump-thump, thump-thump, thump-thump—and the clapping of hands and moving of feet increased with it. The pulse of the lodgehouse quickened as the blood of hundreds of hearts began to course in unison.

Somewhere beyond the circle, a massive floor drum suddenly matched the old woman's cadence, followed almost immediately by smaller floor drums on the circle's periphery. They kept time with a dozen repetitions of the double beat before one of them transitioned into something more complex, more compelling. The others followed suit, matching the beat and amplifying the sound until it consumed everything and everyone. Men dressed in breechclouts moved in a circle to the rhythm of the drumming, their shaved heads and tattooed necks glistening with sweat in the firelight. Outside of their circle, women danced in a circle in the opposite direction, their braids and necklaces flying with each step. Another circle of men danced beyond the circle of women, and yet another circle of women danced beyond the men. Some sang, some yelled, and some howled as if possessed by animals calling to a distant moon from the black night of the forest. They yielded completely until the fire in their souls burned as hotly as the fire in the middle of the lodgehouse. Utterly beyond inhibition, they moved their bodies and raised their voices in a euphoric frenzy.

Each of his senses inundated with what was going on around him, Walks Alone drifted into a euphoria of his own. Then he felt a hand on his shoulder and opened his eyes to see Talks For Us standing above him.

The man raised a finger to his lips. "Don't wake the others," he said. "It's time for us to go."

His head still buzzing with the images of his dream, the boy rose onto his elbows and slowly looked around the inside of the small dwelling where he lived. It was dark except for a dull orange glow in the circle of stones in the middle of the floor and the first hint of daylight around the edges of the skin that hung in the entrance. On the other side of the wigwam, he could see the sleeping forms of Looks Back, the wife of Talks For Us, and Quiet Bird, their four-year-old daughter. The ground beneath them was covered with woven reeds, as was the rest of the interior of the bark-covered wigwam.

Across the room, clay jars and woven baskets rested on low wooden platforms. One basket was filled with dried corn, another with beans. A third sat empty, still giving off the sweet fragrance of the strawberries that had filled it only a few weeks earlier. Walks Alone had learned to recognize the smell as one of the pleasures of early summer, and he was sorry that the season of the berries had passed. Above the jars hung a small amount of dried rabbit meat and some tied leaves of tobacco.

Pushing aside the coarse blanket that covered him, Walks Alone rose to his feet. He secured his breechclout with its leather cord and stepped barefoot into the summer morning. Talks For Us waited thirty yards away, his back to the woods that separated the village and the river.

As Walks Alone walked toward the man he called Uncle, he was aware of how much he admired him, how much he wanted to be like him. Talks For Us stood quietly, looking back toward the boy, a small basket in his hand. In some ways he was much like the other men in the village—he had adopted some of the dress of the whites who were so common in the area, including the amulet that he wore around his neck—but in other ways he was unique, somehow less touched by the outside world. He avoided the alcohol that the other men traded for so freely, simply because his father had avoided it, as had his father before him. He had often told Walks Alone that the whites were inevitable and that the Unami way of life was dying, but he saw no reason to embrace either reality. In the momentary world that always marks the boundary between night and day, his sinewy body looked like little more than a shadow to the boy, but even at his young age Walks Alone believed that his uncle was a better man in shadow than most of the other men were in the full light of day.

"Do you think there will be many fish, Uncle?" Walks Alone asked as he approached.

"Maybe," came the reply. "The river is low now, and the day becomes hot more quickly. Whatever fish we are going to catch are already in the trap. We should go."

Passing quietly through the strange combination of wigwams and cabins that comprised the village, they walked toward the river. Cabins had come with the Europeans, and some Lenape had embraced them. Some had even built fences around them, a practice that Walks Alone found curious. Moving past one of the cabins, the boy and his uncle stepped into the edge of the woods. Over time, most of the brush and fallen trees had been removed from the periphery of the village and the walk was unencumbered and easy, but they soon moved into an area that was more overgrown and most easily traveled on the well-worn paths that cut through it. In some places, even these were partially obstructed by overhanging branches and wiry undergrowth, and walking them in low light could result in cuts and scratches or a poked eye.

They had covered only a few hundred yards of the half mile between the village and the river when Talks For Us stopped, reaching out his hand and placing it against Walks Alone's chest. The boy looked up to see his uncle's other hand placed against his mouth, understanding immediately his silent command to be still.

Less than a hundred yards to the south burned the dull glow of a campfire, the form of a man crouching behind it. As the boy and his uncle watched, the fire grew brighter, an indication that the man was adding wood to it. Within a few seconds it was brighter still—a confirmation that the man was European. Walks Alone understood that no Unami, not even one who had been seduced by the ways of white men, would build such a fire unless it was for a celebration in the lodgehouse. It was more than what was required to either cook or fend off the chill of morning.

Talks For Us knew that, although there was no immediate danger, it was wise to proceed quietly. There were many different kinds of people in the area these days—native, light-skinned whites, dark-skinned whites, and blacks—and it was prudent to be cautious, especially when one was alone or with children. They walked on quietly. A few minutes later, they came to a place where the path became rocky and dropped down a short hill to the river. It was a more difficult walk, especially in the early morning light, but they had made it many times.

"Were they German, Uncle?"

"Probably." Then, after a long pause, he added, "Maybe English, but most likely German. There are too many of both these days." He admitted silently that, for him at least, there had never been a time when there weren't too many whites. "Probably German," he repeated.

At the riverbank, Walks Alone stopped momentarily to look down into the water as it flowed by ten feet below and at least twenty feet away. He had seen the river lower than this, but not often, and he knew that in the rainy seasons the water would only be a few feet below where he was now standing. Although he knew that it was always dangerous because of its swift currents and unpredictable eddies, it seemed less so on this summer morning. As he gazed down into it, the river seemed uncharacteristically lazy, almost as if it would stop to talk if it could.

When he looked up, Walks Alone could see that his uncle was twenty yards ahead of him up river. The boy scurried after him, making up the ground quickly.

"Tell me about my father, Uncle. Tell me about Black Turtle."

The man smiled. "What made you think of your father?"

"I have been thinking about him since I was in the lodgehouse yesterday." He hesitated before adding, "With the old woman."

"She is Four Bears." The tone of his voice shifted and the change was obvious to the boy. "And she is much more than an old woman. She is a healer. She is a shaman."

The boy paused as if absorbing the word before asking, "Is that why she makes everyone treat her with respect?"

"She doesn't make us do anything. And she would never say that she is a shaman. Our people acknowledge her as such."

"Our people? You mean more Lenape than just the people in our village?"

"Yes. She is a shaman to other villages like ours."

"I know she is different," the boy said, "and listening to her talk about our people made me think about my father."

"What did she tell you?"

"That the Lenape have been here for thousands of winters. And that there was a time—a time before the white man came—when there were thousands of Lenape. There were many more villages then, and each village had many more wigwams. Even the women in our village who remember the names of the mothers who came before us cannot remember so far back."

"Yes," Talks For Us agreed, "our people have been here for a very long time, but there are very few of us left."

"She said that many died of sickness that was brought by the whites from far-off places, and that this has happened to our people many times."

"Many times—ten, twelve, more—and once since I have been alive."

"She said that many of our people have moved to the west, to another big river and to big rivers beyond that. After that, we stopped talking and she told me to go and play with the other boys."

"Did she tell you about your father?"

"No, Uncle. She said only that we would talk again soon."

Talks For Us stopped to look down at his nephew. Placing a hand on the boy's shoulder, he said, "I can tell you that it would have made Black Turtle very happy to know that you ask about him so often."

"Did you fish with him?"

"Yes. We fished. We hunted. We did everything together from the time that we were young." He paused before adding, "Nearly as young as you."

"What did you hunt?"

"You know what we hunted, Nephew. I have told you many times."

"Tell me again."

Talks For Us knew that the boy's questions were not about the answers. They were about faith—faith in something that Walks Alone had never seen, or at least didn't remember seeing, and never would see; faith in the feeling that if he heard it often enough it would become as real as if he had lived it.

"We hunted deer and rabbit, ducks and geese," he said. "There was a time when the men in our clan would go on hunts for months at a time, and they would hunt bear and larger game. The women would hunt rabbit and fish near the village, but the men would go on long hunts. That time ended long before your father and I were born. It's different now."

They were a quarter of a mile upriver when Talks For Us turned away from the water and toward a thick area of brush. Walks Alone followed, sometimes stepping over branches as his uncle held them down. They stopped at the edge of a drop-off above a small inlet. A field of rocks lay before them, interrupted only by the few scrawny trees that fought for sunlight and survival below the canopy. As they had done a number of times before, they navigated the rocks carefully but quickly until they stood at the edge of what was less than three feet of water.

The vertical sticks that comprised the weir protruded out of the water in front of them. The back wall was straight and stretched about six feet across the width of the inlet. Walls extended straight out from each side before curving around and back toward the center of the trap. Only a few inches apart at that point, they formed a gateway through which fish could enter to eat bait, but through which they were unable to escape. Instead, they swam in circles, following the curvature of the stick walls.

Talks For Us stepped down into the water and moved behind the trap. Without a word, he turned to look at the boy who was beaming expectantly at the thought of what was about to happen. He reached down into the trap, paused momentarily, and pulled up a large shad with his bare hands. The boy extended the basket so that his uncle could put the thrashing fish into it. Walks Alone had seen his uncle use a net to retrieve trapped fish, and once or twice he had even seen him use a spear, but the most fun was watching him grab them with his bare hands.

"Your father was very good at this," Talks For Us said. "Do you want to try?"

Walks Alone stepped into the water and behind the weir. A fairly large shad circled in the water beneath him. Without taking his eyes off of the fish, he reached down slowly, his hands just far enough apart for the fish to swim between them. A moment later, he jerked his hands together, only to feel the slick sides of the fish pass through them.

"Try again," his uncle said.

The boy reached down into the water, waited for a few agonizing seconds, and then, from a rush of water and fins, emerged with the shad. He held it firmly as it twisted and turned in his grip. Grinning wildly, he carefully deposited it into the basket before looking for more fish in the weir. The three that remained were much smaller, so one by one the boy and his uncle retrieved them from the weir and set them free.

"Only two," Talks For Us said as they climbed up the rocks with the basket.

"But they are good-sized fish," the boy said, "and we are grateful to have them."

They paused on the bank above the inlet and looked back at the water below. Talks For Us drew a small pinch of tobacco from a beaded bag in his belt and released it into the air. "We thank Meesing for providing for us and for all Lenape."

The man smiled as they made the short walk back to the river. He could remember kneeling with his brother above a fallen deer, or walking with him, each with a string of ducks across their shoulders.

"Yes," he confirmed, acknowledging his nephew's words, "we are grateful to have them."

* * *

As she and Roberto ran toward the bridge, Jill didn't know what to expect. *What happened?* she thought. *Is anyone hurt, or worse?*

When they were within a hundred yards, she could see that the truck was on the east end of the bridge and listing to its left above the creek bed. Neither Felix nor Hernando was visible. Once they reached the scene, they were relieved to find both men standing by the creek a safe distance from the truck, the driver side door of which was hanging silently above the edge of the water. Felix was waving his hands frantically and speaking so quickly that Jill couldn't understand a word he was saying. He was obviously shaken. Hernando looked back and forth between Roberto and the truck that balanced on the edge of the bridge.

Roberto tried to calm Felix but the man became more and more frantic, obviously preoccupied by his role in what had just happened.

"*¡Esta bien!*" Roberto yelled above Felix's hysteria. "*¡Este bien! ¿Estas herido?*" Then he turned to Hernando and repeated, "*¿Estas herido?*"

"*Si*," Hernando answered immediately, while Felix continued in his frenzy.

Jill could see that both men were alright, but that Felix was worried that he had done something terribly wrong. "*Esta bien*," she said to him. "It's okay. *Me allegro de que no estes herido.*" She exhaled a huge breath of air behind the words, very happy indeed that neither of the men was hurt. Felix relaxed slightly and his expression began to change, as if he were somewhat reassured.

Seeing Felix begin to settle down, Jill turned her attention to the truck. What had happened was becoming clear to her. Felix had over reacted to Roberto's instructions about crossing the bridge. He had gone too far before turning, and the truck had been misaligned with the bridge just enough for the double rear wheels to ride up onto the four-by-four railing. Jill guessed that the outside tire had missed the railing completely, and that the inside tire was only on it partially before sliding off. The load of rocks had shifted and crushed down into the east bank of the creek, nearly dragging the truck with it. Jill looked at the open door of the vehicle, imagined the two men scrambling out of it, and said a silent thank you that the truck hadn't followed them down. This was a mess, but it was nothing that couldn't be cleaned up.

Then Jill heard Roberto exclaim, "*¡Madre de Dios!*" in the same instant that she saw what he was reacting to. The rocks had shaved away a substantial section of the bank, taking with it huge chunks of earth and heavy grass. From the newly exposed dirt in the side of the bank, the upper portion of a human skull stared straight out at them through the socket of a missing left eye.

Four

The jet rose into the Honduran morning and toward Miami, leaving behind the Sierra Madre Mountains, the capital city of Tegucigalpa, and the Central American summer. Hope Madsen eased her seat back as far as it would recline, planning to sleep on the two-and-a-half-hour flight back to the United States, and perhaps on the subsequent flight from Miami to Columbus. She was tired, and although the previous night's sleep in the Mayan Hotel had helped, she knew that she needed much more rest.

As the plane banked slightly to the northeast, sunlight walked across the wing and into the cabin, making it difficult for Hope to watch the ground below. She had made this trip twice before and knew the plane's path—across the heart of Honduras and up between the valleys of the Aguan and Sico rivers, then past the eastern tip of the Bay Islands before making another northerly turn around Cuba and back to the United States—and as she thought about what she was leaving behind she wondered if she would ever return.

Ten days earlier, she and eleven other volunteers had flown into Tegucigalpa on their way to a ranch where they would work with schoolchildren for a week. "*A ranch*," Hope smiled to herself.

To someone who had never been there, it might have conjured images of a tropical retreat with luxury accommodations, native cuisine, and boundless activities to help one forget the demands of daily life at home. But Hope had known from experience that it was none of those things. Instead, it was a remote outpost where barefoot children with no books of their own could escape the hardships of daily life long enough to learn to read and write, add and subtract.

The ranch was five hours northeast of Tegucigalpa, back in the direction that Hope's plane was now flying. The first leg of the trip extended to the town of Juticalpa, where the volunteers spent the night before setting out for the Agalta Valley and the ranch. They crossed treacherous mountain terrain in vans that were escorted by armed guards, even though the *banditos* in the area seldom bothered the Americans they encountered. *Gringos* never traveled to this remote corner of the world unless they had come to help, a reality not lost on the natives—farmers and banditos alike. The armed guards were a precaution, and no precaution was excessive in a country where carrying a gun and a machete was commonplace. The guards went everywhere with the volunteers; even the ranch itself was guarded and secured.

From her hotel room in Tegucigalpa after a week with the children, Hope sent emails to family members, describing her time in "the lost parts of Honduras." And as her trip to those lost parts neared its end, she knew that she had been privileged to spend time with kids who lived on the edge of the world. She knew that they were no different than other children who were similarly marginalized in the world's most remote places—they were simply doing their best to grow up in the environment into which they had been born. With the tiniest alteration in time and space their lives might have been something different—more privileged or perhaps even harsher still—but this life was all they knew, so they looked out from it with broad smiles and loving eyes, their faces beaming endlessly.

Hope felt blessed to have been of service to the children in the mountains, but she knew that, just as their lives were changing, hers was as well. She had a child of her own, Valeria, named for one of the little girls Hope had taught at the ranch when she had first gone there six years earlier. Her husband's career was becoming increasingly demanding, and even though he had taken the past week to spend all of his time with their daughter, Hope knew that it would become more and more unrealistic for her to travel to remote and sometimes dangerous corners of the world. She thought about the other volunteers on the plane with her, some of them just out of college, and hoped that there would always be people willing to endure the dirt roads into the mountains to help a culture that spent each day in search of its purpose.

As the plane moved into the skies high above the Caribbean Sea, Hope could look down the northern shore of Honduras. Somewhere over there, perhaps even farther than the eye could see on a clear day like this, lay the Mosquito Coast. Hope had never seen it, nor had she seen the many Mayan ruins in different parts of Honduras. She had never been to the beaches in the north or the Gulf of Fonseca in the south, nor had she been to any of the country's many national parks and biological reserves. She had been nowhere other than a remote ranch five hours from the capital city, and she had done nothing other than spend her time with children who were grateful to have it.

The plane banked to the north above the Bay Island of Guanaja, which shimmered below like a solitary emerald in the middle of the gleaming Caribbean.

* * *

"Why do you spend this time with me?"

"Because you are like me."

The answer confused Walks Alone and he paused a long time to ponder it. He enjoyed the company of Four Bears but he didn't see how he was like her. She was an important person to her people, looked up to by the men and women alike. He was just a boy.

Sensing the boy's struggle, the woman added, "Each person in a village has a role; each person has a purpose. Over time, roles have changed as our people have changed, but each person still has his or her place."

"Talks For Us told me," the boy responded, "that there was a time when the men would go on hunts for months at a time. They would hunt larger game than they hunt now."

"There was larger game to be hunted."

"And the women would hunt rabbit and squirrels in the woods, and fish in the streams near the village."

"That's true. And this village, like the other villages, has moved many times, always to be near more fertile ground and more plentiful fish and game."

"He also told me that there were more wigwams in our village then, and many more Lenape villages. He said that there were thousands of Lenape."

"Yes, Young One, there was a time when the land in all directions was the domain of the Lenape. Our people, we of the

Turtle Clan, were here on this side of the river. The Wolf people were in the north, and the Turkey people were on the east side of the river and in the south. In each direction, for as far as man could walk in many days, there were only Lenape." Four Bear's voice became less audible. "And now few of us remain. Many have died of disease. Many others have moved to the west, to places where we can live according to the old ways."

Walks Alone sat quietly, trying to imagine this place in the time that Four Bears and Talks For Us had spoken of.

"I had a dream after we last sat here in the lodgehouse, before I awoke to go to the weir with Talks For Us." He fell silent for a few moments and Four Bears could sense the seriousness with which the boy was remembering his dream. "I dreamt that there were many people celebrating here—more people than I have ever seen in our village or in the lodgehouse. You were drumming and they were dancing wildly, but there were so many that the noise was louder than anything I have ever heard."

Without addressing the dream, Four Bears unrolled a reed mat on the ground near the fire pit. "Lie down here," she requested, and Walks Alone complied without hesitation. She told him to close his eyes and lie quietly as she placed his arms at his sides with his palms flat against the mat. "Take a deep breath through your nose, Young One, way down into your belly, and then breathe it out through your mouth. Breathe it all the way out until none of it is left inside you." Again, the boy did as she asked. "Now do it again slowly," Four Bears said, "and again after that, until you feel as if you and the ground beneath you are one."

As he breathed deeply, Walks Alone became more and more aware of his body. Rather than just feeling an arm or a foot, he was experiencing his entire physical being, and as Four Bears had suggested, he could feel it meld with the earth beneath the mat, the earth that countless generations of Lenape had walked in their lifetimes. Somewhere behind the experience, he was also aware that Four Bears had risen to her feet. He could hear her quiet but deliberate movements and the unfamiliar words that she chanted in a low, barely audible whisper. His next deep breath brought with it the unmistakable smell of burning sage. As Four Bears continued to chant, the sage filled the boy's nose in gentle waves that seemed to carry him along as they ebbed and flowed.

Then, as if it were detached from all things physical, the seemingly disembodied voice of Four Bears said, "Now think of a place near the village—a hole in the ground, or a cave, or even a pond."

For some reason, the boy's thoughts immediately went to the inlet and the weir. He imagined himself standing on the bank, looking down at the sticks that protruded out of the water.

"Now jump into it. Don't hold back. Jump into it completely."

Walks Alone felt his body leap effortlessly into the air and fall feet first into the weir. The thinking part of the boy knew that the water in the inlet was only three feet deep and would never cover him completely, but the feeling part of him submerged easily and completely until he could look up and see the fish that were trapped above. He drifted down into the depths, away from them and toward whatever waited below.

Somewhere, in the void around him, he could hear the steady thump of a skin drum, and he knew instinctively that Four Bears was the drummer. The sound reassured him that he was safe in this mysterious darkness.

In the same moment that Four Bears said, "Tell me what you see," Walks Alone emerged from the water and onto the floor of a lush green valley. Surrounded by beautiful forested mountains and dissected by a deep clear stream, it teemed with the calls and sounds of unseen animals and birds, their voices keeping the rhythm of the drum.

"I see a beautiful place, a green valley fed by a peaceful stream. There is life everywhere. It is all around me."

"Then walk peacefully, and enjoy the journey."

The cool grass beneath his feet, the crystal clear air on his face, the boy walked along the water. He had never been in a place like this and part of him wanted to stay forever.

"Do you see anything else?" Four Bears asked from the suddenly distant world of the lodgehouse.

"I see . . . ," the boy began. Then he stopped and said nothing. Immediately in front of him stood an animal he had never seen before. It was huge, much taller than the largest buck and stouter than the few horses he had ever seen. Its massive head had short but imposing horns and was covered with the same coarse white hair that covered the front half of its body and its rear shanks. It stood taller at the shoulders than in the hindquarters, with a gentle composure that belied its obvious ability to make the earth quake beneath its step. The animal grazed quietly in front of him.

"I see an animal, a large white animal, but I don't know what it is."

Then the animal spoke to Walks Alone. It didn't turn toward him; it didn't look at him or move its mouth; it just spoke to him as if its spirit was speaking to his.

"You will find what you seek," the animal said, "but first you must learn to embrace it . . ." The animal stopped grazing, as if aware of the pain that would remain with the words for the rest of the boy's life. ". . . and it will take longer than you know."

As the boy looked on in bewilderment, the animal added softly, "I will wait with you."

In the next moment, Walks Alone was back in the lodgehouse and aware of nothing other than the lingering smell of sage and the final few beats of the drum.

When he opened his eyes he saw two faces—the first was that of Four Bears, smiling gently back at him; the second was that of Meesing, black on one side, red on the other, staring stoically, watching tirelessly over his people.

* * *

"You don't need me."

The voice belonged to Dr. Roy Cleveland, the Bucks County coroner, and it boomed out of a large, barrel-chested man who looked like an offensive lineman and moved with a limp as if he had once been one. Working his way down the pile of earth and rocks below the skull, he brushed a thick-fingered hand through his graying hair and repeated, "You don't need me. From the looks of things you need an anthropologist."

Jeff Phillips hadn't known Cleveland for long, but he was well aware of the man's reputation for blending a no-nonsense approach to science with an arid and erudite sense of humor. It was the latter that made Jeff think the coroner might be putting him on.

"You're kidding, aren't you?"

A handful of people stood nearby. Jill Martin was down in the creek bed with her father, as was her husband Edward. They stood back from the rock pile, near the edge of the water, at Cleveland's insistence. Roberto from the work crew and Dae Phillips looked on from the bridge, as did a young woman who had briefly introduced herself as being from the local newspaper. Standing on the corner of the bridge where the accident had occurred was Walt McNulty, the county sheriff. He looked on dispassionately, equally interested in and uncertain about what he and the others were witnessing.

"No, I'm not kidding at all," said Cleveland. "Even with a cursory examination I can tell that the skull is very old. It's been here a long time. There's a complete absence of tissue, at least to the naked eye, and significant discoloration. I don't know how much of the skeleton is here or what we'll find when we start digging, but a forensic anthropologist should definitely do the work."

"But we thought there might have been some wrongdoing," Jill replied. "That's why we wanted you and Sheriff McNulty out here."

"It's my responsibility to be here," Cleveland responded, "and there may have been some wrongdoing, but if there was it happened so long ago that Walt won't have to worry about arresting anybody." The comment drew relieved laughter from the small group of onlookers. "Walt and I are going to cover the skull and the immediate area with a sheet of plastic to keep the weather out and the animals away."

"And each of you will have to sign my log book," McNulty said as he headed for his car and the plastic sheeting, "just as a matter of process. I'll need your names, addresses, and driver's license numbers, if you have your licenses handy. Oh," he added, stopping to look up at Roberto, "and I'll need the same information from the guys who were in the truck."

Roberto looked away, obviously unsettled by the request.

"If they don't have licenses," the sheriff added, guessing at the source of Roberto's concern, "tell them to get them, but make sure we know who they are and where to find them."

"What about the anthropologist?" Jeff asked Cleveland.

"I know someone at the University of Pennsylvania. I'll see if she can come up here tomorrow. In the meantime, please stay away from the immediate site."

A half hour later, the site had been covered with plastic, the required information had been recorded in the log, and the cars of the sheriff and coroner had disappeared in the direction of the highway. Roberto was talking to the reporter, trying to explain how the accident had happened, or at least repeating what Felix had told him. She listened to him carefully, taking notes about the accident and the project that precipitated it.

Standing as close as he could without disobeying the coroner's instructions, Edward looked carefully at the exposed portion of the skull. He had been closer to it before the sheriff and coroner had arrived—they all had—but he now saw it from a different distance and altered perspective. A three-inch section of the frontal bone was visible immediately above the eye socket, as were smaller portions of the bones around and under it. But what seemed to make it most identifiable as human was the exposed portion of the nasal cavity. It filled in just enough of a face to cause anyone to look at it with a sense of wonder.

"That used to be a person," he observed from his vantage point. "Look at the way the skull's positioned, like it's staring out at us from deep inside the earth. The rest of him is hidden from sight, as if he doesn't even exist except for the eye with which he's watching us." He pointed toward the section of earth above the skull. "And he's only a few feet below ground. I wonder what that's about."

"You keep saying *he*," Jill cautioned. "Are you sure he isn't a she?"

"No, of course not. But either way I'd like to know his . . ." He paused momentarily. ". . . or her story. Was this a battlefield or a burial ground? Did somebody live out here on this point once upon a time?"

"Whatever the story is," Jeff answered, "I really hope it's just one person's story." He paused and looked across the point toward the crest of the hill above the river. "I hope there aren't more bodies buried out here."

"I'm surprised we haven't found anything else," Jill offered. "I mean, with all the construction over the past few years you'd think more stuff would have popped up."

"Excuse me," came a voice from behind them. "I should introduce myself. My name is Grace Caufield, and I work for the *Courier Times*."

"Jeff Phillips," he said, extending his hand. "And this is my daughter, Jill, and my son-in-law, Edward. You've already met Dae and Roberto. He's done quite a bit of work for us out here."

"It's nice to meet all of you. I've heard about your house and what you've done with this property, but I've never been out here before, not even before you started building."

"It's coming along," Jeff responded.

"I know that you don't know very much right now, but do you mind if I ask you a few questions?"

"I don't know how much help we can be but, sure, ask away."

"Before you start," Edward interjected, "you'll have to excuse me. I've got some work to do up in the barn. It's nice to meet you, Grace." He started back toward the main house along the grassy portion of the creek bed.

"And you," the woman said as he walked away. Then she turned to Jeff. "Why is all of this stuff out here to begin with?"

"As we clear parts of the property and build—and we've built the main house and two smaller houses so far, as well as a barn and an outbuilding—we try to salvage as much material as we can. There's no telling what we may be able to re-use."

"And the work crew was down here retrieving stones for a fountain?"

"It sounds more exotic than it is—or will be. It's kind of the focal point of the entire area across the creek and up the hill from the main house."

"And Roberto told me that his men were taking stones up to the site when this happened."

"That's right. I wasn't down here at the time."

"Roberto and I were down here with his men," Jill said. "We were walking back; they were up ahead of us in the truck."

"And what do you think went wrong?'

"I think the driver made a mistake. Roberto had told him to be careful cutting back across the bridge and I think he was a little too careful. He went too far past and then missed the side of the bridge when he turned. We're just glad no one was hurt."

"The coroner and sheriff didn't seem too upset about all of this."

"You'll have to ask them about that," Jeff advised, "but I agree with you. I'm sure they've both seen enough to know when they should be worked up and when they shouldn't. But yes, I expected more flashing lights and yellow tape, that kind of thing."

"You mean, like a crime scene?"

"Exactly." Jeff looked back at the skull and added, "Maybe I've been watching too much television."

"I thought the same thing," Grace said. "Do you mind if I come back out when the anthropologist is here? I've never seen anything quite like this. It's really interesting."

"No, I don't mind at all. We'll let you know when we know. And yes," he added as the reporter walked toward her car, "it's very interesting."

After the others had gone, Jeff stood alone for a while, thinking about the events of the day. He didn't know what was happening or where it was leading, but he had come far enough to know that there was meaning in this, just as there was meaning in everything.

"What's the message?" he said to the April afternoon. "What's the message," he repeated as he ignored Roy Cleveland's instructions just enough to step forward and pull back the plastic to reveal the skull. Looking into the empty eye socket he asked, "What have you come to tell me?"

* * *

"So, Young One, you have journeyed for the first time."

"It felt as if I was somewhere else."

"Part of you was. But your body was right here in the lodgehouse."

"Can anyone do this?"

"Once, long ago in the time of our oldest ancestors, but most have forgotten."

"You mean they have forgotten how?"

"I mean they will not let their spirits remember."

"I don't understand."

Four Bears looked at Walks Alone with the eyes of a teacher who is too wise to stop learning. "Tell me about the animal you saw on your journey."

"I don't know what it was," the boy replied, "but it was very big and it stood very still, grazing on the grass. And it was white— not the white of the snow, but the white of a cloud, or the white of the water when the river's high in the spring." He continued, describing the animal's huge head, high shoulders, and coarse fur.

"I have seen things on journeys that I have never seen in this world," the shaman began, "so I am not surprised. I have heard stories about strange animals that our men saw on long hunting trips, but those things happened long before I was born."

"But how can I see an animal that I have never seen before?"

"Our ancestors walked to this place from the farthest corners of Turtle Island."

"Turtle Island?"

"Long ago, after the Great Flood destroyed the land, it was rebuilt on the back of a turtle by a muskrat that retrieved soil from beneath the waters. All indigenous peoples know that we live on the back of that turtle, that we live on Turtle Island. Perhaps you saw the animal in your journey through the eyes of an ancestor who once walked this land." She looked into the fire pit of the lodgehouse as if she were peering into the depths of time itself. "Or perhaps your animal only exists in story or legend. Perhaps it is not of our world."

Walks Alone tried to come to terms with the woman's words, but it was difficult for him to imagine that he had seen something that existed beyond the boundaries of the physical world.

"Do you mean like in a dream? Like when I see something in a dream that I have never seen before? Is that what you mean?"

"No," she said, "I mean in the worlds beyond dreams."

"Have you been to these worlds?"

"Some," she answered, looking straight into the boy's eyes, "but only some." After a long silence, she added, "As have you."

"But I don't remember them," he answered.

"I will teach you how to remember, and I will teach you so that you will not forget. But not today; you have experienced enough for one day."

Walks Alone rose to his feet, and as he walked toward the entrance to the lodgehouse he turned to ask, "Do you want to know what the animal in my journey told me?"

"He told you your destiny," the shaman answered softly.

Mystified, but without saying a word, the boy turned and walked away.

Four Bears watched as Walks Alone passed into the light of the afternoon, a single tear gathering in her left eye. Surrendering to the vision that was developing before her, a vision that she knew would not be turned away, she found herself peering into a world she did not recognize. She felt cold and confined, and completely hidden except for the eye with which she now saw a white man. He looked back, staring at her with warm but curious eyes, as if he were asking a question. His clothes were strange to her, his question unheard, but she was overwhelmed by the aura that surrounded him. She could sense his kindness and compassion, both of which assured her that, regardless of how painful, everything was exactly as it should be. The vision dissipated as quickly as it had come, leaving her to ponder what she had seen. She did not understand, and she knew all too well that it was not her place to understand.

"He told you your destiny," she repeated to the emptiness into which Walks Alone had disappeared. "He told you *our* destiny."

Five

He had always joked that he wanted to be doing one of two things when he died: making love or writing. And, having said it so many times, two other things were clear to him as well: the first was that he wasn't joking; the second was that truth is the most liberating thing a person can experience.

Sitting in the big chair near the bed, his notepad and reading glasses on the nightstand beside him, Jeff let his thoughts drift. The soft light of the lamp was gone, the lines of poetry that had come to him in his sleep were recorded, and truth came to sit with him quietly in the darkness.

There was a moment in his life, sometime in the year after he and Dae had met, when he had come to terms with what was truly important to him. He knew that this wasn't an easy thing for a man to do, and it probably had been more difficult for him than for most. When he was younger, others had always been more than willing to project their priorities onto him—team sports; a sixty-hour workweek; a college education; the need to provide for others; staying married for the kids. Whatever importance those things had held for him was overshadowed by the importance they held for someone else. It made no difference if they were his truth.

Some of them were true for him, but in a much different way. He had come to believe that working hard was important, but only when one loves what he does. For him, work became neither a priority nor a truth until it had transformed into creativity. In that boundless place, everything seemed effortless. There was neither labor nor the time in which to bear its burden.

Many things were important to him, but they were all grounded in writing and his relationship with Dae. *How shallow that might sound to someone else,* he thought to himself. *What nonsense that would be to my father.* But he had come to understand that every person has a grounding place—a place that provides the foundation for all they do; a place where they stop retreating from the assaults of life and find the courage to move forward once again. He knew there was power in the ability to recognize that place, to acknowledge its existence, and to use it as the source of his strength.

He arose from the chair just enough to slip out of the sweatpants that he was wearing. As they dropped to the floor, he leaned forward and into the bed. Pulling the duvet to his waist, he moved quietly behind Dae. His first intention was to sleep, but it evaporated in the darkness when he nuzzled against her back.

He rubbed his hand lightly up and down the outside of her thigh, slowly increasing the motion until it was covering the distance between her waist and knee. From the very first time they had ever made love, years ago on the night they met, he had always loved her skin. It was remarkably smooth, with a quality he had come to think of as "depth," as if it were equally flawless a quarter of an inch below the surface. Perhaps it was the result of the little extra weight she carried on her frame—just enough to make her voluptuous. She was unmistakably woman, her body possessing none of the qualities of a girl, and he appreciated it with both his ardor and his adoration.

She began to stir, silently assuring him that she was awake.

"Trouble sleeping?" she asked without moving, softly breaking the dark silence of the bedroom.

"I've been writing," he answered, "and now I'm being selfish."

"You know," she teased, as she began to respond to his touch, "I've always said that I want to be doing one of two things when I die."

"And what would those be?" he asked, only too happy to play along.

"Writing or making love. And truth be told, I'm not much of a writer."

As he exhaled a small laugh, she turned her face to meet his kiss. There in the darkness they made love in the slow, unhurried way that they both treasured. They had the capacity to take each other to a place where nothing else mattered, where nothing else existed, and they each understood the importance of going to that place often.

Afterwards, they lay quietly, her back against his chest. He kissed her neck affectionately as she reached back to gently stroke the side of his thigh with the back of her hand.

"When a man is loved like this," he whispered to the night, "all else becomes possible." Relaxing into the simple truth of the words, he followed his wife, the love of his life, into sleep.

* * *

It was still hours until sunrise, but Walks Alone was awake and staring into the darkness of the wigwam. Sometimes, if he couldn't sleep in the hours before dawn, he would go outside and walk around the interior of the village, knowing that others would be waking soon. But he was reluctant to go outside at this hour, unwilling to risk that Looks Back might awaken and find him gone. He didn't want to worry her.

A few weeks had passed since his journey with Four Bears, and he had spent at least a part of every day with her. She had talked with him about many things, few of which he understood fully but all of which intrigued him in a way he could not explain. Four Bears seemed to know things that no one else in the village knew, not even Talks For Us or Looks Back, and—for some reason that was also unclear—she seemed to want to talk about them with him. She was always patient in explaining things, and willing to talk about whatever he wished. And she treated each of his questions as if it were a helpless bird cradled in her hands, listening to and answering it without judgment. No one had ever treated him the way Four Bears treated him.

They had journeyed together again, three different times, and each time Walks Alone moved fluidly into the netherworld where the white beast waited. Sometimes he would see creatures that were familiar to him—deer, otter, wolves, and turkeys—but the unfamiliar beast was always there. Even if he didn't actually see him, he could always feel the beast's presence. It was as if the animal was unwilling to leave his side.

Four Bears had recently begun to let him drum while she journeyed. At first it felt like play, but he quickly understood that his drumming was important to her, that the repeated thumping helped her spirit move from the mat on the lodgehouse floor to the world of the animals. Helping her filled him with a sense of responsibility that made him at once both jubilant and pensive. The joy he felt was always tempered by the feeling that his help was necessary.

Holding the drum near the side of his head, as Four Bears had taught him to do, he would watch her as she journeyed. She was a small person, shorter than Looks Back and many of the other women in the village, and very slight. As she lay on her back, her clothes seemed to drape on her small frame, her buckskin kilt hanging in the space between her legs, her white shirt settling into the gently defined contours of her slender torso. In the heat of summer, many of the women wore nothing other than a kilt, but Four Bears was always covered. Her long, black hair was tied in braids that showed significant streaks of gray. She wore neither tattoos on her skin nor rings in her ears, and except for her worn shirt, adorned herself with none of the ornaments that the white man had introduced to the Lenape. Her face was angular and chiseled, and as she lay on the mat with her eyes closed, her chin and nose were more prominent than when she stood erect and they were forced to compete with her piercing brown eyes.

As Walks Alone drummed, Four Bears lay perfectly still, her right arm at her side, her left arm across her forehead. He sometimes wondered if anything other than her body was there in the lodgehouse with him. If her spirit wandered too far away, beguiled perhaps into soaring through the sky with an eagle or swimming the currents of the river with a turtle, might it be unable to find its way back? And, if that happened, what could he possibly do to help it? He was always relieved when Four Bears moved a hand or the arm that covered her eyes, silently indicating that she was, indeed, returning.

As he lay quietly in the darkness of the wigwam, thinking about his time with Four Bears, he was filled with the notion of journeying on his own. He drew in a deep breath as he let his body relax into the mat beneath him, just as Four Bears had taught him. He exhaled through his mouth and then drew in another deep breath, his arms at his sides. He imagined himself standing on the bank above the inlet and the weir, the place that he had come to know as his entrance to the world of the animals. The stillness of the summer night clung to his body in a leaf-thin veil of humidity, and he longed for the coolness of the water below. He stepped forward, as if into a dream, and plunged, feet first, into the weir.

The water was cold compared to the air above, and he let it draw him down into its depths, twenty feet, then forty, then more than he could imagine the river to be at its deepest point. He could see nothing, and as he descended, his blindness stirred a wave of concern that perhaps doing this without Four Bears was not such a good idea. His body went deeper, and even though he was breathing easily, he suddenly felt that he wanted to go back. He tried to slow himself, reaching into the water above him in an attempt to swim to the surface. He pulled harder and harder against the water, but each stroke seemed to take him further in the opposite direction. "Just open your eyes," another part of him whispered from the safety of the wigwam, "and you'll be back." But his eyes were open and he was going deeper and deeper.

He flailed his arms wildly, his futile swimming giving way to complete panic. There was nothing around him but black water and it became increasingly resistant as he struggled against it. He knew that it was consuming him. His body was exhausted, his breathing labored, and he was terrified that he might suck water into his lungs with his very next breath.

"Four Bears," he felt himself thinking, "help me. Please help me." Then, as if it were all that had ever been, the river was all that was. It flowed around him, it flowed through him, it flowed within him. Walks Alone and the water his people called Lenapewihittuk were one.

Relinquishing himself to the river, he drew in a deep breath and suddenly found himself in the world of the animals. He had traveled to this world on each of his journeys but he did not recognize this part of it. He was in a forest that was heavier than the woods near the river. In much of it, fallen and decaying trees and dense undergrowth made passage impossible. He was standing near a path that cut through the forest to the west, but it was barely wide enough for him to walk through, let alone for a full-grown man to pass.

The sun was rising behind him, the dense forest dividing its light into beams that cut through the shadows before disappearing in the undergrowth. He moved toward the path, carefully navigating the vines that crawled along the forest floor, wincing against the thorns that cut into his shins. The path provided relief from the brush but brought a different discomfort. He felt confined by its narrowness and restricted by its direction, as if he could only move forward on its terms. The thick canopy above seemed to be pressing down on him, making it difficult to draw in any air that was not saturated with the dank smell of dying trees.

Then, as the sun continued to climb, the path began to widen. Undergrowth flew to the left and right of him, rocks and rotted trees were blown aside. The light of the rising sun converged on the path, illuminating it as it widened into the distance as far as Walks Alone could see. He didn't know where the new path led, but he felt relief at the prospect of finding a way out of the forest.

As he took a few steps forward he heard the thundering of hooves, and he turned back to see three horses running straight at him down the narrow path. They were as white as anything he had ever seen, with eyes that glowed wildly, like embers about to burst into flames. Unable to get out of their way, he stood frozen, hoping that they would somehow avoid trampling him. He closed his eyes at the thought.

They ran by or through him, he didn't know which, but as they passed he could feel the heated breath that blew from their nostrils and the coarse hair that flew from their manes. He opened his eyes and whirled around to see them thundering down the path toward the distant horizon.

Stunned and disoriented, but grateful to be alive, he suddenly became aware of a presence behind him. He turned, nearly falling down in the process, and stared straight into the face of the white beast. It was standing less than ten feet away, its shoulders squared to the widened path the horses had traveled. His first impulse was to be afraid, but it passed in an instant. He knew instinctively that he had nothing to fear. He looked at the animal and asked, "What have you come to tell me?"

In his heart, he heard the reply.

"Such is the path of the Lenape."

He felt a hand on his shoulder shaking him gently, and opened his eyes to find Looks Back kneeling beside him.

"It's time to wake up," she said softly. "It's well past dawn."

* * *

As Jeff Phillips walked along the road between the main house and the bridge, the lines of his poem kept rolling through his head. Poetry happened for him that way, in much the same way that lyrics of songs had always happened for him. Even as a teen in the early '60s, he would only have to hear a song two or three times before he had memorized it completely. Throughout his life, people had commented frequently about his capacity for remembering songs and poems and quotes. Some of them may have remembered the words of people like Gene Pitney, John Keats, and Winston Churchill, but few of them could summon them on demand when the situation called for them.. But it was just a part of who Jeff was.

"How can you remember all of those words?" people would ask. "How can you forget them?" he would reply. And he wasn't being glib or sarcastic. He experienced life in lyrics, and it was only natural that he would absorb the experiences of others through their words.

That's why most of his poetry was written in iambic pentameter. Rhyme and meter made poems memorable, like songs. It made sense to him that people would remember the poetry of the Romantics or Masefield or Frost, even if just a line or two, when they had long forgotten the poems of less-structured poets. But that was only his perspective, and there seemed to be fewer and fewer poets with his perspective.

He had been thinking about the bones in the creek bed, wondering who they belonged to, why they were there, and why they had been discovered in such a curious manner. And he was still concerned that the bones might only be part of the story, that there might be other skeletons buried nearby.

But most of all he wondered what the bones were about. Their discovery had been an accident, but so many pieces had to fall into place for it to happen. One small change in the course of events might have prevented it, but each thing that had to happen had aligned perfectly with everything else. If the truck had crossed the bridge and taken the stones to the upper meadow, the fountain would be finished now and they would all be working on something else, perhaps even the gathering barn in Jeff's vision. But the truck hadn't crossed the bridge; it had slid off of it. And everything else had moved accordingly.

The lines of poetry that had awakened him at 2:00 a.m. rippled through his mind. They had come easily to him, and he had no difficulty remembering them now.

"*One thing shifts and all else follows after,*" he said to himself as he walked, "*nothing moves alone in isolation; by a thread each atom is connected in a strand comprising all creation.*

"*All has meaning, nothing's unimportant, though it may seem so when it first appears.*" Life had taught him the truth of the words, and that there was always more to something than its face value. "*Its purpose may be known in a moment or safely hidden for a thousand years.*" He was haunted by the purpose in this. He wondered about the lessons that it held.

"*On this cosmic jewel we spin together in a karmic ether dark and clouded; thinking we see out with perfect vision.*" In his life, he had misjudged too many things and too many people, usually believing that he saw them clearly. "*We miss meaning perfectly enshrouded.*

"*Through apparent mishap comes this shifting, and I am left to wonder what it's for—What truth lies within its unknown purpose? What meaning waits beyond the opened door?*"

As he neared the bridge, he couldn't help but understand that twenty years earlier none of this would have occurred to him. The bones, as well as the delays they were causing and the attention they were drawing, would have been a nuisance, a frustration to move beyond so that the important things in life could be lived. But, twenty years earlier, he had been pursuing someone else's idea of the important things in life.

"So sorry," he whispered to someone or something in his memory. "I guess I'll just have to go it alone from here." He started humming the tune of some 1960s hit about going on alone. In the next instant another occurred to him, and then a third. *Actually*, he made the mental observation, *there have been quite a few of them.*

When he was about seventy-five yards from the bridge, Jeff could see that a blue canopy had been erected to protect the site where the bones had been discovered. Wanting a better view, he left the road and eased down the bank onto the grassy area of the creek bed. From there, he could see that the corner poles on top of the bank had been cut so that the canopy was only a foot or two above the ground. The poles on the creek side were much longer, anchored in the creek bed about ten feet below the crest of the bank. Plastic curtains had been pulled aside and tied to the corners of the makeshift structure.

The rocks had been removed a day after the accident under the direction of Dr. Emily FitzRoy, a forensic anthropologist from the University of Pennsylvania. Wanting to ensure that no bones had been carried down into the creek bed when the rocks had sheared off the face of the bank, she carefully supervised the work until all of the stones had been removed. She had also decided to disinter the skull and whatever bones were with it from the side of the bank rather than from above, primarily because of the large, flat rock that was buried in the bank almost immediately above the skull. That decision had been made on the previous morning, and she had spent the rest of the day on a partial excavation of the site.

After clearing the area around the skull and some of the cervical vertebrae, she had confirmed Roy Cleveland's findings to Jeff and a small group of bystanders watching the work. "The bones are very old," she had observed. "It's difficult to say exactly how old without testing, but they're very brittle and extremely discolored."

Later in the day she had uncovered what was left of the spinal column, which was little more than a loosely defined row of drum-shaped bones and a few of the wing-like spurs that had been attached to some of them in life. She had found no sign of either the rib cage on the left side or the remains of the left arm.

"Good morning, Mr. Phillips," she said as Jeff approached.

To his surprise, Jeff found himself struck by her beauty as if he were seeing her for the first time, rather than just a day after he had met her. She was so stunning that she seemed she would be out of place anywhere but on the cover of a fashion magazine. It was almost unthinkable that her life revolved around digging in the dirt and removing rocks from the banks of creeks.

She was young, probably in her early thirties, and carried herself with a formality that belied her physical attractiveness. That formality seemed to go with what Jeff imagined to be the staid environs of a university museum in Philadelphia, but the well-formed curves, reddish blond hair, and flashing green eyes of this forensic anthropologist did not.

"Dr. FitzRoy," he nodded in response. "Are you making any progress?"

"Yes," she answered, motioning to a young assistant for something on a nearby table. "As far as I can tell, there's very little of the skeleton left. The entire left side is gone, including the left coxal bone. I doubt that I'll find any trace of the left leg."

"Where do you think it is? The left side of the skeleton, that is."

"It's impossible to tell. I'm guessing—and believe me, with bones this old it's nothing more than a guess—that the body was buried naturally, not by someone else. It may have even been in the water, possibly for a long time. Whatever happened, something took quite a bit of the remains away—maybe the elements, but most likely predators."

Jeff noticed that Grace Caufield from the newspaper was standing on the bridge, listening intently and taking notes.

"This obviously used to be a much wider stream," he offered, "but that was a long time ago."

"This fellow was probably here a long time before the topography changed. A *long*, long time."

"Fellow? How do you know it was a man, or is that just a figure of speech?"

"Look at this." Dr. FitzRoy carefully pulled the jawbone away from the skull, visibly surprising Jeff. "Don't worry," she said, "it detached many, many years ago, but by that time the skull was buried. This is the posterior ramus." She rubbed her latex-gloved finger along the rear portion of the bone. "It's curved inward in males, but it's straight in females. There aren't many clear indications that skeletal remains are male or female, but this is one of them."

"So, what happens next?" Jeff asked.

"Barring surprises, I should finish up today," she answered. "There are protocols to follow, and I'll have to discuss them with Roy Cleveland."

"Protocols?"

"Sometimes, in a situation like this, the coroner's office will want to dig up the surrounding area to make sure that no one else is buried nearby. That will be his call—I'm sure he'll consider it carefully before he starts digging up your property. But first we have to do a formal examination of the remains."

"What does that entail?'

"Everything we find will be removed to the county forensic facility in Warminster. We'll do the examination there."

"What happens to the remains after the examination?"

"You'll have to ask Dr. Cleveland. I would guess that the policy is to release them to the nearest blood relative, but that may prove problematic in this case."

One thing shifts and all else follow after. The words rushed through Jeff's mind. "Is it possible that they could be buried here?" he asked. "I mean, since they were found here?"

"Again," she said, "it's the coroner's decision. But just out of curiosity, why would you care about where they're buried?"

"I don't know." Until the moment in which he had given it voice, the idea had never even occurred to Jeff.

* * *

Other than for celebrations, Walks Alone had never seen so many people in his village. Less than fifty people lived in the ten wigwams and two cabins of the village, but at least three times that many milled about now. As he moved among them, he was surprised to see that many of them were dressed like whites. Instead of breechclouts, many of the men wore pants; instead of moccasins, many wore the much heavier shoes that whites made from the hides of cows. The women were also dressed differently, some even wearing dresses like the European women living on nearby farms.

The men still displayed things that identified them as Lenape, each in his own way. They wore scalplocks—some down to their shoulders—and the familiar tattoos of a snake and a raven on their foreheads, or chains of diamond shapes across the front of their necks. Hatchets with iron or brass heads were tucked into their belts, and the fancy handles of knives protruded from leather sheaths. A few men carried rifles. But most disappointing to Walks Alone was the smell that emanated from some of the men that he passed—the repulsive, pungent smell that came with too much of the white man's liquor.

He had heard Looks Back say that the people of at least five small villages would sit in council today, but even this gathering didn't look like enough people for five villages. He knew that some of the men were working for whites on farms or in mills like the one that had recently been built a few miles away in the place the whites called Durham. And he also knew that there were fewer women to begin with because many of them had intermarried with the Germans and the English.

When one is nine winters old, it's only natural to believe that life always has been and always will be the way it is at that moment, but as Walks Alone made his way through the crowd to the lodgehouse, he was troubled by the understanding that things were changing quickly in the world beyond his village. He didn't know how long the small cluster of wigwams could fend off the realities of that world, but he feared that it was fewer winters than he would like.

Two men stood at the entrance to the lodgehouse, both young and serious, but neither of whom Walks Alone had seen before. No one had been admitted to the lodgehouse yet, and Walks Alone thought that the two men might stop him, but he walked past them quietly and without incident, almost as if he were invisible. He tried to suppress the pride that accompanied this special treatment, but it rose to the surface of his face in the form of a small smile. Four Bears had warned him about such feelings, and he recognized instantly what her warning had been about.

"With humility and gratitude, Young One," she had cautioned, "always with humility and gratitude."

Inside the lodgehouse, Walks Alone could see his teacher sitting on the floor in the shadows at the far end of the building, well removed from their usual place near the fire pit. She sat quietly, staring at the floor in front of her, and the lack of her customary acknowledgment made the inside of the lodgehouse feel even cooler.

"The men at the entrance let you pass," Four Bears observed. "Do you know why?"

"Because you asked them to?" the boy asked in response.

"I didn't speak to them."

"Then why didn't they stop me?"

"Because everyone knows that we have been spending time together, Young One. And everyone knows why." She paused before testing him with a question. "So, how did it feel to walk past them?"

"It made me feel special. It made me feel like I am allowed to do something that no one else is allowed to do, like I can go somewhere that no one else can go."

"Listen to your words, Young One, for they are true. To go somewhere that no one else can go, you must go how?"

"With humility and gratitude?"

"Yes, always, but if no one can go with you . . ."

"I must go alone," the boy interrupted. "I must go alone."

Four Bears did not respond.

The silence around them grew thick and heavy, accentuating the sounds of the people outside the entrance to the lodgehouse. The silence in each of their hearts grew as well, anchored by the meaning the word *alone* holds for like-hearted beings at different extremes of life.

"Soon the people will meet here in council," Four Bears began, "not in celebration, but in council. The whites have met with the leaders of the Five Nations, the tribes who say they hold power over us, the tribes who say they now speak for us. They have made a treaty—a treaty that includes more of the land on which we live."

"But how can they speak for us? How can they say that they hold power over us?"

"They act like the whites. They oppress those who are weaker than they are, and in the process they sell what is not theirs to sell, what is not theirs at all."

"Do all whites act this way?" The question hung in the air like the mask of Meesing on the pole near the fire pit. It possessed a quality of hopelessness that frightened the boy to the point that he wished he hadn't asked it.

"Not all," came the reply. "Onas was different, but he died in the time that you were born."

"Onas? The man the white people call Penn?"

"Yes, but he has been gone for nine winters now. Those who have come after him, including his own children, are not like him."

Talks For Us appeared at the entrance to the lodgehouse, squinting toward the place where Four Bears and Walks Alone were sitting. The woman signaled to him by lifting her right arm straight over her head and people began to file into the building. They moved quickly but solemnly, universally aware of the gravity of the moment. Within a few minutes, the crowd had assembled, not in circle as they did for celebration but in one mass, facing the fire pit. Immediately in front of the mask of Meesing, in the spot where Four Bears and Walks Alone usually sat, Talks For Us climbed onto a short wooden platform that was raised high enough so that everyone could see him. Other leaders from the other villages assumed places on each side of him.

Walks Alone watched his uncle carefully, keenly aware of the dignity that the man brought to the simple act of sitting on a platform. Seated, his back was tree straight, his shoulders back, his head held high. He sat with his legs folded beneath him and the palms of his hands resting facedown on his knees. Talks For Us bore no sign of influence by the white man except for the amulet that hung from his neck, and even that seemed much more like something white melded into something Lenape, rather than the other way around. Walks Alone imagined that there was a time when all Lenape *sachems* and *sakimas* looked like this, and he mouthed a silent prayer to the Great Spirit that many more would follow.

"The white chief Gordon," Talks For Us said to the council, "has met with the leaders of the Five Nations at Coaquannock, the white village on Lenapewihittuk. He met with the Mohawk, the Oneida, and the Onondaga; he met with the Cayuga and the Seneca. They told him that they speak for the Lenape because they have conquered us."

The crowd roiled in a collective buzz that quickly erupted into shouts that rose in the air above outstretched arms and clenched fists.

"They have conquered nothing!" someone across the fire pit shouted. "Least of all the Lenape."

"They are united in their oppression," Talks For Us replied, "and formidable in their strength." He paused, well aware that his next words would stir even more agitation. "They told the white chief that they can sell our land, that they can sell the land of the Unami and the Munsee, including the lands between here and the next river. Tannewhannegah said this on behalf of the Five Nations."

"Where is it recorded that they have the right to do this?" another voice shouted. Walks Alone recognized it as the voice of Turns His Face To The Rain, a cousin to Looks Back and a member of his village. "Where is it recorded that what belongs to the Great Spirit can be sold to anyone, least of all the white chief Gordon?"

"Nothing is recorded," Talks For Us said solemnly, his eyes dropping to the dirt floor in front of the fire pit. "There is no record—no wampum or white man's paper—as there was in the time of Onas. They make no record because they are ashamed of what they do."

Yet another voice in the crowd rose above the din. "How do they do this? How *can* they do this?"

"They do it because they are stronger, because there are so few of us left. They say they will protect us, but they do only what benefits them." Talks For Us spoke with a confidence that made it clear he understood the problem—and a resignation that made it equally clear he could do little about it.

"How can they protect us?" came another shouted question. "They cannot even take care of themselves."

"That is true," answered Talks For Us. "Our brothers trade furs for rum. They trade with the whites and with other red men. Everyone cheats them, red and white alike. And our brothers are so sick for the white man's liquor that they hunt until there is no more game to hunt."

"I have heard," someone shouted, "that they kill even the breeding stock—the animals in the herd that will provide more game in the seasons to come. So sick are they for the rum they receive in trade."

"Yes," said Talks For Us, "even the breeders that our fathers were so careful to let live." He looked out across the crowd, and what looked back was a culture on the edge of extinction. In his heart he understood that it wasn't just his village that was in jeopardy, or even the small group of villages that was represented at this council, it was a way of life, and it was being pushed aside by people who neither understood nor cared about it.

And, somewhere behind his understanding, his wisdom reminded him that the peoples of the Five Nations were also in jeopardy, and that their momentary strength was subject to a fragility of its own. He had heard stories that both the French and the English were building walled villages in the land of the Mohawk and the Oneida, of the Onondaga, Cayuga, and Seneca, and he knew that they, like all of the aboriginal people, would one day be pushed aside by the onslaught of the Europeans. He raised his eyes to the crowd, sitting erect, trying to be strong for his people.

Talks For Us let the council continue until all had said what they had come to say, and when the talking was done the people left the lodgehouse, most in silence, all in frustration.

When they had gone, Walks Alone sat in the shadows with Four Bears. Her head was bowed, her eyes closed, and she held her palms face up, as if in offering.

"I don't understand all that I heard," he said, breaking the silence. "Will we have to move the village?"

"No," Four Bears answered without opening her eyes. "At least not yet." She opened her eyes, but rather than looking at Walks Alone she simply stared at the ground before her. "The treaty with the Five Nations concerns lands between here and the next river. The Lenape who live there are most affected. These lands are still claimed by the sons of Onas and the people who work for them."

"How did all of this land owning begin?"

"I was a child when Onas came to this land. There had been many whites before him. They started coming seventy winters before him. Onas treated the Lenape fairly. We made agreements with him, agreements that the Lenape and the whites would live on the land together." She paused and raised her head to look at Walks Alone. "But the whites believe that they can own the land in the same way that they own the clothes on their backs. They buy it and sell it at their will, without regard for who lives or hunts there, without regard for whose sacred places are there, without regard for whose ancestors are buried there."

"What will happen to us? Will we have to move one day?"

"Yes, and I fear that it will be before too many winters have passed."

Watching the old woman's face as she spoke, Walks Alone saw the profound change in her eyes. They were the same huge eyes that he had looked into many times, but in the lingering shadows they rose like lightless moons in a cloudy night sky.

"In the early darkness of this day," he began, "I tried to journey on my own, lying on my mat in the wigwam."

"And did you journey?"

"Yes—at least I think so—but it was very different than anything I have done with you."

Four Bears said nothing. She sat motionless, looking at Walks Alone solemnly.

"I jumped into the weir, but I did not pass through into the animal world . . ." He paused before adding, ". . . at least not at first." He paused again, as if drifting into a place that was dark and foreboding.

"As I went down into the water it became deeper and deeper, much deeper than any part of the river. Its depth seemed endless. I thought I was going to drown." He hesitated again, and he might not have continued had Four Bears not spoken to him.

"But you did not drown," she said. "You passed through into another place."

"Yes—a dense forest."

"And it was nearly as suffocating as the depths of the river."

"Yes."

"And in that place a path was revealed to you—a path that widened with the rising sun—the brush and fallen trees swept away as if by the hand of the Great Spirit."

He looked back at Four Bears incredulously. His mind swirled with dichotomies. *How could she know? Of course she knows. How could anyone know? If she wouldn't know, who would?* That which made complete sense to him on one level was utterly mystifying on another.

Sensing his confusion, she continued. "And when the path had widened, three white horses appeared behind you, running straight at you, passing by you as if you weren't even there. And then . . ." Four Bears watched his face as a peaceful understanding filled his eyes. She remembered a similar experience in her own life. She recalled vividly the moment in which she first knew that she would walk a path that few were chosen to walk, and she understood that the boy sitting across from her was experiencing now what she had experienced then—a maddening combination of boundless excitement and limitless fear. "And then you awoke from your dream."

"Yes, Looks Back woke me. She said it was past dawn." He stopped short, his voice dropping, the last of the words passing quietly into nothingness. "No, not then," he added quickly. "I woke up after I saw the great white animal. It was standing behind me."

Four Bears said nothing for a few moments, as if wrestling with what the boy had added to the story. "You are blessed, Young One," she said. "We dreamt the dream together, but I did not see the white beast. Did it speak to you?"

"I heard it in my heart," came the boy's reply. "*Such is the path of the Lenape. That's* what the great white animal told me."

Four Bears watched as a look of bewilderment crossed the boy's face. She knew what was happening behind his eyes. A child's brain was processing truths that few grown men and women could absorb. The physical world with which he was so familiar was crashing full force into the spiritual world that he was only beginning to know. She understood clearly that Walks Around would walk with a foot in each for the rest of his life. Each would be his home, but neither would be a home to which he could fully return.

"What does the dream mean?" he said almost inaudibly. "And why did we dream it together?" Questions began to rush from his mouth almost as quickly as they came to him, and his voice rose with each word. "How was the path cleared? What do the three white horses mean? And why did you not see the white beast? Why did he only come to me?"

"I don't know the answer to any of your questions," she admitted. "Perhaps it's not for either of us to know." But, in her heart, she knew that the questions would be answered and that the dark prophecy would be fulfilled.

Such is the path of the Lenape. The blood in her veins seemed to roil with each of the words.

* * *

By four in the afternoon, it had begun to rain, so Jill Martin told Roberto, Felix, and Hernando to stop working on the fountain until the next morning.

"Are you sure, Mees Jill?" Roberto asked. "There's not that much more to do." Roberto didn't mind finishing the job in the morning, but he had been particularly conciliatory since the accident on the bridge.

"Yes, I'm sure. Dad and I are going to check in on Dr. FitzRoy. *Buenas noches*, Roberto." Nodding at Felix and Hernando, she added, "*Buenos noches, amigos.*"

As she turned toward the footbridge, Roberto interrupted, "Not that way, Mees Jill, your father is out there."

Roberto pointed toward the back of the upper meadow, and Jill turned to see her father standing near the trees on the west end of the paddock. "*Gracias*," she responded as she started in her father's direction.

The rain wasn't heavy, but the late afternoon was cool enough to inspire Jill to pull her jacket collar against the back of her neck. As she made her way around the paddock, wild onions in the fencerow greeted her with an unmistakable fragrance of spring, their shoots sparkling with a crystalline veneer of rain.

Beyond the paddock, standing near an imposing oak, Jeff surveyed the surrounding ground, quietly assessing its appropriateness for the task he had in mind. As Jill approached, he looked up and said, "I've been thinking about this spot. It's peaceful here."

Jill didn't respond, but she more than agreed with him. Quiet and removed, the place was very peaceful indeed. The face of the woods that bordered it was curtained in yellow splendor by very old and wild forsythia. In the rain, as it was in the evening, its color was muted, but when the rising sun peeked above the roof of the main house the forsythia burst into a brilliance that Jill might have expected to find at the end of a rainbow. Protected by the huge oak and the woods to the west, the area never suffered in the heat of the afternoon, a blessing for which its lush carpet of vivid green grasses seemed to express its never-ceasing gratitude. The spot radiated an inviting beauty that was nearly impossible to resist, whether robed in spring or resting beneath a covering of new snow.

"I asked Dr. FitzRoy about the bones in the creek bed. If it's not against the law, I think I'd like to bury them here."

She hadn't expected him to say that, but it didn't surprise her. "What did she say?"

"The coroner will have to decide. It'll probably take some time."

"Well, I think it would be a nice thing to do. Whoever those bones belonged to—no, whoever that *was* . . ." She corrected herself mid-sentence, very aware of the fact that neither time nor circumstance could ever change the fact that the lifeless remains had once thrived inside a living being. ". . . would like being laid to rest in a place like this. It's nice of you to look out for him."

"I can't help but think that I'd want someone to do the same for me."

"I thought you wanted to be cremated."

"Yeah, I do." A broad smile crossed his mouth. "Maybe I should have said that I'd like someone to do the same with my ashes, like the archaeologist who finds them hundreds of years from now in the ruins of what used to be somebody's garage."

"Got it," Jill confirmed. "I'll make a note. Let's go see how things are going at the dig." She grinned back at him and added, "That's archaeology speak for *place where the bones are buried*."

"I know what it means," he chided as they walked past Jill's house and headed for the service road that led away from the upper meadow and back toward the excavation site. "And nobody likes a smartass."

The trees on the west side of the creek were just beginning to bud, and it was easy for Jeff and Jill to catch glimpses of the blue canopy from the service road. As they drew closer, they could see a handful of people standing around a table beneath the canopy. Emily FitzRoy and her assistant were easily identifiable, as was Grace Caufield from the *Courier Times*. They couldn't tell who the other person was at first, but they soon realized that it was Roy Cleveland, hidden beneath a rain slicker that seemed to be too much for the gentle spring rain. Leaving the road, they cut down a short expanse of grass and toward the bridge.

"How's it going?" Jeff called out as they descended the hillside. Then he stopped in his tracks, visibly taken aback by what he saw below.

On the table was the partial skeleton that had been removed from the bank. The skull lay looking straight into the top of the canopy, the detached mandible placed immediately in front of it. The sections of the spine, or what remained of it, had been placed in order immediately below the skull. The right coxal bone, which along with the skull was the most recognizable piece of skeleton, lay beneath the pieces of the spine and just ahead of what appeared to be the right femur. The remainder of the right leg and the entire left side of the skeleton were gone. And strangely, especially in light of the fact that so much else was missing, the right arm appeared to be relatively intact. Only the fingers were gone.

Near the jawbone sat a curved piece of what appeared to be corroded black metal. There was something else on the table, something that looked like a pile of small stones, but Jeff couldn't tell what it was from his vantage point.

As he walked onto the bridge, Jeff was struck by the reality of the situation. These were the same bones that had been buried in the creek bank, but now that they were back in the light of day they seemed to assume a much different presence.

"I'm fairly sure," Emily FitzRoy began as Jeff and Jill joined the group beneath the canopy, "that this is all of it. As you can see," she added, turning toward the hole in the bank, "we cleared out quite a space in every direction and didn't find anything else. There were hundreds of these little black and white things. I won't be able to say for sure until I clean them up, but they look like beads to me."

"So now that the bones are out of the ground," Jill asked, "what do you know about them?"

"Not much more than we knew before. Most likely male, and judging from the length of the humerus, about five-foot, eight, or a little taller."

"The humerus is the arm bone?" Jeff asked.

"Yes, it's the long bone in the upper arm, and we can make a reasonable estimation of height by measuring it and multiplying by five. And by looking at the development of bones like the femur," she added, moving her finger along the long bone of the right leg, "we can tell that this person was probably less than twenty to twenty-five years old."

"I don't know much about this," Jill added, "but I'm curious. Were people as tall as they are now when this man was alive? In general, I mean."

"It's a good question," the anthropologist acknowledged. "In general, as you say, no, but knowing so little about these remains, factoring that in would just be speculation."

"So, this was a fully grown male," Roy Cleveland interrupted, "but not very old."

"That's right, Roy, late teens or early twenties."

"So, that's it?" Jeff asked. "Somehow I thought you'd be able to tell more."

"I did, as well," chimed in Grace Caufield. "I guess I've been jaded by movies and television shows."

"Not necessarily," Emily answered. "We can discern quite a bit under different circumstances. The problem is the age of the bones. They're just too old to tell us much."

"Any guesses?" It was clear that Grace's interest was intensifying.

"We're going to do some testing, but short of that I have no idea."

"Why is so much of the skeleton missing?" Jeff asked.

"The real question is—why is so much of it here?" Emily countered. "Naturally buried bones don't always fare this well. The elements, predators, time all take their toll. These remains survived because they were protected somehow. Maybe by a freak of nature, we don't know." She paused, looking again at the cavity in the side of the bank. "And I doubt that we'll ever know."

It began to rain harder, and the sound of the rain on the canopy heightened the solemnity of the scene. The small group moved closer together inside the makeshift morgue.

Jeff continued with his questions. "So, what's next? What's the process?"

The coroner had started to answer the question when Emily interrupted him.

"The other thing is race."

"What do you mean?" Jill questioned.

"Sometimes—and again, I want to emphasize that with bones this old it's difficult to be very precise—we can at least guess at race based on certain features of the skull. If it were Caucasoid, Negroid, or Mongoloid, for example, we might be able to tell by the height of the forehead or shape of the eye sockets. This skull doesn't present any obvious clues in that regard, so even though we can't say for sure what it is, we may be able to reasonably assess what it is not." She lifted it from the table, leaving the jawbone behind and making the skull look painfully incomplete. "We'll most likely never know, and I'm not sure that it makes any difference."

"Do you mind if I take a look?" The voice came from the bridge and the group turned toward it in unison. A man stood there looking down at them. His was nearly comical in appearance, but from his demeanor it was clear that he didn't mean to be. He was wearing a wide-brimmed hat, off of which rain now dripped in every direction, and his white-bearded face was framed on both sides by hoop earrings. A cigarette hung from his lips. His slicker was unbuttoned, revealing a white T-shirt and khaki shorts. Something was printed or painted on the T-shirt—something resembling a half-black and half-red face—but it wasn't very clear through the falling rain. Placing a work boot on the low railing of the bridge, he leaned forward and said, "Maybe I can help."

Six

THANKSGIVING 2010

"Generations stand behind us as we sit here tonight," Jill Martin said to the people seated around the fire pit in the gathering barn. "They cannot tell their stories, but we can tell their stories for them. We can tell the stories of those we remember, and we can tell ours so that the children among us will remember." She waited for a moment, wondering to herself who would be the first to speak. Then, giving voice to the thought, she added, "So who would like to begin?"

The fire burned in brilliant oranges and yellows, warming everything in the center of the building. Jill's brother Harry, home from college for the Thanksgiving holiday weekend, had assumed responsibility for the fire and had moved a number of logs from a storage area near the stage to a place immediately behind his chair. The night was cold and dreary, and he wanted to make sure that the fire was drafting effectively. Its smoke rose quickly into the welcoming copper hood, assuring him that the fire was more than hot enough, but Harry still used the silence that followed Jill's request as an excuse to throw two more logs into the center of the pit.

Her question wafting on the warmth that seemed to envelope the group and everything around it, Jill waited quietly for someone to speak. Except for the couple seated to her immediate left, everyone seated in the circle was family. On the other side of the fire sat her sister, Hope, and her brother-in-law, Scott. Their house, situated across the paddock from Jill's, had been completed in the early spring, and Jill was delighted that they were now so close by. She took great comfort in the fact that their daughter, Valeria, seated on the floor in front of them, and her own daughter would grow up together. Seated next to Hope and Scott were Jill's cousin, Christopher, and his wife, Catherine, and next to them were Chick and Wade, Christopher's parents. Two boys, one a year older than Valeria, the other not quite a year younger, played on the floor in front of their parents and grandparents, randomly moving between playing at Catherine's feet, sitting on Chick's lap, making faces at Valeria, and staring into the roaring fire. Next to Chick and Wade sat Dae Phillips and Jill's husband, Edward.

Three people sat to Jill's left, including a man and woman who were not family but who had become very special friends through the events of recent months. They sat quietly, holding hands, watching the faces in the circle with a mutual intensity. Next to the couple sat Harry's empty chair, its occupant having made an impromptu trip to the area where the firewood was stored.

As Harry returned to his chair, a pile of logs cradled between his chest and arms, a soft voice rose from the other side of the circle.

"I'd like to tell a story," Chick began, "but first I would like to welcome our guests—*our friends*." She nodded at the man and woman who sat to Jill's left in the circle. "It's nice to have you here with our family. I don't think any of us could imagine not having you here with us tonight."

Neither the man nor the woman replied, but both smiled and nodded appreciatively.

"For those of you who may not know, my real name is Robin. My father called me Chick when I was a little girl, and the name just sort of stuck. It's wonderful to be here with all of you, especially at this time of year." Her voice trailed off, as if spirited away by the smoke that rose from the fire pit. "I'm just sorry that Jeff's not here with us."

She paused for a moment, flashing through the mental images that spontaneously preoccupy those who are left behind to deal with death.

"I don't know how well I can do this," she continued, "but I would like to tell a story. And I'm not sure how this works, so if I take too much time please stop me."

"None of us know how it works, Aunt Chick," Hope interrupted. "We're not even sure what *it* is, yet." Then, in an attempt to lighten the mood somewhat, she added, "But if you drone on, we'll be sure to let you know." The comment drew laughter from the others in the circle, leaving the children to wonder about what was so funny.

"I'd like to talk about my mother and father," Chick continued. "But instead of recounting every detail of their lives—and to tell the truth I don't know nearly as many of those details as I would like to know—I want to talk about who they were." Quickly modifying her words, she said, "No, I would like to talk about *why* they were. I mean, at the end of the day, each of us and everything around us is the result of *why* they were, isn't it?"

Another silence ran along the periphery of the circle. For a few moments all that could be heard was the crackling of the fire.

"My mom and dad had difficult lives when they were young," Chick began, "certainly more difficult than anything most of us have experienced.

"My mother was the oldest of four. My grandmother had to work because her husband had deserted his family, so my mother was left to raise her sisters. My mom was married at eighteen, just a few days before her husband went off to fight in World War II. He was lost at sea a few months later." She paused at the thought. Having a son of her own who was career military—a son she had worried about ceaselessly when he was fighting in Afghanistan, Iraq, and other corners of the world—had created one of the most lasting bonds she had ever experienced with her mother. And now, even though her son had returned home safely and was stationed out of harm's way in Oklahoma, the mere mention of her mother's first marriage knotted that bond yet again, strengthening it even more.

"My father had a difficult early life, as well. His father was killed in World War I, three months before he was born. When that happened, his mother re-took her maiden name. I'm not sure why she did that but she did, so my dad lived his entire life with a different last name. And he passed it on to us." She paused again, taking in a deep breath. "One single event, tragic as it was, changed so many things that followed."

"That's interesting," Hope offered. "And I'm struck by the fact that these are things that happened just two generations ago. I can only imagine how much information like that is buried with earlier generations."

"I think," Scott added to his wife's comment, "that there's family information and there's family legend. And over time the two get confused."

"What do you mean?" Chick asked.

"On the face of it one would think that the information is what it is, that it's not malleable. But think about one of the things you just said—your grandmother reverted back to her maiden name after your grandfather was killed in the war. How many things are changed when a person grows up with a different last name—other than the one he or she was supposed to have, I mean?"

"Changed for the worse?"

"Not necessarily. Maybe they're changed for the better, but they're still changed."

"I guess I never thought about it like that. I do know that we know nothing about my paternal grandfather or his family. We just have a name. There are generations of a family just like ours out there. We're related to them and we don't even know who they are."

"That's interesting, too," Scott answered. "You just have a name. I have an uncle who's really into genealogy. He does a lot of research on the Internet. He told me once that his ancestors immigrated to this country from Germany back in the late 1600s. In doing his research, he found thirteen different spellings of his last name."

"How does something like that happen?" Chick asked.

"I only know what he told me. Names were anglicized phonetically. I know that happened quite a bit when people came into this country through Ellis Island."

"My father told me about a similar thing in our family," Wade interjected. "His ancestors were Ukrainian." As he spoke, he reached down to pick up his youngest grandson, who had worked his way along the circle from his mother, to his grandmother, to his grandfather. "My mother's people came from Poland. My mom and dad were both second-generation American, so their grandparents didn't come to this country all that long ago. You'd think that immigration agents would have been recording things more accurately by then."

"There was also a lot of name changing around the time of the world wars," Scott continued. "My uncle also told me that people with Germanic last names didn't want to be associated with the Kaiser or Hitler, so they changed their names to sound more American. I guess church records, especially in the Lutheran Church, are full of that kind of thing."

"May I ask a question?" The voice belonged to the woman of the couple that Chick had welcomed earlier. It was peaceful and considerate. "This is very interesting to me. To both of us," she added, squeezing her partner's hand a little more tightly. "Both of our families have examples of similar things. But I'm most interested in your comment about family legends," she said, looking toward Scott. "What do you consider to be a family legend?"

"Maybe that's not the best way to describe them," Scott answered. "Basically, they're the stories that get passed down from generation to generation. They may be true or they may not be, but over time they become accepted as true."

"I see," the woman said. "We have many examples of those, as well."

"Would you like to share them?" Scott asked.

"Not just yet. Perhaps in a little while."

"I have a great example," Chick offered. "It's something that we all accepted as true for years, at least up until recently." She paused for a moment, watching Harry as he stood to throw another log onto the fire. "It's about how my parents met.

"The story—and perhaps it's the legend—begins with my dad. He was a pretty good football player, and when he graduated from high school he was offered a number of college scholarships. From what I understand, he also had an opportunity to play semi-professional football. He didn't do either. Like a lot of men in that time—the time before the United States entered World War II, I mean—he decided to enlist in the Army, instead.

"He had served for more than three years and was due to be discharged when the Japanese attacked Pearl Harbor. In fact," she said, as if remembering an important piece of evidence, "we have a photo of him throwing a football on some base in Georgia. It's dated December 7, 1941.

"Because his unit was combat ready, it was one of the first to be deployed. I don't know many of the details, other than he was with the Fifth Army in North Africa in 1942. I know he was in combat for nearly three years, and most of the men he went overseas with didn't come home." She paused for a long time, and no one said anything to break the silence.

"Like I said," Chick digressed, "my mom and dad had tough lives. But in reality they probably weren't all that much tougher than those of most folks during that time."

"They sound pretty tough to me," Wade interrupted, placing a reassuring hand on Chick's thigh. "If that kind of stuff was commonplace back then, it's a wonder that anyone came out of it with their sanity."

"I agree," she answered, shaking her head subtly as if doing so would free it of the thought. "Anyway," she went on, "my father served with an uncle of my mother's—Uncle Joe. They had been through a lot together and had become very good friends.

"When they came home, Uncle Joe introduced Mom and Dad, or at least that's what we believed for a long time."

"What do you mean?" Jill asked. "Isn't that what happened?"

"My mom's family wasn't too excited about her being with Dad. She was a young widow—nineteen or so, if you can imagine that—and Dad was neither Italian nor Roman Catholic. Everybody was pretty worked up about it."

"What happened?" Hope asked.

"Uncle Joe took my dad's side—big time. Everyone in the family loved Joe, and in time they came to love my dad as well, but my mother and father never would have been together if it weren't for Uncle Joe."

"So where does the legend come in?" the woman with the peaceful voice asked.

"Five years ago we were at an eightieth birthday party for a close friend of our family. Wade and I were there, as was Jeff. We were sitting at a table, talking with some folks we hadn't seen for years, when a man came up to us and introduced himself. I can't remember his name, but he told us that he owned a shoe repair shop across the street from my grandmother's house—the house where my dad grew up. While we were talking, he said, 'I was with your mom and dad the day your dad came home from the war.'

"We were obviously taken aback by the comment, and I remember Jeff saying, 'You must be mistaken. Mom and Dad were introduced later, by our Uncle Joe.'

"The man said that he also knew Joe, but he insisted that he had seen Mom and Dad together, and even though he was in his eighties himself, he seemed to be remembering the incident very clearly. 'No,' he said, 'your father parked right in front of my shop. Your mom was with him, and he had this huge smile on his face. I'll never forget it.'

"We came away very perplexed, doing the mental arithmetic that often accompanies family legends. Dad was eight years older than Mom, so she was only a teenager when he went into the service. We didn't know if he knew Mom's family beforehand or if he knew her late husband. It was all a mystery. And in retrospect it's not a big deal one way or the other, but that's one legend that certainly took a hit that day."

"So, did you ever find out the truth?" Scott asked.

"No," Chick responded. "There are people we could ask—people who might be able to provide some clarity—but what difference would it make?"

"What do you mean?" Jill questioned. "Isn't there something to be said for truth?"

"Always," Chick agreed, "but there's also something to be said for legend." She paused for a few seconds, trying to frame her thoughts before continuing.

"Do you remember when I said I wanted to talk about *why* my parents were rather than who they were? Well, to me, that's really the point. I mean, they both had very difficult lives. They had been through more by the time they were twenty than most people go through in a lifetime. And I have to believe that when they met and fell in love—however that actually happened—they were focused on where they were going, not where they had been. They wanted to create a life together that was different than the ones they had lived as individuals.

"I'm not saying they were idealistic," she continued, "but it only makes sense that they wanted something better for their children." She looked at her grandchildren—one on her husband's lap, the other on her son's. "For all of us."

Chick paused for a few moments, letting her eyes drift around the circle to each of the people seated there.

"*Why* my mother and father *were* has a lot to do with *why* most of us here *are*. Part of it is physical—if my mother's first husband wasn't killed in the war, or if my father accepted a football scholarship instead of enlisting, or if Uncle Joe didn't intercede for Mom and Dad . . . The ifs are endless, but they really don't matter. That's just the way things happened.

"But part of it is something else—it's more spiritual. What was the purpose in all of it? How did his purpose and her purpose become *their* purpose? And what purpose does each of us pursue because of it?"

As she paused with the question, not really expecting an answer, her attention was drawn to the windows off to her right. The blackness beyond was broken only by the faintest light from the windows of Jill's house at the other end of the paddock. She thought about her brother, her parents, and the generations of people from whom most of the people in the circle had come. Just as her niece had said when the circle had gathered, she knew that all of those people were somehow with them tonight.

"Or should I even think about such things?" she added.

"Of course you should," the woman who had asked about family legends answered. "We are *why* we are because of purpose."

Seven

The bright moonlight painted the landscape beyond Jeff's office window in shades of cream and silver that reminded him of the best black and white films of the fifties. The front lawn, the stone wall, and the meadow beyond coalesced in a palette of non-color that seemed every bit as warm as the soft hues with which the meadow glistened in the afternoon sun.

Beyond the lower meadow, Jeff could see the silhouettes of the trees along the top of the hill that dropped down to the river. Arrow-straight and sharply defined in black, they looked like silent sentries prepared to defend the river against any force that would interrupt its journey along an ancient path.

Jeff had been standing at the window for the better part of an hour. He loved the seclusion of his office and he worked there frequently, although seldom at this hour of the night. He usually preferred to sit in the chair by the bed and write in the soft light of a single lamp, Dae sleeping nearby. But this morning he wasn't writing; he was thinking about the events of the previous day— the work on the fountain; talking with Jill by the large oak behind the paddock; Emily FitzRoy's revelations about the bones spread

out on the table beneath the blue canopy; and the man with hoop
earrings who had appeared in the rain, standing on the bridge as
if conjured by unseen witches.

The man had introduced himself as George Cameron.
"Although," he then added, "a number of people just call me
Crow Feather."

"Which do you prefer?" Jeff had asked a little less than
seriously. He hadn't meant to be dismissive, but he was surprised
that someone would appear out of nowhere introducing himself
as Crow Feather.

"The people who used to inhabit this land would have
preferred Crow Feather, but George is fine."

"Why would the Williams boys have preferred Crow Feather?"
Jeff asked, referring to the men from whom he had purchased the
property.

"Don't know them," came a matter-of-fact reply that implied
the man didn't care about knowing them, "but I'm not talking
about the people who used to own this property. I'm talking
about the people who inhabited this land hundreds of years ago."
Then, after removing his hat and shaking the rain off of it, he
added, "Thousands of years ago."

Now, standing at his office window and thinking about the
ensuing conversation with George Cameron, Jeff thought about
how egotistical his question must have sounded. It would have
been better, he decided in retrospect, to have given the man an
opportunity to explain himself.

Cameron had asked Emily FitzRoy a number of questions,
few of which seemed to pertain to the bones, *per se*. He was
intrigued that she thought the remains were those of a male,

although he seemed to receive the finding as confirmation rather than new information. With the permission of Dr. FitzRoy and Roy Cleveland, he examined the excavated site carefully, as well as the items sitting on the table with the bones.

"Can you describe for me," he began, addressing the young anthropologist, "how the bones were positioned?"

She had responded in considerable detail, walking over to the hole in the bank and using her hands to describe how the bones had been found in a supine position, as well as what bones were missing and what may or may not have happened to them. She then repeated, as she had for everyone else earlier, that most of what she was saying was conjecture, very little of which could be substantiated.

After listening to the information, Cameron had responded in the same straightforward way that he had addressed Jeff's comment about the Williams boys.

"I think our friend here is Native American."

"I considered that," Emily FitzRoy answered. "Artifacts are found on a regular basis here in Bucks County, although skeletal remains are rare these days. But . . .," She paused in a manner that seemed to emphasize what she was about to say. ". . . there's nothing about the remains that would make that obvious."

"If you had found the bones in a seated position or placed on their side," Cameron observed, "I'd feel pretty confident about it. The aboriginal people in this area buried their dead in those ways, usually with food and tools—provisions for the afterlife."

"Do you think that's a tool?" Roy Cleveland asked, pointing to the corroded piece of metal on the table.

"No, I think it's jewelry, and it may be the best clue we'll have in identifying these remains."

"Help me understand something," Jeff began, "I thought the bodies of Native Americans were placed on high platforms in burial grounds."

"That was the case in many cultures," Cameron responded, "but not around here."

"Excuse me," Grace Caufield interrupted. "I'm with the *Courier Times* and I'm gathering information about this for a story. I'm interested in why you think that thing is jewelry."

"I think it's a necklace or amulet, probably European." Cameron sensed the confusion that his observation inspired and he didn't wait for the next question.

"My best guess is that this man was Post-Contact Native American—post contact with the white man, that is. This is probably bronze underneath," he said, picking up the corroded metal, "and the crescent shape indicates that it was worn around the neck. He probably traded for it with a European."

"If that's true," Emily FitzRoy said, "these remains can be anywhere from a hundred to four hundred years old."

"I'd say at least two hundred, but yes, four hundred is a possibility."

"The other thing is this," Cameron continued, poking an index finger through the pile of black and white stones that lay by the bones. "These are beads, and it's doubtful that they were loose when our friend here died. They may have also been some kind of adornment—a belt perhaps—but based on the colors, I'm guessing that they were wampum."

"Wampum?" Grace Caufield asked. "You mean as in money?"

"Yes, very loosely defined. A more precise definition would be 'something of value.' Wampum was used to record important events or family history. As such, it was of extreme value. The beads used prior to the arrival of white men were carved by hand out of shells. They were much smaller than these, and much less uniform. These were either made by Europeans or with European tools."

"We're going to remove everything to the county forensic lab in Warminster," Roy Cleveland said. "Maybe we can make a little more sense out of all this down there. Then we'll decide what to do with the remains. As you all know by now, Mr. Phillips has asked that they be buried here. I have some processes to go through before I can even consider something like that."

Within an hour, the remains and the things that accompanied them had been placed in a black bag, put in the back of Roy Cleveland's SUV, and removed from the property. Even though he could see that the remains were being treated with care and respect, George Cameron watched the process carefully, as if personally responsible for their safety.

Looking out across the moonlit lower meadow, Jeff thought about George Cameron and his observations. Under any circumstances, there was a story behind the remains, but if Cameron was correct, there was a much different story than Jeff had anticipated.

He thought about the conversation with Cameron that had continued after everyone else had left. Standing by themselves beneath the blue canopy, the rain having subsided and a light mist having risen above the water in the creek, they talked about a number of things, all of which had stemmed from a single question from Jeff.

"So, what tribe owned this land hundreds of years ago?"

"White man's question," Cameron answered, shaking his head condescendingly.

"What did you expect?" Jeff answered. "I am white. And while we're on the subject, you're white as well."

"I'm three sixty-fourths Native American," Cameron answered. "And I'm an Outaluck."

"An Outaluck?"

"There are only three kinds of people in the world," George Cameron said stoically, sounding as if he had made the observation countless times, "those who are Native American, those who want to be, and 'Outalucks'—people with only some Native American blood. Outalucks can never be anything more than *part* Native American."

"But three sixty-fourths," Jeff answered, "doesn't seem like very much at all."

"At least I know it. Most people don't know *anything* about their great-great-great-grandparents.

"You have a point there."

"And the people who lived here were more than a tribe; they were a culture."

"What do you mean?"

Picking up a stick that lay on the ground nearby, Cameron squatted and scratched a crooked line in the dirt. "Before the white man came to this country, thousands of Lenape lived along Lenapewihittuk—the River of the Lenape."

"Are you talking about the Delaware?"

"Yes, the Delaware." He poked the stick into the ground near the top of the crooked line. "A tribe called the Munsee, or 'people of the stony country,' lived on the upper river." He dragged the stick to the bottom of the line. "Down here, in what is now the state of Delaware . . ." He dragged it to the right. ". . . and over here in New Jersey were the 'people who lived near the ocean'— the Unalachtigo."

He moved the stick to the place Jeff recognized as the point of Pennsylvania that juts east above Philadelphia. "And in this area, including what is now Bucks County and your property, lived the Unami, or 'people down river.' People from the different tribes often lived together in the same village, but that's where they came from."

Cameron drew a large circle around the crude picture in the dirt. "On both sides of the river there was nothing but Lenape villages."

"Do you think there was a village here?"

"It's certainly possible. The Lenape relied on the river and their villages were always near it, usually along tributaries like this probably was at one time. But they moved their villages on a regular basis, following game to hunt and better ground for their crops."

"So this area was once part of a Lenape, or . . ." Pausing, Jeff apologized, "I'm sorry, what was the word you used for these folks?"

"Unami—people down river."

"So this area was once part of a Unami village."

"There was a very large village south of here in what is now northeast Philadelphia, but there were many villages, usually just twenty or thirty wigwams each."

"Wigwams?"

"Let's get back to your original question," Cameron insisted. "Although you could certainly call the Lenape a tribe, they were much more. They were part of something even larger—the Algonkian-speaking peoples that inhabited most of what is now the northeastern United States. We're talking about a vast aboriginal culture that extends back thousands of years."

"I have to admit," Jeff began, "that when I think of Native Americans I think of the Plains Indians—Sitting Bull, Geronimo, those guys."

"I understand. The tribes that lived in the western parts of North America—and there were many of them—were also grouped in language-based cultures. But by the time Sitting Bull and Crazy Horse met Custer at the Little Big Horn, the Lenape culture here in the East had been gone for a century. The Native American cultures of the West would be pushed aside, as well; it would just happen later."

Jeff stood silently, trying to process the scope of what Cameron was saying.

"And no, the Lenape did not *own* this land."

"Excuse me?"

"That was the other part of your question—'what tribe owned this land?' Land ownership was not a concept to the Lenape, just as it wasn't a concept for most Native Americans. They didn't even have a word for it in their language. It was another thing that white men brought with them to this continent."

"Another thing?"

"Along with guns and disease."

Now, in the darkness of his office, Jeff could envision George Cameron walking back across the bridge and along the service road toward his car, which was parked somewhere out of sight. Although they hadn't agreed to meet again, he knew that they would.

Jeff's office sat next to the main bedroom, and it afforded a similar view of the lower meadow, but few people who came into the house even knew that it existed. The other bedrooms all emptied onto the large round hall in the middle of the second floor, but the office was hidden, accessible only through the dressing area between it and the master bedroom.

As he turned to leave, Jeff could see the surface of his desk, shining like a white stone in the moonlight that flooded the room. When designing the office, he had opted for a flat work surface rather than a traditional desk. It seemed to better suit the way in which he worked—his computer immediately in front of him, papers and books spread out to his left and right. The walls of the room were consumed by built-in bookshelves, most of which had pull-down glass doors like old barrister bookcases. There was no furniture, except for the desk chair and a worn leather chair and ottoman that sat by the windows.

The desk was relatively clear at the moment, the reflection of its surface interrupted only by a tablet of paper, a silver pen, and two books—an opened volume about the demise of George Custer at the Little Big Horn River and Dee Brown's *Bury My Heart at Wounded Knee*. His sleep had been interrupted by the desire to know more about the people who had once lived along the Delaware—or whatever name by which George Cameron had referred to the river—and he was frustrated to find that he had only two books about Native Americans, neither of which appeared to have anything to say about the Lenape. He had purchased the books years apart, more out of admiration for the authors than because of any particular interest in Indians.

Jeff re-traced his steps through the dressing area, moved quietly through the bedroom, and stepped into the second floor hall. Pulling the bedroom door closed behind him, he walked to the head of the double staircase and down the steps to the main floor.

He turned past the majestic water wall that separated the front hallway from the living room, and into a surreal scene that was as alive with the night as anything beyond the walls of the house. The living room had been transformed into a man-made ecosystem fed by moonlight that danced through the windows on the hallway, through the shimmering water wall, and across the lushly carpeted floor. The gentle cascade of water amplified the otherworldliness, as if the river itself had somehow crossed the lower meadow to make its way into the house. Struck by the incredible beauty of it all, Jeff found himself regretting that he alone was awake to see it, that something so moving would be experienced only by a ghost who haunts his own house.

Between the living room and the kitchen sat an informal gathering space, more casual than the former and less functional than the latter. It was nothing more than a place where people could hang out and feel comfortable doing it. One end of the space was anchored by an immense wooden table that Jeff had always seen as a special place for his grandchildren—a place where they could just be kids, spilling their milk and coloring with gleeful abandon. It waited for them expectantly, as if it had seen the future.

At the end of the hallway that stretched across the back of the house, Jeff entered what had come to be known as the plant room. Its huge floor-to-ceiling windows made it a natural place for plants, even though it faced north and the sun only touched it a few hours a day in the heart of winter. It was filled with the flora that Jeff loved and respected. Other wealthy people might have built houses with imposing foyers and dining rooms for twenty guests, but Jeff preferred one in which living things were honored.

Standing by the windows, Jeff looked out across the expanse of land to the north. Bordered by the sloping hillside to the river on the east, it ran northwest for nearly a half mile before ending in a heavily wooded area at the edge of Jeff's property. Like the upper meadow, it was completely natural, untouched since being cleared decades—if not centuries—earlier. Watching the distant landscape dissolve into the moonlight, Jeff could only wonder if there were more bones buried somewhere out there, or if there were artifacts from some distant culture waiting in the rich soil created by the river ages ago.

Suddenly, Jeff gasped, his lungs filling quickly and completely like the airbag of a car at the moment of impact. He tried to exhale, but the effort was met by invisible hands that reached into him from behind and pulled air into his lungs until he thought they would explode. Arching his back against the pain, he fought desperately to remain upright. Then, as quickly as it had come, the air left his lungs and he found himself in the middle of the field beyond the windows.

Moonlight flooded the area around him. Night sounds filled the air—he heard a light breeze in the tops of nearby trees; crickets only a few feet away; an owl perched on a branch overlooking the field. It was easy to imagine field mice and moles rummaging in the high grasses, raccoons and opossums making their nocturnal rounds, and black snakes coiled silently in unseen piles of rocks.

He looked back toward the house, which was now hundreds of yards away and little more than a formless blur in a landscape of moonlight and shadows. In the other direction, he could see the faint glow of the lights of the Wilson & Meyers Produce Company on the far side of the highway. A single set of headlights made its way along the road, clearly visible in one moment and gone in the next, intermittently hidden by the trees and undergrowth of the distant woods.

He stood quietly, peacefully, wondering what this vision was about. He had been out here before, when he first bought the land, and many times since, and he had always taken comfort in the fact that this part of his property was natural and undisturbed, the ward of nature and time.

Then, as if both nature and time were affirming their ability to move the affairs of men at their will, Jeff saw an imposing buffalo standing in the field less than thirty feet away. Its white fur made hauntingly brighter by the light of the moon, the animal stood silently, looking to the east as if unaware that Jeff was standing so close. It didn't look at him; it didn't graze; it just stood there, etched by the moon on the face of an otherworldly coin, staring toward the unseen river.

Jeff wanted to know what this was all about. He wanted to know if the animal would tell him if he asked, or if it would be explained in some other way if he just stood there long enough.

But the vision was gone, and he was back in the main house, on his knees and gasping for air. If the white buffalo was still out there, it was farther out than he could see, a kindred apparition haunting a place of its own.

* * *

Startled out of her dream by a loud noise, Dae Phillips lay quietly, trying to determine if she had heard something from inside the room, outside the room, or the recesses of her dream. She looked around as she got out of bed and into her robe, quickly determining that the noise had not come from inside the room. She walked over to the windows and opened the curtains, letting in the gray light of the overcast morning. There was nothing unusual on the lawn or beyond the stone wall, other than the greening grasses that moved back and forth at the whim of the light wind that rose and fell in the meadow.

She moved silently toward Jeff's office, making a mental note about the placement of things as she moved through the dressing area. Everything seemed to be in its place, but she could see immediately that the door to the office was closed. Jeff seldom closed it, not even when he was working, so Dae was fairly confident that she had found the source of the noise. Her suspicion was confirmed when she opened the door and found the windows cranked opened and the curtains riding the gentle gusts that passed through the screens. The door had been blown shut. She secured it with a brass doorstop cast in the form of a turtle and then closed the windows.

As she turned to leave, she saw two books on Jeff's unusually neat desk. A paperback was lying opened and face down, *Son of the Morning Star* recorded in black letters above a picture of a feathered lance crossed with the pennant of the Seventh Cavalry. It was one of her husband's favorite books, and she wondered if he was reading it again or if he had been referring to it for some other reason. Next to it was *Bury My Heart at Wounded Knee*, a title she recognized but did not know much about. She didn't know why the books were on Jeff's desk, but it was easy to guess that they had something to do with his conversation with George Cameron the previous day.

There was something else on his desk—a pad of paper with lines of poetry scrawled on the top page. She looked in the wastebasket by the desk and saw crumpled pieces of the same paper, the discarded chronology of the birth pangs of creativity. Pulling the pad closer, she read the lines of the poem.

> On time's lost landscape stands a buffalo,
> Its coarse white hair made brighter by the moon—
> Pale specter in a sleepless vision,
> Unknown magician's otherworldly rune.
>
> What's the meaning of its silent message?
> Is it a mystery to words immune—
> Prophecy revealed in the moonlight
> To be fulfilled in sunlit afternoon?
>
> Is it witness to events transpired
> Or harbinger of something opportune?
> Has it come to offer vindication
> Or cast a light on what will happen soon?

Images of a white buffalo filling her head, a head that only minutes earlier had been lost in dreams, Dae walked back through the dressing area and toward the shower.

* * *

As soon as she turned onto Jacksonville Road, Emily FitzRoy began looking for Eagle Way, which, according to her GPS, would soon be coming up on the left. Even with the warning, she might have missed the turn had it not been for the sign on the cyclone fence that announced the county forensic facility. Eagle Way amounted to little more than a service road through an industrial park, and as Emily approached the facility she was struck by how out of place it looked among the metal-sided, mostly windowless buildings that sat behind it. The one-story building was obviously only a few years old, and its clean lines and crisp façade appeared better suited to the bustling campus of a community college than to this austere village of warehouses.

A few minutes later, Emily was greeted by Roy Cleveland in the lobby of the facility.

"Welcome, Dr. FitzRoy," he said, extending his hand. "Can I get you a cup of coffee?"

"Thank you," she answered, "it's nice to finally be here. And no, I don't care for anything. I'm just anxious to get to work."

"Well, at least let me show you around before we get started."

"I'd like that. I've heard so much about this place."

"All of the public areas are off of the lobby here. That conference room over there is for meetings, press conferences by the district attorney's office, that type of thing. His offices, by the way, are over there on the other side of the lobby."

He turned and pressed an access card against the magnetic security lock next to the door behind him. The lock clicked and he pushed the door open, continuing with the impromptu tour.

"This is Audrey Simmons," he said as they entered the room. "She runs things around here. Audrey, this is Emily FitzRoy, the anthropologist from Penn I told you about."

The woman rose from her chair behind the desk and extended a hand. "It's nice to meet you, Dr. FitzRoy, and please don't believe the part about me running things."

"It's nice to meet you as well, Audrey."

"These are our administrative offices," Cleveland continued. "My office is down the hall, as are the offices of the deputy coroners. And through here . . ." He turned and used his access card again. ". . . is the business end of things.

"This room," he said, pointing to the right, "is for family members that may be called upon to make identifications. We want them to be as comfortable as possible and have whatever privacy they require. They can make identifications through the window here, but we also have closed circuit television if they're more comfortable with that. As you know, there's not much need for in-person IDs anymore, but the room's here if we need it."

Pushing open the door on the opposite wall, he said, "This is the main cooler. We can accommodate seventy bodies here."

As they stepped inside, Emily could see six gurneys in the middle of the huge room. It was clear that four of them held adult bodies, the white coverings following the contours of the corpses beneath. On one, two discolored feet of what was obviously a relatively tall person protruded beyond the end of the covering. The remaining two gurneys held what she guessed to be children, their remains less defined beneath black plastic sheets.

"This is a big room," she observed. "Much larger than I would have guessed."

"Because we're between Philadelphia and New York, we have to be prepared for just about anything—plane crashes, train accidents, even terrorist attacks. I'd hate to see this room at capacity, but it's not out of the realm of possibility."

"Unfortunately not."

A few steps down the hall from the cooler they made a left into another hallway.

"These offices are for the autopsy assistants and visiting law officers. And down here," he added as they walked through large doors that opened automatically, "is the main examination room."

It was a large room, eighty-five to ninety feet in length, with three fully equipped autopsy stations, the state-of-the-art components of which Cleveland described proudly as they walked from one end to the other. At the far end, they paused outside of an adjoining room that was comparatively smaller but appointed every bit as well as the stations they had just passed.

"What's this?" Emily asked. "It looks like a completely self-contained unit."

"Exactly. It's for situations in which we suspect a possible biohazard or infectious disease. The idea is that one person, or a minimum number of people, could do everything that needs to be done. There's even an overhead lift so that a body can be moved easily by a single individual."

"It's all very impressive, Roy, obviously a significant investment by the county."

"Thanks. I think we're fortunate to have it. Now, if we can work our way back to the hallway, I'll show you where we process decomps."

The door at the end of the main hall opened into what looked like a garage, a large, open room with an automatic overhead door on each end.

"This area is about privacy, too," Cleveland began. "We can unload a body in here out of view of the public, the press, and helicopters. It's just a big garage, but it serves a very useful purpose. And through here . . ." He opened a door on the opposite wall and they stepped outside into a covered passageway between the main building and an isolated room. ". . . is the examination room for decomposed bodies or, in the case of the bones from the Phillips place, skeletal remains."

Emily FitzRoy could tell instantly that the room was different. A smell seemed to permeate everything, even the stainless steel fixtures and instrumentation. It wasn't the unbearable smell that always accompanied the advanced stages of death, as much as it was the permanent reminder that the smell had once filled the room. Even the numerous vents that constantly sucked the air out of the room, twenty-four hours a day, seven days a week, could not erase the subtle, sober residue of old death.

"I know," the coroner said softly, responding to the look on Emily's face. "It never really leaves completely. We haven't had a body in here in more than two weeks and there's still a faint trace of the smell. When it can no longer be repulsive it settles for just being haunting."

They stood quietly for a few seconds before Cleveland broke the silence once again.

"Okay. The locker rooms are back across the way. The holding cooler is on the other side of the garage. I'll meet you there in a few minutes."

Fifteen minutes later, the coroner and anthropologist had moved the skeletal remains into the examination room from the holding cooler where they had been taken upon arrival. Dressed in scrubs, more out of procedure than necessity, they had placed the bones on an examination table in the same manner in which they had been arranged beneath the blue canopy on the Phillips property.

As Emily pushed the table against the retention sink in the autopsy station, the bones seemed to openly defy all of the leading-edge technology that surrounded them. They presented no hair or tissue that could be used for toxicology testing; no tendon or ligament that might provide the smallest insight into the cause of death; no drop of blood or fluid that could in any way help identify the human being in whom they had once lived. Stripped bare and fully exposed, they clung to their secrets as if secrets were all they had left.

Pulling a suspended microphone down to face level, the coroner said, "Today is Thursday, 9 April, 2009, and this is the examination of skeletal remains found on the Bucks County property of Jeffrey Phillips near Riegelsville. Attending are Roy S. Cleveland, county coroner, and Emily L. FitzRoy, forensic anthropologist on staff at the University of Pennsylvania.

"The remains are skeletal and partial, and there is no obvious or apparent reason why this is the case. The bones are extremely brittle and significantly discolored, suggesting that they are quite old. Would you care to add anything, Dr. FitzRoy?"

"Only that the remains were unearthed in the bank of a creek during a construction-related accident on the property. They did not appear to have been ritually buried, and the absence of so much of the skeleton seems to confirm this. The body may have been exposed to weather and predation for an extended period of time, which could account for the fact that much of the skeleton is missing. I excavated a considerable portion of ground on all sides of the remains and found no additional bones or bone fragments."

"It should be noted," Roy Cleveland added, "that two unidentified items were found at the site—a heavily corroded piece of metal in what appears to be a crescent shape, and a considerable number of loose beads. Both the metal object and the beads will be analyzed by Dr. FitzRoy tomorrow at the University of Pennsylvania." As he handed an ID tag to Emily, he continued, "We're now tagging the remains with Identification Number BCC 2009-0038 and beginning a standard photographic sequence."

As Roy snapped the required series of photographs, Emily addressed the few characteristics of the remains that could be identified.

"We believe the remains to be that of a male based on two things: the curvature of the posterior ramus and the size of the sciatic notch. Only the right coxal bone remains, with the ilium, ischium, and pubis all relatively intact, and it is clearly that of a male. It should also be noted at this point that the jawbone is completely separated from the skull.

"Regarding height and age . . . Based on a humerus length of 35.12 centimeters and allowing for deterioration, we estimate a height of between 5'9" and 5'10". The bones appear to be fully developed, so we're estimating that the deceased was at least twenty years old.

"Race is indeterminable, and although the bones appear to be that of an active individual, there's not enough evidence to estimate body weight."

After the bones were photographed, they were transferred onto a radiolucent table in the x-ray area.

As he slipped his arms into a lead vest, Roy observed, "We're not supposed to need these if we stand at least six feet away and use the remote, but I think it's a worthwhile precaution."

"Thank you," Emily said in obvious agreement, "I think it is as well."

Shaped like a letter C, the mobile fluoroscopy unit was large enough to pass over the plastic table easily without disturbing whatever was being x-rayed. Roy moved the machine into place above the skull, took a few steps back, and activated the x-ray using the remote control. The image of the skull appeared on a nearby monitor.

"I want to take some snapshots of the skull," he said, "then we'll move on to the larger bones. I can enlarge the image on the monitor like this," he added after taking the first shot, "and I can take a snapshot of the enlargement. I also have the option of downloading pictures to disc."

Moving the fluoroscopy unit into place above the humerus, he repeated the process.

"Look at that," Emily said as the image of the arm bone appeared on the monitor. "The density of the bone is very poor, both from the exterior in and from the marrow wall out. There appears to be some remaining stability in between, but not very much."

"They're deteriorated alright, but we still don't know how much of the deterioration is due to age and how much of it can be attributed to the conditions under which they were interred."

"I agree, Roy. If it's okay with you I'd like to do an ultraviolet test, and I think we should test for nitrogen as well."

"Yes, of course. Eventually we'll have to do something with these remains, and having a better idea about how old they are may help us with that." Moving back within range of the microphone, Roy recorded their intention to do the additional tests before adding, "We're not conducting a toxicology test because of the complete absence of soft tissue, and DNA testing appears to be of little value at this time. Do you concur, Dr. FitzRoy?"

"I do, Dr. Cleveland. I don't mean to be glib, but what would be the point?"

"This shouldn't take long," the coroner suggested as he lifted the humerus from the table. "I'll be in the small lab next to the main examination room."

As she waited alone with the remains in the silence of the decomp examination room, it was easy for Emily's imagination to wander. She had spent her share of time in morgues and other unnerving locations, and she had seen more strange things than most people could imagine seeing, but she was still susceptible to fantastical musings, especially when they came wrapped in this kind of mystery.

"What is your story?" she said to the remains, almost as if she expected the disconnected skull and mandible to rise magically in some cartoonish levitation and answer her question.

"What is *my* story?" she imagined the skull saying in response. "I'm dead and have been for a long, long time. And when you're dead the *only* story is the one you wrote while you were alive. What is *your* story?"

"I spend my time with people like you," the anthropologist responded somewhat defensively, wondering what inside of her had allowed an inanimate object to turn the question around. "I try to answer questions like *who* and *where* and *when*, questions like *why* and *how*."

"So you spend your life trying to figure out mine? What's the point of that?"

Clever boy, Emily thought to herself, *but I'm the doctor here.*

"There's always a point," she finally offered. "Answering those questions can set the record straight. It's important work, and I intend to dedicate my life to it."

"Set the record straight for whom?" the skull asked, as if it didn't give a whit about the anthropologist's life work.

"For the people who come after, for those who have to go on living."

"What about me? Can you set the record straight for me and my people?"

The question took Emily by surprise, since she saw the answer as so obvious.

"I might be able to," she answered, "if I knew who you were. And if I knew who they were."

"What if you never find out? Can you set the record straight just because it's the right thing to do?"

The door clicked open and Roy Cleveland stepped back into the decomp room, the humerus in his latex-gloved hand. The sound jolted Emily from her fantasy, the skull's imagined question languishing in her head. It felt as if her conversation with the skull had only taken a minute or two, but when she looked at the clock she saw that Roy Cleveland had been gone for nearly forty-five minutes. The skull stared silently at the ceiling above, as if no longer interested in talking now that the coroner had returned.

"Well," the coroner started, "there's a complete lack of fluorescence."

"So we're looking at a hundred years," Emily observed from the edge of her stupor. "A hundred years, minimum?"

"And the nitrogen is just under 2.7 percent, so I would say two to three hundred years is more like it."

"But we still have to account for the conditions." As she spoke, Emily became increasingly aware of her return to reality. "We didn't find these bones in a crypt in the desert. Being buried in a creek bank like that should have accelerated the deterioration process."

"No doubt, but at least we have a better idea. We will probably never know how these bones were protected, or why they were protected, but here they are, trying to speak to us."

The young anthropologist smiled, thinking about her imaginary conversation with the skull. "What happens now?" she asked.

"For the moment, they go into cold storage. Then we have to figure out what to do with them. The law says they have to be released to the nearest blood relative."

"How in the world are we going to determine that?"

"I don't know." The coroner paused and looked down at the lifeless bones arranged on the table in front of them. As he returned the humerus to its position among the remains, he added, "I guess we'll just have to figure out the right thing to do."

* * *

Grace Caufield sat in a remote corner of the offices of the Recorder of Deeds in Doylestown, a pile of large and obviously old books on the table in front of her. Earlier in the day she had reviewed her information about the discovery on the Phillips property with the managing editor of the *Intelligencer*, a sister newspaper to the *Courier Times*. The editor agreed with Grace that the story had potential, but she was quick to add that—for the moment at least—potential was all it had.

"Put together a high-level piece for Sunday," the editor had suggested. "Just lay out the basics. And then start doing some research. You may want to look into the history of the property. There may be something there."

Opting for some exercise, Grace had walked the half mile from the *Intelligencer* to the county offices on Court Street. It was a good day to walk, sunny and warm, the pleasant side of the coin that the weather gods seemed to flip daily in April. It presented nearly incomprehensible contrast to the drear and rain of the previous afternoon.

She had been greeted at the offices by an affable, gray-haired woman who told Grace that she had been working in the office for nearly forty years. And after hearing about the accident on the Phillips property and the subsequent discovery of the skeletal remains, the woman was more than willing to help.

"Our records date back to 1684," the woman offered proudly. "That was just two years after William Penn first came to this area to claim most of the land around here."

"I don't understand," Grace responded. "How did he claim it? Did he put a flag in the ground?"

"No, it wasn't anything like that." She paused for a long moment before continuing, as if trying to remember events that she had participated in personally. "The history of this area goes back to 1609. That's when Henry Hudson of the Dutch East India Company discovered the Delaware River. I don't remember when, sometime in the summer, I think. Then Peter Minuet and the Swedes were here in the late 1630s."

"Those are famous names. I remember them from elementary school history."

"Of course, we all do. The Dutch settled the area after driving out the Swedes in 1655, only to be driven out themselves by the English less than a decade later."

"So William Penn was *not* the first Englishman to be here."

"Hardly. The English had been here for almost twenty years before he arrived. The land was granted to Penn by Charles II as repayment of a debt to Penn's father. That happened a year before William Penn actually came to this country."

"How do you know so much about all of this," Grace asked, "especially if your records don't go back that far?"

"It's the nature of this work," the woman answered. "It's only natural to uncover a piece of information and then wonder what happened *before* that. And this area is so rich in history that it's not difficult to fill in the blanks."

"So when you say that the land was granted to Penn, exactly what land are you talking about? Are you referring to Bucks County?"

"Sort of. At the time, you see, Bucks County included all the lands around Philadelphia County. Today, there are seventeen counties in what was called Bucks County when it was given to William Penn. And that includes the entire state of Delaware."

"Seventeen? That must have been some debt."

"Indeed. And Penn came here to oversee affairs in his 'Province of Pennsylvania' in 1682."

"And the records in this office start two years after that. Isn't that what you said?"

"It is. They go back to 1684."

The reporter didn't say anything for nearly a minute. She was trying to digest what she had just learned, while wrestling with the same question that the woman had apparently asked so many times.

"What happened before all of that?"

"What do you mean?"

"Before Henry Hudson discovered the Delaware River. What happened before that?"

"The land was inhabited by Indians. I don't know much about their history, and we certainly don't have anything about it here."

"So, how did the Indians feel about the King of England giving the land to William Penn? Didn't they have anything to say about it?"

"I can't say. I've heard that Penn paid them for their lands, but I don't know why he would have done that if King Charles had already given them to him."

"Well, thank you," Grace responded. "It's all very interesting. Now, what can you point me to that will shed some light on the property I asked about?"

Seated beside the pile of books that the woman had brought in response to her question, Grace began working through them. It soon became obvious to her that the most recent indices covered relatively brief periods of time—from 1999 to the present; from

1994 to 1998; for the five years before that; for the eight years before that; and so forth. For the most part, the indices covered five- to nine-year periods dating back to World War II. The index before that included deeds recorded between 1920 and 1941, and the index before that included everything from 1684 until 1919.

Even without any of the supporting detail, the indices themselves provided valuable insight into the history of the area. The buying and selling of the sprawling farms that had issued forth from the fertile soil of the ancient river had taken two hundred and thirty-five years to record; the effects of industrialization between the two wars had taken a mere twenty-one years; and the suburbanization that followed World War II was so vast and so rapid that it had to be segmented according to eight much more manageable spans of time.

What will it be in the next three hundred years? Grace thought to herself. *Will these records eventually be indexed by individual year*—or less?

It took Grace most of the afternoon to piece together a timeline of ownership of the Phillips property. Much of the time was spent understanding the process—knowing what to look for, how it was identified, and how to locate it in reverse chronological order.

She found out that the land had belonged to the Williams family since 1895. A man named Carl Williams bought it in that year and left it to his son Richard when he died in 1934. When Richard died in 1943, a date which caused Grace to guess that he may have been killed in World War II, his wife assumed sole ownership of the property. The land later passed to her sons, Benjamin and Eldon, from whom Jeff Phillips bought it in December of 2004.

Between 1860 and 1895 the property had belonged to a man named Johann Christopher and his wife Adele. That was also the first time that the land had been sectioned in its present-day form.

Prior to that, the land between the creek and the crest of the hill belonged to something called the Rutherford Company. By cross-referencing the name, Grace found out that John A. Rutherford bought the property and opened a sawmill on the hillside in 1832, the same year that the nearby canal was completed and opened for business. It was easy for her to envision milled lumber being loaded onto canal boats for shipment to points south.

The land on the west side of the creek was part of a huge tract that was once owned by a man named Josiah Musselman. His was the last of five generations to own the tract over a period of one-hundred and twenty-five years.

The Rutherford property had changed hands three times prior to the time that John Rutherford purchased it, dating back to 1735.

The single column of owners on Grace Caufield's notepad had divided into two columns, one for the west side of the Phillips property and one for the east side. Both columns ended in the year 1735. When she looked at the family names of the people who had sold both tracts, she was surprised to find that they were one and the same—Thomas and Richard Penn.

A half hour later, she had done a quick check of a handful of other properties in the area and found that they, too, had been sold by Thomas and Richard Penn in the mid- to late-1730s. She was unable to identify the ownership of any property that predated ownership by the two men.

The woman who had helped her when she first came in stopped by to tell her that the offices would be closing in fifteen minutes.

"That's alright," Grace said, "I think I'm finished for the day."

"Just leave the books," the woman said. "I'll put them away tomorrow."

"By the way, do you know who Thomas and Richard Penn were?"

"Yes, they were two of William Penn's sons. He had a number of children during the course of two marriages—I can't remember how many—but it was Thomas and Richard who protected many of the family's interests in this country following their father's death. By the way, I did a little research for you while you were working."

"Research? Into what?"

"Well, you asked about the Indians that were here when Henry Hudson arrived. I found out that there's a small display at the Mercer Museum down the hill on South Pine. I haven't seen it, but the director suggested that it might be helpful. And they don't close until five."

"That's really kind of you. I'm a little threadbare right now so I think I'll wait until another day."

A few minutes later, Grace was back in the sunlight of the waning afternoon and walking back toward the parking lot of the *Intelligencer*. As she walked, her mind raced with a number of thoughts and questions. Regardless of where it ended, most land ownership in the area began with William Penn and his sons. Which of the people she had read about owned the Phillips property when the person whose bones had been found was buried there? Was it even possible to determine that? Would the examination by the coroner and forensic anthropologist uncover any new information? What about the man on the bridge at the Phillips place; what did he have to say about this? And what was going on prior to the day that Henry Hudson sailed into the Delaware Bay in 1609?

* * *

Grace Caufield's article ran in the Sunday editions of both the *Intelligencer* and the *Courier Times*. It wasn't front-page material. In fact, it was found in both newspapers in sections that were dedicated to summaries of the week's news.

Mystery Surrounds Remains
Discovered Near Riegelsville

Grace Caufield, *Courier Times* Staff Writer

Shrouded in a mystery that may never be solved, skeletal remains were found earlier this week on the property of Jeffrey H. Phillips, R.R. 2, Riegelsville. The bones were unearthed from a creek bank on Monday, during a mishap in which a load of rocks slid from the flatbed of a truck as it crossed a small bridge. No one was injured in the accident.

Bucks County Coroner Dr. Roy Cleveland was called to the scene, as was Sheriff Walter McNulty. Cautioning that little about the remains could be determined without formal testing, Dr. Cleveland said that the bones appeared to be extremely old.

Based on Dr. Cleveland's observations, Sheriff McNulty said that foul play has been ruled out for the time being and that no criminal investigation would be conducted.

On Tuesday, responsibility for the site was assumed by Dr. Emily FitzRoy, a forensic anthropologist at the University of Pennsylvania. After a preliminary examination, she agreed with Dr. Cleveland's comments about the age of the bones, citing that they were "very brittle and extremely discolored."

The remains included only a portion of the skeleton, the most identifiable pieces of which were the skull, a humerus, a femur, and a portion of the pelvis. The bones were all from the right side of the body, raising questions about the fate of the left side. Dr. FitzRoy noted that because the remains appeared to have been buried naturally, they may have been exposed to weather and predators for a period of time. "That may account for the fact that only partial remains were found," she said.

"It has been quite some time since my office has been involved in something like this," Dr. Cleveland confirmed at the scene. "Bones were found on a property above New Hope in 1984, but they were eventually identified as the remains of a deer."

Asked by Dr. Cleveland to oversee the exhumation, Dr. FitzRoy conducted her painstaking work at the site for a day and a half before being satisfied that there was nothing else to be found. At that time, the remains were removed to the county forensic facility in Warminster, where Dr. FitzRoy and Dr. Cleveland formally examined them on Thursday morning.

Following the examination, Dr. FitzRoy confirmed by telephone that the remains were that of an adult male of undetermined age and race and approximately five feet, nine inches in height. She further confirmed that a series of procedures, including fluoroscopy, ultraviolet testing, and testing for nitrogen content, indicated that the bones were between 200 and 400 years old.

Further details, including information about what will be done with the remains, have not been made available by the coroner's office. "Under law," Dr. Cleveland noted, "they must be released to the nearest blood relative. But in this case I'm not sure how a relative can possibly be identified."

There are two clues that may help in that regard, both of which are artifacts discovered with the remains. One is a piece of badly worn and discolored metal that has been determined to be bronze. The other is a handful of black and white beads. Both were examined on Friday by Dr. FitzRoy at her office in the Museum of Archaeology and Anthropology at the university.

"I have heard at least one opinion that the bronze object is a piece of jewelry," Dr. FitzRoy revealed, "and a hole in one side of it does suggest that a cord or rope could have been tied to it at one time, but its purpose cannot be confirmed without further examination."

When reached by telephone on Friday, Mr. Phillips indicated that he and his family were quite taken aback by the discovery of the bones and have pledged to cooperate with both the coroner's office and the sheriff's office in solving this mystery.

"One minute we were preoccupied with things around here," Phillips said, referring to his family's continuing work on the property, "and the next we were completely distracted by the discovery of these remains. I don't know if we'll ever know any more than we do right now, but it would sure be interesting to understand what happened here."

Jeff Phillips didn't see the *Courier Times* until much later in the day. When he finally had a chance to look at it, he was seated in a large comfortable chair in the plant room—the room in which he had been standing prior to his vision of the white buffalo. After reading Grace Caufield's article, he rose from the chair and went to find Dae. As he walked, he whispered to himself, *"One thing shifts and all else follows after."*

PART TWO

"Being Indian is not blood as much as it is culture."

— Tony Hillerman

Eight

AUGUST 1729

It was almost a half-day's walk to the village where she grew up, or what remained of it, and almost all of it was hard against Lenapewihittuk. Carved originally by her ancestors, who walked in single file along the river for thousands of years, the path had grown wide enough for two in many places. Its timeless length was interrupted only by water making its way to the river—rocky creeks rushing down wooded hillsides and quiet streams snaking lazily through rare flat areas of lush grasses and reeds.

The boy was older now, but not old enough, and it was that single fact that troubled her more than anything else. If circumstances had been different, she would have brought him along more slowly. She would have responded to him differently when she first saw him peering into the emptiness of the lodgehouse. At worst, she would have shooed him away impatiently, knowing that his heart would keep insisting that he return. At best, she would have nudged him away gently, as if to say, "Come back when the time is right." But the practices

that were once driven by generations of tradition were now being
dictated by something else—an unnerving sense of urgency in the
face of gathering darkness. Her task was to prepare him for a life
he would never live, and for a fate neither of them could ever fully
comprehend. The task was formidable, and made more so by the
lack of time in which to complete it.

As they made their way along the river, she pondered in her
heart what was happening to him now—what was happening to
him in the few hours it would take them to walk from his village
to the forks of the sacred waters; what was happening to him
without his knowledge.

We live many lives within each life, she thought to herself.
*And we make our way between lives in different ways. Sometimes we
walk excitedly, full of anticipation about what is about to happen;
sometimes we walk in fear, unsure about what may happen and our
ability to handle it. We walk in sorrow; we walk in joy. We walk in
laughter; we walk in tears.* She looked up at the boy as he moved
along the path, ten paces ahead. *But the most perilous of journeys
is the one we make without knowing it. We move from place to place
unaware that the life we are living will never be the same.* In her
heart, she knew full well that the boy was making such a journey.

Sometimes he would walk by her side, and they would talk
in detail about the Lenape way of life and how it had changed so
dramatically in just a few generations. They would talk about the
way in which their history had always been remembered through
a perfect oral tradition, and how that tradition had been diluted
as their history blurred with the histories of those who were not
Lenape. They would talk about the way in which their lineage
had always been marked matrilineally, and how that practice had

become more difficult as the Lenape intermixed and intermarried with Europeans. They would talk about the winter migrations and seasonal festivals that had marked the passage of time for countless winters, and how the migrations had all but ceased and fewer and fewer Lenape were left to celebrate the festivals.

Sometimes he would catch sight of a creek tumbling down the hillside and dash up ahead in anticipation of finding the right combination of rocks on which to make his way across. He moved quickly, almost frenetically, barely able to contain his excitement. When he spied a fish, he was quick to tell her its name and remind her of the best way to catch it, proudly confirming knowledge that he had gained at the side of Talks For Us. Keenly aware of everything that was going on around them, he would identify birds in the air and small animals that scurried in the brush along the path.

In one moment, he was very much a man, in the next he was just as much a boy, and his movement back and forth between the two was painful for her to watch. He should have been allowed to be fully one and then fully the other, but there was no time for such a metamorphosis.

"Young One." She mouthed the words quietly, almost imperceptibly, but he turned to face her instantly, as if he had sensed what she had said more than he had heard it. He walked back to the point where she was leaning above something in the brush.

"What is this?" she asked, moving aside some leaves to reveal a sprig of white, bell-shaped flowers.

The boy recognized the plant immediately, but he hesitated in his response long enough to run his fingers down the length of the stem from which the flowers hung.

"Wintergreen," he answered.

"What is it used for?"

"Many things. The leaves can be made into a tea that soothes the stomach and relieves pain. It also helps with fever. The leaves can also be fermented and used to flavor meat and fish, or they can be smoked with tobacco."

"And the berries that it bears in the winter?"

"They soothe the stomach when eaten."

"Will you gather some . . ." A shallow cough exited her mouth, interrupting the request. ". . . leaves for us?"

As he had been taught by Looks Back, the boy reached down and cleared the area around the plant. The upright stem rose about four inches from an unseen vine that he knew grew just below the surface of the ground.

"May I have some tobacco?" he asked, extending a hand toward Four Bears, and he wasn't the least bit surprised that the tobacco was in his hand while the words were still on his lips. He laid the tobacco on the ground by the side of the plant that faced the river, the side that faced the rising sun.

"We give thanks," he said softly, gently touching the tobacco with the fingers of his right hand, "for all that is provided for us by the Great Spirit."

Then, taking care not to disturb the plant, he moved the surrounding brush aside to reveal more like it. From these, he gently pinched shiny, leathery leaves until he had gathered fifteen or twenty of them. He turned and handed them to his teacher, who placed them carefully in her pouch.

As they continued their journey, the warmth of the morning slowly gave way to the heat and humidity of the early afternoon.

They were on a part of the path that ran between the river and a wide clearing of high grass, completely exposed to the midday sun. It felt hot on the boy's skin as he moved silently along the river, his eyes surveying the grass for signs of animals. He took two or three more steps before noticing that Four Bears had stopped. When he looked up, he saw the figures of two men standing in the shadows at the far end of the meadow.

Both of them knew that there were many different kinds of people in the area these days, and that most of them were not Lenape. A stranger could be friend or enemy and represent opportunity or danger. It was difficult, if not impossible, to know. These were white men, and Four Bears knew that few white people used the native paths that ran up and down the length of the river. They were more likely to travel the inland routes. She and the boy were exposed in this situation, and her instincts told her that they were in danger.

As the men approached, Four Bears and Walks Alone stood quietly. In the middle of the clearing there was no place for either of them to run, should running be required. The possible safety of the trees was twenty-five yards behind and fifty yards ahead.

The men were less than fifty feet from them, eyeing the woman and the boy carefully as they walked slowly toward them. The tall one wore a dirty shirt and dark pants that were torn above one knee. A rifle was slung on his back, supported by a leather strap across his chest. The shorter one had a stocky build and his clothes were both cleaner and less worn than those of his friend, but not by much. In his belt, he carried a pistol and a sheathed knife. What bothered Four Bears most was the same thing that Walks Alone had begun to recognize as a harbinger that bad things were nearby—even from a distance, both men stunk of alcohol.

The stocky man leered at Four Bears, surveying her from head to toe without saying a word. It was impossible to know what he was thinking, but with the passing of each agonizing second it became increasingly difficult for Four Bears to believe that it was good. He looked at the boy quickly, possibly to see if he was carrying a weapon, and then returned his stare to Four Bears.

Walks Alone felt a strange combination of fear and reassurance. He was clearly afraid of the two grown men that stood on the path. If there was trouble, what could he possibly do to protect himself and his teacher? But he knew that he could not, that he would not, run. Whatever outcome lay ahead, he had to do whatever he could to keep Four Bears from harm. The inevitability of helping her filled him with the strange confidence that whatever was about to happen was supposed to happen, even if it included injury—or death.

As he stood perfectly still, aware of the beads of sweat that gathered at the top of his spine and trickled down his back, the boy's attention was drawn to the distant shadows from which the men had emerged. It looked as if a figure was standing there, and, for a moment, Walks Alone thought that it was the white beast of his journeys. It stood quietly, looking at him, its image blurred in the white haze of the noonday sun. He thought he heard the animal speak, although he didn't know how he could possibly hear it from this distance, and the words came to him in swift reassurance—"I will wait with you."

The stocky man saw that Walks Alone was distracted and turned quickly to see what he was looking at. Emerging swiftly and resolutely from the shadows, the figure of a Lenape man moved toward them on the path. He was dark and muscular, his skin glistening in the sun from his brow to his shins. Wearing only a breechclout, he carried a large knife in his right hand, drawn from the sheath at his side. The edges of his mouth were turned down and his eyes were focused on the two men like the eyes of a yellow hawk focused on rabbits in a field.

The tall man grabbed the leather strap of the rifle as if to lift it from his chest, but the other man quickly placed a hand on his arm, silently telling him not to do it. He jerked his head to one side, and an instant later both men had stepped around the woman and boy and were moving at a half-run down the path. Four Bears turned to watch them disappear into the distance.

Walks Alone didn't watch them. He stood transfixed, watching the man who now approached them. Up close, he looked even stronger, the definition of his body amplified by his nakedness. He stopped a few feet away, his expression softening, his eyes releasing their gaze on the disappearing danger.

The boy had seen this man before. He was from the village at the forks—the village to which they were walking—and Walks Alone had seen him at councils and celebrations. But the man had always been dressed in buckskin or wrapped in an animal hide. Now he stood before them as a warrior, his skin glistening with the bear grease that some Lenape men smeared on their skin in the summer to avoid sunburn. As he sheathed his knife, he looked down at the boy and smiled.

Four Bears turned around, looked at him gratefully, and said, "*Wanishi*, His Sprit Watches. Wanishi, my friend." Then she added, "Will you please walk with us to Lechauwitank?"

As they neared the place at the edge of the clearing where the path moved into the coolness of the shadows, Walks Alone looked for any trace of the white beast, but he saw nothing. Then he looked back at the face of the man who now walked beside Four Bears. Somewhere ahead waited the place where two rivers merged in a confluence of sacred waters, but it was difficult for the boy to imagine a place more meaningful than the shadows through which they were passing, or a moment more profound than the one he had just lived.

* * *

To Jeff Phillips, the completed fountain was a subtle affair—unpretentious, unassuming, inconspicuous—and he couldn't have been more pleased with it. As he stood before it in the mid-morning brightness, he considered the differences between it and the fountain in his original vision, and he could conclude only that it had ended up looking exactly as it was meant to look. The word that kept coming to his mind was "integrated." The fountain seemed as integrated into the landscape as the trees that surrounded the upper meadow and the wildflowers that grew in the paddock fencerow. It had only been there for a few days, but in some strange way that made little sense to him, it was already difficult for Jeff to remember when it hadn't been there.

It was lower than he had envisioned it originally, only about three feet above the ground, and oblong rather than round, the foundation having been completely reshaped by Roberto and his cousins. Jeff remembered how they had reacted when he asked them to take down the rocks they had arranged so perfectly in a circle. They had laughed about it in their casual and good-natured way, but Jeff suspected that at least some of the Spanish that followed was poking fun at his indecision.

The altered shape of the fountain provided more surface area, and the pipe in the center had been shortened so that it protruded less than six inches above the water. Rather than rising into the air in ostentation, the pumped water simply gurgled a few inches before falling back into the pool and rippling gently toward its edges. Jeff imagined that the water plants Jill and Dae had been discussing would make the end result even more tranquil—even more integrated.

"Know what I think?"

Jeff turned to see Dae approaching from the direction of the main house. She was dressed in shorts and a casual camisole and the gentle smacking of her flip-flops marked each of her steps, but her womanly frame and the striking features of her face seemed to him like timeless art in the dappled sunlight that surrounded her. From the moment they first met, Jeff had always loved spending time with Dae, and as she drew closer he thought about how nice it would be to spend the rest of the day with her at the shore, or shopping in New Hope, or just walking down by the river.

"No, what do you think?" he responded as she kissed his cheek. "Or should I be afraid to ask? Do I have to tell Roberto that we've decided to go with the original design?"

"You're funny," she mocked. "No, I like it. I like it because there's water up here now. I know the creek's just down the hill, but it's not quite the same as having water up here. It's as if we moved a small part of the river to this place."

"Interesting. I hadn't thought about it that way." He paused for a moment, silently surveying the elliptical shape of the pool.

"So what do you think about the new layout? Does it work for you?"

"It doesn't matter. It'll work for the fish."

"Fish?" The surprise in Jeff's voice was obvious. It was becoming increasingly clear to him that what he had envisioned originally was not a finished thing but the seed from which something more complete would grow. He smiled outwardly at the thought, but in his heart he knew that the idea was something to be pondered.

"Jill and I have been talking about it. We're thinking about koi."

"Aren't they like big Japanese goldfish?"

"I don't know about the goldfish part, but we're talking about the same thing. Jill and I like the idea."

"I do, too. It hadn't even occurred to me until you mentioned it, but I like the idea, too. You know . . ." Jeff's voice fell off, as if he had decided that what he was about to say was better left unexpressed.

"What?" Dae asked. "I know what?"

Looking out across the upper meadow, Jeff began, "Just a few years ago this was just an overgrown meadow. Now things are thriving up here—Jill and Edward, and a baby on the way; the horses, the paddock, and all the flowers; this fountain, about to become a home for water plants and fish; and the barn that I keep thinking about." He paused before adding, "And if things work out, maybe Hope and Scott will build a place up here."

Jeff's stare dropped to the ground, and Dae knew immediately where his thoughts had gone. "It's okay, Jeff. And Harry and his sister? What about them?"

"It's too much to think that they may live here someday. I just can't let my dream go that far. I've never been very good at marriage, and I haven't always been a good father, but not having her in my life cuts like a knife."

"Maybe that's what all this is about—a second chance."

"Could be," Jeff replied. "Maybe this ground and I are both getting a second chance."

The observation made Dae smile, partly because she agreed and partly because her perspective was slightly different. "You, maybe, but who are we to say how many chances this ground has had? Maybe it's had hundreds or thousands of chances. None of our stuff may be here hundreds of years from now. I wonder if people like us will stand on this spot and talk about giving it a second chance."

Jeff smiled at her comments. She was right of course, and even though she said the words with a calm that made them sound understated, he heard them with a subtle edge that alerted him to their lesson.

"Anyway," she continued, "I came up here to tell you that Walt McNulty called. I brought your cell phone in case you want to call him back." Handing him the phone, she added, "I'm not sure why you even have that thing. You never have it with you."

The edge to those words was anything but subtle, and he smiled at the playful irritation with which she walked back toward the house.

Jeff turned toward the paddock as he retrieved the sheriff's number and punched the call button on his cell phone. McNulty wasn't at his desk, but the receptionist in the office assured Jeff that it wouldn't be difficult to find him.

"Just give me a minute," she asked before putting the call on hold.

While he waited, Jeff started along the fence of the paddock. The horses moved toward him slowly, certain that he had something to feed them. He patted one of them on the neck as he walked by.

"McNulty."

"This is Jeff Phillips, Walt. I'm returning your call."

"Thanks, Jeff. I just want to let you know where we are with this—which is basically where we have been. The woman from Penn and the folks at the forensic lab have wrapped up their work. Their report confirms most of what they suspected to be true right from the beginning."

"What about ethnicity, Walt? Were they able to confirm that the remains were those of a Native American?"

"No, they weren't. Neither could they confirm that the individual was white, black, or yellow. Hold on a second. I'll get the report."

About thirty seconds later, the sheriff's voice returned to the line.

"The formal terms are Caucasoid, Negroid, and Mongoloid. Apparently they're the only races that can be identified with any degree of certainty."

"So what are we dealing with?"

"I don't know. You would probably be better off speaking with Roy Cleveland or Emily FitzRoy, at least on that particular issue."

"Okay." Then, after pausing to consider if he even wanted to ask the question, he added, "You may not have had time to think about it, but where are you with my request to bury the remains here?"

"Right now, they're in cold storage at the forensic lab. Technically, they could be kept there indefinitely. I spoke with the coroner about this 'nearest blood relative' thing and we both agree that there's absolutely no way to determine that. I don't know what will happen, so I'll just ask you to be patient."

"Not a problem, Walt, but I do want to repeat the offer. Whoever that man was, his remains should be treated with respect, especially after what appears to be so much time."

"It's good of you to believe that, Jeff, and believe me I haven't forgotten your request. It's just going to take some time to let everything play itself out."

"Thanks, Walt. You know where to find me."

By the time he hung up his phone, Jeff had walked to the back of the paddock and was standing near the spot that he thought would be a good resting place for the bones.

"Maybe I'm pushing too hard here," he said to himself. "Maybe I should just leave this alone."

The sun was directly overhead, and for a fleeting moment most of the things in the upper meadow were without shadow. The forsythia by the woods had lost most of its bright yellow foliage and the less-vibrant branches seemed drab and lifeless without it. In the darkness of the trees, the place felt less transitional, less celebratory, than it had seemed when everything was in bloom. The air felt heavy with uncertainty and delay, and Jeff wondered if the remains would ever spend as much time in this place as they had in the bank of the creek.

* * *

The boy hadn't noticed that His Spirit Watches had left the path. He may have been listening to something Four Bears was saying or lost in a reverie that required no company, but whatever the distraction, he had lost sight of the man who had come to their aid in the clearing.

A few hundred yards later, Four Bears nudged the boy's shoulder, silently directing him into the trees to the right. They only walked a handful of paces before joining His Spirit Watches on the bank above Lechauwitank, the place where the two sacred rivers became one.

"There is purpose in everything," she said just loudly enough for Walks Alone to hear, "but one is left to wonder why there seems to be so much more purpose in some things, so much more purpose in some people . . ." She took in a deep breath, as if inhaling the very site at which they stood. ". . . and so much more purpose in some places."

Just below them, Lenapewihittuk lazed quietly through the heat of the summer day, but the boy knew that the river was anything but lazy, and that it had the power to pull a man as large as His Spirit Watches under without warning. A good swimmer might escape the deceit, but not before understanding that the river was just as capable of taking life as giving it.

Off to their left, Lechewuekink dropped over low falls and into Lenapewihittuk, completing a perilous journey that began far away, as Four Bears had told him, ". . . in the place where the sun sets in the summer." The waters merged with urgency, as if anticipating a destiny that awaited them to the south, but without relinquishing the elegance of powers that had been joining in the dance for thousands of years.

Across the river and only a short walk from the bank, an escarpment rose high above the ground, as if its black face was a living thing reaching for the sun. Walks Alone could not imagine scaling it, yet he found himself wondering about what he might find if he did. The imposing cliff continued downriver as far as he could see.

The place was awe-inspiring. Even a boy could understand why his people regarded it as sacred. Each color seemed to emanate from everything around it, like the green of the distant trees that seemed to borrow simultaneously from the blue tints of the water, the yellow streaks in the leaves of plants, and the shadowy striations of the escarpment. And even more striking was the way in which the resulting hues seemed to change at will in support of the altering opacity of the water or the shifting translucence of the sky. Each thing was brilliant and perfectly defined, as if it were the only thing, yet all things merged completely in an image that was impossible to forget.

His Spirit Watches turned and walked back through the trees, leaving the woman and the boy on the bank above the river. Four Bears turned to follow him. Lost in a wonder that had consumed countless Lenape before him, Walks Alone looked out at the confluence of waters, drawing the scene into all of his senses at once, as if trying to make it a part of him.

The boy didn't remember walking back through the trees and joining Four Bears and His Spirit Watches on the path, yet a few minutes later he was rushing to catch up with them.

They walked together until they came to the river called Lechewuekink, following it for a short distance along a path that ran between the river and another equally high, and equally formidable, escarpment. At a place where it widened, tucked back against the base of the cliff, sat a very small Lenape village of seven or eight wigwams.

Walks Alone noticed immediately that the village was different than the one in which he lived. There were fewer signs of assimilation into the white culture—no log cabins or rail fences, and no cattle or other livestock. A few people milled about, and they were dressed much the same as the people in his village—an obvious combination of native and European—but the gathering of huts seemed to be a little out of place, as if it were a few winters behind.

"There were once more Lenape here," Four Bears said to him, as if she could hear the question that was forming in his head. "This wasn't a big village, like the villages of a hundred winters ago that had many wigwams, but it was this size three times over."

"So, why are these people still here?" the boy asked quietly.

"There have always been Lenape here, Young One. This is a sacred place for us. I would like to say that there will always be Lenape here, but . . ."

"But that's not true, is it?" The interruption was respectful, based more in wisdom than ego.

"No, it's not true. In fact, those of us who are here now may be the last to live at Lechauwitank."

"How do we give up our sacred places? After so many of us have come to this place to watch the lives of these rivers run together into even greater life, how can we come here no longer?"

"As usual, Young One, your wisdom runs ahead of you. This place will always be sacred, but only in our memories, only in our dreams."

"What about the people who replace us? Will this be a sacred place for them?"

"The Great Spirit makes something sacred. He makes it a part of people; he puts it in their hearts. If he puts this place in their hearts, then yes, it will be sacred for them."

"And if he does not?"

"Then we will trust that he has not done so for a reason."

"This I promise . . . ," the boy began softly, ". . . I will come here as an old man. I will bring my grandchildren here and tell them what this place was and what it meant to the Lenape. You are my teacher and I promise you that I will do this."

The woman looked away without saying anything. She tried desperately to keep the darkness in her heart from overshadowing the simple beauty of his words and the feelings that inspired them, but its oppression was too great and she surrendered to it with tears.

It was not lost on the boy that Four Bears did not acknowledge his promise, and he knew there was a reason for this as well—a reason that was perhaps better left unsaid.

The boy was confused when His Spirit Watches walked past the wigwams and started up an incline that ran along the base of the escarpment. They followed him for about fifty yards before losing sight of him in a small grove of trees. When they entered the grove a few moments later, they found a solitary wigwam nestled in it shadows.

"Is this where he lives?" the boy asked.

"It is," the woman replied, still pondering what she knew to be the hopelessness of the boy's promise.

"Why is he apart from the others?"

"Because he is different than them."

"Different? In what way?"

"In *many* ways, Young One. In many ways." She didn't wait for the boy's questions. It was important for him to know the answers. They were one of the reasons she had brought him here, and they were important. "His Spirit Watches lives in the old ways," she began. "Like the bear grease he rubs on his skin to turn back the sun and hide his scent when he is hunting. Very few Lenape men do that now."

"How does he get the bear grease?"

"In the old way," Four Bears laughed, glad for the question and its innocence. "He goes up into the mountains to hunt in places where the bear still lives."

"What other old ways does he honor?"

"He wears no white clothes and no white ornaments. He dresses in a breechclout when the weather is warm and in buckskin when it is cold. He sleeps beneath animal skins, not woolen blankets."

Walks Alone looked at the woman expectantly, eager to hear more about His Spirit Watches. The boy imagined that in meeting this man he had been magically transported to an earlier time—the time of his father, or perhaps his father's father.

"The head of his hatchet is sharpened stone," Four Bears continued, "not the iron or bronze brought here by the Europeans, and . . ."

"But his knife . . . I saw his knife in the clearing, and it had a fancy handle."

Four Bears was patient with the boy's interruptions. She knew that he didn't mean to be disrespectful. To the contrary, he was completely immersed in this opportunity to learn about the past.

"He took that knife from an enemy," came the woman's reply, and Walks Alone was reminded immediately of the imposing form of His Spirit Watches as it rushed toward them in the clearing. It was the last thing that the enemy from whom His Spirit Watches had taken the knife had seen, and Walks Alone could only imagine the fear the man must have felt.

"What else?" the boy asked hungrily. "What else?"

"He is not Lenape."

The words hung in the summer air like a thunderstorm. They had materialized out of nothing, and once conjured it seemed as if nothing short of the strongest wind could drive them off. The boy looked at her quizzically, the maelstrom of questions in his head making it difficult to maintain his emotional equilibrium. Every Lenape knew of people who had been captured by natives and had become a member of the tribe over time, but this was different than that. This was about a man who followed the old ways of a people he did not belong to, and he followed them while many around him were content to abandon them. "What kind of man does that?" he asked himself. "What kind of man does that?"

"His Spirit Watches is of the Nanticoke people who once lived below the mouth of Lenapewihittuk. Some are still there. It was said that they were witches and sorcerers, that they could destroy an enemy through the mere force of their breath."

"Did you believe that?"

"I believed that they were not much different than us, but they used the legend to their advantage."

"And how did His Spirit Watches come to this place?"

"Most of the Nanticoke left their homes and moved toward the setting sun. His Spirit Watches chose to stay behind. He would not leave his home. He walked up Lenapewihittuk until he found us. This happened when your father and Talks For Us were the age that you are now. Some of our people feared him, believing that he would grow to be a sorcerer, and wanted to put him to death."

"But that is not the Lenape way."

"No, that is not the Lenape way. Eventually he walked here to Lechauwitank with his adopted people, and, once touched by this place, he stayed. Now he has become more Lenape than most Lenape."

"But why . . ." Walks Alone left the question in mid-air, trying to process what he was hearing. "But why . . . "

Four Bears said nothing, and she resolved to remain silent until the boy had asked the question that was confounding him.

"But why would a man who is not Lenape follow the old ways of the Lenape people?" He looked straight into the woman's eyes, anxious for her answer.

"Because he believes in his heart that they are worth following. They are his truth."

As Four Bears answered, Walks Alone continued to look into her eyes. He would not allow himself to look away, fully aware that something important was passing between them. He felt her words flow into him; he felt his heart absorb them.

"Will he speak to me?" the boy asked, still not looking away. "Is that why you have brought me here, to see the way that His Spirit Watches lives?"

"Yes, in part. He has much to teach you. He has much to teach all of us. But his greatest lesson is this: one is Lenape in one's heart. If his heart is good, the blood in his veins is of little matter, but if his heart is bad, there is no purity of blood that can make it otherwise."

"Is it this way with others? Is it this way with all men?"

"With all men and through all of time, it is this way, Young One. The Great Spirit has made it so."

* * *

Jeff Phillips stood at the awkward confluence of three streets in Philadelphia, waiting for the light to change. Behind him lay most of the urban campus of the University of Pennsylvania; up ahead were two outliers—Franklin Field and the Museum of Archaeology and Anthropology.

A minute later, having wondered if the onslaught of traffic on 33rd Street was ever going to permit pedestrians to cross, traffic light or otherwise, he turned out of the shadow of the massive brick façade of the south stands of Franklin Field and into the courtyard of the museum. Bounded by a sweeping brick drive that curved between entry and exit ways on South Street, the courtyard contained an impressive garden, the centerpiece of which was a lavish fountain. Trees, some familiar to Jeff and some unknown, surrounded the fountain in a perfectly integrated design that suggested an elegant antiquity, as if everything else in the area had grown up around it. Classic statuary, now darkened by patina, accentuated the sense that one was stepping back in time.

A few minutes later, Jeff was standing at the secured entry to a series of offices on the second floor of the museum, waiting for

Emily FitzRoy to meet him. The walk from the elevator in the center of the building had not been a long one, but it had revived in him an old and recurring notion. The corridor was lined with photographs, paintings, and display cases, all telling silent stories about remote cultures, few of which still existed. Information about each culture was accompanied by artifacts that had been excavated from distant resting places many decades ago.

Focused on his meeting with Dr. FitzRoy, he had walked past all of the artifacts as if they had never existed. It had not been a matter of disrespect, because he had felt anything but disrespectful, but he had rushed by the things that human beings had created in homage or reverence, or possibly just to survive. A living, breathing person had forged each of them from the ground on which he or she lived, transferring his energy into something that would transcend its immediate purpose and become timeless. As he waited for the anthropologist and took the time to look around, he felt a strange gratitude for what these artisans had created, even though he had no idea who—or why—they were.

"Mr. Phillips," a voice behind him said, and he turned to find Emily FitzRoy holding open the door. "Please come in."

As he turned to face her, he found himself yet again caught off guard by her beauty. She looked back at him through black-rimmed reading glasses that made her green eyes look larger and even more commanding of attention. His instincts had been correct. She was completely out of place in a museum.

"Thank you, and please call me Jeff. I'm much more comfortable with that."

"Did you have any trouble finding us?"

"No. Parking was problematic, as I'm sure you know. I parked over on Walnut Street, a few blocks up, but it gave me an opportunity to walk down through the center of campus. It's a great walk."

"Yes, it's beautiful." She turned and started down a center hall with offices on both sides. "I would give you a tour, but there's not much to see back here. These are mostly faculty offices."

"And that?" Jeff asked, nodding toward a room full of books behind what looked like the door to a jail cell. "What's that?"

"Our research library," the anthropologist answered. "There are some very old things in there, and it usually requires credentials to work with them."

"Credentials?"

"There's probably an academic definition, but it really means that you're not allowed in there with a peanut butter and jelly sandwich." The words exited her lips on a smile.

Jeff grinned back her. It was exactly the kind of down-to-earth comment that endeared a person to him. It eschewed protocol but still made its point. Her response couldn't have been more perfect, unless of course she had just said, "PB&J."

The door to Dr. FitzRoy's office had a smoked glass window on which her name was painted in heavy black lettering. Once inside, she invited Jeff to sit down in one of the chairs in front of the desk. She sat in the other, rather than in the high back chair behind her desk, a gesture that Jeff attributed to a lack of ego or self-importance—another endearing quality.

"How can I help you, Jeff? How are things up at your place?"

"Everything seems to be fine. I asked to see you because of a recent conversation with Roy Cleveland. He told me about your findings from the examination, and that they were pretty much in line with the things you said out at the site."

"That's true. There's really not much to add, at least that can be added with any degree of accuracy."

"I thought you might be able to shed some light on the type of people who used to live in the area in the timeframe we're talking about. I think you said two to four hundred years ago."

"Scientifically, that's correct. I know it's quite a range, but it's probably as close as we're going to get," she paused for a moment before adding, "and in all honesty, I think we're fortunate to be able to get that close."

"What do you mean by *scientifically*? What else do you have to go on?"

"The man on the bridge . . . his name was Cameron, wasn't it? His observations about the artifacts seemed to confirm the timeframe, although Dr. Cleveland and I found nothing to confirm that the remains were those of a Native American. So we have some cultural clues to go with the science."

"That being the case, who might that man have been?"

Emily FitzRoy was taken aback by the look in Jeff Phillips's eyes. Whatever the discovery of the remains had meant to him at first, it had obviously become something far more serious, something more intense. The sincerity with which he asked the question spoke to something running below the surface—a desire to do something, a need to take some action.

"What is this about, Jeff?" she asked without answering his question. "Why is this so important to you, if you don't mind my asking?"

Jeff looked across the desk as if Emily FitzRoy were sitting there rather than in the chair next to him. If she had been sitting there with the desk between them, if he had found her to be a different type of person—more self-absorbed, less approachable— he might have avoided the question, but the humanness he sensed in her inspired him to answer.

"I feel as if there's more to this than just finding bones on my property. I believe that there's a reason *why* we discovered the bones. I believe there's some purpose in this."

Thinking about her experience in the county forensic facility, and remembering her imagined conversation with the skull, Emily answered pensively, knowing full well that her words might take her to the threshold of a place that she did not necessarily want to enter.

"For some reason," she began, ". . . for some reason that I do not understand, I think I agree with you. But I'm not sure what else I can do at this point."

"What else *might* you do? What are the options?"

"Well, for one, I could take a team out to your place and excavate the entire area to see what else we might find. There may be clues there that will get us a little closer to the truth, but . . ."

"But what?"

"But there's no legitimate reason to do that. The condition of the bones, the position of the bones, and even the amount of remains that were found suggest that they were not buried by someone else. I could spend the university's money and impose on your time and resources to look for a burial ground or a settlement, but there's absolutely no justification for doing so."

"Is there anything else?"

"I can't think of anything, and yet I have to admit that I'm willing to help in any way I can."

"I appreciate it, but why *is* that?"

"Because, like you, I think there's a definite reason for all of this. Maybe it's a hunch, maybe it's something more."

Jeff listened to her words carefully, straining to hear the many unspoken things that seemed to be wedged in the spaces between them.

"I'm sorry to ask again, but can you tell me anything about the people who were in this area hundreds of years ago? Anything at all?"

"Unfortunately, it's not my area. I've picked up some things since I've been here, mostly through osmosis, but I've spent most of my time in other parts of the country—if not other parts of the world."

"Well, if you think of anything . . ."

"Let's say," she interrupted, as if she hadn't even heard him, "just for the sake of argument, that Mr. Cameron is correct and the remains are Native American."

Jeff shifted forward onto the front edge of his chair.

"There's an exhibit at the end of this floor, in the other direction from the elevator, about Native Americans in this area. I was down there when it first opened, but it was crowded and I didn't get to see much. Maybe it will be of some help."

"May I make one more request?"

"Yes, of course."

"Would you be kind enough to walk down there with me?"

Nine

He didn't know how long he had been asleep when Four Bears touched his shoulder, but it felt like it had been hours. Walks Alone had been sleeping soundly, lost in the place of complete relaxation that waits beyond the dream world. If someone else had awakened him—Looks Back or Quiet Bird—he would have begged to be left alone, but the mere touch of his teacher's hand was enough to wake him as completely as a storm passing overhead. His Spirit Watches was not in the wigwam, and the boy wondered how long he had been sleeping alone.

Dressed only in his breechclout and moccasins, he walked out into the summer night. The landscape was an uncomfortable combination of shadows cast by the full moon that was rising above the river. Its light danced on the water in flashes of white that rose with the current and then melted into the blackness below. The trees on both sides of the river watched in a similar balance, half illuminated by the moon and half invisible in the shadows. The air itself was likewise confused, hanging with humidity in one moment and rising in the next on a breeze that came in fits and starts.

"Walk with me, Young One." Her voice was calm and reassuring but unquestionably serious. She had awakened him for a reason.

They followed a path that gradually ascended the escarpment as it took them farther upriver. After a few minutes, he turned to look back along the path, trying to see the wigwam of His Spirit Watches or the wigwams farther below, but everything was lost in shadow. The moon, which became brighter as they climbed higher above the river, seemed to conspire with the trees, preventing him from seeing clearly either where he had been or where he was going.

They finally emerged at the top of the path. The landscape was forested, but its relative flatness welcomed the moonlight in a more generous way than the rocks and water below. The night breeze was more consistent up here, and Walks Alone let it touch his face and chest as it pleased.

The boy smelled the fire before he saw the sweat lodge. Then he saw both. The imposing form of His Spirit Watches knelt by the pit, which was only a few feet from the entrance to the lodge. The fire was hot but very low, an indication that it had been burning for a long time. There were no flames, just searing red embers. In their midst, five round rocks glowed with the heat.

Walks Alone looked at Four Bears, his questions in his eyes, but said nothing. He was very familiar with sweat lodges. All Lenape were. Each village, no matter how small, had one somewhere nearby, usually very near the water. He had heard of a time when villages were larger and had two sweat lodges, one for the men and one for the women, but he had never seen that.

And regardless of how many sweat lodges a village had, they were still used for the same purposes: to bathe, to heal the sick, and to heighten the senses before important events, like councils.

This sweat lodge looked very much like a wigwam, except that there was no vent for a fire. The black of its bark coverings blended into the darkness so perfectly that it would have been difficult to see at all were it not for the light of the moon.

His Spirit Watches lifted his hand toward the opening to the lodge. "Wanishi," he said to Walks Alone. "I am grateful to be a part of this."

Walks Alone removed his moccasins, knelt down, and crawled through the entrance. He was surprised when Four Bears followed him, but he said nothing. As he watched, she spread a deerskin near the pit in the center of the dirt floor and motioned to him to lie on it, which he did without hesitation.

Four Bears lifted her medicine bundle from a belt beneath her shirt. He had seen it before, but not very often, and only in brief glimpses that made him feel as if he were trespassing in his teacher's most personal space. She drew the talon of an eagle from it, as well as a strip of hide that still bore the hair of a bear, and placed both in her lap.

His Spirit Watches entered the sweat lodge, balancing a glowing rock on two stout pieces of tree branch. As he placed the rock in the pit, he chanted a ceremonial prayer to the Great Spirit, a prayer that Walks Alone had never heard before. Then he withdrew and, rising to his feet outside the wigwam, pulled a skin across the opening. The light of the full moon suddenly shut out, the inside of the sweat lodge was illuminated only by the glow of the single stone in the pit.

"It's time for you to prepare," Four Bears said to Walks Alone. "You are younger than I was when I prepared, but my spirit guides tell me that you must do this now." She paused for what seemed to the boy like a long time. "I hear the questions to which you do not give voice. You want to know what you are preparing for, and it is prudent to want to know. If you are not prudent and practical you will not be able to help your people." She scooped water from a bowl near the pit and poured it slowly over the stone, causing a hissing cloud of steam to rise into the air. "At the same time, you should resist too much practicality, because the mysteries of life are neither revealed nor resolved for those who are too practical to accept them." She paused again, and he knew that she was somehow listening to his heart. "You are afraid, and that too is as it should be, but you are trusting, and for that I am grateful. Wanishi, Young One." A ghost of steam rose into the air as she dripped more water onto the stone.

"Close your eyes, Young One, and let the vapor take you. I will remain here to watch." The boy could feel the first beads of sweat exiting the pores in his face. "Let the vapor take you to your spirit guides, to the white beast and all else in his world."

Walks Alone didn't notice when His Spirit Watches brought a second stone into the sweat lodge, but he heard the words of his prayer and the amplified hissing of steam rising from more than one stone. As a familiar scent filled his nostrils, he could picture Four Bears sifting red cedar needles between her fingers and onto the stones. He was aware of the muscles in his back and buttocks as they relaxed completely, joining him with the deerskin as if he himself were the deer.

"Before the Great Spirit can come into you," Four Bears said softly, "before you can accept its gifts and walk in its service, you must empty out all that is within you. You must be as empty as a clay jar before you can be filled with the water of life that is the Great Spirit. It was this way for me, for my teacher, and for his teacher. It has always been this way."

Walks Alone heard the words—he heard them and he understood their symbolism—but he heard them from a great distance, as if they were reaching out for him as he drifted off the edge of the escarpment and through the summer night, toward the river below. The sweat that dripped from his physical body became indistinguishable from the essence that seemed to be issuing from his soul, and he released both willingly.

He fell toward the river without fear, trusting in the teacher who waited with his physical body. At first he was on his back, his arms stretched toward the stars, but then his body tipped forward and he glided feet-first into Lechewuekink. Enfolding him in the arms of its cool current, the water carried him toward the sacred confluence of rivers. A moment later, he tumbled over the falls, safe in the foam that churned in the massive rocks, and into the waiting depths of Lenapewihittuk.

He shot down through its coolness, unaffected by its dangerous currents, undaunted by its blackness, as if it held only good things for him. As he fell through its murky bottom, he had a vision of the muskrat retrieving mud from below the waters and taking it to the surface and the waiting turtle. He felt the same mud fill his nostrils, but, instead of suffocating him, it filled him with the understanding that Turtle Island is truly timeless.

He found himself in the lower world, sitting on the bank of the river, its waters rushing past the rocks just a few yards below his feet. The summer morning was cloudless and unusually crisp, causing him to think that the Great Spirit had misplaced a morning from autumn. He sat quietly, feeling no need to get up and move elsewhere, content that his journey would find him. The sky was blue and seemingly endless, and he wondered if it held the path back to the sweat lodge.

Suddenly aware that he was not alone, the boy looked to the side to see a rattlesnake coiled silently only a few feet away. Its head was pointed straight at him. His initial reaction was to move away as quickly as he could without making a movement that would cause the snake to strike, but the inclination was swept away almost immediately by the realization that it meant him no harm.

"What have you come to tell me?" Walks Alone asked.

The snake said nothing but continued to look straight at him, its triangular head resting on its coiled body.

"You bring the wisdom of transformation," he said to the serpent, answering his own question. "Like you, I must shed my old skin in order to move on toward my destiny. And . . ." He paused, carefully considering the importance of the words he was about to say. ". . . I must not look back."

The rattlesnake raised its head into the air, an action that Walks Alone instantly understood to be acknowledgment, rather than aggression.

"I ask you to watch over me as I make these journeys, and to help me apply what I learn on behalf of all people. I ask that you do this to help me honor the Great Spirit."

The snake turned away from Walks Alone, lowered its head to the ground, and slithered into the underbrush. As it disappeared from view, a barely audible voice assured him, "It shall be as you have said."

The boy started to rise, but, before he could stand up straight, he was swept into the air and back toward the physical world of the sweat lodge. A moment later, he was staring at the glow of four stones in the pit.

"Welcome back," Four Bears said quietly. "Here, let me help you up."

The boy was soaked with perspiration, and as he rose to a sitting position it felt for a moment as if he was too weak to support his own weight. In an effort to regain his equilibrium, he instinctively allowed his weight to shift against his teacher. He tried to move away quickly, unwilling to presume anything that concerned Four Bears, but she placed an arm around his shoulders, silently assuring him that everything was alright.

"I am grateful for your respect, Young One, but we must lean on each other." He heard her words, but he also felt her struggling, and he was uncomfortably aware of the cough that followed her exertion.

She helped him back through the entrance and into the night, where His Spirit Watches waited with a large bucket of water from the river. He moved behind the boy and gently poured it across his shoulders, letting it cascade down the entire back of his body. Then he moved in front him and repeated the action. The water refreshed Walks Alone, and he used it to rub some of the perspiration away from his skin. As he did, His Spirit Watches raised the bucket into the air and gently poured the remainder of the water over the boy's head.

Momentarily revived, Walks Alone began to speak excitedly, anxious to talk about his journey. "This came to me . . .," he blurted.

"Be still, Young One," Four Bears cautioned, placing a hand to his lips. "You must hold these things in your heart. They are not for us to know."

As His Spirit Watches reached for a smaller bucket, the shaman added, "You must drink now and rest, and then we will return to the sweat lodge."

Walks Alone looked down into the fire where another cluster of stones was glowing like a constellation of small orange moons.

* * *

"This story is bugging me. If it's not the most frustrating thing I've ever worked on, I don't know what is. There's definitely something here—I know it—but there's no way to get at it. Every road is a dead end. I really can't justify spending any more time on it. I need to be realistic about that."

Grace Caufield thought she was saying these things to herself, but when a woman coming toward her on the sidewalk looked at her quizzically, it occurred to her that she may have been saying them aloud, or at least louder than she wanted to. In some ways, the mystery behind the bones wasn't a mystery at all. A truck had dumped a load of rocks into a creek bed, and the fallen rocks had exposed a skull. Somewhere along the line someone had died, and his remains had been discovered years later through a freak accident. If there was any more to it than that, no one seemed to know how to find it.

"Dead ends," she said, this time loud enough to hear the words, as if hearing them would substantiate their truth and inspire her to move on.

She paused long enough to confirm the address on the mailbox and then pushed open the wooden gate that guarded the small, overgrown front yard. It was obvious that it hadn't been properly cared for in quite some time. The flowerbeds could not be distinguished from the grass in the yard, the plants and shrubs having grown high enough and wide enough to obscure everything behind and beneath them. Occasional blooms protruding up through the sea of branches and leaves confirmed that, at some point in the past, someone had planted flowers with care, but the attention had long since stopped. A brick sidewalk ran from the gate to the covered front porch, where random sections of missing mortar had been filled in by moss and thick tufts of green grass. A well-worn path jutted from the walk and around the side of the house, but even it was having difficulty fending off the vines that crept out of the adjacent flowerbeds. Grace knew there was a fine line between the managed chaos of an English garden and a once-elegant landscape that was running to riot, and it was clear to her that this was the latter.

The man who answered her knock was slightly bent over, but he pushed the door open with a certainty that suggested an inner vitality. His bright blue eyes looked out at her over thin reading glasses that he obviously hadn't cared to leave behind.

"Ms. Caufield, I presume?"

"Yes, Dr. Henry. And please call me Grace."

"Well, *Grace*," he answered, emphasizing her name in response to the invitation, "please come in."

As she stood momentarily inside the front door, she could see into the living room on one side of the hall. It was dark and cluttered with books and papers that had obviously been left where they had last been used. The room wasn't dirty; it was just disorganized. Or perhaps, it occurred to her, it was perfectly organized in a way that she did not understand.

"My study is this way," the man suggested, leading her toward two doors on the other side of the hall. One of them was open, and as he walked through the doorway, she was quite certain that he had been in the room when she had knocked.

A few things in the room stood out: a huge, dark wooden desk that sat about six inches above the floor on round wooden feet; a high desk chair upholstered in very worn black leather; two leather easy chairs positioned immediately across from the desk; and a wooden cart that held three or four decanters of what appeared to be alcohol. Everything else was books. They were everywhere— shelves of them, stacks of them, boxes of them—causing Grace to wonder if she had ever seen such an aggregation of books outside of a library.

"Please," he said, motioning toward one of the easy chairs. "Can I offer you something to drink?"

"Thank you," she responded, "but no." As he lowered himself into the other easy chair, she continued, "I'm told that you're something of an expert on the history of this area, and I was hoping that you could answer some questions for me."

"I will if I can. What are your questions?"

"I'm interested in the period of time from two- to four-hundred years ago, and the people who lived here then." She paused before qualifying, "Here in Bucks County, I mean."

"You're talking about three or four centuries, and that's quite a span of time. Can you be more specific?"

"Unfortunately, no. That's as close as I can come."

"So, this concerns your article—the one about the remains that were discovered near Riegelsville?"

"You saw it?"

"Yes. I read just about anything I can get my hands on."

Grace tried to suppress her grin, but it rushed onto her face as involuntarily as a heartbeat.

"I'm sorry," she began, "but I . . ."

"It's okay, Grace. I guess I was stating the *very* obvious." He smiled widely, assuring her that he had taken no offense. "The beginning of the seventeenth century is when Europeans began coming to this area.

"What do you mean by 'Europeans'?" she asked. "Which Europeans?"

"Well," he answered, "certainly the Dutch. Henry Hudson is credited with discovering the Delaware, or what he called the *Suydt* or South River. A few years later, Cornelis Mey, the man for whom Cape May is named, built Fort Nassau just below what is now Gloucester, New Jersey.

"But the Swedes were also here. Peter Minuet founded what the Swedes claimed to be the first permanent settlement in Pennsylvania in 1638."

"Who was right?" Grace opened a tablet and began taking notes.

"I tend to come down on the side of the Dutch, primarily because of their other activity in the area, like Hendrickson's discovery of the Schuylkill River in 1616. But the point was moot by 1655. By then, the Dutch had pretty much driven the Swedes out of the area."

"What about before all of that?"

"I assume you mean before 1609?"

"Well . . . yes, if that is before Henry Hudson discovered the Delaware River."

"The entire area—the entire East Coast, really—was inhabited by Native Americans. I would never say that the early seventeenth century was the first time a Native American saw a white man—there were European fur traders in eastern Canada in the 1500s—but it was certainly the time when contact between the two cultures began on a more widespread basis. It was the time of Jamestown, Plymouth, New Amsterdam . . ."

"Which became New York?"

"Yes," he answered before finishing, ". . . and the southern portion of what is now the Delaware River."

"What kind of Native Americans were in this area? People have told me about the Lenape, although I've heard people refer to them as the 'Lenapee.'"

"*Le-nah-pay* is the correct pronunciation," he said, sounding it out, "and they lived primarily in the areas around the Delaware and lower Hudson rivers. So, you're talking about eastern Pennsylvania, northern Delaware, most of New Jersey, and southern New York. They called it Lenapehoking."

". . . ho . . ." Grace mumbled, trying to spell it phonetically.

"It's h-o-k-i-n-g. Lenape*hoking*."

"And how many people lived in Lenapehoking?"

"Thousands. Some people believe there were as few as fifteen thousand, others say there were as many as forty. No one knows for sure, but there were thousands."

Grace underscored one of the notations on her notepad before looking at Dr. Henry pensively. "I feel as if I'm jumping ahead, but I have to ask. What happened to them?"

The man smiled, as if to confirm that she was indeed jumping ahead. "Quite a bit, actually. I'm sure we'll talk about it in more detail, but here's an interesting perspective to consider. At the end of the seventeenth century, there were still fewer than ten thousand Europeans in the area the natives called Lenapehoking. A hundred years later, there were three *hundred* thousand. One could say that the Lenape simply lost a numbers game."

After making another note, Grace pursued the point. "Please forgive me, Dr. Henry, but there must be more to it than that. I mean, we're talking about a whole tribe of people."

"What we're talking about," he cautioned in response, "is an entire *culture* of people in what is now the northeastern United States. The Algonkian-speaking peoples . . ." He paused, seeing that Grace was making a note of the word. "You'll find it spelled a number of different ways, but the spelling isn't as important as the fact that it included a number of native tribes that were bound together by both language and cultural practices"

"So, it was more than just the Lenape?"

"Absolutely. It included the Iroquois tribes in the north. Among these, there were the Mohawk in the east, the Seneca in the west, and the Onondaga in between. They were known as the Elder Brothers. And there were two Younger Brothers—the Oneida, who were affiliated with the Mohawk; and the Cayuga, who were affiliated with the Seneca. There were others as well."

"But they were all part of this Algonkian-speaking culture?"

"Yes. They had their differences of opinion, but they all belonged to that culture."

"How did they get to the Northeast originally?"

"Whoa. Now you're really jumping ahead—or back as it were." Rising out of the easy chair, he added, "I'm going to have a glass of water. May I offer you one?"

"Yes, thank you. That would be nice."

A few minutes later, Dr. Henry returned to the study with two tumblers of ice water. He handed one to Grace and took a short sip from the other as he returned to his chair.

"The origin of the aboriginal people really isn't my field, so I would encourage you to speak with others about it. My focus has always been the later Woodland Period."

"When was that?"

"Most of my colleagues in prehistory define it as 1,000 BC to AD 1,600. It was preceded by the Archaic Period, which began around 8,000 BC, and the Paleo-Indian Period, which began around 10,000 BC."

"Are you saying that the Lenape were here twelve thousand years ago?"

"I'm saying that the ancestors of the Lenape were probably here then, yes."

Grace wasn't sure about what to do with the information. She made notes and underscored the numbers, but they seemed too vast to be meaningful. The date of the discovery of the Delaware River by an Englishman seemed trivial in the wake of so much time.

"And going back to your question," Dr. Henry continued, "they walked across the continent, most likely from the Bering Strait."

"I always thought those stories were legends."

"There's interesting research that genetically links aboriginal people in the Delaware River valley with people from Asia."

"So, they walked here?"

"Yes, and in time they began to walk back. Today, the remnants of the Lenape people are in Oklahoma and Kansas."

"What happened, Dr. Henry? What happened to the Lenape who were here?"

"There are many forks in the road that leads to the answer to *that* question. It's anything but *as the crow flies*. With your permission, I'd like to postpone that discussion until you've had a chance to do some reading."

"Some reading?"

"Yes, I'd like to loan you two or three books—if the idea appeals to you, that is. But before we conclude, I have a question for you."

"Yes, of course. What is it?"

"May I infer from all of this that you believe the remains that were found are those of a Native American?"

"Someone suggested that. There are reasons to believe that may be the case—the artifacts that were found with the bones, for example—but none of the scientific evidence supports it conclusively."

"Then why pursue it? If there is no proof, that is."

"If there's a story here I would like to know what it is. As impossible as it may be to get to it, I'd like to try."

"But what if the remains are those of a white man, someone perhaps who happened to have the artifacts with him?"

"From what I understand, the remains of a white man—or a black man, for that matter—could probably be identified as such. But it really doesn't matter. One way or another I would like to find out. So I'm willing to walk that road you referred to." She paused before adding, "Even though I sometimes think it's a waste of time."

A few minutes later, a number of the man's books tucked under her arm, Grace Caufield closed the front gate behind her. As she started down the sidewalk, she heard Dr. Henry call to her. She turned to see him standing in the doorway, a puzzled look on his face.

"I don't know much about the newspaper business," he began, "but is it possible that the road *is* the story?"

She smiled and walked away without responding.

* * *

When Walks Alone and Four Bears crawled back into the sweat lodge, the stones had been removed but the air was still heavy with moisture from the first session. Walks Alone knew that it would not take long for the inside of the lodge to be as humid as it had been when his first journey ended. He lay down on the deerskin without waiting for instructions from his teacher. It was still wet with the residue of sweat from his body.

"Each of us," Four Bears began, "has a mind, a body, and a spirit. The mind and body are very strong, and each is more than willing to be in control. The spirit is shy. It waits quietly for its chance, but when that chance arises, it assumes a place from which it cannot easily be removed."

She placed the strip of bear skin from the medicine bundle onto the boy's chest and pressed it to his heart. "Here your body is weakening. Here the darkness and seclusion can play tricks on your mind. But here your spirit is free to wander as it will, free to seek its power. May the strength of the bear go with it." She placed the eagle talon in his hand and, wrapping his fingers around it, added, "And may the instincts of the eagle guide its flight."

His Spirit Watches transferred a single stone from the fire beyond the door to the pit in the floor of the sweat lodge. Walks Alone watched as His Spirit Watches mouthed a quiet prayer and withdrew, dropping the skin across the entrance as he left. The inside of the sweat lodge lapsed into silence, the odor of red cedar once again rising in the air.

Closing his eyes, the boy tried to journey to the lower world. His body was weak, depleted by dehydration, and he thought it would be easy to shed his skin like the rattlesnake and leave the physical world behind. But he could not. He was distracted by everything around him—the piece of hide on his chest, the talon in his fist, the wetness of the deerskin, the sweat that rose on his forehead and dripped onto his eyelids and down the sides of his face. As if he had nothing to say about it, the frustration in his mind joined hands with the restlessness in his body, and they came forward together to take control of his being.

The boy was about to open his eyes when he felt a small pressure in the middle of his chest, and he knew that Four Bears was pressing her fingers against the strip of bear skin. He inhaled a deep breath, part of which was voluntary and part of which seemed borrowed from otherworldly lungs, and fell not into a journey but a deep sleep. He fell into its depths until he could fall no further, and there he dreamed.

Once more, he found himself by a river, but it didn't look like Lenapewihittuk. It didn't look like any river he had ever seen. It cut through a deep gorge in currents that rushed against huge rocks in explosions of white foam and toppled into treacherous holes that seemed to swirl down into nothingness. Everything in the river screamed of danger; everything told him to stay away.

Somewhere behind him, he heard the piercing call of a large bird and he turned to see a raven on the branch of a nearby tree. It leaned forward on its perch, its head pointed down toward him, and raised its formidable wings into the air, as if preparing to fly off. But it did not leave; it just stayed there, screaming at him.

Walks Alone felt his heart race but he was not afraid. His people revered the raven—the keeper of secrets, the clever magician who teaches one to confront his fears. "What is your lesson?" he asked calmly, in stark contrast to the frantic rants of the bird. "What is your lesson?"

The bird began to settle, its frenetic act lost on the boy below. "For you, I bring the gifts of magic and healing," said the bird, "for there will be much to heal."

"Do you mean people? Will you give me the power to heal others?"

"You will care for the sick and dying, and you will look after the souls of those you cannot heal, but . . ." The bird leaned forward again, staring down at the boy with powerful eyes that drew him toward their blackness. ". . . but it is your destiny to heal a greater wound—a gash that seems beyond healing."

"When will I do this?"

"The cutting began long ago."

"I do not understand."

"I did not say that it is your destiny to understand the wound. I said that it is your destiny to heal it."

"What else have you come to tell me?" the boy asked.

"I will tell you this . . . ," answered the raven, ". . . the sweat of your body has soaked the deerskin until it can hold no more. Is it not uncomfortable? Does it not make you want to wake up?"

And, with that, Walks Alone opened his eyes.

He tried to raise himself onto his arms, but it was impossible. The stones in the pit glowed relentlessly, as if they would not be satisfied until they had drained the last bit of energy from his body. And, in his heart, he feared that they would be satisfied soon.

"Do not move," the voice of Four Bears demanded. "Do not move."

The skin across the entrance was lifted and His Spirit Watches crawled into the sweat lodge. Carefully reaching beneath the boy's drenched body, he raised him into the air and, moving across the dirt floor on his knees, carried him out into the night.

Laying the boy facedown on a large piece of bark that he had covered with reeds from the river, he poured water on him again—first on his back, then on his chest, and then on his face and head. He put a huge hand behind the boy's head and raised it so that he could drink from a ladle of water. Walks Alone drank voraciously, causing His Spirit Watches to draw the ladle away from his lips a number of times, giving his young body a chance to assimilate the restorative fluid.

Long minutes passed, during which Four Bears and His Spirit Watches said nothing. They watched the boy carefully, knowing all too well that the necessity of his trial brought with it risks that could not be ignored. He was badly dehydrated, and whatever water he was absorbing now would not be nearly enough to replace what he had lost.

Four Bears remembered when she had walked the path into the depths of who she was. She remembered the things that she had seen on her journeys and in her visions and dreams—the things that she still held in her heart, never having spoken of them to anyone. But now her heart was consumed by something else, something that both she and His Spirit Watches knew and feared—the knowledge that the boy had to return to the sweat lodge one more time.

* * *

As he walked with Emily FitzRoy toward the exhibit at the far end of the second floor, Jeff Phillips's attention was drawn immediately to the high arch that formed the entrance. Across the top, "Fulfilling a Prophecy" was inscribed over a field divided into four rectangles of different colors—orange, gold, red, and crimson. A subtitle announced "The Past and Present of the Lenape in Pennsylvania." On each side of the entrance was a list of places that had been named by Native Americans hundreds of years ago. There were at least fifty of them in total.

There were names of places that had since been absorbed into the city of Philadelphia: Wissinoming, Aramingo, Passyunk, Manatawny, Wissahickon, and Shackamaxon. There were names of nearby towns: Neshaminy, Holicong, Conestoga, Sanatoga, Perkiomen, and Manayunk. There were names of Pennsylvania towns that were farther away: Shamokin, Erie, Shickashinny, Towanda, Analomink, Tamarack, Monocacy, Allegheny, Pocono, and Susquehanna. And there were names of places beyond Pennsylvania: Cinnaminson, Hoboken, and Manhattan. There were names of counties, names of school districts, names of rivers, names of creeks, and names of state parks.

"It's strange," Jeff began as he scanned the list.

"What's that?" Emily asked.

"Our daily lives touch so many places from another time, but we rush past them on our way to whatever we deem important. Some of these names are familiar to me. My wife and I have walked along the Wissahickon Creek, and we've spent Saturday mornings shopping in Manayunk. We've hiked above the Susquehanna and in the Poconos. But I never stopped long enough to wonder about the origin of the names or what they meant."

"I know exactly what you mean. I grew up in Sullivan County in southern New York State, and when I was a girl I spent three consecutive summers at Camp Netimus in Pike County, Pennsylvania. It's near the village of Shohola. I learned early on that the camp was named for an Indian chief, but it wasn't until I first saw the word Shohola here on this arch that someone told me it's Lenape for *place of peace*. If I ever go back to that area it won't be hard to remember that a people once thought of it that way."

Just beyond the arch, they stopped to watch a film about something called the Prophecy of the Fourth Crow. A woman's voice recited each part of the prophecy in the Lenape language, followed by a man's reading of the English translation. The man then interpreted the meaning of each passage of the prophecy.

"It was said four crows will come. The first crow flew the way of harmony with Creator."

"*The first crow is the Lenape people before the arrival of the Europeans.*"

"The second crow tried to clean the world, but he became sick and died."

"*The second crow is the death and destruction of our culture.*"

"The third crow saw his dead brother and he hid."

"*The third crow is our people going underground and hiding.*"

"The fourth crow flew the way of harmony again with Creator. Caretakers, they will live together on the earth."

"*The fourth crow is the Lenape becoming caretakers once again, and working with all people to restore this land.*"

The exhibit was divided into four parts, one for each of the crows in the prophecy.

The first included information about the ancient culture and featured a number of artifacts.

"Look at this," Jeff said, looking down into a glass display case. "This is wampum." A short, twisted length of small white beads had been situated under a magnifying glass so that it could be seen more easily. "But it doesn't look much like the beads that you found in the creek bank."

"The description here," Emily began, "says they're made from mollusk shells, and that would coincide with what George Cameron said that afternoon. These were carved by hand. The beads we found were tooled, presumably by tools introduced by Europeans."

As they moved into the second part of the exhibit, their attention was drawn to a wooden mask immediately in front of them. Identified as a ceremonial mask of Meesing, it had been mounted on a post so that it faced the entrance to the exhibit, as if meant to watch all who entered.

A map hung on a nearby wall, an artist's depiction of what the Delaware River valley may have looked like when it was inhabited by the Lenape. It had been commissioned by the Philadelphia City Planning Council in 1934. The Lenape word *Coaquannock* was drawn on the portion of the map where the city of Philadelphia would one day stand. Strangely transfixed by the map, Jeff followed the familiar line of the Delaware River as it tracked northeast to the area where he now lived. And as he did he saw the land—*his* land—in a completely different way.

"Look at this."

His reverie interrupted by Emily's words, Jeff stepped back from the map to see what she was referring to. A framed reprint from the *Pennsylvania Gazette* hung on the wall in front of her. It was dated July 12, 1764. "What about it?" he inquired.

"Down here," she answered, pointing to an announcement near the bottom of the page. "This is an ad, if you can call it that, calling for Lenape scalps: $134 for male scalps, $50 for female scalps."

"I wonder what they did to deserve that."

"I don't know, but I didn't know that type of thing happened in this part of the country. I thought it was part of the history of the West."

"Sounds like it may have been a part of the history of the East, as well." Jeff was trying to ignore the images that the ad conjured, but they would not be ignored. As he moved on to the next part of the exhibit, they walked with him.

There was information about the immigration of the Dutch, the Swedes, and the English, and subsequent movement into the area by the Germans, the Mennonite, the Quakers, the Amish, and Africans. And there was a display about something called the Walking Purchase of 1737, described as an event in which the Lenape lost a portion of their lands nearly as large as Rhode Island.

The third part of the exhibit focused on the departure of most of the Lenape people to points west. It illustrated how those who left did their best to maintain their way of life, and how those who remained behind did what they could to honor their heritage, even as they were being absorbed into a different culture.

"Look at how they marked common household items," Emily observed, looking at a displayed blanket. "This design looks like a simple decoration, but it's the repetition of a cultural symbol that was important to them. It says that it symbolizes the cardinal directions and the creator of all things."

"And that child's doll," Jeff added, pointing to the corner of the display case. "It has a face of each side of its head, one for a public white world and one for a private Lenape world."

"This is daunting. These are the creations of a culture trying to hang on against overwhelming odds. There are many examples of this type of thing throughout history, but it's still sobering to think that it happened here, in our backyard."

"Sobering, indeed." As Jeff contemplated the meaning that *backyard* held for him in this instance, he understood just how sobering it really was.

As they continued into the fourth part of the exhibit, they encountered display cases containing information about people of Lenape descent who still lived in Pennsylvania. Photographs and documents described many of the things that they did to celebrate and preserve their Lenape heritage.

"I wonder if any of these people are pure-blooded Lenape," Jeff said without looking away from a photograph of a group of people in a display case. "I wonder how many sixty-fourths each of them is."

"I'm not sure I understand what you mean," Emily answered.

"It's something that George Cameron told me about. He said that he was three sixty-fourths Native American, and an Outaluck. What did he mean by that?"

"He said that there are three kinds of people—those who are Native American, those who aren't, and those who are part. They're 'outaluck' because they can never be any more than part Native American."

"Were any of George's ancestors Lenape?"

"He didn't say, but he's certainly passionate about these people. If they weren't Lenape, I wonder where all that passion comes from."

"Maybe there's more to his passion than ancestry. Maybe it's something of a quest for him." She hesitated, not knowing if she should say what she wanted to say. Somewhere deep in her consciousness something, or someone, tugged at her. She imagined five generations of people standing behind George Cameron, three of whom were different than the others, but whose blood had found a way to flow through his veins in a more compelling way.

"What is it?" Jeff asked, sensing her reticence.

"Maybe," she confided, "he's only doing what he believes is the right thing to do."

* * *

When Walks Alone crawled into the sweat lodge for the third time, he went alone.

The inside of the lodge seemed devoid of air. Humidity consumed it so completely that it seemed impossible to the boy that it had not condensed into rain. It felt difficult to breathe, and although he had never felt confined or trapped in a sweat lodge, as some others had, the crushing weight around him now caused him to look nervously toward the entrance. He thought anxiously about the relative coolness of the summer night that waited just beyond the bark walls, and wondered if there was still time to return to it. But he stayed.

Crawling to the deerskin, he lay back into its unnerving wetness. So much of his sweat had soaked into the hair and the hide beneath it that he felt as if it was more him than deer. He knew that he would never again be able to look at a deer standing in the pouring rain and not remember the hideous feeling that he was feeling now.

His Spirit Watches entered with a glowing stone and placed it in the pit. He prayed again, but this time he said a different prayer, one that somehow seemed more fervent, more necessary. Then he crawled away, closing up the entrance as he withdrew.

Walks Alone closed his eyes and sucked in a deep breath that transported him, almost instantaneously, into another realm. But instead of lapsing into a dream or falling through air, water, and land to the lower world, he found himself drifting high above Lenapewihittuk. He could see the cliffs on both sides of the river and the moonlight as it danced on the water between them. The heavily leaved trees swayed quietly in the breeze, occasionally revealing a small fire in the distance. He drifted higher and higher into the night, as if he were meant to touch the moon.

He thought about the rattlesnake; he thought about the raven. He thought about Four Bears and His Spirit Watches; he thought about Talks For Us and Looks Back. He thought about his father. He thought about good things, and he also found himself thinking about things that were not so good. He thought about the two men that had stopped Four Bears and him in the clearing, and he wondered if they were somewhere down below. He found himself hoping that the Great Spirit would help them find a truer path. He thought about the white beast and the things that the beast had said. He thought about his destiny, and he looked toward the stars with a prayer that he would be worthy of it.

He drifted up and up, and when there was no more drifting, he found himself looking upon a strange and unimaginable site. In the distance, he saw a village of large dwellings, grand stone structures that seemed to be carved in the face of the sky. Taken together, all the villages of all the native people he had ever heard of were not as big as what he was seeing now. He could only wonder how many people lived in such a place.

Suspended in the clouds and framed by snow-covered mountains, the village waited stoically with a permanence that seemed unassailable. Streaks of lightning flashed above the mountains and behind the clouds, illuminating the village in mysterious shades of white and silver.

Walks Alone watched breathlessly, and for an agonizing moment he was filled with the fear that he had died in the sweat lodge, that his body had finally drained out into the waiting hide of the deer, and that he was looking upon the home of the Great Spirit. But as quickly as the thought came it left, and in its place came the understanding that he was drifting back toward the escarpment and the sweat lodge.

An instant later, he opened his eyes to find that he was out in the night air and on the large piece of bark. His Spirit Watches poured water over him with a sense of purpose that seemed as intense as the atmosphere from which the boy had just been removed.

Four Bears stood a few feet away, her back to him, her arms stretched out to the sky above. The moon slipped behind a cloud, leaving just enough light to illuminate the outline of her body.

His Spirit Watches raised the ladle to the boy's lips but he pushed it away, wanting to say something, having to say something, even if he did it on a final, thirsting breath.

"This came to me . . ." he whispered, ". . . I will hold it in my heart, but you must know that this came to me . . ."

Without turning around, without dropping the arms that were raised to the Great Spirit in gratitude, Four Bears interrupted the boy. "It's called the Place with No Words, Young One." She coughed harshly, as if trying to dislodge something in her throat. "It's called the Place with No Words."

Ten

More than a full day had passed since Walks Alone's experiences in the sweat lodge. It had been close to dawn when the last of his journeys had ended, and even though he had been awake for most of the night, he had been too excited and too alert to fall asleep. But dehydration and exhaustion had eventually held sway and carried him into a sleep that lasted through the rest of the day and into the following morning.

As he lay looking out at the first light of morning from the wigwam of His Spirit Watches, each of his senses felt as honed as the edge of an axe. He was certain that he could hear the fish as they jumped above the currents of the river and catch the scent of the wildflowers and herbs that hid by the path that would eventually lead him home. He was still weak, his body not yet fully recovered, but he had never felt so alive in his young life.

When he stepped out into the morning air, he saw His Spirit Watches sitting on a rock by the path down the hill from the wigwam. He held something in his hands, something that commanded his attention so completely that he didn't notice the boy until he had taken a few steps toward him. Walks Alone could not imagine what it was.

"*He*," His Spirit Watches said as he looked up. "How do you feel?"

"A little weak," came the reply, "but the sleep helped." Then, looking down the path past the place where His Spirit Watches sat, he asked, "Where is Four Bears?"

Without responding, the man returned his attention to whatever he was holding in his hands.

"My teacher," the boy repeated, "where is my teacher?" The words came out in a demanding tone that Walks Alone did not intend. His Spirit Watches was not the kind of man of whom one made demands. And besides, Walks Alone knew that he could never repay the man's kindness and service, and he didn't want to appear ungrateful. He stuttered something unintelligible, trying to compensate for his tone.

"She is not here," His Spirit Watches said without looking up. "She will return later."

The boy wanted to know where she was—for some unknown reason he felt as if he *had* to know—but he remained silent, unwilling to risk saying something inappropriate again.

"This is a difficult time for her," the man said. "I know you don't realize it, but this takes almost as much out of her as it takes out of you. And . . ." His voice fell off, as if he had thought better of continuing.

"Please say what's in your heart," Walks Alone said. "Please say what's in your heart."

"She worries about you, more than I have ever seen her worry about anyone."

"I don't understand. Why would she worry?"

"Because yours is a great destiny, and the Great Spirit has chosen her to lead you toward it. He has chosen you, but he has chosen her as well."

"Do you know what my destiny is? Has she told you?"

"No. And I don't need to know. The Great Spirit has brought me from a distant place to help, and help is what I will do. Why he has asked this of me is unimportant."

"Are you going to take me back to my village?" the boy asked.

"Perhaps in time," the man answered, "but there is much to be done before you can go back."

"Much to be done?"

Without answering the question, His Spirit Watches told Walks Alone to go back to the wigwam and wait for him. He said that he could drink as much water as he wanted, but he was to eat nothing. The boy walked back up the hill without questioning the instructions.

When His Spirit Watches approached him a short time later, the boy could see a stone-headed hatchet tucked into the belt that held his knife and a quiver of arrows and a bow on his broad back. On the cord of his breechclout was the thing that he had been working on when the boy had found him sitting by the path. It was a deerskin pouch, a little larger than the pouches that most Lenape men carried, bound with a dark leather thong. He stopped at the wigwam long enough to retrieve a water skin and then started up the path toward the clearing where the sweat lodge sat. Walks Alone followed after him, understanding beyond any doubt that he was supposed to do exactly that.

They climbed to the top of the escarpment and crossed a long flat section of forest before beginning their ascent up a formidable incline. The morning was hot, and the boy feared that the climb would be rigorous, but he knew it would be even more so without the protection of the dense canopy above. In the two hours that followed, they stopped to drink from the water skin, and they stopped to fill the skin whenever they found water, but, other than that, they stayed on the move.

Walks Alone had many questions, but he asked none of them. He knew that talking required energy and he had to save as much of his as he could. He also sensed that His Sprit Watches didn't want to talk. The man was focused and resolute, climbing the mountain with an unstated purpose that seemed to echo across its forested face. But, even in his determination, he moved at a pace that made sense not for him but for the boy, and for that Walks Alone was very grateful.

They walked for the remainder of the morning, traversing long stretches of woods, rocky outcroppings, and occasional clearings of high grass. The flat areas along the ascent provided breaks from the steep climbs, and His Spirit Watches would use them as an opportunity to let the boy rest, for long periods of time if necessary, and regain his strength.

It was after midday when the light in the tree line grew brighter, and Walks Alone knew that they were nearing the top of the mountain. A few minutes later, he followed His Spirit Watches into a small clearing. Far below them and out as far as they could see, countless treetops followed the contour of a magnificent valley, through the middle of which cut the dark river. Walks Alone had never seen anything to compare to it. He sucked in a huge gasp of air, and he didn't know if he was reacting to the climb or the incredible beauty that stretched out for miles in front of him.

"In the winter," His Spirit Watches began, "when the leaves have fallen from the trees, you can see the snow on the floor of the valley. When the sun meets the whites and blues and silvers of the snow, you cannot help but think that the Great Spirit lives here. Why would he live anywhere else?"

They stood looking out across the valley, neither saying anything, both absorbing the beauty as if it were air for their lungs or blood for their veins. They stood there until Walks Alone, suddenly consumed by an inexplicable combination of fear and joy, broke the early afternoon silence.

"I'm here to keep my vigil. That's why you brought me here, isn't it?"

"It is."

"But it shouldn't be for another winter."

"For you, and those like you, time is less important. Things don't happen according to a plan or schedule; they happen when they're supposed to happen. This is your time to keep your vigil."

Emotions and words flooded through the boy in a torrent as deep and imposing as Lenapewihittuk itself. He had many things to say and many more to ask, but each time he began he stopped himself short, knowing that words were meaningless. This was about becoming a man, if only a man of eleven winters, and he knew that there was no direction in which to walk other than straight ahead.

"You may take any of these things," His Spirit Watches said, touching the knife and hatchet simultaneously, "or you may take them all."

"The bow," the boy said softly but with assuredness, "and the knife."

His Spirit Watches handed the weapons to the boy and then drew the water skin from his shoulder and placed it on the ground in front of him. Then he removed the deerskin pouch from his belt.

"I made this for you." He handed it to the boy, and for the first time Walks Alone saw doubt and vulnerability on the man's face. "It's not for me to make your medicine bundle, so I will understand if you want to find another."

"Didn't you just say," the boy began, "that things happen for people like me when they're supposed to happen?"

The man nodded.

"Then it *is* for you to make this for me. It is as it should be."

His Spirit Watches smiled gratefully and took a few steps backward before turning in the direction from which they had come. "May your spirit guides be strong, and may they walk with you always."

As he watched His Spirit Watches disappear into the trees, the boy rubbed the highly tanned deerskin of the medicine bundle. The words of his massive friend rolling through his head, he picked up the water skin, took one last look into the valley, and moved on. He knew that Four Bears was with him, if only in spirit. He knew that His Spirit Watches and Talks For Us were with him. He knew that his father was with him. And he knew that somewhere on top of the mountain the great white beast waited patiently.

* * *

She was so accustomed to awakening and finding him gone that it was becoming more familiar than finding him asleep next to her. It wasn't that Jeff didn't sleep well; he just didn't sleep much. He never complained about it. He never used it as an excuse. He never napped later in the day in an attempt to catch up on his rest. And although he had always said that there was just too much to do to spend one's time sleeping, she knew that the deeper truth was that her husband just didn't know how to relax. There were no circumstances under which he would admit it, but she believed that he was afraid to stop for fear that he would never start again.

Finding him gone, she would usually roll over and go back to sleep, but this time she felt compelled to get out of bed and look for him. Not finding him in his office, she threw on a light robe and went out into the round upstairs hall. She paused for a moment at the top of the stairs, thinking that she might hear him moving around on the first floor, but there was nothing but silence. Tying the sash of the robe, she descended the steps.

A minute or two later, having surveyed the downstairs between the front hall and the sunroom, she found him in the sitting room on the north end of the house. He was sitting on the floor with his back against the large sofa that faced the massive floor-to-ceiling windows and the vast meadow beyond. He stared out into a night that was so bereft of light that she could only wonder what he was really looking at.

"Hey," she whispered, not entirely committed to interrupting his reverie, "are you okay?"

"I'm fine," he answered without looking up. "Are you having trouble sleeping?"

"Me?" She couldn't help but laugh. "No, I'm not the one in this relationship who has trouble sleeping." She sat down next to him in the faint light of the room, her back to the sofa as well. Resting her folded arms on her knees, she added, "What are you doing down here in the dark?"

"Thinking."

"About what? Anything I can help with?"

"You help with everything. My life is what it is because of what you bring to it. You know that, don't you?"

"I know you wouldn't say it if you didn't feel it in your heart, so thank you." She waited for what seemed like a long time, not wanting to confuse sentiments that didn't belong in contiguous sentences. "But something tells me that's *not* what you were thinking about."

"What's this all about, Dae?"

"You mean finding the bones, don't you?"

"Yes."

"I don't know. Maybe it's just that. We found the bones, we treated them with respect, and we did what the law requires. Maybe that's all there is to it." She reached over and placed her hand on his arm. "I'm sure it's happened many times before."

"I'm sure it has, too. But if this is just an oddity of life, something to experience and move beyond, why is it having such an effect on me? And what's worse . . ."

She waited for the end of the thought, an end that did not come. "What's worse?" she finally asked.

"What's worse is that we can't do anything about it. We just don't have anything to go on."

A silence grew in the room, a silence as dark as the night beyond the windows. They both knew that she would respond as she always responded, with the truth—a truth that would give a name to his conundrum, turn him square shouldered to face it, and move him toward its resolution.

"That's what this is really about, isn't it? *You* can't do anything about it. Not *we* can't do anything about it, *you* can't."

Her words hung in the air, waiting for him to grasp them, and they hung there with a permanence that seemed unassailable, even by gravity itself.

"But where do I start?" He was dodging, looking for an opening, and they both knew it, but she had described the real problem perfectly and no half-hearted avoidance was going to change that.

"Tell me," she began, with just enough edge in her voice to let him know that she would only go so far with this game, "when has not knowing where to start *ever* stopped you?"

"Look," he relented. "You're right. This is about me wanting to solve this puzzle, and that's something I will probably never be able to do. But, for whatever reason, I just can't let it go."

"Then don't. Do what your heart tells you to do. And if that's not enough . . ." The rest of her words exited on a laugh that let him know she was squarely on his side, whatever the outcome. ". . . then you're really screwed up and I can't do anything to help. Now come back to bed with me."

He followed her through the house and toward the staircase. As they neared the water wall he was keenly aware of its steady, mesmerizing sound. All but invisible in the dark, the constant sheet of water that cascaded down its face could have convinced any passerby that it was really a mountain stream, tumbling its way to the river. An unexpected wave of peacefulness filled his body as he followed his wife up the steps, untied her robe in the darkness, and made love with her.

* * *

Walks Alone had been in the forests near the village many times, and he had learned how to survive in them. Talks For Us had taught him well, as had Looks Back and, more recently, Four Bears. But he had always been with one of them, and seldom had they been more than an hour or two from the relative safety of the village.

This was different. He was at least four hours from the small gathering of huts below the escarpment, a place with which he was unfamiliar and that he only knew lay in the general direction of the river. He was neither afraid nor confident, and his young mind was becoming increasingly aware of the intricate tangle of feelings that stretched between the two extremes.

There were things to fear—unanticipated things like the men who had approached Four Bears and him in the clearing only a few days earlier; and things of which to remain aware—expected things like dangerous animals and sudden changes in the weather. He was grateful that his senses were so honed, even though he found himself wishing that the honing had sapped less of his strength.

What he felt most was uncertainty. He knew what was expected of him—he was expected to keep his vigil until his spirit guide revealed itself, and then to kill an animal, most likely a deer, and return with it not as a boy but as a man. The first seemed simple. The white beast had revealed itself to him many times, and although he had never seen an animal like it, he was certain that it was his spirit guide. "If it's not," he thought to himself, "what *is* it?" The other was not simple at all. He knew how to hunt, but killing an animal was much different than finding it, especially when one was hunting alone. And what if he did kill a deer or some other animal? How would he ever manage to drag it back down the mountain? And how much time would his vigil require? Would he be on the mountain for hours or for days?

Knowing that he would eventually have to carry whatever he killed down to the river, he decided to lessen the distance by heading in that direction to begin with. Securing the weapons that His Spirit Watches had left with him and draping the water skin from his shoulder, he set out in the direction from which he had walked earlier in the day. After walking for less than an hour, he felt as if he needed to rest and give his taxed body an opportunity to recover. Even though it would still be light for a few more hours, the sun was already beginning to drop into the trees behind him. He decided to prepare for a night in the forest.

He came to a small clearing that he and His Spirit Watches had not passed on their climb, and he knew that he was not re-tracing their steps as closely as he wanted to. He was moving in the right direction, but the forest was different now. Its colors and shadows, and even its smells, made it seem like a different place. The ground was lighter, dustier, and the smell of decaying trees on the forest floor more acrid. In the clearing, a large rock jutted out of the ground in such a way that its flat top was about eight feet above the angle of the hillside below. It seemed to watch stoically with a strength the boy wished he could borrow for whatever ordeal awaited him.

In the next hour, he built a small lean-to in the trees behind the top of the rock. Little more than a covering of heavily leaved tree branches, it was only big enough to cover the length of his body, but it would keep away the rain and morning dew. Leaving the bow, the quiver, and the water behind, he moved out onto the top of the rock, sitting at its edge with his legs folded beneath him. His stomach made a low, growling sound, and his thoughts turned to food. He now knew why he had been instructed not to eat, and that whatever he ate next would be the result of his own ability to find it. He resolved that he would hunt at first light.

Immediately below him, something moved in the brush, and he watched silently as a squirrel emerged into the failing light of the forest floor. It paused momentarily before resuming its frenzied examination of fallen leaves and branches. "Not easy to hit with an arrow," he thought to himself as he watched the squirrel scurry back into the undergrowth.

Closing his eyes and sucking in a deep breath of mountain air, the boy could feel himself relax into the cool permanence of the rock beneath him. And, in that relaxation, he allowed his thoughts to drift.

When he opened his eyes, Walks Alone was in a vast and open land. It was winter, but not the winter of Lenapewihittuk. There was no gentle blanket of snow on the forest floor; no crystals of ice on bare tree branches, shining in the morning sun; no crisp air that awakens the senses to the reality that there is beauty in all things, even the subtle death that walks with the last of the seasons. In this place, there was nothing *but* winter, and it was harsh and unforgiving. It crushed down on everything in great blankets of cold and ice that seemed immune to even the most remote possibility of spring. The sky was pewter, sunless, devoid of life. Not one bird seemed courageous enough to risk a journey across its dark face.

He was with a small band of men, all of whom were well known to him, one of whom was a member of his family. They all had much more hair than Lenape men. Their heads were unshaven and without scalplocks, their faces covered by thick beards. Heavy animal pelts covered their bodies from head to toe and untanned hides protected their feet. They crouched silently behind an elevated section of craggy rocks, watching the stand of trees to the right of the icy ground below. They waited patiently, saying nothing, the frozen stillness broken only by the sounds of excited breathing in the frigid air.

A sound issued from the trees, ending as quickly as it had come. The six men leaned forward, anticipating the appearance of prey, but nothing emerged from the trees. The waiting was agonizing for Walks Alone, his body racked with paralysis from staying so still in the cold. The sound came again, louder this time, preceding the emergence from the trees of a huge, tusked beast. Its coarse brown hair was caked with mud and snow, and it moved on legs that were as stout as trees, pounding the ground with merciless thuds. It was twice as tall as any animal Walks Alone had ever seen, and its menacing tusks curved upward in long, lethal arcs. The animal took a few steps toward them, causing the band of hunters to squat lower behind the rocks, and then it paused, cautiously surveying the open space before it. Walks Alone wondered if the animal would ever reach the ground below the rocks, and he feared that if it took much longer he would be too cold to raise his spear against it.

Finally, the beast took another step toward the hunters, then another, and then another still. Walks Alone felt his right hand tighten on the wooden shaft of his spear, its sharpened stone head hard against the side of his face. As he looked toward the man standing to his right, a plume of frozen breath billowed out into the air between them. His body trembled with excitement and fear, and he felt even colder than he had a moment before. If something went wrong and he somehow ended up beneath the massive legs of the approaching beast, he was certain that they would snap him in half like a shard of ice.

It all happened in a spark of energy that ignited in a vacuum, lost to everything except its single purpose. The beast was immediately below the rocks and the hunters were scurrying over them, screams rushing from their mouths and spears rising toward the unbroken dullness of the sky. The surprised animal turned its head toward them, trumpeting in protest, and jerked backward. An instant later, a spear whistled into its throat, causing it to thrust its head upward in a long and primal shriek. The sound crushed into Walks Alone's ears, making them vibrate with pain.

Another spear flew, striking the animal in the hindquarters, causing it to cry out yet again. Walks Alone hesitated for what seemed like an endless moment, waiting for the clean target behind the shoulder of the animal's foreleg, and in that moment something happened with a sickening slowness that seemed to defy time.

As one of the hunters threw his spear, he lost his footing and lunged forward. The spear went flying above the animal; his body went flying directly into the beast, bouncing as harmlessly as snow off of its formidable mass. Walks Alone hurled his spear with as much force as his frozen body could muster. It struck the beast's shoulder just as the animal's tusk impaled the hunter on the ground. Their agonizing cries split the frozen air in horrifying unison.

The beast toppled over onto its right side, pulling its own victim into the air on its tusk. The hunters jumped down from the rocks, retrieving their spears and stabbing the animal repeatedly until it stopped bellowing for air. It was only then that the sickening gurgles in the throat of the impaled man became audible. He was severely injured, but not dead.

The band of hunters used knives to split open their kill and hack away as much of its meat as they could carry with them. They ate as they hacked, smears of still-warm blood on their faces.

The impaled man screamed in agony against Walks Alone's clumsy effort to free him from the tusk. As blood rushed from his punctured midsection, his screams became weaker, quickly dissipating into little more than futile gasps. Knowing that he could do nothing else for the man, Walks Alone drew his knife and turned to hack at the beast, hunger burning in his stomach.

When the hunters had eaten as much as they wanted and cut free as much as they could carry, they began walking in the direction of the dim light that was moving toward the horizon. They moved quickly and with purpose, knowing that once they were gone, other animals, and perhaps other hunters, would find the animal they had killed.

Walks Alone remained behind long enough to look for one last time into the wounded man's all-but-lifeless eyes. Then he rushed to catch up with the others.

* * *

Emily FitzRoy had been hoping to find information about the earliest ancestors of the Native Americans who eventually settled in the Delaware Valley. Her Internet research had led her to stories about something called the "Lenape Stone," including a presentation to the Bucks County Historical Society by a man named John Bailey on July 18, 1882, which she found to be intriguing reading—especially from a twenty-first century perspective.

> *Having briefly described the people of the latter part, at least, of the "Stone Age," we wish to call your attention to an event of Indian history—an event engraved or transcribed on stone, like the sculptures on the temple walls of Assyria or the hieroglyphics on the sarcophagi of Egyptian tombs—an event whose record presents additional evidence that man was coeval with the huge mastodon and other large animals of an undeterminable period; also an event that no doubt occurred in this country and county.*
>
> *In 1872, a young man named Bernard Hansel, while plowing his father's field, LOCATED ON THE EAST SIDE OF THE DURHAM ROAD, ABOUT TWO MILES NORTH OF BUCKINGHAM MOUNTAIN, found a part of this stone, or breastplate, as it may be termed. Nothing in particular attracted his attention, except the few lines drawn upon its face, and it was placed with his collection of arrowheads, of which he had found great numbers in the same field.*

Since that time, he has been on the watch for the other part, and was rewarded by finding it a few months ago while plowing the same field, and near the same spot where the first part was found. This is a singular incident, as they may have broken apart centuries ago; and without the latter part, we would fail to read the first correctly. It might be well to state that the field in which so many relics have been found is near five springs, and was a hunting or camping-ground, being near this great Indian pathway that existed from the Delaware at Point Pleasant, through Bucks, from thence to the falls of the Susquehanna.

The stone is of liver color, perhaps of slate or shale limestone; present length, four and one-half inches; width, one and three-quarter inches; and one-quarter inch in thickness.

In order to more fully illustrate the engraving, we have prepared a rough enlarged facsimile; the details are six times the size of the original.

The artist, in depicting this event, has probably given us as much history in the same space as we would expect of our artists of the present day; and, Mr. President, when the leading painter of America, Benjamin West, in his historical painting of "Penn's Treaty with the Indians," represents men of mature years who were but children and did not arrive in this country until seven years after the treaty, and when William Penn, the prominent feature, was here until the treaty was ratified; while the costumes were not

worn for nearly a century after; and the three-story
building did not exist; when this great artist is allowed
to fancy and produce something of a fictitious nature for
the history of the founding of this Commonwealth—
then we should allow some license to the savage, with
his rude engraving tools, if he should not make perfect
curved lines and his perspective should be a trifle faulty.

Interesting point, Emily FitzRoy thought to herself, *especially in 1882.*

She found his discussion of the authenticity of the stone intriguing, although her training assured her that similar debates had been going on around the world since archaeologists first started digging in the dirt, but she was particularly engaged by his brief discourse regarding the historical accuracy of Benjamin West's painting. If a comparatively recent painting was so inaccurate and flawed, what *could* be taken at face value? Just about anything could be called into question. She wanted to give Mr. Bailey the benefit of the doubt, but the condescending benevolence of his admonition to "*allow some license to the savage*" prevented her from going too far with that.

Our interpretation of the engraving is that the scene or
action represents an encounter with one or more huge
animals. In the cut, only one is in view, a mastodon
*(*Mammoth Elephas primigenius*), the same as*
described as belonging to the European Stone Age.
The tusks and proboscis are plainly visible, while the
perpendicular lines on various parts of the body must
indicate the long hair with which the animals were
covered, necessary for the cold climate.

The fossils of the mastodon or hairy elephant are found in many parts of Siberia, and in 1799, an animal nearly complete in its parts was found imbedded in the ice on the Siberian coast. They roamed over Central Europe, from Ireland to the Ural mountains, and from thence across northern Asia to Behring's Straits, to Canada and the United States.

If we allow the stature of the Indians represented in the engraving to be five feet in height, and if the artist has given us a correct proportion and delineation of the monster, it would measure twenty-six feet in length, eighteen feet in height, twelve feet in depth of body, and in length of tusks on the curved line thirteen feet. These measurements have been exceeded by remains found in many places in this country.

One of the braves has a drawn bow, and an arrow pierces the side of the monster, which signifies that they could fight him with their arrows. Near this brave stands another, with his spear set upright in the ground, or placed perpendicular, showing that their spears are useless; they could not get close enough to use them. A third party is reclining on the ground near a large stone, smoking his pipe. Some of them were cowardly and hid themselves, and left braves to do the work. Still another is under the monster's feet. We would infer that some were killed by him. He is more destructive than the forked lightning, which is beautifully depicted.

He is as tall as the tree tops. He is more powerful than the sun's rays; more changeable than the moon, which is now a crescent; wonderful as the course of the planets . . .

"Alright, Mr. Bailey," Emily muttered to herself, "let's get back to the Lenape Stone." She continued with Bailey's story.

On the reverse side of the stone are various symbols of tribes, perhaps those connected with the event. Most conspicuous are the turtle, eagle, sea-snakes, and reindeer, or elk, with large antlers. Also, plainly outlined on one end, is their early history. Large, crooked lines represent water, and a large fish floats in it, while a number of crossed lines are over the water. Near the water lines, five points, or peaks, are represented. Next is a mountain peak with its rocky sides. Directly over the mountain is a cross, and on the off-side of the mountain from the five peaks, is a square tablet, and within its borders are ten dots regularly spaced off.

This history would read: That they crossed the great water; they were acquainted with the five peaks of the Cascade range, their ancestors lived within view of them; they crossed the mountain of rocks or the Rocky mountains, and the ten dots mean there were ten tribes at the crossing, or ten generations, epochs or cycles had passed since the crossing; they kept a record of great events, and every fifty-two years was a cycle, when great feasts were celebrated, and every three hundred and twelve years, or six of these cycles, was an extra epoch. Maybe ten of these extra feasts had passed.

Emily conjured a mental image of a young boy working in the fields of his family's farm a few years after the end of the Civil War. His plough unearths part of a flat stone that bears unusual markings. Thinking nothing of it, he puts the stone with his collection of arrowheads, most of which have also been found in the fields of the farm. Ten years later, he finds the other part of the stone.

The conjoined halves of the stone reveal markings that depict men hunting a mastodon on one side and a series of pictures on the other.

And from this, she thought to herself, *we know about the prehistory of the Lenape people. Or at least people were talking as if they knew about it in 1882.*

Although she liked the story, she regarded the authenticity of the stone as little more than something to be bandied about at historical society meetings. What concerned her was that there was a time, and it wasn't all that long ago, when people took such information as fact, or at least gave it credence because it was believed by supposedly "learned" people. As she knew all too well from her own experience, recorded history was heavily influenced by such perceptions. The importance of mitigating these distortions, to the extent that they could be mitigated, was why she had become a forensic anthropologist.

As it invariably did, Emily's work on the Internet took her from link to link and deeper into time. She had already studied much of the information she was now finding on various websites, but she had never considered its relationship to a specific people on the eastern coast of what would one day become the United States.

She found that the dates of the last Glacial Period varied according to source—and its place in prehistory ensured that the dates would always be little more than estimates—but it ended around ten thousand years ago, having lasted for about one hundred thousand years. Much of North America was covered in ice during that time, and it was shaped differently than the continent that exists today. What is now known as the continental shelf was exposed, extending coastlines like that of New Jersey by at least fifty miles. On the other side of the continent, a land bridge connected Asia and what would one day be known as Alaska. It was across this narrow piece of land that hunters of big game crossed to a different continent.

Emily understood that although there were many schools of thought and widely ranging speculation about the peopling of North America, many scholars agreed that the land bridge across the Bering Strait served as the gateway for the continent's aboriginal people. By the time the bridge had disappeared, roughly eleven thousand years ago, they had walked the length of the Pacific coast and across the continent to the Atlantic.

Following yet another link, Emily moved on to something called the Paleo-Indian Period, which lasted for two thousand years, from the end of the ice age to approximately 8,000 BC. During that time, inhabitants of the eastern part of the continent lived in a harsh climate that was believed to be eighteen to twenty degrees cooler than the climate of today. The land was a combination of marshland and tundra, roamed by mammoths, mastodons, and other mammals that were much larger than the animals that would one day inhabit the continent in their place.

Some of the information about the period suggested that people lived in small, nomadic groups in shelters that were simple and as mobile as possible. Vast areas of land were required to support relatively small numbers of people who hunted caribou, walrus, and the larger mammoths and mastodons with spear points of stone or bone. Every part of a slain animal was used—meat, marrow, and organs provided food; bones and hide were made into crude tools; and sinew and strips of hide were made into bindings. It was a harsh, tenuous existence, created by unpredictable food sources, imbalanced diets, disease, and the countless hazards of the environment. Sickness and injury were common, and, in most cases, nothing could be done about them. The injured and elderly were simply left to die.

Her research looped back around to another presentation to the Bucks County Historical Society, this one by a man named Charles Laubach, in July of 1892. Entitled *Prehistoric Man in Bucks County*, it touched on a number of related themes. As she scanned through it, a number of items caught her attention.

> *The discoveries in this region give tangible results of man's great antiquity in the valley of the Delaware. Several sites, circles of stones, hearths, small boulders burnt and cracked by fire, discolored earth, etc., have been found in this vicinity, deep under gravel deposits of post-glacial times. These deposits, lying immediately south of the terminal moraine, give us approximately their own age and connection with the last Glacial epoch. To say that man was here before the close of the Glacial epoch fixes a minimum point only, as to his*

antiquity. How long he was here previous to that time must be determined by other considerations.

Mr. Laubach went on to describe a number of sites in Bucks County where ancient artifacts had been discovered. Emily found one of them particularly interesting.

In 1862, after a heavy freshet whereby about twenty acres of river drift were washed away along the Delaware River at Riegelsville, Bucks County, we picked out of the embankment remaining, at a depth of forty feet from the surface, some sixty arrowheads manufactured of argillite. It may be claimed that this river drift deposit is comparatively recent, yet viewing it from an archaeological standpoint, it is extremely old, dating back to the thawing of the great ice sheet.

That's not too far from the Phillips property, she thought as she smiled to herself. *I guess that part of the river has a knack for revealing its secrets.* Tired of sitting in front of her computer, Emily stood up to stretch. She had been reviewing information on websites for nearly three hours. A great deal had been written about a period of time that, like most of the relics that survived it, was buried deep in prehistory. Very little of it was conclusive. Some of it was the result of sound scientific practices, but even science had its limitations when so much time had elapsed. *And besides*, she thought to herself, *conclusiveness isn't the point. These people—the people we call Indians, or their ancestors, at least—were here for a long, long time.* Pushing her chair away from her desk with the backs of her legs, she headed for the elevator and the small cafeteria on the main floor of the museum. *A very long time.*

The open entrance to the cafeteria was off of a hallway that ran the length of the building. She walked in and picked up a tray, surveying the menu that had been recorded on a chalkboard on the wall behind the counter. A minute later she was seated at a small table in the windowed dining room of the cafeteria, staring at but not seeing the oatmeal cookie and salad of mixed greens in front of her.

Emily was no stranger to either history or antiquity, but her training and experience had always placed both in remote corners of the world. Even though she knew otherwise, and as dismissive as it now felt to her, she had never thought of North America as a very old place. Americans believed that Philadelphia was an old city—the "Cradle of Liberty"—even though it had only been in existence for a little more than three hundred years, but the land on which it was built was much older, and on it rocked a much different cradle, one that had been allowed to fade into obscurity. Preoccupied with the thought, she picked up her tray and started back toward her office.

By cross-referencing "Lenape Stone," Emily found information about the symbols that accompanied the drawings engraved in its sides. Often compared with other artifacts known as the Grave Creek Stone and the Davenport Tablets, the Lenape Stone was singled out for its symbology, including the use of the trident in three different places.

Her exploration of the trident took Emily to an account by Major W.H. Emory of the United States Army, who made a military reconnaissance from Fort Leavenworth, Missouri, to San

Diego, California, beginning in 1846. In his report to Congress in 1848, Major Emory described hieroglyphics and characters carved in the rocks of tablelands above the Gila River in New Mexico. He made plates of the same, which he included in his report.

> *One of the plates shows us a bident and a trident close together, an orante, several crosses, the astronomical sign of Leo, which is also the letter "ga" of the Primitive Buddhist alphabet before the time of Asoka, the symbolic meaning of which, according to the "Lalita Vistara," is this: "Profound is the law of entrance into the production of connected causes" (i.e., the beginning or first of connected causes belongs to a law too deep to penetrate).*

A quick cross-reference of *Lalita Vistara* revealed that it means Birth of Buddha. Emily also double-checked *orante*, which she only vaguely remembered to be a figure with open arms—a representation of the soul at peace in paradise. She also looked up Emory's reference to Asoka, finding that Ashoka the Great was an Indian emperor whose forty-one-year reign ended in 232 BC. She read that although his name means *without sorrow*, he was so moved by the suffering caused by a successful military campaign that he eschewed war and resolved to consolidate his vast empire through nonviolence. *An elightened man*, Emily thought to herself as she sat back in her chair. Forty-five minutes had passed and the salad and cookie had not been touched. *He did the right thing for his people.*

She imagined the final minutes of her time in the county forensic lab and her conversation with the skull.

"Can you set the record straight for me and my people? Can you set the record straight just because it's the right thing to do?"

"Whether or not these were your people," she said to the image in her head, "the answer to your question is *yes*."

* * *

It was dark when Walks Alone opened his eyes. He was cold, much colder than he should have been on a summer night. He rubbed his shoulders and his torso, trying desperately to feel warmer, but the rubbing didn't help. What he was experiencing was not the cold of the forest but of the winter of his vision. And it was somehow made worse by the memory of the look in the man's eyes as the life drained from his body. Walks Alone didn't know why the vision had come to him, but he did know that he would not be forgetting it soon.

He had not built a fire and he was unwilling to risk foraging for wood on a moonless night. He knew that there were too many dangers that could not be seen, and too many more that would be able to see him all too well. He crawled beneath the lean-to, raking debris from the forest floor behind him. It wasn't much, but piled closely to his body it would provide some protection against the dead of night. His hand on the handle of the knife at his waist and the branches of the hastily made lean-to hard against his back, he tried to sleep. He began to shiver again, and he knew that he was now experiencing neither the cold of the forest nor the residue of his vision. This was fear, as raw and primal as the forest floor.

Night passed without rest as Walks Alone watched in the netherworld between wakefulness and sleep. Fatigue and the sounds of the forest pulled him back and forth in a ceaseless tug-of-war, as if for the amusement of the spirits of the night. It was not until the faintest light of morning had crept into the trees in the direction of the river that his mind and body were able to relax into sleep. A dream waited there.

Walks Alone found himself standing with a small group of people near a wide stream. Off in the distance a vast river cut a wide and imposing path, bisecting the land with its relentless flow. Above the distant horizon, the morning sun cast blinding streaks of light across the surface of the water.

There was no snow, no oppressive winter, yet the season of the year was unclear. Parts of the land above the river were carpeted in greens and golds, but others were obscured by black bogs of surface water. The air was too crisp for summer, and it rode a nearly constant wind laced with chilly shards that stung his eyes and the exposed skin of his face. Yet he and the others were searching in the brush for berries and wild plants, in seeming defiance of the season.

Upstream from them, a second group of people stood by the bank of the stream, dropping weighted nets into the water, an occasional piece of thin ice floating in the water nearby. One man pulled a net from the water, a fish thrashing violently in its tangles.

As the sun rose higher in the sky, the two groups eventually merged and moved together through the high grasses and toward the edge of a distant stand of trees. Walks Alone knew that their village was there.

There were only thirteen or fourteen shelters in the village—some of them constructed of rocks, but most nothing more than tree branches covered with skins—still it was the largest village Walks Alone had ever seen. He estimated that as many as fifty people lived there. Few of the people in the village looked up as the men approached. The women simply continued with the work of tanning hides or making baskets; the children helped as required or played nearby. All were dressed warmly in hides, protected from the chill that seemed to permeate the entire environment.

As the men dispersed toward their individual shelters, a second, smaller group prepared to leave the village. They carried sturdy baskets that seemed suited to neither fishing nor carrying plants, and Walks Alone knew they were going to quarry stone for tools: axes and adzes; and weapons: spear points and knives.

Like the other men who had returned from the morning journey to the stream, Walks Alone settled into the seemingly ceaseless activity of the village, digging out a canoe with a man who lived in a nearby shelter. He knew that he was related to the man but the relationship wasn't clear. It didn't seem to matter. He was part of a community—a kinship of sorts—that worked together to scrape its subsistence from the water, the grass, the trees, and the muck of the surrounding land.

The process of digging out the canoe was slow and tedious. After the outside of the log had been shaped into a rough version of its eventual form, sections of the inside were burned before being hacked away by an adze.

He was hard at work with a stone-edged adze, sweat building beneath the hide that covered his torso, when a sudden commotion broke the quiet focus of the people at work. The hoarse shouts of an unseen man issued from the trees, and, when he emerged into the village, Walks Alone could see that it was one of the men who had left for the quarry. He waved his arms wildly in the air, screaming loudly in a strange language that Walks Alone somehow understood. Game had been spotted, and judging from the man's gestures, there was a lot of it.

Men grabbed spears and knives and rushed together in the direction from which the messenger had come. Walks Alone joined them without hesitation.

They ran through the trees and underbrush, dodging low-hanging branches and leaping across muddy rivulets, until they emerged on the far side of the forest. Then they ran again, this time across a wide expanse of grassland that seemed to join with the sky on the distant horizon. Walks Alone sucked in deep gasps of breath as his side cramped with pain, but he kept running. When he was certain that he couldn't take one more stride, the group came to a sudden halt.

They were standing above the delta of a wide stream, the ground sloping away from their feet on its way to the flatland in the distance. There, in the high grass between the slope and the stream, a huge heard of animals grazed quietly. They were huge, dark beasts with square humped shoulders and narrow hindquarters. Their massive heads were covered with long hair that tapered below their mouths in coarse beards. They were a familiar and welcome sight to the Walks Alone who stood with the others at the top of the slope; they were a strange but reassuring sight to the Walks Alone who was dreaming in the lean-to. Not one of them was white, but if one had been it might have been mistaken for the great beast that came to him in his journeys, visions, and dreams.

As he started down the slope with the others, weapons held firmly at their sides and guarding against any sound or movement that might frighten the bison, he was filled with the certainty that everything was as it should be. It always had been. It always would be.

Eleven

Dr. Henry's books spread out in front of her, Grace Caufield sat down at her kitchen table with a cup of coffee. She had been up much of the night reading—at the table, in her favorite chair in the living room, and in bed—only retiring after assuring herself that she would continue reading in the morning. Dr. Henry had done a good job of choosing books about the natives who had occupied Pennsylvania and New Jersey prior to the arrival of Europeans. She had found *Indians in Pennsylvania*, a book by a man named Wallace, to be particularly insightful, as well as David Zeisberger's *History of Northern American Indians (1910)*. Zeisberger was a Moravian missionary who lived among the Lenape in the late 1700s, but he spent most of his time with them along the Muskingum River in Ohio, years after the Lenape culture in the Bucks County area had all but vanished. Grace found his observations to be extremely valuable because he had actually lived among the Lenape, but she found herself wishing that he had lived among them in a different place and time.

Other missionaries from the Moravian Church had done the same thing, and Grace found it interesting that although the

Lenape had always treated the missionaries with the deference and respect that was fundamental to their culture, they had never been moved to adopt any spiritual path other than the one they had followed for centuries. As Wallace noted in his book:

> *Delaware, Iroquois, and other Indian peoples, after the Christian missionaries began to spread their doctrines, found much to attract them in the new religion, but were repelled by many of those who professed it. The men whom the Indians met in the border country were—with some honorable exceptions—far from the best representatives of Christian civilization. Contact with them inevitably colored the Indians' attitude toward the whole white race. The Shawnee chief Kakowatchiky explained this to Count Zinzendorf in 1742 when he said that the difference between the Indian's religion and the white man's was that the Indian had it in his heart while the white man had it on his lips.*

Even though her research into the Lenape had included a mere four or five hours of reading, Grace was already troubled by the realization that every account was that of a white man. There was no first-hand information, primarily—she realized—because the Lenape had no written language. Everything was translated, written, and, in varying degrees, filtered by people who were not part of the Lenape culture.

Another of the books, *Handbook of the Delaware Indian Language*, by a contemporary linguist named Scott Wenning, seemed highly authentic in its considered approach to the spoken language of the Lenape people, but even Mr. Wenning had based much of his work on the writings of the Moravian missionaries.

As the introductions to the books illustrated clearly, much had been written about the Lenape, or the Delaware as they had come to be known, and she was curious to read the other perspectives, both positive and negative, that undoubtedly waited to be discovered.

Rising from her chair to get another cup of coffee, Grace was struck by the notion that the rest of her reading could wait until later in the evening. She needed to get out of the house for a few hours, and wondered if there was some way she could incorporate that need with her fledgling research. The woman at the offices of the Recorder of Deeds, she remembered, had mentioned something about an exhibit at the Mercer Museum, and a visit seemed like the perfect solution. Grace headed for the bathroom, taking the second cup of coffee with her. In less than an hour, she was at the museum.

If this isn't Doylestown's most interesting landmark, Grace thought as she looked at the austere castle beyond the windshield of her car, *I can't imagine what is.*

On the hill above the parking lot, the seven-story concrete museum sat ponderously. Grace's immediate impression was that rather than being built from the ground up, it had been dropped from the skies by gods that could find no place for it in their heavens. And, once imbedded in the ground so completely, no force could possibly dislodge it.

Once inside, she learned that the castle was the creation of Henry Chapman Mercer, "a Renaissance man," according to an attendant at the front desk, who had been recognized as a historian, an archaeologist, and a ceramist. He had also been a collector of more than fifteen thousand artifacts and had built the castle as a home for his collections.

Grace entered the interior of the building and looked up into the high central court that contained an unlikely air squadron of artifacts. Suspended high above her were a whaling boat, a stagecoach, and a Conestoga wagon, along with huge farm implements that seemed as lost to history as the agrarian age that had spawned them.

Crossing to the far corner of the building, Grace started up the concrete steps to the upper floors. The soles of her running shoes made almost no sound as she climbed. *There's something about stone or concrete steps*, she thought. *There's something permanent about them, something timeless.* She tried to imagine what wooden or metal steps would feel like in their place, but the idea left her as quickly as it had come. These steps, she concluded, were perfectly suited to carry a person back into time.

She climbed from floor to floor, following a curious pattern in which the steps to the next floor were at the far end of the building from those she had just climbed. In between, corridors guarded by black metal railings overlooked the central court and the individual rooms and alcoves on the floors above and below. She paused at the railing on the fifth floor long enough to look at the map she had been given at the front desk. It showed areas dedicated to various disciplines and trades—woodworking, metalworking, surveying, fruit preservation, and the healing arts among them.

"Where was all this stuff before it was here?" she asked the openness above the central court before continuing her walk.

At the end of the walkway, another set of steps took her up to an area that seemed to be set off by itself. An inscription on the wall at the top of the steps announced: *Early Encounters: The Lenape and the European in the Delaware Valley.* Although the entrance hinted that the exhibit was quite permanent, Grace found it difficult to reconcile the placement of such an exhibit with a nearly overwhelming collection of tools. She made a note to ask about both before leaving the building.

The space was quiet and claustrophobic. The air didn't move at all and she was certain that she might begin to sweat just standing in it. Although three narrow windows admitted daylight into the room, it was obvious to Grace that the lights in the display cases were quite necessary.

The very first display resurrected in Grace's thinking two issues about which she had made notes while reading Dr. Henry's books. She paged through her notebook, looking for entries about diseases so that she could compare them to the information in the display case. "Tuberculosis," she confirmed to the empty room, "was part of Lenape life before contact with Europeans. So were arthritis and asthma." She underlined each of the words in her notes. "But smallpox, measles, influenza, and diphtheria were not. They had been . . ." She paused for a few seconds, searching for the word that might best describe both the situation and its cruel irony. *Inherited*, she thought, scribbling in her notes. *They were inherited.*

Then she read a quote that both confirmed her use of the word, albeit in an even more ironic way, and raised the other issue with which she had been preoccupied. It was supposedly said to William Penn by a Lenape chief named Tenoughan. "What is the matter with us Indians, that we are thus sick in our own Air, and these strangers well? 'Tis as if they were sent hither to inherit our lands in our steads."

Tenoughan's reference to himself as an *Indian*, and his use of words like *thus*, *'tis*, and *hither*, all of which Grace doubted, made it clear to her that these were the words of a European speaking for a Lenape chief. "When do you get to speak for yourself?" she asked the painting of the Lenape chief in the display case. "When do you get to speak for yourself?"

The ironies continued, and Grace soon found herself wondering if she was just being cynical about all of this. Another display case featured a drawing of a Lenape family whose existence had presumably been improved by contact with Europeans. They appeared to be quite happy that they now had brass kettles instead of clay pots and blankets instead of animal skins. Grace certainly didn't believe that everything about contact with Europeans was negative for the Lenape, but she was haunted by the notion that they were probably doing just fine before the white man's arrival.

On the other side of the small room, three large displays provided information about each of the three periods into which the history of Native Americans in the area had been divided— the Paleo-Indian Period, the Archaic Period, and the Woodland Period. She read with interest about how the three compared in areas such as land use, spirituality, and health.

Just beyond the three displays, Grace came to a large map of eastern Pennsylvania and New Jersey, including the entire length of the Delaware River. The zigzagging line of the river made the map so familiar that Grace felt suddenly transported into a more contemporary history. She was struck by the amount of land occupied by the different clans of the Lenape people at the end of the Woodland Period, and she was even more impressed by the vast expanse of geography that was inhabited by the Algonkian-speaking culture to which the Lenape belonged. It stretched north to Canada, east to the Atlantic Ocean, and south into Delaware.

Then she read notations on the map that lent to it an eerie reality. "Ten thousand," Grace repeated to the room, making a note of the number of Europeans who lived in the area a hundred years after the first appearance of the Dutch. "Three hundred thousand," she said incredulously, noting the number that would be in the area a century later. *And everything that had evolved in the thousands of years before that*, she thought to herself, *would be all but gone.*

"Excuse me . . . ?"

Grace hadn't realized that someone else was in the small room, and as she turned to face the sound of his voice, she stepped back in obvious surprise.

"I didn't mean to startle you." A tall man in a blue blazer stood near the entrance. "Abby," he began, "the girl at the front desk, told me that someone from the paper was up here." He held out his right hand as he added, "My name is Robert Dawes. I'm the director here at the museum. Is there some way I may be of service?"

"Grace Caufield," she answered, shaking his hand. "And if you don't mind, I do have some questions. To begin with, why is this exhibit here? I mean, it's very informative, but it doesn't seem to go with all the tools."

Dawes smiled, taking in the observation but saying nothing.

"I'm sorry," Grace volunteered, uncomfortably aware that she might have offended the man.

"There is no need to apologize," he answered, the confirming smile still on his face. "Mr. Mercer was a rather eclectic collector. The history of the Lenape people makes up much of the history of Bucks County, and I think that's what the exhibit is meant to acknowledge. It is different than, say, a room dedicated to the tools used in glass blowing, but no less critical to the history of the county."

"If not more," Grace offered, a sheepish grin following the words almost immediately. "I'm afraid I've done it again . . ."

"It's alright," he interrupted. "I try to avoid such comparisons, but I understand your point."

"Where did these artifacts come from? Were they found in archaeological digs?" The questions piled together. "Did Mercer find some of them himself? Were they all found in Bucks County?"

"Yes, many of them came from digs, and I'm sure that Mercer found some of them. I would have to check the museum catalogue to say with certainty." Dawes adjusted his eyeglasses, thinking about her list of questions. "As to whether or not they were all found in Bucks County, I'm not sure. Some were probably found elsewhere and given to the museum."

As she scanned her notes, Grace shook her head back and forth slowly, a mannerism that did not go unnoticed by the museum director.

"Is something wrong?" he asked.

"No, not really." Then, in a rapid reversal of direction, she said, "Well, *yes*. I think this is all wrong. I'm no expert on the Lenape, but it doesn't seem right that the story of such an old and pervasive culture should be relegated to a small room on the sixth floor. I'll bet a lot of your visitors don't even come up here."

"You're passionate about this, then." It was, at the same time, an observation and a question.

"I'm certainly *becoming* passionate about it."

"And exactly what is it that you're passionate about?"

The question hit Grace straight on. For a fleeting moment, she felt as if she had walked into one of the castle's concrete walls.

"I'm not sure—the injustice, perhaps. These people were part of the human race. In fact they have been *the* human race for most of the history of this county."

"Someone once said—" The man adjusted his glasses again. "—it was Emerson, I believe—that 'The end of the human race will be that it will eventually die of civilization.' He may have been on to something there."

Grace smiled back at Robert Dawes. His comment had put her at ease and that, she thought, was saying a lot. A maelstrom of questions, observations, and opinions was swirling within her head and within her heart, and still he had put her at ease. Her smile widened.

* * *

When Walks Alone awoke, it was mid-morning and the sun was already bright in the trees. He was uncomfortably aware that the rhythm of his life was different here in the woods, alone. There was no wigwam with Talks For Us or His Spirit Watches sleeping nearby, protecting him from any danger the night might hold. There was no fire burning to embers that kept watch through the night. There was no food and only a small supply of water. But it was most different because of the disconcerting reality that he didn't know how long he would be on the mountain. He knew only what he had to do before he could return, and that task alone was more than enough to fill him with apprehension.

Not wanting to endure another night without a fire, he resolved to begin the day by gathering wood. There was plenty in the trees behind the rock, so he gathered even more than he thought he might need. Although he placed most of it within easy reach of the front of the lean-to, he stacked some under the shelter to keep it safe from the elements.

Pushing the knife into his belt and slinging the quiver and bow across his shoulder, he set out in search of food. He started up the mountain toward the brightness that shone in the canopy, certain that he would find something to eat there.

After a short time, Walks Alone found an area of dense brush, nearly as tall as he was and twisted in an unapproachable knot of vines and scrawny branches. Raspberries peeked out of the tangle with a seductive redness that glowed in the morning sun. He moved toward the raspberries carefully, well aware that snakes liked them, too, and that his bare legs would be exposed to the brush while he was picking. He poked the bow into the brush and rustled it vigorously, hoping to drive away anything hidden beneath it, but even having done that he proceeded to pick the berries quickly. When he had a handful, he drew away from the brush and ate them immediately. He thought that he had never tasted anything quite so good, although he knew his judgment was clouded by acute hunger.

The boy was hungry enough to pick more berries—but reluctant to eat too many of them at one time—so he decided to move on. He didn't have a pinch of tobacco to place on the ground where he had found the food, but he still stood quietly, facing the sun, and thanked the Great Spirit for its generosity.

As he turned to walk away, he thought of the medicine bundle that His Spirit Watches had given him. Drawing it from his belt, he opened it slowly to find not only tobacco, but a piece of flint and the tail feather of a golden hawk. He smiled appreciatively as he placed a small amount of the tobacco on the ground near the raspberries. From his crouched position, he could see the reflection of the sun on the shiny black scales of a snake moving in the underbrush, and he mouthed another quiet prayer. "Enjoy your meal, brother," he said as he departed.

He had been walking through the trees for more than an hour when it occurred to him that he was probably past the place where His Spirit Watches had shown him the valley. He walked in what he thought was the direction of the river, finally emerging at a point that was farther up the mountain, but from which the green valley looked equally beautiful. The wind moved in the treetops below, inspiring an undulation of color—greens and whites and silvers—that mesmerized the boy. It was almost impossible for him to look away, and he may not have, had it not been for the sound he heard in the trees behind him.

Turning slowly and reaching for his knife, he saw a deer standing about twenty paces away. The buck was young, with only two points on its antlers, and it seemed too preoccupied with finding its own breakfast to worry about the boy. The quiet breeze that moved in the trees was in the boy's face and he guessed that the deer had not caught his scent.

The process of replacing the knife in his belt and drawing the bow from his shoulder unfolded in an agonizingly slow combination of motion and silence. His right hand passed the bow to his left before returning to the quiver and the feathered shaft of an arrow. He drew the arrow so slowly, so quietly that he was afraid the deer might be spooked by the nearly deafening silence. The arrow eased into place, leveling toward its target, its white stone head momentarily glinting in the sunlight. His heart pounding, Walks Alone squinted at the buck's shoulder and pulled the leather thong tight across his body. The deer looked up just as the arrow hissed into the air.

In a suspended moment in which each of his senses seemed as sharp as the arrowhead itself, Walks Alone heard the arrow crush through the bone in the deer's left shoulder. The animal lunged forward, its leg collapsing beneath it, its outstretched neck smacking the ground, and then pulled back to a standing position in an instinctive reaction to flee. It started through the trees as quickly as it could move on three good legs, its wounded shoulder dropping toward the ground with each labored step. Having moved less than twenty-five yards, it crashed to the ground in a headlong tumble that left it lying on its side.

As Walks Alone approached the deer, he could see that it was wounded badly but not dead. Obviously terrified, but no longer able to run, it could only wait to die.

The boy had seen many deer killed, and he had even killed one himself, but that was while hunting with Talks For Us. He had never been in a situation like this, and he found himself wishing that the arrow had either been more efficient or missed the buck altogether. Wracked with compassion for the bleating animal, he reached for the knife at his side, drew it into the air with two shaking hands, and thrust it down into the neck of the deer. Its head jerked upward a single time and the animal went limp, its small, final sounds lost to the silence of the forest.

Kneeling by the fallen deer, Walks Alone retrieved some tobacco from the medicine bundle and placed it on the ground. "I honor your life, my brother, and I thank you for your sacrifice in this, my time of passage. May the Great Spirit carry you to an endless forest."

His body still coursing with adrenalin, his heart still pounding with exaltation, Walks Alone set about the task of dragging the deer back to the lean-to. It had taken him an hour to walk the distance earlier; it took more than twice that to return with the deer. Finally reaching his makeshift camp, he dragged the carcass to the base of the large rock, where he used the knife to remove the arrow and skin the buck. Setting aside enough meat for a meal, he buried the entrails in the ground, using only a sharpened stick to dig the hole.

Part of him wanted to eat and then begin the journey back down the mountain, but another part cautioned that it would take longer to descend the mountain with a deer than it had taken to climb it with His Spirit Watches. He reluctantly decided to wait. He used vines from the forest floor to secure the carcass to a tree near the lean-to, judging that they were strong enough to support it until dawn.

His arms stained with the blood of the deer, Walks Alone went to look for water. It would be difficult to find this high up, especially in the summer, but he wanted to wash the blood from his body. The sun had peaked in the sky and was already descending toward the far side of the forest, so he decided to walk with the shadows of the trees at his back. He wasn't planning on going too far, and he knew that if he paid close attention to the ground he was covering he would be able to find his way back to the lean-to.

The shadows had grown longer, but it was still long before sundown when he found what felt like the top of the mountain. It stretched out in a short plain, the relatively flat ground of which was interrupted by outcroppings of rocks and groves of pine trees. Crossing a span of grass to one of the outcroppings, he found a pool of stagnant water that was more than adequate for his needs. A few minutes later, the green scum on the surface of the water and the mosquito larvae just below it were sharing the pool with the blood of Walks Alone's deer. It wasn't like washing in a stream or cleansing one's self in the humidity of the sweat lodge, but the boy was grateful to have found the pool.

The walk back was as easy as he thought it would be, the lengthening shadows pointing the way perfectly, and it filled him with a sense of confidence. He had been fortunate that the deer had found him, rather than the other way around, but his aim had been true, or at least true enough to hit the animal. His vigil could not have gone better. He had survived the night, and he had done so with neither company nor the warmth of a fire, and he had slain a deer. He was no longer a boy but a man, and he moved through the trees with an assurance that befit his new status.

There was a brief instant of mutual shock when the boy and the bobcat first saw each other. Walks Alone stopped in his tracks, less than twenty paces from the lean-to, as the bobcat backed away from the deer carcass, blood on its face.

Adrenalin pumped into the boy's legs in primal preparation to run. But he knew that, even if he could outrun the animal, there was no place on the mountain where he would be safe from it. He had never seen an animal like this before, and few of the people in his village had ever talked about seeing one. He thought he remembered hearing that a bobcat would not attack unless it was rabid, and that it would most likely run when confronted by a human, but he was suddenly very aware of the difference between *talking* about what a wild animal might do and standing face-to-face with one in the woods.

Walks Alone stood as still as his shaking body would allow, looking straight into the animal's eyes. As it took a slow step toward him, Walks Alone was certain that he was being measured. He suddenly felt helpless, as if everything he had ever learned had deserted him. There was nothing he could do, no course of action he could rely on; there was only resignation. And, from that resignation, rushed the ancient urge to scream, to invoke the animal in himself in an attempt to frighten the bobcat.

"I-eeeee!" his lungs bellowed. "Iiiiii-eeeeeeeeee!" The sound ripped through the silence of the surrounding forest before evaporating in the afternoon shadows.

The cat charged; its taut body—which Walks Alone judged to weigh at least half as much as he did—eating up the distance between them in fiercely determined strides.

The boy felt the handle of the metal-bladed knife, the knife with which he had slain a deer and become a man, and drew it from his belt. As the animal jumped into the air, the boy straightened his arm and thrust violently upward, hoping with the last of his hope that his timing would be good. The blade buried itself in the bobcat's ribs, but not before its razor-sharp claws had raked Walks Alone's shoulders. His eardrums were pierced by the hideous shriek of the cat in the same instant that his lungs exploded in a hoarse, searing cry of pain. He thrust the knife again, focused on what he was doing, trying to ignore what was happening to him. He thrust it as hard as he could and as often as he could, resolved to use his final breath to kill.

* * *

"We're only open on weekends, but I'll be here Saturday and Sunday if you want to drive up."

The invitation had come from George Cameron, and as Jeff Phillips drove down Fish Hatchery Road he wondered why he had accepted it. It wasn't that he didn't like Cameron, because, in some way that he couldn't quite put his finger on, he did; and it wasn't that he thought he didn't have anything to learn from the man, because he knew that he had much to learn, and that we seldom get to choose either our teachers or the wrappings in which they arrive. He just felt overwhelmed, like a child on the first day of school.

The Museum of Indian Culture sat hard against the road in a quiet creek valley near Allentown. As Jeff pulled into its small parking lot, he could see that the building was nothing more than an old stone house that had been converted into the museum. A wide expanse of grass sloped from the back of the house to the creek bed below, and then continued on the other side of the creek before ending at a stand of tall trees. There was a smaller stone building at the bottom of the grade, leading Jeff to conclude that the grounds had probably once been part of a small farm.

Seeing no other cars in the parking lot, Jeff remembered that the museum opened at noon. "Fifteen minutes," he muttered to himself as he looked at his watch. "I guess I'll take a walk."

He had only gone a few yards down the hill when something to his right caught his eye. A section of the grass had been fenced off in a way that made it look like a fort from an old Western movie.

The gate to the fort, which consisted of two doors made of the same rustic-looking slats as the fence, was secured with a chain and padlock, but the doors could be separated enough for a man to squeeze through. In the space beyond, Jeff could see what looked like a dome-shaped dwelling faced with tree bark. "Crow Feather's not the kind of guy who would mind if I take a look," he said to himself as he ducked under the chain and squeezed between the doors of the gate.

Once inside, he could see that the dwelling he had seen consisted of a frame made of branches that had been set in the ground in a circle and then bent toward the center to form the domed roof. The frame was partially covered with huge sections of tree bark that appeared to have been unwrapped after a long vertical slice had been made in the trunk of the tree. The sections at the base of the frame were overlapped by the sections above them. He moved around to the back of the structure, where the frame had not yet been covered, and took a closer look at the interior. Against the far wall, a low platform had been constructed of tree branches. He imagined that it might be a bed, but he wasn't certain.

Jeff wondered how many people lived or gathered in this type of dwelling, and he mentally compared it to the massive house in which he and Dae lived. As he had been many times before, he was reminded of the lack of balance that seems to permeate life—and lives.

"It's called a wigwam." The voice came from the direction of the gate, and Jeff stepped to his right to see George Cameron unlocking the padlock.

"And it's a house?" Jeff asked.

"Yes. It's the kind of structure the Lenape in this area lived in during the Woodland Period."

"Hello, Crow Feather," Jeff said, extending his hand.

"*He,*" came Cameron's reply. "That's a Lenape welcome."

"I hope you don't mind that I came in here. I arrived a little early and decided to take a look around."

"It's fine. In fact I wish *more* folks were so insistent about looking around."

"I'm interested in your comment about the Woodland Period. What does that mean?"

"Basically, it means the time between 1,000 BC and the 1600s, when the first Europeans came to this area."

"So, the Lenape were living here in wigwams like this one two thousand years ago?"

"Yes, and long before that."

"How many people lived in a structure this size?"

"Usually a family unit—three or four people. The Lenape culture was matrilineal, so families were structured according to the maternal bloodlines. Larger family groups would have lived in something like this." Cameron turned toward a different part of the fort and a framed structure that looked to be about forty feet in length. It also had a rounded roof, but bark had not been attached to the frame. "It's called a longhouse, and ten or fifteen people could have lived in one this size."

"And how many wigwams and longhouses were in a village?"

"Fewer than you might think. Twenty would have been a fairly large village when the culture was flourishing. Villages became increasingly smaller in the years following the arrival of whites."

"The obvious question, I guess, is 'Where did the Lenape go?'"

Cameron smiled and said, "I have to open the museum. C'mon inside."

They walked across the grass to the main building, passing what looked like the main door to the old house and entering through a door closer to the parking lot. The area immediately inside was narrow, with barely enough room for a chair and a shelf for pamphlets. On one side, a room had been converted into a small gift shop. On the other, a hallway led to the remainder of the rooms on the main floor.

"I'll be right with you," Cameron offered. "Feel free to look around."

While Cameron did whatever he had to do in the gift shop, Jeff started down the hallway. To his right was a small room with packed bookshelves. Just beyond it was a room with what appeared to be display cases.

At the end of the hallway, Jeff emerged into what he guessed was the largest room in the museum. It was lined with shelves and display cases, all of which held various artifacts. An impressive-looking diorama had been set up on the far wall. Jeff would have expected to see something like it in a more sophisticated museum, rather than in this small, converted farmhouse.

The scene inside included a Native American woman and young boy. She was dressed in buckskin and wore hoop earrings. He was naked except for a loincloth, and he had long black hair. Various artifacts and foodstuffs were spread on the ground in front of them, an obvious representation of the staples that were fundamental to their daily lives. The outdoor landscape painted on the wall behind them included a wide stream surrounded by lush green grasslands.

From a smaller adjoining diorama, the figure of a native man stared out into the room. According to the placard behind the glass, the man's appearance represented what a Lenape man might have looked like after contact with Europeans. He wore his hair in a scalplock, which looked like a ponytail at the back of an otherwise shaved head, and his tattoos and loincloth looked decidedly Indian, but his cotton shirt and knee-high hosiery, as well as the wool blanket across his shoulders, did not. The man also wore a brass amulet around his neck. It was highly polished and secured by a leather thong, and at first Jeff didn't associate it with the piece of black and corroded metal that had been found with the remains in the creek bank. An instant later he made the connection, and the figure in the diorama suddenly became much more relevant.

"Is *this* what the man may have looked like?" he asked himself as the skull and handful of bones came to life before his eyes. He wanted the figure to look at him and smile or nod, to somehow acknowledge its connection with the remains, but it only continued to stare from the confines of the enclosure.

"What do you think?"

The sound of Cameron's voice startled Jeff, shaking him from his fascination with the figure in front of him.

"Is this our guy?" Jeff asked. "I mean, is this what he may have looked like?"

"That's what I think. The only clues are the amulet and the tooled wampum, and they definitely give us a timeframe. And . . ."

"And," Jeff interrupted, "if the remains belonged to a white man, Emily FitzRoy and Roy Cleveland might have been able to confirm it."

"We're on the same page. Can we say with one hundred percent certainty that the man was Lenape? No. But the odds are good that he was Native American, and that makes the odds even better that he was Lenape."

Jeff's mind was racing, and the feeling of being overwhelmed returned.

"Getting back to the question I asked outside, where did these people go? What happened to them?"

"There's a lot to it, Jeff, and if you talk to enough people you'll get many different answers."

"What do *you* think?" Jeff insisted.

"I think at least three things happened. The first was disease. When the whites arrived from Europe, they brought illnesses that the Lenape could not fight off."

"Things like smallpox?"

"Yes, smallpox is the disease most people think about when it comes to the Indians, but there were other things—things like measles and the flu—that did their share of damage, as well."

"They had no diseases?"

"I didn't say that. They had more than their share of problems—tuberculosis and asthma, for example—but they had no immunity to what the whites brought with them."

"You said there were three things, George. What were the other two?"

"One was the dilution of their culture."

"What do you mean?"

"As more and more people came into the area—and I'm talking about whites, blacks, and even other natives—the Lenape culture became increasingly threatened. The ways they hunted and fished changed, as did their ability to move their villages as they pleased.

"The whites introduced many things to the Lenape, and the truth of the matter is that the Lenape took advantage of many of them. Rifles were a lot more efficient than bows and arrows, and blankets were easier to obtain than hides. And metal tools made a significant difference in the way the Lenape lived. But . . ."

"I knew there was a 'but' coming. *But* not everything the whites brought was beneficial?"

"That's right. They also brought alcohol, something to which the Lenape had little resistance, and it made them do things they never would have done without its influence."

"Like what?"

"The whites traded blankets and rifles and alcohol for pelts, and the more the Lenape wanted those things, the more they were willing to get pelts at any cost. By the time it was all said and done, they were killing breeding stock—the young animals that would eventually mate and ensure a future supply of game—and that's something their ancestors wouldn't have even thought about doing."

"What's the third thing?" Jeff asked.

"The second and third things are related. Over time, the Lenape lost their lands—or I should say their homes—to the whites. More and more people came into the area, forcing the Lenape out and farther and farther west. Many of them were content to go, driven by the need to maintain their way of life. They thought they could get away from the whites, but they couldn't."

"What was the land thing about? You said the Lenape were forced out. Does that mean they were thrown off their lands?"

George Cameron scratched his white-bearded chin slowly, his eyes surveying the carpet.

"Not exactly. This is a tough one for me. I have trouble talking about it with any objectivity." He paused as if deciding whether or not to continue.

"Just say what's on your mind."

"No one knows how long the Lenape and their ancestors were here in this part of the world, but most agree that it can be measured in thousands of years. The King of England gave most of what the Lenape called home to William Penn's father. Penn first came here to claim it in 1682.

"The Lenape were a highly hospitable people. In fact, there's a quote that goes something along the lines of 'A true Indian never deems anything too good for his friends or a visitor.' And in all fairness, William Penn was very hospitable to them. He treated them very fairly."

"I sense another 'but' coming," Jeff interrupted.

"Not really. The early relationship was good. Penn gave things to the Indians and the Indians agreed to co-exist with the Europeans. They didn't know any more about land leasing than they did about land ownership, but that's what they thought the whites were doing—leasing the land, in a manner of speaking. The idea was reinforced each time Penn paid the Lenape for the same land, which happened a number of times."

"So where was the problem? What happened?"

"There were a number of treaties, the most famous of which was recreated in a painting by a guy named Benjamin West: 'Penn's

Treaty with the Indians.' It's complete bullshit. The clothes of both the Europeans and the Indians aren't even close to what was worn in that period; a number of the Europeans in the painting were in Europe at the time; and there's a fictitious brick building in the background that would lead one to believe that the area was already being built out. It's just crap!"

Cameron's agitation was obvious to Jeff, as was his passionate digression.

"Anyway," Cameron continued, "as long as Penn was involved, things went well. After he returned to England, taking his integrity with him, they deteriorated. The whites who made subsequent treaties had different motives, and the Lenape were penalized accordingly. The entire thing went on for almost sixty years before ending with something called the Walking Purchase in 1737."

"I saw something about that," Jeff remembered, "at the University of Pennsylvania. What was the Walking Purchase about?"

"Well, to begin with," Cameron started, a growing redness in his face, "there was no *walking* and there was no *purchase*!"

Jeff smiled at his passion. He didn't know exactly what inside of Cameron was responding, but it was clearly more than his "three sixty-fourths" native heritage.

"In 1734, representatives of the Penn family presented a deed to the Lenape leaders. Dated 1686, it claimed that the Penn's held the rights to much more of the land on which the Lenape lived. It was a complete and utter forgery.

"There were two subsequent meetings to discuss it, one in 1735 and one in 1737. Believing the deed to be a truthful representation of what their leaders had agreed to almost fifty years earlier, and wanting to lessen rising tensions with whites in the area, the Lenape leaders agreed to the terms."

"Which were what?"

"That the Penn family was entitled to as much land as a man could walk in a day and a half."

"So, what happened?"

"The four Lenape sachems, or chiefs, thought that the whites would walk along the river, stopping occasionally to shoot squirrels or smoke a pipe, as one of them said. Instead, they hired runners who ran due west over land that had been secretly cleared weeks earlier.

"Then James Logan, who represented the Penn family, insisted on drawing a right angle to the northeast from the point to which the fastest of the men had run, which made the amount of land involved about twelve *hundred* square miles. That was easily twice as much as the Lenape expected to lose. It was really the straw that broke the camel's back."

"How so? What do you mean?"

"The Lenape were understandably upset about the whole thing. Some pretty ugly stuff ensued. People on both sides were killed. Eventually, Logan brought some Iroquois down from the north to police the Lenape. He ended up screwing them, too, but they served his purpose at the time."

A family walked into the room where Jeff and George were standing. The mother was carrying a child who appeared to be about a year old; the father was leading a preschooler by the hand.

"You'll have to excuse me," Cameron suggested. "People are starting to come in."

"Thank you, George. I'd like to talk again, if it's okay with you."

"Come up anytime," Cameron responded. Then, after telling the couple who had just entered the room that he would be right back, he walked with Jeff toward the door.

"If you go home through Easton, you can see the place where the Lehigh River flows into the Delaware. The Lenape called that confluence of rivers Lechauwitank, and they held it as sacred.

"I know exactly where that is. There's a little park there."

"And then take the road off of Route 611 that leads up to Durham. You'll see a marker where the runner who completed the Walking Purchase stopped for lunch on the first day. If you're interested, that is."

Less than an hour later, Jeff was standing at a wrought iron fence in a small park in Easton, Pennsylvania. Immediately below him, the waters of the Lehigh River cascaded over manmade falls into the Delaware. Jeff wasn't sure why someone had decided to "improve" the falls by covering rocks with concrete, but he found himself wishing that he could see the confluence as the Lenape had seen it. To his left, the Delaware flowed effortlessly on its southern journey, framed by the distant escarpment on which sat the town of Phillipsburg, New Jersey. Across the Lehigh and to his right, another escarpment towered high above the landscape. He knew that the top of it leveled off toward I-78 before ending at the base of what was called Morgan's Hill. From that point, the mountain rose and leveled alternately a number of times before peaking high above the stunning valley below. He had been up there many times. His father had been raised on the mountain; both of his parents were buried in a churchyard near its top.

Leaving the park, he drove across the iron bridge that spanned the Lehigh and prepared to turn south onto Route 611.

Immediately in front of him, the road crossed under a railroad bridge and rose up the escarpment and out of sight.

Route 611 was a tight, two-lane road that was wedged in between the river and a series of hills, rocky outcroppings, trees, and in some cases, very old houses. Anything but a modern road, it seemed to go where time and circumstance had permitted it to go, almost as if it was following an old walking path.

As he drove, Jeff thought about the mannequin in the diorama, imagining him to be the man in the creek bank. Alive and vital, with bone and muscle and skin restored, he saw him step out of his Plexiglas tomb and assume his rightful place in the green lushness of the forest by the river. He watched as the man paused briefly to take one final look at the sacred confluence of waters before disappearing along the banks of the Delaware.

* * *

It was more than a mile from the top of the escarpment to the foot of the mountain, and His Spirit Watches had walked most of it at odds with himself. He wanted to go up to look for the boy, who had now been gone for two nights, but he knew it wasn't permitted. His instincts pulled at him, haunting him with images of what could befall the boy up on the mountain, but his abiding sense of tradition and deep respect for the old ways told him to resist.

The sun was almost directly overhead when he reached the trees. He moved into them hesitantly, praying to catch a glimpse of Walks Alone. Then he stopped, as if frozen solid in the August noonday sun. His face contorted in the combination of emotions that overcame him simultaneously: pride, awe, admiration.

From the trees on the incline, Walks Alone descended on obviously weakened legs. In his left hand, he carried the two pointed antlers of a deer. Across his right shoulder lay the head and spotted hide of a bobcat, its eyes staring lifelessly toward the bright sunlight beyond the trees. Dried blood covered the boy's right arm, but it was impossible to tell if it was his or the cat's. Rivulets of fresh blood traced down his left arm, and there was what appeared to be a puncture wound above his left eye. Blood was smeared all over the left side of his face, as if the boy had rubbed the area repeatedly.

His Spirit Watches dropped to one knee as Walks Alone approached, allowing the boy to collapse across his massive left shoulder. Then he stood up, turned toward the river, and ran. He ran as fast as he could.

Twelve

"It's nice to see you again," Robert Dawes offered, extending his hand as he walked toward her, "but I have to admit that I didn't think you would be back so soon."

Reaching out her own hand, Grace Caufield said, "I told you that I was passionate about this, and it feels as if I'm becoming more so."

"Where would you like to talk—in the exhibit room, or in my office perhaps?"

"Your office, if you don't mind. The exhibit room makes me a little uncomfortable."

A few minutes later, they were sitting across from each other in the sitting area of his office, cups of coffee on the low table between them. The room, like Dawes himself, was stately, but without the slightest hint of ostentation, and Grace could not ignore the feeling that the combination attracted her.

"So, Grace, how can I be of service?"

"I have been speaking with my editor about a feature article for the paper—an article about the Lenape."

"I see," Dawes said, reaching for his coffee. "And what about the Lenape is newsworthy, at least to the extent that it would merit a feature article?"

"It's a fair question," Grace conceded, "especially when one considers that information about them has been available for such a long time. There really isn't much new to tell, except . . ." Her voice trailed off, as if she were distracted by some idea or image floating through her mind.

"Forgive me. I'm not one to finish the sentences of others, but I think you're about to say something about the remains that were discovered on the Phillips property."

"Yes, of course. No one knows for sure that the bones are Native American, yet I find myself wanting to find out all I can about the Native Americans who lived here hundreds of years ago. I know it doesn't make any sense, and it's certainly not news, but . . ." She stopped short again, and Dawes sensed that this time she had nothing to add.

"I would agree that information about the Lenape has been available for a long time," Dawes began, "but I'm not so sure that there's no news here. I don't know the last time that Native American remains were discovered in this area, but if the possibility that these remains are Lenape gives you the opportunity to write about the Lenape people, well . . ." He raised his arms out in front of him, his palms facing up. ". . . that seems like a way to tie history and news together."

Grace looked at him appreciatively but said nothing.

"So tell me, Grace, have you started writing this article?"

"I've outlined most of it. The first part is about William Penn and how he represented the line of demarcation between the

Europeans who preceded him—the Dutch and the Swedes—and the ones who came after him. The difference between the two was profound for the Lenape."

"I'm not an expert on Lenape history, but I agree that there was quite a difference between what was here before Penn and what followed."

"And there's another angle," Grace began, "that may be worth writing about. Not many people are aware that the Algonkian-speaking culture of the northeastern United States included tribes from the Abanaki in Maine all the way down to the Nanticoke and Cony in Maryland. People know a little about the Iroquois tribes in New York, but to most folks, Indians are a part of the American West, not New Jersey and Pennsylvania."

"What you're talking about isn't a feature article," Dawes observed, shifting forward on his chair, "it's a book. In my opinion, Americans have blotted out the history of Native Americans in this part of the country. I'm not sure why—maybe it's guilt, maybe it's something else—but except for stories about the origins of Thanksgiving and Indians selling Manhattan for trinkets, we just choose to ignore that part of our history."

Grace watched the man's face as he said the words, and for the first time she saw the seed of passion that had already taken root in her. Now it was he who looked away pensively, as if struck by the meaning of his own words.

They talked for another fifteen minutes before a woman interrupted to tell Robert Dawes that someone from Washington, DC, was on the phone and needed to speak with him immediately.

"I would like to continue talking," Grace said. "Perhaps we can share some more ideas."

"Of course," Dawes answered, "I would enjoy that."

He held a hand out to her as they walked toward the door, an uncharacteristically boyish flush on his cheeks.

"At the risk of appearing untoward, would you like to talk over dinner?"

Grace found neither the invitation nor the idea to be improper. To the contrary, she liked both very much.

* * *

"Is he going to die?"

"He is very sick, but he will remain with us."

His Spirit Watches was concerned about the boy, so concerned that he would not leave the sweat lodge or the nearby area to either eat or sleep. He wanted to know how Four Bears could be so sure that the rabies was not life threatening, but he would not even think of questioning her.

"You have a good heart," Four Bears said to him. "You want to know how I know that the boy will not die, such is your worry for him, but you set aside your own fear out of respect for me."

She retrieved a nearby bowl and used a pestle to ensure that the dried leaves in it were finely ground. Then she poured hot water into the bowl and stirred the tea repeatedly with the pestle.

"Lift his head for me."

Placing an arm at the base of the boy's neck, he elevated Walks Alone's head so that he could drink. The shaman placed the bowl against his lips and gently let some of the tea drip into his mouth. From his semi-consciousness, the boy swallowed some of the liquid, but most of it dribbled onto his chin.

"The disease was not advanced in the cat," she said slowly.

"It will not reach the boy's brain. The nightshade will help him recover, but too much of the tea is dangerous, so we must watch him carefully. And," she added, now laboring to speak, "you must leave us long enough to find more yarrow. We will need it for poultices."

A shallow cough exited behind the words, then a second that was much deeper. She tried to suppress a third cough, covering her mouth with her sleeved forearm, but it came anyway. It was deep and hoarse, causing her to grimace in pain, and when she withdrew her forearm, her shirt sleeve was stained with a small clot of bright blood.

He watched her closely, reacting to each painful movement as if it were happening to him. And, in his heart, he knew that he would gladly accept the pain in her place. He prayed silently to the Great Spirit, asking him to somehow make it so.

"You should not be doing this," he said, the words coming out in a passionate but scolding tone that he regretted immediately. "I'm sorry," he added quickly, trying to atone, "but you are not up to this."

"You are my good friend," she answered, "and you are my brother as much as you would be if the Great Spirit had given us the same mother and father . . ." Another cough rose up, followed by a small crimson smear on her bottom lip. ". . . but that is not for you to say. Please, my friend, the yarrow, and only the highest leaves and flowers." She coughed yet again. "The plant is most potent there."

He didn't want to leave, knowing that they both needed him, but he also knew that the boy's recovery depended on an adequate supply of plant remedies. The high clusters of tiny flowers would not be difficult to find, and he would be back soon. As he turned to leave the sweat lodge, he heard a voice from behind, and for a moment he thought that someone else was there other than the boy and the woman.

"He will not die because it is not his destiny to die this way."

He turned around, assuming that the words had sounded strange because of the woman's strained voice.

"It makes my heart glad that dying here is not his destiny," he said. "Thank you for telling me."

Four Bears looked at him quizzically as he turned to leave.

While His Spirit Watches was gone, Four Bears devoted the little strength she had to attending to the boy. Her friend was right—she was not up to this. Whatever was wrong with her lungs had grown much worse, and it had done so quickly. The coughing had begun in the winter, but she couldn't remember exactly when. She may have been coughing without realizing it for days, perhaps longer, too focused on the needs of others to be distracted by the minor irritants that come with inclement weather. It had been many winters since she had felt fully healthy, and those moments had usually come in the spring and the fall.

A single stone glowed in the pit in front of her. The steam in the sweat lodge was now intended for a different purpose—to help cleanse the boy's system—and she instinctively sought the narrow crevice between cleansing his system and depleting it. Sweating would help; dehydration would not. She ladled a little more water onto the stone, and a modest amount of steam rose into the air above the pit.

She struggled to think clearly, knowing that the boy's welfare was in her hands, but many things entered her thoughts—some leaving too quickly, and others staying much longer than she wanted them to. She thought about the journey back down the river to the small village where Talks For Us and Looks Back waited for the boy. And now, for the first time, it occurred to her that she may not be strong enough to make the walk. She knew that His Spirit Watches would look after the boy, and she smiled at the notion that the boy's destiny, as well as the destiny of his people, might be entrusted to a Nanticoke man—a sorcerer so fearsome that the mere blowing of his breath could vanquish his enemies. The mental image caused her to laugh out loud, an exertion that quickly dissolved in yet another cough.

The claw marks on the boy's shoulders and the puncture wound on his forehead concerned her more than the possible worsening of the rabies. She was watching them closely, constantly looking for signs of infection along their jagged, pink edges. The wound in the left shoulder was the most worrisome. It was the deepest and had required cauterization with the metal blade of a knife. She knew that the resulting tissue damage would take much longer to heal.

The boy had been lucky. He might not have fared so well against a larger cat—the image of a cougar jumped into her head, and she scraped the air in front of her face in an effort to brush it away—or one that was more rabid. She washed the wounds gently before applying more poultices of yarrow. The boy stirred when they touched his left shoulder, but he did not wake up.

The coughing had increased during the spring, but it had never become debilitating. She had continued to go wherever she needed to go, do whatever she needed to do, and serve her people as she had always served them. Sometimes the smoke from a fire or a smudging bowl would irritate her lungs, as had the penetrating dampness of a winter morning, but nothing had ever kept her from living her life. Sometime in early summer that had changed, and she had begun to realize at the deepest level of her being that there was much less life to be lived.

She knew what it was *not*, because she had spent a lifetime caring for the sick and dying. Tuberculosis would have been less insidious; pneumonia would have been more debilitating; and pleurisy would have been more painful. The chest pains, the blood, and the shortness of breath had been slow in coming, unwelcomed guests who had taken months to make their ominous journey. But she did not know what it *was*. The not knowing had been troubling at first, but somewhere on the path along Lenapewihittuk, as she had walked with a boy who was traveling from one place, and one life, to the next, it had given way to the peaceful realization that she was doing likewise.

She dipped the tip of her index finger into a small bowl that sat nearby, and then gently touched the finger to the boy's lips. She dipped her finger again, this time smearing a film of the liquid on the boy's forehead. As she applied the tea, she whispered a fervent prayer that asked for much more than Walks Alone's recovery.

"Great Spirit, this trial is but one small step in this boy's journey around the medicine wheel of life. We both know that it will not be easy, and that it will seem to end badly before its full purpose is revealed. I pray that you will allow me to walk with him for as long as it is your will, and that you will send others to walk with him when I cannot. His journey to the center of the wheel will be troubled and unsettled, and it will take many winters. Give him a good heart and the patience he will need to find you. May it be thus."

She dipped her finger into the bowl a third time, but now she touched it to her own forehead, praying once again.

"May the mystical powers of this vervain be with us as we live, and die, according to our destinies and according to your will."

Walks Alone moved again, his head momentarily jerking back and forth before once again settling into stillness. He was dreaming, and she hoped that his dreams were good. A cough started to rise from her chest, but rather than resisting it, she relaxed, silently inviting it to come forth. But, as if suddenly offended by her willingness to accept it, the cough dissipated painlessly in the depths of her lungs. She touched another drop of the vervain to her forehead and closed her eyes, welcoming whatever message—and whatever messenger—the Great Spirit might send to her. At first there was only the sweat lodge— the isolated heat of the single stone in the pit; the light, almost imperceptible mist that it breathed into the air; the aromas of dried leaves, teas, and poultices; and, somewhere beneath it all, as if hidden from all but the sharpest of senses, the iron smell of blood—hers and the boy's. Then there was nothingness.

She imagined that she was small, no taller than the shortest finger on her hand, and naked, unencumbered by the things that human beings wrap around their spirits. Walks Alone looked like a sleeping giant to her, his chest rising and falling like great bellows, his breath rising into the air above his face on deafening exhalations. The stone in the pit glowed violently, a formidable sun to which she was already much too close, its heat pulsating in the skin of her face. From its surface, huge vaporous clouds billowed into the air, climbing to the nearly invisible top of the sweat lodge before falling back to the earthen floor in torrents of rain.

She climbed to the edge of the nearest bowl, standing there quietly for a breathless second, and pitched forward into the sea of vervain tea. The liquid was warm and comforting against her skin, inviting her deeper and deeper into it, like a womb inviting the return of a newborn. She yielded to it completely, tumbling over and over, arms and legs splayed, on a boundless voyage beyond time and space. There was no pain; there was no coughing; there was no blood. There was no worry about the boy or his destiny. There was no longing for the old ways of her people.

With each breath, the tea drew deeper and deeper into her healthy lungs, into her bloodstream, into her cells, and into her soul, until she and the vervain existed as a single entity in the same magical realm. The plant's magic was her magic, and she breathed it upon the world in a sweeping blessing of all people, all animals, and all things—the two-leggeds, the four-leggeds, the no-leggeds; the formless and those encumbered by form.

The Great Spirit spoke to her, and she turned in the direction of its voice, prepared to take one final step along her spoke on the medicine wheel. And then she found herself in the lower world.

She was in a grand field of vervain—thousands of plants, reaching up in tall graceful stems and branching into slender shoots of small, bright lavender leaves. She walked through them in the fully clothed body with which she walked through life, inhaling their fragrance into her lungs, their purple shoots brushing against her thighs. Her hair was down, touching her shoulders in one moment and wafting on the afternoon breeze in the next.

She heard a rustling off to her right, the slow plodding movement of a large, grazing animal, and she knew what it was without turning around. She took in a breath of air saturated with the fragrance of vervain and turned to face the white buffalo.

He stood quietly, head down, searching for whatever grass grew on the ground beneath the endless purple flora. He didn't acknowledge her, nor did he have to. They had known each other for a long time.

"It is said," a voice came from her left, "that it is a great honor to see another's spirit guide."

She looked the other way to see Walks Alone, his head down, his right hand brushing slowly back and forth above the tops of the vervain. But, instead of a boy, she looked upon the form of a grown man, his powerful chest and arms darkened by the summer sun. He raised his head and looked at her with eyes that were warm and kind, but held too much sadness for one so young. He was tattooed at the neck—the alternating ring of snakes and birds that had once been a favorite adornment of Lenape men—and his hair dangled from the back of his head in a thick scalplock. The knife of His Spirit Watches was sheathed at his waist, and the amulet of Talks For Us hung from his neck. She reached out and touched him, tracing her fingers along the features of his face, across the side of his neck, and down the heavy scar that ran between his shoulder and his chest.

"It is a great honor," Four Bears answered, "but I could say the same thing to you."

"I know that now," Walks Alone said softly, "but I didn't know it when you were caring for me in the sweat lodge."

"But that's exactly when you knew it."

Walks Alone said nothing.

"Why did you not tell me about the white beast? Why did you not tell me that you knew what it was? Why did you not tell me that it guides you as well?"

"He guides many of us, and each in his purpose. It was for him to choose the time and place. And, as you see, he has chosen here and now."

Walks Alone gazed at the tops of the vervain, a question hanging on his lips.

"What is my destiny? Please tell me, my teacher, what is my destiny?"

"This is neither the time nor the place. The purpose in this is him." Without turning, she motioned almost imperceptibly toward the buffalo. "He has told you that he will always wait with you. I will wait with you as well, but only for as long as the Great Spirit wishes."

The words coursed through Walks Alone on a quiet wave of fear that swept effortlessly across the expansive ether between the physical world and the world of the animals. He stirred in his unconsciousness on the floor of the sweat lodge.

"Does that mean," he asked, "that you will not go with me? Does that mean that I will not see you again?"

"You will see me one more time in the physical world. I have something else to tell you."

"I don't want to know. If it means that we will no longer talk and that you will no longer be my teacher, I do not want to know."

"Open your eyes, Young One. The fever is breaking. You have kept your vigil and slain the deer. You are a man now."

A great wind rose up around them in a purple cloud of vervain. It encompassed them completely—Walks Alone, Four Bears, and the white buffalo.

In the sweat lodge, Walks Alone opened his eyes to see the familiar and relieved face of His Spirit Watches.

* * *

The holiday weekend ushering in summer began with a temperate Friday evening, and the weather forecast promised that it would become even more beautiful as it lazed toward Memorial Day. To Jeff Phillips, it felt like the perfect start to a summer that seemed to hold only wonderful promise. The past two months had passed in a perfection of their own, but for him that could only be assessed in retrospect. The discovery of the remains in the creek bank had been disruptive, even unsettling, but it had set in motion a series of events that now seemed strangely appropriate. He could not imagine what April and May might have been like if a few inches of dirt had kept the skull from ever looking out into the world.

Things had developed with a slowness that added an air of synchronicity to the events of recent weeks. If Jeff's request to bury the remains on the edge of the upper meadow had been quickly granted, things might have gone only that far. But delays had given everyone an opportunity to think about things, and to vacillate in their feelings about them. When April had arrived, bearing the many promises that always accompany it, Jeff had known nothing about the Lenape, and very little about other Native American tribes. His reading, at least as far as he could remember, had consisted of the two books in his study. The rest of what he knew about Indians had come from old movies and television shows. But now he knew much more. He had been affected by the discovery of the remains, affected by an awareness of unfinished business regarding things he knew absolutely nothing about. He had been frustrated at first, bewildered by his lack of control over events concerning the bones, but—as was always the case—things had begun to align once he was able to relax into the understanding that his control was of absolutely no relevance.

Others had been affected, as well. Emily FitzRoy's interest had progressed well beyond her forensic responsibilities at the discovery site. Talking with her had left Jeff with the impression that she had been surprisingly distracted, not by what waited in other parts of the world, but by what was buried in her own backyard. George Cameron's interest in the Lenape was clearly intense, which made Jeff somewhat leery of his seemingly passive interest in the discovery of the bones—he seemed to be watching, and waiting, from afar. And Grace Caufield may have been the most affected of all. She had told him about the Mercer and its director, and about the way in which a proposed feature article had transformed into the possibility of a book. Although he didn't know how that would play out, it was clear to him that she had started down a path from which she would not soon waver.

Now his own path was being widened by a curious inevitability. He had always believed in destiny, and he had come to understand that, for him at least, it could only be viewed from one perspective. His concept of destiny was not looking back on one's life with the certainty that what had happened had always been meant to happen. He preferred to think of it as the conscious combination of possibility and choice in a universe with room for many outcomes. He didn't know what outcomes might be served by the bones, by the gathering barn, by his vision of the white buffalo, or by the figure of the Lenape man in the glass case at the museum, but he did know that they were traveling his path with him.

Jeff looked out onto the length of the ground that ran from the house to the unseen trees to the north, the ground on which he had seen the white buffalo. He wanted to see him again; he wanted to hear his message; and he closed his eyes in a conscious attempt to move into an altered state. The house was quiet in the early morning hours, although he thought he had heard someone stirring earlier, and he was sure that he would be able to drift away at will. He drew in a deep breath, and then another, trying to relax both his mind and his body. A gentle peacefulness settled over him, and he seemed to meld with the couch, with the plants in the room, and with the late spring morning that was bursting into being on the other side of the glass.

He felt a hand on his forearm and, certain that had he moved to another realm, he opened his eyes. Nothing had changed except for the presence of four-year-old Valeria, who stood quietly in her pajamas by the arm of the couch. She smiled at him from a face surrounded by long dark hair that needed brushing but seemed perfect nonetheless.

"Good morning, Kiddo," Jeff said. "Where's your mom?"

"She said," the child began, pausing to lift her well-worn teddy bear onto the arm of the couch, "that I should come down and see you."

"Oh, she did, did she? We'll that's just fine with me. Are you hungry?"

His granddaughter nodded and Jeff rose from the couch, having found an altered state that he had not anticipated.

They sat at the huge table in the space between the kitchen and the living room—the table that Jeff had always seen as a place for the children—eating Cinnamon Life and talking about many things: what Valeria had been doing in pre-school; the fish that Dae and Jill were going to put in the fountain; what her teddy bear had been doing lately; and whether or not it would be hot enough to go swimming. They talked about absolutely nothing, and yet the conversation was as rich and full, as meaningful and rewarding, as any he had ever had.

And as he talked with Valeria, Jeff couldn't help but think that he hadn't had nearly enough conversations about nothing with his other children. He cherished the time he now had with Jill, and he wanted so much for Hope and Harry to live here as well. But more than anything he wanted to have Harry's sister back in his life. He wanted to be sitting at the table with her, talking about absolutely nothing.

"Would you like some more cereal," Jeff asked, "or maybe some strawberries?"

The child shook her head, a residue of soy milk on her bottom lip. She poked at it with a napkin until her grandfather guided her hand to the right place.

"Hey, I've got an idea. Let's go down to the plant room."

Valeria's mouth curved in a huge smile as she jumped down to the floor.

"Do I have to get dressed first?"

"Nah, you can go like that. But what*ever* you do, don't tell your mom. Okay?"

"Okay," she squealed, heading for the steps.

In a property made up of nothing but favorite places, Jeff's favorite place was the plant room and its greenhouse. Like the rest of the house and the grounds, he had seen them, almost in their entirety, long before he had built them.

They occupied all of the lowest level of the house, flush with the ground that sloped past the Creek House and down to the footbridge to the upper meadow. The greenhouse lacked perfect natural light, which Jeff had compensated for with perfect light, perfect water, and perfect climate control in the plant room. It was a large space—immense in relation to the Lenape structures he had seen—the focal point of which was a small gazebo in its center, with two small benches and a quiet, inconspicuous fountain. The sides of the gazebo were covered in gloriously flowering vines— an inseparable blend of white jasmine and purple clematis. In pots on the ends of each bench, grand profusions of variegated fig cascaded in a splendor that belied the relatively short time it had taken to cultivate it.

One inside wall was lined with tables that were normally reserved for young seedlings—flowers, herbs, and various fruits and vegetables. Most of them were empty now, the weather having warmed enough for the seedlings to be moved outside to various gardens and beds on the property. Some held late-summer bloomers that would be moved outside over the next few weeks, and inside plants that would be moved upstairs as needed. A few held the thirty to forty poinsettias that would mature over the summer and flower, with the appropriate coaxing, just before Christmas.

Part of the back wall was occupied by a long potting table, which Jeff regarded as the indulgence to end all indulgences. For as long as he had loved caring for plants, he had wanted a place where he could pot them, re-pot them, and experiment with different soil mixtures, all without worrying about cleaning up afterwards or getting dirt on the floor. If there was ever a place where he could find inner peace, sitting on a stool in front of that bench, his hands sifting soil around the roots of plant, was it.

The short west wall, which ended at the greenhouse, was dedicated to bromeliads and other tropical plants. They hung in baskets; they grew from pots on an elevated platform; they jutted out from small formations of flat rocks and contrived piles of small logs. Jeff was particularly partial to the Guzmania bromeliad. They were beautiful plants with lush green leaves and vibrant blooms, and they were not particularly difficult to grow. But Jeff loved them for a different reason—they demanded patience, something that had not come to him easily.

The short wall on the other side of the greenhouse had been converted into one large planter—walled off, filled with soil, and converted into a permanent indoor garden. Part of it was planted in roses, and part in impatiens. There were day lilies, Gerbera daisies, and geraniums. There was even a small silver garden, an area set aside for succulents and cacti.

"I've been saving a special plant for you," Jeff said to the child. "I thought you might like to plant it here in the greenhouse."

"The boat," Valeria squealed. "First tell me about the boat."

"Again?" he asked. "You want to hear about it again?" He took her hand as they walked toward the potting table.

"Sometimes, people spend a lot of money on fancy things. Some like fancy cars, some like fancy boats. Well, this is my big, fancy boat."

"That's funny," Valeria offered. "It doesn't look like a boat."

"No, Kiddo, it doesn't look like a boat." He paused, wondering what age Valeria would be when the metaphor made sense to her. "But you'll understand some day."

On the potting table, a small, brightly colored plant waited in a shallow green dish.

"This is called a flowering quince, Kiddo. It's a Japanese tree, and it's just a little older than you are."

"I'm four years old," the child confirmed.

"Oh, I know," Jeff assured, "and this tree is about six years old."

"But trees are big."

"Yes, many trees are big, but they all start as little trees, like this one."

The child carefully examined the single shoot that formed the delicate trunk and the brightly colored flowers on its branches.

"Let's find a place for it over here. Okay?

"Okay!" she exclaimed, trailing after her grandfather.

Choosing a place not far from the silver garden, and after asking Valeria if she thought it was a good place for the tree, he drew a circle in the dirt that was about a foot in diameter.

"One day, a long time from now, your tree will be big enough to fill up this whole space. We'll train it to grow in whatever shape we want it to grow. Does that sound like fun?"

Valeria agreed that it sounded like fun, and they set about the work of transplanting the quince from the bonsai dish to the permanent garden. Standing beside her grandfather, her bare feet already dirty, she leaned over to put tiny handfuls of potting soil around the base of the small tree. Jeff guided her hands just enough so that she did the work but it was still done properly. She worked quietly, concentrating on the application of each handful of soil. He was impressed by her focus, and he found himself hoping that she would carry it along with her as she grew older.

When they were finished, he began to brush the potting soil from her hands.

"Does my tree need water?" she asked.

"*You* need water," he answered, "but yes, it would be good to water your tree, too."

"Can my tree and me get water together?"

The question was perfect in every way, and inspired a series of images in Jeff's mind—images of living things being cared for and watered.

"Maybe I should just turn on the sprinkler system. Then everything in here will be watered, including you and me."

"Yay! Let's all get watered!"

In an instant of sheer joy, Jeff walked to the small control panel by the door and turned on the sprinklers. A gentle spring rain consumed every growing thing in the plant room and greenhouse. Only the potting area was spared. The child jumped up and down in the garden, the Japanese quince near her feet, her pajamas soaked, her hair matted against her face. She was euphoric. His T-shirt and sweatpants also soaked, Jeff walked over and lifted his grandchild into his arms, and they danced in the rain together.

"See, Pop-Pop," she said gleefully, "it *is* a boat!"

They had completed their third jubilant whirl around the floor near the gazebo when Hope walked into the greenhouse.

"Are you two having fun?" she asked.

"Yes!" Valeria shouted. "We're having fun in a boat!"

* * *

The restaurant was elegant but completely approachable, the kind of place that served great food in an inviting atmosphere without, as Robert Dawes had assured her, being "the least bit snooty." The fact that a word like snooty occupied a place in his vocabulary made him even more attractive to her. His physical presence and quietly sophisticated manner would have been more than enough; the quiet glimpses of a sense of humor provided by words like snooty were just icing on the cake.

Their conversations were becoming increasingly relaxed, even though they were underpinned by a sexual tension that was obvious to both of them.

"You haven't talked much about the feature article," he said. "Has that idea gone by the board?"

"Not entirely," she replied. "It's still a possibility, but there's still that concept of linking history and news."

"Can you think of anything else you would like to pursue?" The question hung in the air between them, causing them both to grin. "Ideas, I mean—ideas to write about."

Grace hesitated, more interested in responding to the question they had both heard the first time. "A few," she acquiesced. "I'm really interested in events leading up to the French and Indian War."

"Interested in what way?"

"I've been reading about the way in which different Indian tribes took sides, some with the French, some with the English. I had always assumed that the Lenape had sided with the English, mostly because of their history with William Penn. That was true at first, but it changed."

"I have always believed that allegiances in the French and Indian War were fairly cut and dry," her dinner companion offered, although admitting to himself that he was indeed interested in other things. "The French and their allies, like the Iroquois, were interested in peltry. The English were interested in land."

"That's true, but the Lenape fell somewhere in between. They were so upset about being cheated out their lands and forced out of their homes and hunting grounds by the English that they just switched their allegiances to the French. Things weren't much better for them with the French because the Iroquois had extended their own hunting lands down into the mountains of Pennsylvania, but it shows how pissed off they were at the English."

"Pissed off?" Dawes smiled at her use of the slang, but his profession had taught him that one couldn't get too close to history without eventually resorting to it.

"Yes, pissed off," Grace repeated emphatically. "And they had every right to be."

A brief silence fell between them as they focused on their dinners rather than the affairs of the Lenape.

"May I change the subject?" Robert asked.

"Please," Grace replied, followed by a spontaneous, "say something romantic."

The comment did not catch him off guard, but the completely relaxed way in which she said it did. "Well, you may find this romantic, in a unique sort of way." He looked up from his plate and straight into her eyes. "I have decided to re-do the Lenape exhibit at the Mercer. I'm going to move it down to the ground floor and expand it quite a bit."

"Why are you going to do that?"

"Isn't it one of the first things you asked me about—why the exhibit was so removed from the rest of the museum? I thought you had a point, and you still have one."

"You're going to move it because of my comment?"

A broad smile curved his lips as he said, "Yes. Don't you find that romantic?"

Even though she knew there was more to the move than her request, she nodded as if acknowledging his motivation.

"Perhaps," he began, reaching across the table to take her hand, "we should set aside the history of the Lenape for a bit, and create some history of our own."

She squeezed his hand in response as his invitation moved to the forefront of the many things she now found herself incapable of setting aside.

* * *

Walks Alone sat on a deer hide on the ground near the entrance to the sweat lodge, a small bowl of the nightshade tea cupped in his hands. Each time he raised the bowl to his lips, His Spirit Watches paid close attention to how much the boy was drinking.

"Just a little each time," he said. "The bowl should last all morning. Sip it *that* slowly."

He was satisfied that the boy was recovering, and he knew that Four Bears was satisfied as well. If she had any doubts at all, she would be sitting with them.

"Where is my teacher?" the boy asked.

"She is feeling better today, and she has gone down to the river."

"Do you mean that she has stopped coughing?"

"No, not stopped, but she's not coughing as much. And she has more energy."

Walks Alone studied the tiny bits of ground leaves in the bottom of the bowl. He shook it gently, causing them to swirl into the tea like tiny bits of dirt on the wind. He had never picked any of the nightshade plants, but he had watched Four Bears do so, explaining as she worked that the plants were used for healing in small, measured doses, but potentially lethal in larger amounts. The Lenape regarded all plants with reverence, whether they healed, provided food, or both, but the nightshade plants demanded much more. They required timing, balance, and abiding patience. He raised the bowl toward his lips, but then set it on the ground in front of him without taking a drink.

"I'm hungry," he said. "May I eat?"

"Yes," the man answered, relieved to hear that the boy wanted food. Handing him a piece of dried deer meat, he added, "For now, suck the juice from this, but again, go slowly."

The boy worked the venison with his tongue until it began to yield its juices. It was less than he wanted, but it tasted good. Rising from his cross-legged position, he tried to stand, but he teetered momentarily, causing His Spirit Watches to lunge toward him frantically. He caught his balance and eased himself back into the seated position.

"I am still light headed," he said, spitting the deer meat into his hand.

"You are still *weak*," came the man's reply. "The air is good for you, but you must not try to do too much."

"When will I see Four Bears? I want to talk with her about my journey. I saw her there and I want to tell her."

"Soon. You will see her soon."

Seemingly content with the answer, the boy stretched out on the deer hide and gave in to the weakness he was feeling. Within a few minutes, he had fallen asleep.

His dream was troubling, and he lapsed in and out of it in a way that made it feel even more so. He was standing with Four Bears in the field of vervain. When they just stood quietly, absorbing with each of their senses the seemingly endless peace of the place, his dream would continue. But if he began to ask her the question he wanted to ask, the dream would be interrupted by what he experienced as a hazy wakefulness. Through barely opened eyes he would see His Spirit Watches seated quietly only a few steps away. Then he would simply close his eyes and drift back into his dream. As before, it would continue only as long as he refrained from asking his question.

"Why are you doing this?" he asked Four Bears.

It was a question, but not the one he wanted to ask, and it seemed to alter the cadence of the dream.

"Are you sure it's me? Do you think it could be *you*? Perhaps you don't really want to know the answer. Perhaps that is why you keep waking up."

"But . . ." he answered, knowing that she was speaking the truth, "you said there is one more thing to tell me. What is it? What is the one more thing?" The question asked, he prepared to open his eyes, but he did not wake up, not even for a moment.

Four Bears stared quietly across the vast expanse of vervain. Whatever she was about to say was coming from a place of deep contemplation, and she had been thinking about it for a long time.

"Does it matter to you," she began, "that His Spirit Watches is not Lenape?"

The question was hardly an answer to his question. He felt as if she was avoiding the answer, as if she was stalling for some mysterious reason, but that was not his teacher's way.

"No," he answered, trying to be patient, "it doesn't matter at all. His Spirit Watches is Lenape in his actions and in his heart. And that is enough for me."

She looked straight into his eyes and said, "Say it again. Say it so your heart hears the words for all of time."

"That is enough for me," he repeated. "That is enough for me."

She reached out to touch his hand, smiled warmly, and said, "Sleep, Young One. Sleep and be well. We will talk again soon."

Walks Alone's eyes opened just wide enough to see that His Spirit Watches was keeping his vigil, and then closed again, carrying the boy into a long, deep sleep.

When he awoke, it was nearly dark. His Spirit Watches sat in the same place, and Walks Alone wondered if his friend had moved at all during the day. Moving slowly, the boy rose to a seated position, crossing his legs under him. Once upright, he noticed the form of Four Bears, sleeping beneath a blanket only a few feet away.

"I have been sleeping all day," he offered.

"Yes. Your body needed the rest. Drink some water, and take the juice from another piece of venison. If your stomach accepts that, you can eat some more."

"When did Four Bears return?"

"Just a little while ago. She fell asleep quickly."

"When can I talk with her?" the boy asked, but he already knew the answer. His Spirit Watches was watching over them both, and he was going to ensure that each of them got whatever they needed to recover.

The boy sat silently until well after dark, staring into the fire that His Spirit Watches had built as night had edged closer. He thought about his journey from the steam of the sweat lodge and his frustrating dreams of the field of vervain. He wanted to know what Four Bears had to tell him, and why she had asked him how he felt about His Spirit Watches. It was a strange question, and he wondered if his dream was just playing a trick on him.

The night was dark, and the orange flames provided the only light in the otherwise black landscape around the sweat lodge. The boy and his friend spoke sparingly, as if words were far less important than tranquility and the healing that walked with it.

Walks Alone eventually broke the silence enough to say, "I want you to know, my brother, that you are my brother. And you always will be."

"Wanishi," the man said. "You are my brother as well."

"But I want you to know . . ." Hesitant to continue, the boy allowed his voice to trail off into nothingness.

His Spirit Watches said nothing, knowing that the boy would continue if and when he was so moved. He looked into the flames of the fire.

Whatever time passed was far more difficult for the boy than it was for His Spirit Watches. He wanted to express himself, but he was unwilling to offend his friend in any way.

"But I want you to know," he finally continued, "that you are my brother, even though we are not of the same Lenape blood."

Raising his eyes from the fire, His Spirit Watches said, "Thank you for speaking your truth. Thank you for your courage." He looked above the flames and directly into the eyes of Walks Alone. "Too much is made of blood. This is the Great Spirit's world. It is not the Lenape world or the Nanticoke world. It does not belong to the white man; it does not belong to the black; and neither does it belong to us. It belongs to all men, and all that matters is walking in it with a good heart. If your heart is good, you are a brother to every man. If your heart is bad, you can be a brother to no one, regardless of the blood in your veins. Your heart is good; my heart is good; and we are brothers."

If Walks Alone had anything to say, he quickly forgot what it was. Even at eleven, he knew that some words cannot be followed.

When he awoke the following morning, Walks Alone noticed immediately that Four Bears was gone once again. He felt as if he could have eaten anything in whatever quantity it was available, but he set his hunger aside for something more important.

"She is at the river," His Spirit Watches said before the boy could even ask. "She is at the place where we walked through the trees to look at the forks. You will find her there."

Without saying a word, Walks Alone started for the river. He walked down the path from the sweat lodge to the wigwam of His Spirit Watches, and then down the face of the escarpment to the handful of Lenape wigwams clustered there. As he passed the wigwams, three women paused in their morning work to watch him. They said nothing, but maintained a studied stare that he found disquieting. He recognized one of the women—he had seen her at a council in the lodgehouse in his village—and the others may have been familiar to him as well, but he wasn't certain.

At the base of the escarpment, he walked toward the forks, which was only a short distance ahead. The morning was bright and clear, and the birds sang to it as they watched him from the leaved canopy high above. With each step he walked faster, somehow ignoring his hunger and the need for the food that would help him complete his recovery. The events of recent days had left him dehydrated and in need of sustenance; they had lifted him to unimaginable heights and driven him down into depths he could not comprehend. He had looked at death from each of its sides, having killed and having nearly been killed; he had learned to walk in two worlds, and he had discovered that he could walk with his teacher in both. He had crossed the space between being a boy and being a man, and even though his body had not yet grown fully, the child that once lived within it had disappeared forever.

Beyond the trees that bordered the river, he found Four Bears sitting in the grass, staring silently at the place where the two rivers converged. She didn't turn to acknowledge him, nor did she have to.

"How do you feel, Young One? You found your way here, and that can only be a good sign."

"How do *you* feel?" he asked in response. "Are you still coughing? Are you still coughing . . ."

"Blood? Yes, I am still coughing blood."

"What can I do? How can I help you?"

"Nothing. I know that it will be one of your most difficult lessons, but there is nothing you can do."

He sat on the grass next to her, facing the river, his left arm nearly touching the sleeve of her shirt. Without moving his head, he could look down and see the blood on it—the blackened stains that had been there for a long time, and the bright red smears that had only arrived recently. For the longest time he said nothing, and she said nothing in response. They just looked out on a place that had drawn their people since the oldest of their ancestors had first looked upon it thousands of winters earlier.

"As I lay in the sweat lodge," he finally began, breaking the silence, "journeying from the depths of my sickness, this came to me. I met you in a field of vervain, you and the great white beast. He is your guide as well as mine, yet you never told me."

"And this came to me," she said. "I met you, but not you as you are now. I met you as a grown man—a grown Lenape man. And yes, the white buffalo is my guide as well, as he was the guide of my teacher and his teacher before him. He is how I knew you. I sensed things about you from the first, but *he* is how I knew you."

"Why did you not tell me?"

"There was no need. He has told us both."

"And this came to me as well . . ." The boy spoke hurriedly, remembering the way he had awakened from his dream each time he was about to ask the question. "You said that you have one more thing to tell me. Will you tell me now? I later dreamed that I asked you again and again, but each time I awoke before you could tell me. Then I dreamed that you answered with a question about His Spirit Watches." He paused, thinking about all that he had just said, before repeating, "Will you tell me now?"

"I asked how you felt about His Spirit Watches as your brother, even though he is not Lenape. I asked because . . ." She paused, knowing how her words would walk with Walks Alone for the rest of his life. "I asked because you are not all Lenape. Your mother was white."

Everything rushed together in his head like the water rushing over the falls at the forks. His mind conjured images—the look on the face of His Spirit Watches as he rushed to their rescue on the path; the sound of the arrow splintering the shoulder of the deer; the feeling of the claws of the bobcat as they raked his own shoulders; the journeys, the visions, the dreams. Not one single moment of any of them had felt like this.

Without waiting for the boy to speak, Four Bears said, "Your mother's people were German. They were called *redemptioners*. I don't know where the word comes from but it means your mother's mother and father were slaves. They sold themselves into slavery for passage to this land. They remained slaves until they paid the cost of their passage."

"What happened to her?" The words were burdened by hesitation, as if the boy could not imagine hearing one more word of unexpected news.

"She died giving you life."

It was more than the boy could stand to hear. He closed his eyes and hung his head, as if doing so would somehow make all of this a dream from which he could awake. The reality of the words being too much to absorb, he grasped for something— anything—of which he could make sense.

"And that is why you asked about His Spirit Watches. We are the same; neither of us is full-blooded Lenape."

"Yet you both have proven yourselves in my eyes, and now in the eyes of our people."

The boy rose to his feet, and the words finally came out in the screams of frustration that could no longer be contained.

"How can that be? The white beast spoke of my destiny and the destiny of my people! How can that be? How can the destiny of the Lenape lay with someone who is not Lenape . . ." He shook his head, trying in vain to loosen the fragments of disbelief that had lodged there. ". . . or is only half Lenape?"

"Young One," she began. She tried to rise to her feet, but the exertion caused her to stagger backwards. She reached out a hand for the boy, and he was stunned to see that she was so light that he could easily keep her from falling. For a moment, everything else moved aside as he tended to his teacher.

"You must take me back to His Spirit Watches. We must go now."

Helping Four Bears to her feet, Walks Alone put his arm across her back and under her right arm. She was so weak and frail that his own depleted body had more than enough strength to help her move toward the trees.

"Wait," she said as she turned, leaning into the support of his body, and looked for one final time at the sacred waters.

Thirteen

THANKSGIVING 2010

A pause in the conversation gave way to a spontaneous moment of silence. No one requested it; it just happened, as if the ancestors who were being discussed had magically manifested a tribute to themselves. Even the children were quiet and still, if only to wonder about why everyone else had stopped talking.

Then Wade spoke.

"I haven't had occasion to do this very often in my life," he began. "Sitting around a fire like this, I mean. I may have done it at summer camp when I was a kid, but if what I'm experiencing right now is any indication, I was much too young to appreciate it." He drew in a deep breath, as if he was about to speak, but said nothing.

After a few seconds, the man sitting next to Harry asked, "Please go on. What *are* you experiencing right now?"

"What is it about this atmosphere?" Wade asked in response. "I've never placed much stock in the otherworldly—if I'm using the word correctly, that is—but this feels otherworldly to me. Being here like this with all of you, with three generations of our family, makes me want to talk about things that I usually don't talk about. Is it the fire? Does it have something to do with gathering around the hearth?"

"The fire has something to do with it," the man answered. "But what else do you see?"

The question took Wade aback. He didn't mind being asked, but he was surprised that he couldn't think of an answer to something so simple.

"I don't know. I see people of different ages, most of us related, sitting in a circle and talking. Am I missing something?"

"Not at all. In fact, you just said it. You see people sitting in a *circle*."

"Why does that matter? Wouldn't it be the same if we were sitting in the living room of the main house?"

"Perhaps. And please don't misunderstand me—I think it's wonderful whenever people get together to talk. But I have been taught that there's something truly otherworldly about a circle."

"Please go on," Wade suggested, gently sending the man's words back to him. "What do you mean?"

"Think of this circle of people as a wheel," the man replied. "Each of us, even these young children, occupies a place on the outside of the wheel. In the center of the wheel is the Creator, or God, or Spirit, or however you want to hold him—or her for that matter—in your heart.

"There are at least four spokes in the wheel, although there can certainly be more—one for the East, one for the South, one for the West, and one for the North; the four cardinal directions. Each of us walks a life along the outside of the wheel, eventually making our way along one of the spokes to the Creator."

"Does it matter which spoke we travel?" Edward asked.

"Indeed it does. Each of the directions is associated with an archetype—the models we strive to emulate as humans. The archetype of the Warrior is usually associated with the South, for example; the archetype of the Magician is associated with the West. But there are others—the Hero, the Wise Man, the Trickster—there are many, in fact.

"One may travel the path of the Child to reach Creator, or one may travel the path of the King. Or one may emulate a combination of archetypes."

"I wrote a paper on the Grail Legend last spring," Harry commented. "Percival, Galahad, Arthur, and the others, all represent archetypes."

"Exactly!" the man exclaimed. "It's a great example. So, bringing this full circle—if you'll excuse a very bad pun—what you may be feeling, Wade, are the life journeys of the people gathered here in this circle. The fact that we're discussing the lives of people we love, or loved, coupled with the fact that all of us are sharing this exact time and place in our individual journeys, makes this specific circle both unique and powerful. It will never happen again."

"I guess it's not as simple as I thought," Wade observed.

"To the contrary," the man answered, "it couldn't be *more* simple. We can participate consciously, but even when we are unaware we participate, whether we like it or not."

"So, Uncle Wade," Harry said softly, staring across the tops of the orange flames in the pit, "what does being in this circle make you want to talk about?"

"Probably some fabrication," Hope interjected, "about the way one of his distant relatives taught Betsy Ross how to sew, or how his Uncle Barney actually walked on the moon a year before Neil Armstrong."

"Hey!" Wade protested, causing one of his grandsons to look up at him from the floor. "I don't deserve that!"

"Yes, you do," Chick scolded. "You've been telling these kids tall tales since they were old enough to listen. Can you answer Harry—seriously?"

"Not many people know this," Wade began, "but my Uncle Giuseppe . . ."

It was impossible to tell who groaned first or loudest, but Chick, Hope, and Jill all reacted in unison.

"No, seriously," Wade said, "I want to talk about my dad." He looked into the fire for a few seconds before continuing.

"My father was born in Colorado. His mother died when he was young, and my grandfather sent him back east to stay at an orphanage until he could set up a life for both of them in New Jersey. My grandfather died when my father was a sophomore in high school, so Dad had to quit school and go to work.

"On his first day in a textile mill in Passaic, no one told him to go home after his twelve-hour shift, so he kept working through the second shift, as well. When the foreman from the first shift came in and found out what had happened, he told Dad that he would still have to work his regular shift, so my father started out by working thirty-six consecutive hours.

"I've always admired him more than anyone else I have ever known, and I've always been grateful that he passed along the gene responsible for his work ethic."

"It's a great story," Scott said, "but is work ethic a matter of blood?"

"Probably not," Wade answered. "It's probably more a matter of watching what the people we love and respect do, but I'd like to think that it can be passed along."

"I guess a lot of things get passed along," Jill observed, and everyone in the circle, including the couple to Jill's left, knew that she was thinking about her father.

"If I may," Catherine began, "I'd like to tell a story. It's not profound—at least I don't think it is—but it's interesting.

"One of my three-times great-grandmothers—and," she digressed, "I think that means there are thirty-two people at that level of our family tree—actually had an affair with Edgar Allen Poe. It wasn't illicit or anything like that . . ." She paused, as if considering the difference between family information and family legend. ". . . at least I don't think it was. It happened before Poe married his thirteen-year-old cousin when he was already twenty-six. Now *there's* something to talk about around the fire!"

The comment drew laughter from everyone in the circle—the kind of self-assured laughter that comes with knowing that other family trees may actually contain more dysfunction than your own.

"Anyway," Catherine continued, "my great-great-great-grandmother and Poe apparently had a fairly serious thing going on. And even though they eventually went their separate ways, something remained that resulted in there being two Edgars and three Allens in that part of my family. It's just a story, and it happened a long, long time ago, sometime in the early 1830s if I remember correctly."

The woman to Jill's left chuckled in response to Catherine's comment, and it was apparent to everyone that she had something to say.

"What?" Chick asked. "What is it?"

The woman's stare dropped to the floor. She was obviously embarrassed.

"I'm so sorry," she said without looking up. "That was very rude."

"No, it's alright," Catherine added. "I wasn't offended."

The woman's partner placed a reassuring hand on her back before saying, "Our people believe that everyone should have an opportunity to speak, even these young ones if they are so inclined. And we believe that no one should dominate the conversation, not even the eldest and the wisest. I think that my wife was reacting to Catherine's observation that 1830 was a long time ago. I think she would respectfully offer that it was little more than yesterday."

"Perhaps," Hope offered, "it is *we* who have offended *you*. I think I understand why your wife laughed. I have worked with children in the most remote parts of Honduras. They are part of an ancient culture, one that may have been there for thousands of years. The people of that culture understand little about the history of this country, but when they hear that it's only a few hundred years old, they chuckle at its infancy."

"Oh, no," the woman offered, raising her eyes to meet Hope's. Then, looking at Catherine, she added, "We are not offended. It's just that our people were here for thousands of years before the United States came into being.

"Our ancestors walked the very ground on which this wonderful barn is built. They held their own council fires in this same earth. They lived and died by the leave of the ancient river that flows beyond the crest of the hill to the east. They fished in the nearby streams and hunted in the surrounding woods. They held as sacred the confluence of the Delaware and Lehigh, only a few miles from here in Easton. And by 1830 none of their descendants—none of our people—remained in this river valley. And to us, and I say this with the utmost respect . . ." She stared directly into the flames, comforted by her husband as he rubbed her back in a gentle circular motion. ". . . it feels as if it happened only a few days ago."

She raised her eyes from the flames to the copper hood immediately above her, where the images of a wolf and a deer had been hammered into the copper with glorious precision.

Fourteen

"You spoil her, Dad."

"I don't see her enough to spoil her, so you should be grateful."

"So, if Scott and I accept your invitation to move here, will you spoil her more?"

Jeff Phillips stopped in the middle of the footbridge by the Creek House. He had been looking forward to this conversation with Hope, but like most things with her, he knew that it wasn't going to happen until she wanted it to. The invitation had always been implicit, but he and Dae had formalized it at Christmas. The most important variable was Scott's business career, which he insisted on pursuing regardless of family money. Jeff respected that, so all he could do was ensure that they knew they were welcome—and be patient. He had come to understand that so many things turned out better when he was patient.

"Does that mean you've made a decision?"

"It does, and I guess I'm just going to have to do what I can to keep you from spoiling her."

They hugged joyously, there in the middle of the footbridge, one of them looking forward to the new life that lay ahead, the

other flustered by good news. In his life, Jeff had known victories
and defeats, and he had always tried to maintain a steady keel
through both. He believed that nothing was ever as bad as
it seemed and nothing was ever as good, but there were still
moments of joy—moments like this one—that left him euphoric.
And euphoria flustered him. He turned back toward the house,
then immediately reversed direction to walk to the upper meadow
with Hope, and then turned back once again to find Valeria. He
wanted to do everything at once.

"Valeria is with her responsible grandparent right now,"
Hope kidded. "I'm sure that Dae has things under control. Why
don't we take a walk?"

"So," Jeff began, trying to settle down as they started up the
hill to the upper meadow, "I guess there's going to be quite a bit of
activity up here this summer. If the construction crews are going
to come in to build your house, I'm going to have them work on
the barn at the same time."

"Whoa!" Hope exclaimed. "Slow down a little. Scott and I are
definitely going to do this, but I don't know if we can move that fast."

"You should do it in whatever time works for the two of you.
The house will be waiting for you when you get here. Okay?"

"Yes, Dad. It's great." She smiled to herself as they walked past
the paddock and toward the back of the meadow. She had known
that he would react this way. In fact, it was the only reason that
she and Scott hadn't accepted the invitation when it was made
during the holidays.

"Can you stay this week?" Jeff asked.

"Scott has to go back on Tuesday morning, but Valeria and
I can stay."

"I'll ask Ed Davies to drive out here on Tuesday morning. We might as well get started right away."

Three days later, both partners in the New Hope architectural firm of Davies and Kleinfelter were walking the upper meadow with Jeff and Dae, Jill and Edward, and Hope and Valeria. It was decided that Hope's house would sit on the northwest corner of the meadow at roughly the same angle that Jill's house sat to the southwest. Between the houses, facing due east, the grove of forsythia would be left untouched in anticipation of the bones that would eventually be buried there. If that didn't happen, the site was large enough to be used for something else, including another house.

It was decided that Rick Kleinfelter would create the plans for Hope's house, and that he would work directly with Hope and Scott, traveling to see them if necessary. The plans for the gathering barn, as Jeff continued to call it, would be left to Ed Davies.

It was also decided that, Jeff's enthusiasm aside, Hope and Scott would plan and build their house at a more measured pace, giving Scott adequate time to affect the required changes in his work. It was a given that he would be spending time in either New York or Philadelphia, depending on the final arrangements, and there were many details that had to be worked out. It wasn't going to happen quickly, but it was going to happen, and that was more than enough for Jeff.

Ed Davies listened intently as Jeff described his vision for the gathering barn. He knew that they would have to share the vision in order for him to make it a reality, and that was happening fluidly.

"I understand what you think it looks like," he said at one point, "but I have a more fundamental question: What is its purpose?"

The question made Dae laugh to herself. She knew that purpose always came later where Jeff's visions were concerned. He saw what was to be; he created what was to be; and then he let it adopt its own purpose. For him, it was a matter of faith, and she knew no one who had more.

"I think," Jeff answered, "the operative word is 'celebration.' Dae and I want our families—and their families—and others we may not even know yet, to have a place to gather and celebrate life. At first, I thought that a big, open space would be sufficient, but then I realized that something else is required. People don't go to a wedding without remembering other weddings that they've been to, or without talking about their own wedding or their parents' wedding. They do the same thing with births, and graduations, and even deaths. The remembering is what the fire pit is all about—the remembering and the story telling that usually accompanies it. I may be wrong. The place may end up being used to store furniture and boxes, but that's not what I see. And I can only go by what I see."

The clientele of Davies and Kleinfelter was well-to-do, but Ed Davies knew few people who could indulge their visions the way Jeff Phillips could indulge his. What was sadder, he thought as he listened to Jeff talk, was that he knew few others who even had visions. Most of them wanted grand and opulent things that would speak to their positions in life, and they were willing to pay handsomely for them. Jeff didn't give a damn about what anyone else saw as his position, or if anyone else ever came to his property to assess it. He was simply honoring what he envisioned for himself and for his family. It was, Davies sensed, a deeply personal thing.

"If I can borrow your notes and sketches," he suggested, "I'll put some things together for you. It should be a fun project. I don't know that I've ever done anything quite like it."

An hour later, some rough measurements having been taken and some additional discussions about both the house and the gathering barn having taken place, the small group dispersed. Ed Davies and Rick Kleinfelter left by way of the service road that ran above the creek and past the bridge where the bones had been unearthed. Hope and Valeria accompanied Jill and Edward to their house, Jill having promised her niece a horse ride after lunch. And Jeff and Dae headed back to the main house. They were past the Creek House and halfway across the yard when a car pulled to a stop a few yards away at the end of the drive. A man dressed in a blue blazer and open-collared shirt got out of the car.

"Mr. Phillips?" he asked.

"I'm Jeff Phillips. How can I help you?"

"My name is Seth Williams," he replied, "I'm a member of the Delaware Nation in Oklahoma, and I'm here because of something called NAGPRA."

"Williams. Are you related to the people who used to own this property?"

The man smiled, as if aware of some joke to which Jeff and Dae were not privileged.

"No, I'm not. At least not in the way you think."

"I'm sorry, Mr. Williams, what is NAGPRA?"

"NAGPRA—the Native American Graves Protection and Repatriation Act—which was passed by Congress in 1990."

"And I assume that this pertains to the remains we found down by the bridge?"

"It does, but there's no need to be alarmed. I would just like to make you aware of what NAGPRA is and how I may be able to help, if at all."

"I'm sorry," Jeff said, turning toward Dae. "This is my wife, Dae."

As she shook the man's hand, she asked, "Would you like to come up to the house for some lunch, or something to drink perhaps?"

"Yes, thank you. Something cold to drink would be nice."

A few minutes later, they were seated in the living room with glasses of lemonade.

"So, Mr. Williams, can you tell us a little more about this congressional act?"

"Yes, of course." He paused to take a sip of lemonade. "The act requires any institution that receives federal funding to return human remains and cultural items upon request by federally recognized tribes."

"Cultural items being what?" Dae asked.

"Well, they certainly include funerary objects, but they also include things that are handed down from one generation to another."

"I'm interested in the *federal funding* part," Jeff asked. "What does that include?"

"Just that. If an entity doesn't receive federal funding, the act doesn't apply."

"I don't mean to jump ahead," Jeff added, "but that excludes us."

"Yes, I understand. I'm only here to tell you about NAGPRA, what it means, and what others in your place have done because of it. Native American remains cannot be expatriated from private land. It's really up to the property owner to decide what to do with them. He can put them on the mantel or sell them on eBay."

"Please say that you're kidding," Dae exclaimed. She was smiling, but the words preceded a nervous laugh that confirmed she was not amused.

"I wish I were," Williams answered. "Unfortunately, it happens all the time. Remains are discovered frequently, both accidentally—as was the case here—and during planned excavations. Many people who find Native American remains treat them with great respect, but others do not."

"The problem here," Jeff suggested, "is that the remains found here cannot be positively identified as Native American. Without that, isn't this conversation academic?"

"Perhaps, Mr. Phillips, but I would encourage you to think about some things. Let's assume that they are Native American. In fact, let's go one step further and assume that they're Lenape, which isn't a huge jump based on where they were found.

"One option would be to turn them over to Lenape descendants, if they could be found. But even if descendants could be located, it's doubtful that they would want the remains."

"That surprises me," Dae interrupted. "Wouldn't they want to bury them in accordance with their own traditions?"

"Yes, but they could do that without removing them from where they were found. In fact, many tribal elders prefer that remains stay where the people they once belonged to lived and died."

"I think I see where you're going with this, Mr. Williams. You think we have a legal right to have them interred here."

"Yes, I do."

"But why go to the trouble of coming here to tell us that? Wouldn't things just unfold that way on their own?"

"Possibly, but others may challenge you. I have spoken with Sheriff McNulty and Dr. Cleveland, as well as with Dr. FitzRoy at the University of Pennsylvania. Each of them told me about what happened, how you responded to it, and what you would like to do. I would like to see you be successful."

"I don't mean to be rude, Mr. Williams, but I'm still missing something here. You could have done this over the phone. Why would you travel here from . . ." He paused, thinking back on the conversation in the yard. ". . . Oklahoma, was it?"

"Anadarko, Oklahoma. And to answer your other question, Mr. Phillips, I am Lenape, although we are more often referred to as Delaware these days. I owe it to my ancestors, including the one whose bones may be in the county forensic facility, to make this trip. I'm honored to do it."

Jeff moved forward onto the edge of the easy chair, placing the half-empty glass of lemonade on an end table.

"Now I understand. And thank you. I won't insult you with assurances about what we will or will not do, Mr. Williams. We'll let our actions speak for us. Would you like to see where the remains were found?"

"If I'm not mistaken, I saw the place on the way in. I stopped at the bridge and got out of my car. I hope you don't mind."

"We don't mind at all," Dae offered. "Feel free to stop again when you leave. And stay as long as you like."

Jeff offered, "We made a decision some time ago that if we were given responsibility for the bones, we would bury them in the upper meadow in front of a tall stand of forsythia. Would you like to see the site?"

"Very much," Williams responded. "I would like to see it very much."

Ten minutes later, they were standing in the shade of the tall trees in the back of the upper meadow. As Jeff explained why he thought the lush green grass in front of the forsythia was the perfect resting place for the bones, Seth Williams could do little more than nod his head in complete agreement.

Jill stood in the center of the paddock behind them, leading the tethered Bandit in a slow, monotonous circle. A gleeful Valeria sat in the saddle on his back, her shrieks of joy interrupting the stillness of the day. Hope walked next to the horse, vigilant but not concerned.

"There's a small town in Kansas," Williams finally began, more than satisfied with what he had seen, "called Piper. A builder built a housing development there—a place called Delaware Ridge. A Delaware man named Neconhecon is buried there, in a grave that was designated as a historical site in 1982."

"Was he a famous man?" Dae asked.

"A chief, of sorts, and the leader of the Wolf Clan. He lived in the mid-1800s and signed an important treaty in 1861."

"Someone recently told me about the Lenape clans that once inhabited this area," Jeff said. "One of them was the Wolf Clan—the Munsee, if I remember correctly."

"You do," Williams replied. "The developer left vacant the lot where the remains of Neconhecon are buried. It's between two houses, and the people who live nearby look after the grave as if one of their own people were buried there."

"Perhaps he *is* one of their own people," Jeff suggested. "Perhaps we're all more closely related than we think."

"I'm very glad to have met both of you," Williams said as he turned to leave. "And, with your permission, I will stop down at the bridge again."

"For as long as you like," Dae repeated. "For as long as you like."

* * *

Walks Alone and Four Bears had only walked as far as the small grouping of wigwams when they were met by the three women whom Walks Alone had seen earlier.

"I am Storyteller," one of them—the one whom Walks Alone had remembered from the council—had said when they arrived, "and you must give her to us now." She had spoken with great reverence, as if reluctant to address Walks Alone in any other way, but she had been firm in her insistence that he entrust the shaman to their care. And it was she who had emerged from the wigwam at midday to tell him that Four Bears had died.

His Spirit Watches was waiting with Walks Alone by then, and the two of them were unable to do anything other than rise to their feet and stand there in desperate silence. Whatever words either had to say belonged to another time.

"You may see her," the woman said to His Spirit Watches, and he moved stoically, head bowed, toward the entrance to the wigwam. His massive form disappeared into it, remaining there for what seemed like a full winter to the boy. Walks Alone didn't know what was happening, or if he would be allowed to see his teacher, but he was grateful for the time that His Spirit Watches had with her. His friend was more than worthy of it.

His Spirit Watches returned to the day, a look of emptiness in his eyes. He wasn't crying; he didn't even look sad. His face was utterly without emotion, as if waiting for some feeling—any feeling—to return. Storyteller followed after him.

"You may come in," she said to Walks Alone.

The inside of the wigwam was dark and quiet, the other women attending to the body of Four Bears. The smoke of burning herbs filled the air, and he drew its sweet fragrance deep into his lungs. The body of Four Bears lay face down on the hide of a black bear, all but the crown of her gray head covered by a blanket. Her face was turned away from him, and he wanted more than anything to ask that he be allowed to see it once again, but he remained silent.

"She told us two things," the woman said softly. "The first was that you be allowed to see this."

She drew the blanket away from the old woman's head and down below the space between her shoulder blades, revealing a tattoo of the white beast. It had been drawn in the dark stain that he normally associated with body markings, but filled in with a white that he had not seen before. He didn't know how it had been accomplished, but he resolved in that moment to find out.

Storyteller spoke again. "The other was this: that *you* lead us as we bury her."

Walks Alone stepped back, not knowing what he had expected but knowing that it hadn't been this. He gulped the fragrant air, hoping somehow that it held words with which he could respond.

"I," he stuttered, "I . . . don't know what to do."

"She said," the woman answered, "that whatever you do will be what she would want to have done; whatever you say will be what she would want to have said."

His life pressing down on him, driving him to its primordial core like the current of Lenapewihittuk, Walks Alone broke down and cried.

* * *

The events of the past few days rolling in his head like the thunderstorm that was building in the night beyond his office window, Jeff Phillips pushed away from his computer. With most of his family so nearby, the holiday weekend had felt like a joyful blessing.

For a brief moment, he had forgotten about it all—the remains in the creek bank; his meeting with Emily FitzRoy at the University of Pennsylvania; his encounter with the white buffalo; and his conversation with Crow Feather at the little museum in Allentown. Life—in the form of a dance with his granddaughter in the rain of the greenhouse, and the knowledge that she and her parents would soon be living in a house in the upper meadow— had temporarily pushed everything else aside. But, as if on cue from some cosmic hand, a man had appeared in the driveway and brought back into focus everything that had to do with the bones.

He had been thinking about the mannequin in the museum. Its lifelike grace and dignity had given him a three-dimensional appreciation of what a Lenape man might have looked like. He wondered about when he lived and died, what his life was like, and what caused his death. Even though he knew that the mannequin was not the man who had been discovered in the creek bank, it was easy to imagine that they were the same.

Jeff rose from his chair, pulled shut the window, and went to bed. Somewhere above the river, a flash of lightning cut through the late night sky, illuminating the lines of poetry on his desk.

Man Behind the Glass

A whisper in his old and unknown voice
Comes rippling through this long and sleepless night;
Concentric circles carry forth his song
Of ancient wrongs now longing to be right.

The wounds that he felt centuries ago
Embed themselves so deeply in my chest
That even a guarded breath reminds me
Of timeless pain that will not let him rest.

The hopes that he carried in his lifetime
Rush forth to merge with mine within my soul;
I take them in, praying that fulfillment
Will fill the emptiness and make us whole.

The perils and pleasures of our journeys,
And every path we follow on our own,
Are the destiny that we now follow
Together, so that neither walks alone.

PART THREE

"This we know: the earth does not belong to man, man belongs to the earth. All things are connected like the blood that unites us all. Man did not weave the web of life, he is merely a strand in it. Whatever he does to the web, he does to himself."

— Chief Seattle
1852

Fifteen

NOVEMBER 2002
(SEVEN YEARS EARLIER)

As he drove through the early evening rain, Jeff Phillips muttered to himself. "What am I doing?"

He was cold and uncomfortable, and the heat in the car didn't seem to be doing much to make him feel less so. He had been caught in the rain on the walk between his meeting on 45th Street and the parking garage at the hotel, and even though his raincoat had kept his clothes from getting wet, his head had been soaked. And now he couldn't shake off the chill.

"What am I doing to Dae? What am I doing to my family?"

He had always loved autumn and was fond of noting that October was the best time of the year, and that it would be perfect if it wasn't followed by November. Weather like this was the reason why. This rain wasn't the same thing that fell through the emerging warmth of spring or accompanied the thunder and lightning of mid-summer storms. It was completely inhospitable

on its own—a combination of cold and humidity that cut to
the core of one's being—and it made everything around it seem
equally inhospitable.

"What am I doing to myself?"

And it didn't help that the days had grown shorter. By the
end of his meeting, the business day had only begun to draw to
a close, but darkness had already descended. Now, as he drove
down the New Jersey Turnpike, the long, light-splashed evenings
of summer seemed a lifetime away.

The deal with the global banking company—the deal to
which he had dedicated most of the past year—had fallen through.
"Well, not exactly," he said to the headlights in the northbound
lanes. "It's just delayed." But he knew that he was rationalizing.
He understood clearly that the largest financial institutions in the
world don't delay eight-digit computer initiativess without a good
reason, and his client hadn't given him one. Something else was
going on—something that he didn't know about; something that
he probably couldn't do much about if he did know. The deal
wasn't delayed; it was slipping away completely.

A lot of things had slipped away in the past year. Everything
had changed since those airliners had plowed into the World
Trade Center on September 11th. In the weeks immediately
following the attacks, everyone and everything had lapsed into
a state of mutual confusion and uncertainty that had provided
an ironic sense of order. But as things had begun to sort
themselves out, some details had made more sense than others.
Some factors had begun to recover immediately, while others
had slipped into an abyss from which recovery would be much
more problematic. Jeff's business had been one of the latter,

and the way out of the abyss had since grown increasingly difficult to see.

For Jeff, computer sales had always been a series of ups and down, victories and defeats, just as, he imagined, it was for everyone who participated in it. Experience had taught him to maintain an even keel because nothing is ever as bad as it seems. He gave voice to the remainder of the thought, "And nothing is ever as good." But, on this particular November night, when everything seemed to be sloshing around at the foot of the abyss without so much as the smallest drain to take some of it away, he was seeing things with unusual clarity. The unvarnished truth of the matter was that he didn't care whether things were good or bad because his need for balance had long ago become anesthetized apathy.

"What am I doing to myself?" he asked the night.

As the miles passed, he thought about his professional life, and he didn't like what he was thinking. He had once heard someone make a distinction between a job and meaningful work, and no day had passed since in which he had not thought about the difference. He had chosen his career path, or perhaps it had chosen him, because it had seemed like a good opportunity to make money. "Meaningful" had been less important then, and as he drove down the New Jersey Turnpike, he felt as if the concept had all but evaporated from his life.

His job had its moments—moments that challenged his intellect, moments that inspired his creativity, moments that truly engaged him—but for the most part it held little that he found truly meaningful. Both he and the company made money from his work, but who, he often asked himself, really prospered? Whose life was changed for the better? Who was afforded an opportunity that never would have come their way if it hadn't been for his work? "What," he asked himself with increasing regularity, "is the purpose in it?"

He had met and worked with some people who were really worth knowing—people who had a strong sense of themselves and a genuine concern for others—but they had been few and far between. He had come to believe that most of the people he knew in the business world saw life as nothing more than the earning of money, and that they valued little beyond their own immediate interests. And, of late, he had grown even more cynical, increasingly certain that it wasn't just business people who lived their lives that way.

He remembered with some sense of longing the words of a CEO he had worked for some years earlier. He had returned to the office after another meeting in which a deal had been lost. "It's really bad," he had said to his boss, "and I accept full responsibility for it." The man had responded by saying, "No, *Bosnia* is really bad. This is just a setback, and we'll move beyond it." In his career, he had known few business people with that kind of perspective. If he had met more of them, he might have felt differently, but that CEO had made most of the others look trivial, small, and less *meaningful*.

"I'm fifty-two," he thought to himself as he took the exit for the connector to the Pennsylvania Turnpike, "and I haven't done a damn thing with my life." Listening to his own words, he imagined what Dae would say if she were in the car with him. As she had many times, she would say that he was being tough on himself, and although he had agreed with her on most of those occasions, he knew that this time he would say, "But not tough enough."

He merged onto the Pennsylvania Turnpike and began the twenty-five minute trip to the exit for Route 309, the road that would take him home. *So, what would be meaningful?* he thought to himself. *What would make a difference?*

Many things ran through his head: a business of his own, one that would help other people, the environment, or both; teaching, perhaps even at the college level; working for a non-profit organization, perhaps in a fundraising capacity; doing something with Dae, something that would integrate their mutual interest in health and well being; creating something for children. It would be risky, and almost certainly generate less income than he was making now, but if it provided the opportunity to do something truly meaningful, it might be worth it. It started to rain harder and he increased the tempo of the windshield wipers.

As he exited the turnpike and turned onto Route 309, he could feel himself becoming a little more comfortable with the night. He was finally drying out, even though it had taken the entire trip for the collar of his shirt to feel like something other than a wet washcloth. And he was recovering from the disappointment of the meeting, relaxing enough to entertain thoughts about possible ways to resurrect the deal—ways that might even allow him to close it before the end of the year. He was looking forward to a hot shower, which was now only a few minutes away, and to curling up with Dae on the couch. "Things are never as bad as they seem," he said to the night.

His cell phone buzzed and he picked it up to see a text message from Dae: *We need coffee, if you have a chance to stop. Be safe.* Jeff smiled to himself. There was a small grocery store about a mile up the road.

He moved as quickly as he could toward the front door of the store, but not quickly enough to avoid the water dripping off the edge of the overhang. It made a curiously direct hit at the base of his neck and ran down onto his nearly dry collar. He shook his head, part in amazement, but mostly in exasperation. "Not my night," he said, as he walked into the store.

"Hello, Mr. Phillips," a voice said before Jeff had a chance to shake off the rain. "Where have you been?"

Jeff looked up to see the cherubic face of the man who owned the little store. "Hello, Sam," he responded. "I've been working on a big project for the last two or three weeks. There was a big meeting about it in New York, today."

"And . . . how did it go?"

Jeff scrunched his face and shook his head.

"I'm sorry. Maybe things will turn around. You know what they say: nothing's ever as bad as it seems."

"In my heart, I know that's right, Sam, but my head doesn't always see it that way."

"Well, I hope you never have to look at things like I had to—from a bed in the intensive care unit—but believe me, nothing's . . ."

Jeff smiled and shook his head in agreement. ". . . ever as bad as it seems," he completed the saying, thinking about Bosnia.

"I just need a pound of coffee, Sam, and then I'm going to go out and enjoy some more of this rain." Jeff disappeared briefly down a familiar aisle, returning almost immediately with the coffee.

"*That's* the spirit, Mr. Phillips," the man replied, only half in jest. He ran the container of coffee across the scanner and added,

"That'll be six dollars and three cents, please."

"I like that," Jeff observed.

"What's that, Mr. Phillips?"

"That you say 'please,'" he responded. "And, in a moment, you'll say 'thank you.' And I like the fact that you call me 'Mr. Phillips,' even though you know you don't have to. You're a good businessman, Sam, but you're a better man." He thought about what he had just said and the things he had thought about on his drive.

"Thank you, Mr. Phillips," Sam offered, his hand reaching out with Jeff's change. "I *think* that covers everything you just said." He smiled widely, causing Jeff to do the same.

"Oh," Sam called out as Jeff reached the door, "would you like some lottery tickets? Big jackpot, you know."

Jeff reached into his pocket and withdrew the ninety-seven cents in change. "Can't do it, Sam. My meeting ran long and I used all my cash for parking. I probably should have used a credit card, but I was really in a hurry to get out of there."

"What was the change—ninety-seven cents?"

"Uh-huh."

"Well there's three pennies sitting here by the cash register. A lady left them earlier. She said someone might need them."

"I don't know if *need's* the right word, Sam."

The man punched a few buttons on the face of the lottery machine and a ticket popped out of the slot. "You owe me ninety-seven cents, Mr. Phillips."

As Jeff put the change on the counter he said, "Thank you for your kindness, Sam. You just made my day, and I genuinely appreciate it." He turned and left the store.

A few minutes later, Jeff pulled into the garage at his house in Blue Bell. He began to feel better almost immediately upon seeing the garage door ease down, slowly shutting out the November night and it's irritating rain. When Dae wrapped her arms around his neck, he felt better still.

"How was your day?" she asked, only to hear him briefly describe the outcome of the meeting. She didn't press him for details. He didn't like talking about business when it was good, and he disliked it even more when it was bad. He would always take the time if she really wanted to know because he felt that he owed her the information, but her instincts told her that it was best to let it pass this time. "Why don't you take a long, hot shower? When you come down, we'll eat."

"Sounds good." As he headed for the stairs, he added, "Thanks, Babe. Thanks for letting me be me."

"I love you," she responded. "Why wouldn't I want you to be you?"

After dinner and the last forty-five minutes of a show on the History Channel, they found themselves lying together in bed, her hand gently holding his. They were both tired, and each knew that sleep would come easily.

His eyes closed, and aware of little other than the touch of Dae's hand, he let himself drift off. His last thoughts of the day were the outcome of the meeting in New York, the walk through the rain to the parking garage, and the long drive home. His thoughts could have been about the best parts of his day—Sam and his kindness, Dae and her love—but instead they were about the worst. So it was in the mindset of his own choosing that he fell asleep.

It was almost three in the morning when Jeff's eyes opened suddenly, the images of his dream churning vividly in his head. In his dreams, every meeting had been long and boring; every relationship had become antagonistic; every discussion had deteriorated into something adversarial; every walk to his car had been made in the freezing rain; and every drive home had provided nothing other than endless time to think about all of it over and over again. "It's not true," he reassured himself. "I've had so many great experiences." And he believed what he was saying as he spoke it to the darkness of the bedroom, but he knew that if he closed his eyes something inside of him would dream otherwise. Not wanting to go back to sleep just yet, he got out of bed and went downstairs to get something to drink. The first floor of the suburban colonial was dark except for a faint light above the stove in the kitchen, and silent except for the late fall rain that continued to hit the windows.

He was drinking a glass of cold water when it hit him—the unmistakable feeling in his lungs. The imaginary hand reached into him from behind and pulled air back into him until his lungs ached with the pressure. He closed his eyes and reached for the counter, thinking that he might collapse, but he remained upright. The pressure in his chest subsided and he opened his eyes to see Sam the grocer standing on the other side of the counter.

"Hello, Mr. Phillips," the man said. "Are you feeling alright?"

"I'll be okay," Jeff replied. "These episodes sneak up on me."

"I understand."

Jeff started to say something but stopped short, thinking about what Sam had said and wondering exactly what it was that he understood. "Why am I seeing you like this, Sam?"

"Oh, it's nothing. I just stopped by to say that there are better things to dream about—things that may serve you better."

"I have no doubt. But sometimes I just can't turn it off."

"The negativity?"

"Yeah. I guess you could call it that."

"You should work on that, Mr. Phillips. I don't want to see you end up in intensive care." Sam turned, as if moving toward an unseen doorway in the small dining area on the other side of the counter. "Oh, there is one more thing." He held out a lightly closed fist before dropping three pennies into Jeff's hand. "I hope you will always find what you need." Then he looked into Jeff's eyes and added, "Take care, *Jeff*."

As Jeff returned to bed, the vision returned with him, and it stayed with him until almost five o'clock, when he finally drifted back into sleep. It preoccupied him so completely that the negative thoughts from his dream were unable to get even the slightest handhold in the crevices of his mind.

When Jeff awoke, it was almost eight o'clock on Saturday. Unaccustomed to sleeping so late, he pushed the blankets aside and went to the closet to find his exercise gear.

"What time is it?" Dae asked groggily.

"Eight o'clock already. I guess I had a tough night. I'm going for a walk; want to come along?"

"You go ahead," Dae suggested. "I'm going to grab another thirty minutes."

"Sure," Jeff smiled, not believing a word of it. "Sweet dreams."

The rain was gone, but the morning was overcast and chilly. Jeff turned onto the short suburban street that connected with the main road back to town. He felt surprisingly good for someone who had been awake for two hours in the middle of the night, and he quickened his pace much sooner than he normally would have. About a half hour later, he was within a hundred yards of the small grocery store and he decided to stop in to say good morning to Sam. It occurred to him to tell Sam about his vision, but he thought better of it.

As he approached the store, he saw that it was closed. A small sign in a nearby window listed the store hours, including "Saturday: 8:00 a.m. to 6:00 p.m." Jeff didn't have to look at his watch to know that it was well past eight.

"Can I help you?" a voice asked from behind.

Jeff turned to see a young woman standing on the sidewalk, a small ring of keys in her hand. She fingered through them methodically, apparently looking for the one that opened the front door.

"It's not important," Jeff offered. "I just wanted to say hello to Sam."

"He passed away last night," the woman said. "He was my great uncle. My mother asked me to come down and open the store."

"I'm *very* sorry for your loss," Jeff answered. "Do you mind if I ask how he died?"

"He had another heart attack. He just died in his sleep. And I appreciate the thought, but we really weren't very close. I didn't know him that well."

"That's unfortunate," Jeff suggested. "He was worth knowing." He turned to resume his walk, the image of Sam standing by the register rolling through his head.

"I thought," the woman called after him, "that you were here to check your lottery ticket."

"No," Jeff answered, "I just wanted to see Sam. I just wanted to say good morning and thank him."

"Somebody won it, you know."

"Won what?"

"That big jackpot. Somebody won it last night."

"No, I didn't know. I just wanted to say good morning."

Jeff resumed his walk, now resolved to walk a little farther than usual. He was sad that Sam was gone, but grateful that his friend had slipped away without spending more of his life in intensive care. The night before, inside the store and beyond the drear of a cold, rainy November night, the man had caused a small bit of sunlight to cast its warmth on Jeff and his life. He was grateful that Sam had not suffered.

As it turned out, Jeff didn't know how much more had happened on the previous night. He wouldn't find out until Monday that six tumblers had dropped into alignment deep within the lock of some cosmic safe, and that three pennies, passed from a stranger through a friend, and his ninety-seven cents had become two hundred and sixteen million dollars.

Sixteen

SEPTEMBER 2009

"Do they really call it a powwow?"

"Apparently."

"I'm sorry," Dae said emphatically, "it sounds a little politically incorrect to me."

"It certainly evokes a stereotype," Jeff admitted, "but maybe that's just us—or me. Why don't we withhold judgment until we've had a chance to check it out?"

"That's fine with me, and I don't mean to judge anything or anyone. I guess it was just a gut response."

"You certainly don't have to explain it to me. I get where you're coming from."

As they headed up Route 611 through a perfect September afternoon, neither Jeff nor Dae knew quite what to expect. The flyer had described a gathering of something called the Lenape Nation of Pennsylvania, but they didn't know if that meant a few people or a few thousand. It said that there would be dancing, food, and vendors of authentic Lenape crafts, all of which conjured images of a street fair. But they both needed a respite from the nearly constant activity at the property, as the gathering barn approached completion and Hope's house took form, and this day trip seemed like the perfect answer.

"Refresh my memory," Dae began, "where did you hear about this event?"

"It was back in the spring when Emily FitzRoy and I went through the exhibit at the University of Pennsylvania. It was put together with the involvement of this Lenape Nation, which I checked out on the Internet later. The website included an announcement about the powwow."

They had decided to take old Route 611, which hugged the river between Riegelsville and Easton. There was a newer Route 611—a more modern highway that bypassed the two-lane curves of the road they were on—but it wasn't nearly as scenic.

"Too bad that it's only eight miles to Easton," Dae suggested, "An hour of this would be good for my spirit."

"It's peaceful," Jeff answered, "and it's easy to see why the Indians liked it so much. It's like our place, except right on the river."

The road curved back and forth, following the contours of the Delaware. To the left were forested hillsides and rocky outcroppings, interrupted periodically by open fields or houses that sat hard by the road. To the right, the Delaware Canal snaked between Route 611 and the river. In some places, the land on the east side of the canal was wide enough to live on, so houses had been built there in spite of the danger of flooding. Somewhere in a distant pre-history, the river had cut its determined path through the mountains between central New York and the tidewaters of

Trenton, leaving just enough room for houses, roads, and canals that it would periodically wash away as testimony to its timeless power. But, on this September day, its power was content to remain dormant and flow lazily to the south.

As they approached Easton, Jeff pointed out the place where the Lehigh flowed into the Delaware. "This place was sacred to the Lenape," he said.

"I remember you saying that," Dae responded. "I don't know how many times I've been up here, and I never knew anything about the history of the place. There are a number of historic locations in Easton, some of which are designated by fancy markers, but most of them have something to do with the Revolutionary War. There was obviously a lot of history here before that."

They swung to the right, across the Lehigh River, and then took an immediate right onto the road that led to the park overlooking the forks. A few minutes later, they were walking hand-in-hand from the small parking lot to the iron fence above the falls.

"I wonder what this place looked like when the Lenape were here," Dae said. "I'll bet that it was beautiful when it was all green and forested."

"It's difficult to imagine," Jeff responded, "with all the buildings that are here now. And the parking lots and the bridges—somehow it doesn't seem sacred."

They followed the fence along the periphery of the park until they were looking east across the Delaware at the town of Phillipsburg, New Jersey. An iron bridge spanned the river immediately in front of them, connecting Northampton Street in

Easton with Union Square in Phillipsburg. The square was little more than an aggregation of buildings clustered at the base of the escarpment. Most of the unseen town sat on top of it.

Dae pointed to steps that ascended from Union Square straight up the face of the escarpment, climbing above the buildings toward a long row of houses that clung to the edge of the cliff. "That looks like quite a climb," she said. "I wonder if people still use those steps."

"I can only imagine climbing them with shopping bags or groceries," Jeff confirmed, "or maybe with a small child in your arms. But someone obviously used them at one time."

A short time later, they were back in their car and headed out of Easton. In less than a mile, they came to a place where the road curved to the right and made a huge sweeping arc around the base of a hill before continuing west.

"That curve always frightens me," Dae noted. "Why did they design the road that way?"

"From what I understand," Jeff explained, "there's a cemetery up there that pre-dates the American Revolution. There was talk about moving the cemetery when the highway was built, but it met quite a bit of resistance. We should stop up there some time. I'll bet it's really interesting."

They continued west before turning north. About fifteen minutes later, they exited the highway and curved down the ramp into the little town of Wind Gap. They had to ask three people for directions before they found someone who was able to direct them to the park where the powwow was being held.

The field in which they parked was still sloppy from two days of rain. It was passable, but only because the foot-high grass provided a buffer of sorts between their shoes and the water puddled beneath it. They slogged through it purposefully, collapsible lawn chairs in bright blue sheaths slung over their shoulders. "I hope the information on the Internet was right," Dae observed. "It wouldn't be right to carry these things around in this mess and not use them."

"Two adults," Jeff said as he peered into a small shack at the woman seated on a chair. As he handed her the admission fees he noticed that she made two neat hash marks on the tablet beside her, indicating that two more people had paid.

"I wonder," Jeff began, "if you can tell us what this is all about. The powwow, I mean. We've never been to one before."

Jeff guessed that the woman was fifty, but she moved with an effort-conserving slowness that suggested she was much older.

"Powwow heap good fun," she said dryly in a surprisingly deep voice. She broke into a broad smile before adding, "No, I'm just playin' with ya."

Jeff and Dae smiled back cautiously, remembering their conversation about stereotypes.

"A powwow is a gathering of native peoples, but all are welcome. We sing, we dance, and we socialize, but more than anything else, it's an opportunity for us to honor our culture. Excuse me for a moment." Two people approached from the parking area, handed the woman fifteen dollars, and started down the dirt road beyond the shack. As they left, she studiously added two more hash marks to the tally on the tablet. "There'll be all kinds of dancing," she finally resumed, "social, tribal, specialized. There's food, crafts . . . I think you'll enjoy it."

"Thank you," Dae said. "And thank you for your sense of humor."

"No problem," the woman said. As Jeff and Dae turned to follow the other couple down the road, she added, "And don't forget, as members of your tribe you can participate in the tribal dances."

"Oh," Dae said, looking over her shoulder, "we're not members of a tribe."

"Really?" the woman replied, her voice contorted in an awkward combination of question, incredulity, and wisdom. "Really?"

"I wonder what she meant by that," Dae offered.

"Not sure," Jeff responded. "Maybe she knows something we don't."

They set up their lawn chairs on the periphery of a large roped-off circle, in the middle of which a fire of three or four fairly large logs burned slowly, pushing a light column of white smoke into the sparkling blue afternoon. On the far side of the circle, a large canopy had been set up, under which men and drums waited patiently.

A large man in a red plaid shirt and Western hat stepped to a microphone, his long hair tied in a single braid that hung down the center of his back. He welcomed everyone, explaining that the circle was sacred and that anyone entering it should do so through the makeshift arbor that had been set up specifically for that purpose. "Please remember," he repeated, "to honor our circle. Please do not break it."

After another man said a prayer to the Great Spirit, the host came back to the microphone to announce the introduction of the colors and the entrance of veterans. Drums and voices rose in an energetic cadence as the people at the arbor began to move into the circle. One carried the flag of the United States; a second carried the familiar POW-MIA flag; and a third carried an American flag with the face of a very old Native American superimposed on the field of red and white stripes. Behind them walked a number of men and women, some in dance regalia, others in regular street clothes. After the flags were secured to the front posts of the canopy, apparently to remain there for the duration of the powwow, the host announced "The Star Spangled Banner" and everyone stood to hear it played.

Jeff whispered to Dae as the last bars of the National Anthem drifted above the canopy. "That was impressive."

"I agree," she whispered back. "The ceremony was nice, but the level of respect was awesome."

As they eased back into their lawn chairs, the host announced the grand entrance and everything in the circle jumped to life. Voices rose in unison, drums pounded, and men and women in native costumes, some of them extremely ornate, proceeded through the arbor. The colorful costumes were exhilarating to look at, and it was clear to both Jeff and Dae that the people who wore them had gone to great lengths to put them together. It was also apparent that a number of different native cultures were represented. Dancers dressed in regalia that seemed appropriate to the Plains Indians moved around the circle with people in clothing that appeared to be from the southwest, or possibly even Mexico. Others wore costumes that spoke to a specific period like the French and Indian War. It was a dazzling combination of color and creativity.

A tribal dance was announced and a number of the dancers remained in the circle to participate. As they moved around the periphery, they motioned for people sitting outside the circle to join them. Jeff felt a strange compulsion to do so, but when Dae declined, he decided to stay in his lounge chair. Later that night, lying awake in the dark, he would wonder why he hadn't joined the dance.

A large ring of tents with the wares of various vendors had been set up twenty-five yards outside of the main circle. A number of the tents offered foods, some of which were advertised as authentically Native American. Some sold books, videos, and CDs of Native American music. Others offered T-shirts, weapons—bone-handled knives and brass-headed hatchets—arrowheads, and spear points. Still others had jewelry and beaded belts and neckwear. And there was at least one vendor who was selling bird feathers, turtle and abalone shells, and animal furs.

Dae bought a heavy bracelet of elongated, polished shells that ran parallel to the wrist, and Jeff found a book about the Lenape in the Delaware Valley, playfully confirming for Dae that he now had *three* books about Native Americans.

"We're grateful for your interest in our people," the woman behind the plywood counter said as she handed Jeff his change. "Wanishi."

"You're welcome." Then, giving in to a curiosity that had been building since he and Dae had left home, he added, "Are you part of the Lenape Nation?"

"Yes," she replied. "I'm the secretary of the Nation."

"And, if I may ask, how many people are in your group?"

"About three hundred, most of us here in Pennsylvania."

"I don't mean to be rude, but are you full-blooded Lenape?"

"Oh, heavens, no. I have Lenape ancestors on my mother's side, but they're pretty far back."

Jeff looked at her quizzically, as if he was reluctant to ask more questions.

"Then why do you do this?" Dae interjected, all too willing to ask. "I mean, if you're no more Lenape than you are Irish or Italian or something else, why do *this*?"

"I appreciate the honesty of your question," the woman said extending her hand. "My name is Lydia Baker."

"Dae Phillips, and this is my husband, Jeff."

"It's nice to meet both of you, and to have you here with us." Then, returning to the conversation, she said, "It's cultural. Lenape values and the Lenape sense of things—things like living with a good heart—work for me. It's just cultural."

"I appreciate *your* honesty," Dae answered. "And I know what you mean. Belief systems are extremely important. They can make all the difference in a person's life. We don't all have to believe the same thing, but we should all believe *something* at the core of our being."

"That's a nice way to say it," Lydia Baker replied. "Very nice." Then, looking between Jeff and Dae, she added, "Here's someone you should meet. This is Raymond Last Elk Tully. Raymond is the chief of the Lenape Nation."

"Jeff Phillips," Jeff said, shaking the man's hand. "And this is my wife, Dae."

"Welcome to our powwow. It's always exciting to welcome newcomers . . ." He stopped mid-sentence, squinting at the couple as if trying to connect dots in his memory. "*Jeff Phillips*. Why is your name familiar to me?"

"I can't imagine," Jeff answered, "unless it has something to do with the remains that were found on our property last spring."

"Exactly!" Tully exclaimed. "I remember now. I read about that in the Bucks County paper. Someone sent me copies of that woman's articles."

"Yes, Grace Caufield."

"Did anything ever come of that? Were the authorities able to make a more precise identification?"

"No, not yet. In fact, the remains are still in the county facility in Warminster. We've had some inquiries. A man from Anadarko, Oklahoma, came out to see us, but . . ."

"Someone from Anadarko was out at your place?" Tully interrupted.

"Yes," Jeff responded cautiously, a little suspicious that a cat may have been let out of a bag he knew nothing about. "Forgive me," he added, wanting to change the subject, "but I'm interested in how you became a chief."

Tully hesitated, as if he wasn't quite ready to move on with the conversation, but then continued. "I was appointed by the clan mothers. It has always been the Lenape way."

"And what are your duties?"

The man paused, his eyes looking toward the ground, and it was clear to Jeff that he had unwittingly crossed another line. A temporary silence rose between them.

"I didn't mean . . ."

"No, it's alright. I get that question a lot. It just triggers quite a few things for me."

Jeff wanted to ask what had been triggered, but he thought better of it.

"My duties are organizational, like the duties of any president or chairman of an organization would be, I guess, and largely ceremonial. The problem is that the nation is not federally recognized."

"*Federally recognized?*" Dae asked.

"The federal government recognizes between five and six hundred Native American tribes in the United States. We're not one of them, so the leaders of our nation are not permitted to do what the leaders of recognized tribes are permitted to do."

"Like what?" Jeff asked, his interest intensifying. "What does that entail?'

"A federally recognized tribe has the right to form its own government and enforce its own laws. Tribal sovereignty is respected and acknowledged. For the most part, a recognized tribal government can do what a state does, but it also has the same limitations. It can't make war or coin money, things like that." His voice fell off and his stare dropped to the ground once again. "Without recognition, we can't honor our traditions—the way we marry people, the way we bury them, the way we welcome them into the world.

"And there's usually land involved," he continued. "The federally recognized tribes usually live on reservations, lands set aside for them by the government. We don't have that; in fact, our resources are quite modest. It's as simple as that." Then, having thought about what he had just said, he qualified, "It's not simple, but it's as simple as that."

"So, no Lenape tribes are recognized?"

"Two Delaware groups are recognized—the Delaware Tribe of Indians in Bartlesville, Oklahoma, and the Delaware Nation in Anadarko. Their recognition was formally restored earlier this year."

"I don't mean to be glib," Dae started, "but can't you just tag on to their recognition?"

"Actually it's an excellent question, but the answer is no, we can't. One of our tribal ways is that people are no longer recognized as members if they leave the tribe. Most of our ancestors—those of us in the nation that is—stayed behind when our people moved west. In some cases, they were protected by colonists, many through intermarriage. In others, they didn't go for personal reasons. But they all gave up membership in the tribe. So, in a manner of speaking, we don't really belong."

"It's extremely interesting," Jeff observed, "and it's kind of you to talk with us about it."

"It's kind of *you* to show such interest," Tully replied. "Now, if you'll excuse me, I have some things to attend to."

As they returned to their lawn chairs, Dae said, "I don't know about you but *that* was a lot more than I bargained for. Every time we turn around, more information comes to light. I had no idea that we would get into a conversation like that today."

"Neither did I," Jeff answered. "Believe me, neither did I."

* * *

Robert Dawes stood motionless in the central court on the second level of the Mercer Museum, an eclectic array of artifacts and implements, including a covered wagon and a boat, suspended in the air above him. On any given day, the sounds of activity in the museum would rise and fade quickly within the building's hulking concrete superstructure, but this was not any given day. It was the latest in a series of days during which construction crews had been working in one corner of the second level.

Recessed three steps into the floor, the area was situated between rooms dedicated to printing and glassblowing, and the tools and artifacts in those rooms now listened along with the director as construction noise rumbled out into the massive open space of the central court.

The noise wasn't troubling to Dawes. To the contrary, it testified to change—inspired change, at that—and he welcomed it. Conjuring anything fresh from a building full of antique tools and artifacts was extremely difficult, but this opportunity to move and expand the Lenape exhibit was allowing him to do exactly that.

His plan had met some initial resistance from the board of trustees of the historical society, but their reluctance had softened when Dawes showed them how the exhibit could be moved with a minimal amount of disruption to the building. The large corner room on the second level provided an opportunity to nearly triple the size of the exhibit without knocking down existing walls. Most of the renovations revolved around adding lighting, wall mounts for signs and placards, and supports for display cases, some of which would be in the center of the room.

What had been the most challenging was arranging for additional artifacts from various sources in the northeast. Some things had come, or would soon arrive, from other historical societies in Pennsylvania, New Jersey, and New York. Others would be provided by the National Museum of the American Indian in Washington, DC. But Dawes was most surprised by the things that had been loaned by private citizens. Authenticating them was an ongoing process, but it was obvious that many things had been passed reverently from generation to generation.

Both Emily FitzRoy and Grace Caufield were working closely with Dawes, and their joint vision included a display about why the Lenape had left the Delaware Valley and where they had gone. Emily, who had recently returned from South America, had taken responsibility for that portion of the project, believing that there were multiple sources for information and artifacts.

While still in South America, she had sent an email about the project to the Delaware people living in Oklahoma, and had indicated a willingness to travel to Bartlesville, Anadarko, or both, when she returned to the United States. In her most recent communication with Dawes, she had indicated that she was trying to get the people in both communities to meet with her.

Leaving the openness of the central court, Dawes walked to the corner where the new exhibit would be housed. Strips of overlapping plastic hung across the entrance, doing their best to keep construction dust from drifting out into the court. As he reached to separate them, he noticed that they had only been partly successful, and that a heavy layer of white dust had covered the facing windows of the adjoining exhibits. It was in the air, as well, and it drew up into his nostrils like an acrid baby powder.

"Hey," a familiar voice called from behind, and he turned to see Grace Caufield walking toward him from the stairwell.

"Hey, yourself," he responded. "Did you talk with your boss? How did it go?"

Squeezing his hand, Grace kissed his cheek, allowing her lips to linger there as long as decorum would permit. "Yes, we talked."

"And?"

"And it's going to be quite a year. He wants me to continue working on this." She nodded toward the strips of dusty plastic.

"And he'll give me the time to write the book if I agree to let the paper publish excerpts. All of which is fine with me . . ."

"Is there a *but* on the way?"

"No, I think it's an *and*, as in *and* he still wants me to cover anything pertaining to the remains found at the Phillips place, *and* he wants me to do a feature article about the new exhibit before it opens."

Dawes smiled. "You're right—it's going to be quite a year." He took her hand and led her to the middle of the floor, away from the plastic strips and white dust. As they walked, he asked, "So, what do you think you're going to write about?"

"Well," Grace began, "there are three or four books in this, or at least that's what I'm thinking at the moment. I'm intrigued by the period of time between 1701 and 1737, which is basically the thirty-six-year period between the time that William Penn left Pennsylvania for the last time and the time of the Walking Purchase."

"Yes," he smiled, "we've only talked about it a hundred times, give or take a few."

"For all intents and purposes, that period marked the death of the Lenape culture along the Delaware River. The story of how an entire culture could be brought down in such a short period of time would make a great book." She paused momentarily, wondering if she was about to put the cart before the horse. "It's probably premature," she added, "but I already have a working title: *A Sin Against God*."

"Where did *that* come from?"

"A man named George Cameron said something to me. I think I told you about him. I met him out at the Phillips property.

Anyway, he said that, 'Killing a Native American is a crime against man, but killing his culture is a sin against God.' I really like it."

"I do, as well. It's a terrific quote." Dawes paused for a moment, pondering the title. Then he added, "So, is this going to be a history book?"

"Maybe, but I've also been thinking about a historical novel. There have only been a few written about the indigenous cultures in the northeast, and there haven't been *any* written recently."

"Wow! Interesting."

"What? That so few have been written?"

"No, that you're going to write a historical novel. I guess I never thought of you as a novelist."

"You know," Grace said slowly, searching her memories of their brief time together, "I don't think I have ever heard you say 'wow.'" A wide smile crossed her face. "I think it suits you."

Dawes leaned over and gave her a small kiss on the lips. "Wow!" he said again as he drew away slowly. "Wow!"

* * *

Emily FitzRoy had been in Peru since mid-July and, having the luxury of no classes in the fall, had been able to extend her trip into September. Being the advisor to three doctoral candidates required that she return to Philadelphia soon, but, for the moment, she was relishing the final few days of her trip.

Her time in Peru had begun in the Moche Valley, only a few miles inland in the northern coastal area. She had been working with a team of anthropologists from various universities, studying the effects of destruction by Spanish treasure hunters during the colonial period. Much of the team's work had focused on two adobe brick structures that sat on opposite ends of a quarter-mile plain—Huaca del Sol, the Pyramid of the Sun; and Huaca de la Luna, now called the Temple of the Moon. Both structures had been built by the culture that inhabited the Moche Valley between 100 BC and AD 800.

Although both interesting and useful to Emily, the fieldwork had not been particularly rigorous. There had been no isolated camp in some windy desert location, no rainforest outpost ten hours from civilization. To the contrary, many of the sites in Peru were frequent destinations of tourists, many of whom arrived by cruise ship, so Emily had enjoyed both the field work and the civility of modern hotels in Peruvian cities between the north coast and the capital city of Lima—all while still being able to check in on her projects at home through the convenience of an Internet connection.

It was at the Hotel Libertador in the city of Trujillo that she had first met Lynne Pendleton, a forensic anthropologist at the University of Michigan. While collaborating on a project with a group from Berkeley, Lynne had been in a number of meetings with a doctoral candidate whose work Emily had directed two years earlier at Penn. That common acquaintance had led to a budding friendship and many conversations, one of which led to the subject of the remains in the creek bank on the Phillips property. Emily had taken Lynne through the entire process, up to and including the examination of the remains in the county forensic facility.

"I understand," Lynne had observed, "why you didn't do a toxicology test—there was no soft tissue to use—but why didn't you test the DNA?"

"We talked about it briefly," Emily had admitted, "but neither the coroner nor I saw any reason to do it."

"With bones that old, I would normally agree with you, but based on everything else you've told me, I think it's worth a shot."

"Are you suggesting that we might find markers that will help us confirm that the remains are Native American?"

"That's exactly what I'm suggesting. I mean, what do you have to lose? You're down here for another month and the bones are tucked away in a freezer in Pennsylvania. Time is hardly an issue."

"No, time is not an issue, but you know how controversial that whole thing is. The simple truth of the matter is that most people don't want to believe that we all come from a common source."

Emily hadn't followed up on the suggestion immediately. The testing that her colleague had talked about would not confirm anything with one hundred percent certainty, but it might provide some clarity. She had spent some time on the Internet, finding out where she could send bone samples, what kind of tests she could request, and how long it would take to receive the results. Eventually, following another conversation with Lynne Pendleton, she had decided to call Roy Cleveland.

"I understand what you're asking for," Cleveland had responded, "but I'm still not sure what good it will do."

"In all honesty, it may do absolutely none, *or* it may help you get those bones out of your freezer."

They hadn't talked long, mindful of both the cost and quality of a phone call between Trujillo and Warminster, but by the time they had finished, Roy Cleveland had acquiesced.

Two days later, Cleveland had followed up with Jeff Phillips.

"There's been something of a development here, Jeff," he began, "and I just want to bring you up to date."

"I appreciate it, Roy. What's going on?"

"We're going to have a full set of DNA tests run on the bones. It's possible that the tests will turn up markers that will tell us a little more about the remains."

"What are you looking for?"

"Markers in the genome."

"Genome?"

"A genome is the complete set of genes that each of us carries. There are between thirty thousand and forty thousand of them. A person's genome is the combination of the genes of his or her parents and, for the most part, it's all scrambled up. But every once in a while there's a mutation—a mutation that doesn't get scrambled up and is passed down through generations. It's called a marker.

"Some markers are passed through females—they're found in mitochondrial DNA—and some are passed through males along with the Y chromosome. They can be used to trace where a person's ancestors came from, at least in some cases, so there's an outside chance that this testing will tell us something."

"I understand. At least I think I'm following you."

"The tests seem to be most relevant among descendants of aboriginal peoples because the gene pool, if I may say it that way, is less diluted."

"That makes sense as well. So, what do you need from me?"

"Nothing, actually. I just wanted to keep you in the loop. I'll let you know when we get the results."

A few weeks later, as she sat in her quiet room at the Hotel San Antonio Abad in Lima, a small plate of food and a glass of wine on the table in front of her, Emily opened the overnight express envelope that had arrived from Arizona. She took a sip of the wine and read the first page.

Tests had been conducted on both the mitochondrial and Y-chromosome DNA. The first test, which pertained to maternal lineage, had focused on a set of five hundred sixty-nine genes in Hypervariable Region 1 of the mitochondrial DNA. The results had been compared to the Cambridge Reference Sequence—the standard mitochondrial sequence originally published in 1981 by researchers in Cambridge, England, and the catalyst for the Human Genome Project. The second test, which pertained to paternal lineage, had focused on twelve markers in the Y-chromosome DNA.

The mitochondrial test had revealed a marker from Haplogroup H, which could be traced back to a lineage that re-colonized the European continent at the end of the last ice age. It was by far the dominant Haplogroup from which women in Europe were descended. The Y chromosome test had revealed the M3 marker from Haplogroup Q3, which could be traced to a man born in North America more than ten thousand years ago, after the ice bridge across the Bering Strait had disappeared. Almost all aboriginal people in North and South America were thought to be descended from his lineage.

A knock on the door interrupted Emily's review of the material and she answered it to find Lynne Pendleton standing in the hall.

"Hello, Lynne. C'mon in."

"No, I don't want to intrude. In case we miss each other in the morning . . ." She reached out to hug Emily. ". . . I just want to tell you that I have really enjoyed working with you."

"And I with you," Emily responded as they hugged. "It's been a real pleasure. But," she added as Lynne turned to leave, "I really think you should come in. There's something I want you to see."

"Does that mean the DNA test results finally arrived? What great timing!" As she followed Emily into the room, she asked, "So, what's the story?"

"It appears as though our man may have been biracial."

* * *

It was after eight when Dae awoke from her dream, much later than she wanted to be in bed. There was too much going on, too much to be done, and she had work to do. Jeff had let her sleep. He always let her sleep, and even though she usually found it endearing, she wished that he hadn't done it on this particular morning.

She had not been sleeping well. They had been going to bed earlier of late, usually exhausted from working outside all day, and she had been waking up after four or five hours of sleep and lying awake for an hour or more. She would go back to sleep eventually, usually around four or four thirty, and sleep until seven. That was when she dreamed—the thirty to forty-five minutes before she awoke for the second time.

Her dreams had been troubling and she had no idea why. Everything was going better than anyone could have hoped. It was a busy time, even a chaotic time, but the seemingly endless buzz of activity spoke to a vibrant future—a future to be worked toward with excited anticipation.

Her dreams had also been bizarre, which was the exact word she usually used to describe them to Jeff. They were full of images and events that made absolutely no sense, as if they were the residue that was left over when all of her other dreams had been accounted for. With no place else to go, they seemed content to visit her at six thirty in the morning.

But this morning's dream had been different, and she wished again that Jeff had awakened her earlier. Her father had been there again, as had Jeff's mother. The gathering barn that was now under construction had been completed, and Dae, Jill, Hope, and others were sitting in a circle around a beautiful fire in the pit in the middle of the floor. They were talking about their parents and grandparents—loved ones from previous generations who had inspired the stories they were telling now.

As they talked, Dae was aware that others were standing around the periphery of the circle—*many* others. Her father was standing behind her, his hand resting gently on her shoulder. She raised her hand to touch his, and the mere act of touching him again caused her to cry. The others in the circle seemed unaware that she was crying, except for a woman who sat two chairs to her left, a woman she had never seen before. Looking past the man she was sitting with, she met Dae's eyes with a compassion that felt to Dae as if it had a physical presence. It was primal and unfettered; it was warm and comforting.

Others stood behind Dae. Jeff and Chick's mother was there, looking across the circle at her daughter, her grandchildren, and her great-grandchildren. Dae was keenly aware of the loving energy the woman seemed to be sending to each of them, and that awareness filled her with a peacefulness to which she would not be able to assign a word when she awoke. Jeff's sister-in-law was there, a woman who had succumbed to cancer years earlier, as was a sister-in-law of Dae's who had fought her own battle with cancer, dying just a few months before Dae and Jeff had met. At first, she was surprised to see them together, but with her very next heartbeat she understood that it could not be otherwise.

There were others around the periphery, most of whom Dae did not recognize. They stood behind Chick and Wade; they stood behind Hope and Scott, behind Jill and Edward, and behind Christopher and Catherine. A man came up to stand behind Harry, a man who looked very much like Jeff, and Dae knew immediately that it was Jeff's father. He smiled the same warm smile that Dae had seen in countless photographs, and she found herself wishing that they had known each other.

A number of people stood behind the couple to Dae's left, and many more stood behind them. They were ten, sometimes fifteen deep, filling the floor of the gathering barn with their timeless presence. There were circles of beings within circles of beings, all listening peacefully to the stories that were being told.

Deep within her dream and suddenly uncomfortably aware that Jeff was not nearby, Dae got up from her chair and turned toward the windows behind her. She saw him standing outside in the chilling November night, and motioned to him to come inside. Then, in the same instant that she feared he would not come in, she awoke with a start.

"Why didn't you wake me up earlier?" she asked of the absent husband who was undoubtedly working in the new barn. "Why did you let me sleep?"

She was fixing her hair, preparing to join the others in the upper meadow, when she felt someone watching her from the bathroom door. She turned to see Valeria standing there, dressed in a hooded sweatshirt and ready to participate in the irresistible activity in the upper meadow.

"Hi, Honey," Dae said. "Did they ask you to come find me?"

"No," the child answered. "I asked Aunt Jill where you were and she said I could come up here."

"Well, I'm glad you did. Have you had breakfast, yet?"

"A peanut butter and jelly sandwich!"

"It sounds like your grandfather has been cooking."

"Yup! Pop-Pop made it!"

"Would you like some eggs, or maybe a little cereal?"

"No, I just want to see the fish."

"Okay, but can I grab some coffee on the way out?"

"Sure!" With that, the child headed for the steps.

A few minutes later, they were approaching the gathering barn—Dae with a cup of coffee in her hand, Valeria holding a plastic sandwich bag full of bread and crackers for the koi.

The barn sat to the northeast of the main paddock. It was many times larger than the tractor shed it had replaced, but its two-story frame and high-pitched roof merged just as effortlessly with the high trees that sat behind it. It had been completely framed out, and most of the work crew was high above the ground putting shingles on the roof.

"*Buenos dias*, Mees Dae!" Roberto called from the roof, a hammer in his hand. "What a beautiful day!" He raised his arms above his head like a bird about to take flight.

"Good morning, Señor Roberto," Dae responded, echoed by the same, but far more gleeful, greeting from Valeria.

Siding had been affixed to the walls of the barn, and it was now even more evident where the high windows would go. There were ten of them on the side of the barn facing the main house and Dae knew that there would be ten on the west side, as well.

Leading Valeria by the hand, she stepped inside, where the sounds of hammering on the roof were dramatically amplified. To Dae's left, the area that would become the small apartment that Jeff had seen in his vision had been framed out and cabinets and counter tops were being installed in the kitchen. Through the open studs, she could see the steps going up to the second floor, where two bedrooms and a bathroom would be located. On the far end of the building, the stage had been framed out as well, its face already finished in stone. The same stonework had climbed halfway up the walls on both sides of the stage, and it now waited patiently to be finished.

In the middle of the floor sat the fire pit. To one side, Jeff, Jill, Ed Davies, and a man whom Dae assumed to be the coppersmith were looking at drawings spread out on a table in front of them. Valeria let go of Dae's hand and raced toward her Aunt Jill, who turned to greet her, carefully squatting behind her very round belly.

As Dae drew closer to the group, she could hear Jeff talking. "I definitely want a brown bear. 'Where the bear walks, there is wisdom.' I don't remember where I first heard that, but I have always liked it."

"I like it, too," the unidentified man said, "obviously."

"Good morning," Dae interrupted, as she looked at Jeff with an annoyed 'why-didn't-you-wake-me-up' look.

Jeff smiled back at her, obviously unaffected. "Dae, this is William Bear. He's going to do the copper work for us."

"Hello, Mrs. Phillips," the man said, extending his hand.

"Mr. Bear," she acknowledged, eliciting a giggle from Valeria.

"Is his name really Mr. Bear?" Valeria asked.

"Yes," Jill interjected, "and your name is going to be Trouble if you don't hush up while we're talking."

Valeria made the familiar motion of zipping her lips closed before giving in to a wide smile, delightfully preoccupied with the notion that the man's name was "Mr. Bear."

William Bear pointed to the large sheet of paper that had been spread out on the table, explaining that it was a scaled-down version of the face of the copper hood that would be suspended above the fire pit. A few cutouts of animals had been placed on the paper in locations the group had already decided upon. A stack of similar cutouts waited nearby.

"Some of this," he began, speaking directly to Dae, "is traditional. Virtually every indigenous culture in this country, and most others for that matter, honor the cardinal directions. Certain animals are associated with each of them. The eagle is the animal of the east, although some cultures honor other birds. The song sparrow is one that comes to mind. The dog is sometimes associated with the south, so we have been talking about using that. The mouse is another possibility. I think it's an elegant way to mark the cardinal directions on the hood."

"It is elegant, Mr. Bear." Then, as if there could be no doubt about what she was about to suggest, Dae added, "But I like the mouse for the south."

"So," Jeff interrupted, "I guess that brings us to the west." Everyone laughed, including Jeff, but in his heart he knew that whatever Dae was thinking would eventually reveal itself to be exactly right. The mouse on the copper hood would turn out to be as perfect as the koi in the fountain outside.

"The west is the bear," the coppersmith said, "and I think your husband has decided on a brown bear. Now the north, which is usually thought of as a place of wisdom, can be honored with the owl, and sometimes with the buffalo."

"That's easy," Jeff said. "We'll go with the buffalo." He paused briefly, unsure about the feasibility of what he was about to request. "And can it be a white buffalo?"

"I can probably work something out," Bear suggested. "Let me think about it."

Eight other animals were chosen to be placed in pairs between each of the animals of the cardinal directions. The deer and the otter were selected, as were the snake and the raven, although Valeria made it clear that the picture of the snake did not appeal to her at all.

"And," Jeff said, "I want to honor the people who once lived in this area."

"So," Bear answered, "the shad would be an excellent choice, as would the totems of the three Lenape clans—the wolf, the turkey, and the turtle."

"Wow," Jill exclaimed, "you seem to know a lot about them."

"A little bit. I have some Lenape blood in me, but it's pretty far back. I just know a little bit of the history."

"I think these are good choices," Jeff said. "How should we place them?"

"If," Bear began, "we were to spread the Lenape totems around the circle it might look like this." He placed the shad, wolf, turtle, and turkey to the right of the eagle, mouse, bear, and buffalo respectively. "Then, if we put the deer to the left of the eagle and . . ." He placed the remainder of the pictures on the sheet of paper.

A long silence ensued, during which everyone studied Bear's arrangement carefully. The work crew had apparently stopped for a break, and their hammering had departed with them. The only sound was made by Valeria, singing under her breath as she squirmed restlessly at Dae's side.

"Okay," Jeff said, as if he had just worked out the answer to the puzzle, "let's do this . . ." He began to move the pictures around with a disarming certainty. "The shad and the otter go next to the eagle, and the wolf and the deer go next to the mouse." He picked up four more pictures and rearranged them as he added, "The snake and the turkey go next to the bear, and the raven and turtle go next to the buffalo. That spreads out the Lenape symbols, as well as the bird energy; we still have some canine energy near the south, and . . ."

Everyone was looking at him. No one was nearly as concerned with the placement of the totems as they were with the manner in which Jeff was arranging them. He was resolute and confident, as if he had done it a hundred times before.

"What?" he asked, looking up at their stunned faces. "What's the matter?"

"Nothing," Jill offered on behalf of the group. "We're just . . ."

Before she could finish, the voice of Walt McNulty interrupted from the entrance to the gathering barn. "Hello, everyone," he said as he started toward the small group, Roy Cleveland walking with him.

"Sheriff," Jeff acknowledged. "Dr. Cleveland. What's important enough to bring the two of you out here together?"

"This is quite an undertaking," McNulty said, surveying the inside of the imposing barn. "I heard you were expanding up here, but I had no idea you were doing *anything* like this."

"We have a couple of projects going on," Jeff responded, before introducing Ed Davies and William Bear to the sheriff and coroner. "So, what brings you out here?" Jeff repeated.

Roy Cleveland spoke briefly about the DNA tests that Emily FitzRoy had requested, and the way in which he had followed up by sending bone samples of the remains to a company in Arizona. He added that it had taken almost a month to get the results, but that Dr. FitzRoy had received them on the last night of her trip to South America.

"What they revealed," Cleveland began, "is that the remains appear to be those of a man who was half Native American and half Caucasian. Dr. FitzRoy believes that the mother was of Central European descent. She wasn't any more specific than that, but she and I are going to debrief once she returns to her office at Penn."

"What does that mean with regard to the 'nearest blood relative' thing?" Dae asked.

"I think," Cleveland answered, "and I hope I'm not speaking prematurely here, that we're okay from the Native American standpoint. Your conversation with the fellow from Oklahoma seemed to confirm that. As far as the other half of the equation is concerned, I seriously doubt that anyone will come forward after three centuries."

"Roy and I were talking about it," McNulty interjected, "and we thought one possibility would be to have the woman from the *Courier Times* do an article about the DNA findings. If someone comes forward after it's printed, we'll deal with the situation accordingly; if not, Roy and I agree that the remains can be buried here."

"That sounds fair," Dae answered. "We've waited six months; we can certainly wait a few more weeks."

"I agree," Jeff chimed in. "It sounds like a reasonable approach. It was good of you to come out here to tell us. Can we get you anything?" Then, after pausing for effect, he added, "*Like a hammer?*"

"No," Cleveland laughed, "but I wouldn't mind a short tour. I never got farther than the accident site before. It would be nice to see what you're doing up here."

"I'll tell you what," Dae offered. "I'll show the sheriff and coroner around and all of you can finish the planning for the copper work."

"I'd say we're pretty close to finished," William Bear noted, looking at Jeff's arrangement of the pictures. "And I think it's going to look absolutely great."

As Sheriff McNulty, Dr. Cleveland, and Dae walked out into the sunlight, Valeria running after them, the remaining group moved toward the fire pit to iron out a few more details about the copper hood. The hammering on the roof started up again, and the ever-hopeful industry of the upper meadow resumed.

* * *

**Genetic Science Weighs In
On Identification of Remains**

Grace Caufield, *Courier Times* Staff Writer

In an interesting turn of events in the identification of centuries-old remains discovered near Riegelsville in April, genetic science may have provided the most tangible evidence to date.

The remains, which were discovered following a construction accident on the property of Jeffrey H. Phillips, R.R. 2, have been in cold storage at the Bucks County Forensic Facility in Warminster for nearly six months, awaiting any identification that might link them to a nearest blood relative to whom they can be released.

"We were prepared to keep them indefinitely," Dr. Roy Cleveland, Buck County coroner, said recently, "but these latest findings may enable us to either give them to descendants or bury them in accordance with the laws of the State of Pennsylvania."

The apparent breakthrough came as a result of DNA testing requested by Dr. Emily FitzRoy, forensic anthropologist at the University of Pennsylvania. Dr. FitzRoy is the same anthropologist who exhumed the remains from a creek bank on the Phillips property and later examined them with Dr. Cleveland in the county forensic facility.

Having recently returned from a summer project in Peru, Dr. FitzRoy explained that in early August she asked Dr. Cleveland to send bone samples from the remains to the Genographic Project at the Arizona Research Labs in Tucson. The Genographic Project specializes in tracking human migration across the globe through the identification of markers, or mutations in the human gene structure, that are passed from parent to child.

"We requested that both the mitochondrial and Y-chromosome DNA be tested," Dr. FitzRoy explained. The mitochondrial DNA includes markers that are passed from mother to child. The Y-chromosome DNA includes markers that are passed from father to son."

The results of the tests, received by Dr. FitzRoy just prior to her return to the United States, suggest that the male whose remains were found on the Phillips property may have been descended from a Native American father and a Caucasian mother. "The DNA bore two markers," Dr. FitzRoy said. "The M3 marker from something called Haplogroup Q3 was found in the Y-chromosome DNA, strongly suggesting that the subject was part Native American. The M3 marker, which can be traced to a man who was born in North America nearly 10,000 years ago, is prevalent among aboriginal people in North and South America.

"The Haplogroup H marker, which was found in the mitochondrial DNA, is common among women in Europe. It can be traced through a lineage that extends as far back as the re-colonization of Europe at the close of the last ice age."

According to a number of sources, intermarriage between whites and Indians in the Delaware River valley was not uncommon in the 1700s, a period of time which coincides with the possible age of the remains, but it usually occurred between white men and Indian women who worked for whites in various capacities. In most cases, the women were integrated into white families. The reverse—Native American men marrying Caucasian women—was less common.

"Mr. Phillips has asked that the remains be buried not far from where they were found on his property," said Walt McNulty, Bucks County sheriff, "and based on discussions with at least one Native American organization that is one possible outcome. But state law requires that the remains be released to the nearest blood relative, if one can be identified, so we still have to consider maternal descendants."

According to a spokesperson at the Genographic Project, DNA data from aboriginal people is extremely useful because it is largely undiluted, especially in situations in which people have lived in the same geographic area for hundreds, or even thousands, of years.

The five-year Genographic Project maintains that all living humans may be descended from people who lived in Africa more than 60,000 years ago. The global migration routes that they walked in the ensuing millennia, carrying with them DNA markers like the ones found in the remains of the biracial man discovered near Riegelsville, have led each of us to the time and place we occupy today.

According to Emily FitzRoy, "The project is controversial to say the least. Not everyone is willing to believe that we all come from a common place and common ancestors. Think of the impact on issues pertaining to race, religion, and politics. To me, it's mindboggling."

* * *

"*That* is complete bullshit!"

A small voice from the sofa across the room echoed, "Bullshit."

"*Where* do these fuckin' people get off hypin' this shit?"

"Fuckin' people," the small voice repeated. "Hypin' shit."

Reggie McCarthy jumped up from the easy chair and threw the newspaper to the floor, his face flushed with anger, veins pushing against the skin of his temples. He smashed his foot down onto Grace Caufield's article, slipping awkwardly before catching his balance. The near fall made him even angrier.

"Who is this bitch?" he shouted. "And where does she get off writin' this shit?"

"Writin' shit," his older brother, Darwin, repeated from the sofa. "Writin' shit, hypin' shit."

Reggie thumped around the small, congested living room of the two-story house on Center Street, tightly clenched fists at his side. He jerked first in one direction, then in another, and then in a third and fourth, not knowing where to turn or what to do next.

A woman's voice shouted loudly from the top of the steps between the living room and dining room. "Shut the fuck up, Reggie! No one wants to listen to that shit! Least of all me!"

Reggie said nothing, shooting a middle finger toward the steps as he continued to circle the room in his now-silent rant.

Darwin watched Reggie's every move, transfixed by his brother's anger but terrified of its physical manifestations. Over a period of years, Darwin had slowly adopted the practice of mimicking everything that Reggie had said, especially when he was angry, saying it more slowly in hopes that the intensity might somehow be drained out of it. There was probably a medical term to describe what he suffered from, but it had long since been forgotten, along with the other details of conversations with specialists in birth defects and disorders of the brain. His mother called him "shy," a term that she remembered from a movie, although she couldn't remember which one, but everyone knew that it was just another way to say "not right." And after early abuses from his father, the breakdowns of his eventually widowed mother, and the maturation of Reggie into what his mother called "one worthless piece of shit," any shot that Darwin McCarthy ever had at "rightness" had grown as dim as the forty-watt bulb at the foot of the cellar steps.

Slowly settling down, more out of exhaustion from anger than a desire to alter his state of mind, Reggie moved between a pile of magazines and two mostly dead plants in front of the window that looked out onto Center Street. He stood there, staring out at the inactivity of the evening, and muttered to himself.

"There ain't no white man that comes from a nigger. Those scientists are fucked up! That shit ain't nothing but stirrin' up trouble!"

"Stirrin' up trouble," Darwin repeated.

"And who cares about some fuckin' bones, anyway?"

"Fuckin' bones anyway."

"I don't give a shit if some no good injun was porkin' a white woman hundreds of years ago, and nobody else in this country gives a shit about it either. What the fuck? They're dead now. Why even drag that kind of shit up?"

"Porkin' a white woman. What the fuck?"

"This is just the media spreadin' its lies. I hate this shit! I'm gonna give this bitch something to write about!"

He turned around and stormed from the room, shouting at his brother as he disappeared into the kitchen. "And stop sayin' what I say, you *imbusel*."

"*Im-bu-sel*," Darwin repeated slowly, mimicking his brother perfectly.

Seventeen

OCTOBER 1734

He had tried repeatedly to find her on his journeys to the animal world, to talk with her in the field of vervain, the white buffalo standing nearby, but his efforts had been in vain. His journeys and visions had continued, and, in many ways, they were even more powerful than before, but only when they were for the benefit of someone else who required his shamanic help. His ability to journey on his own behalf had diminished. Everything had happened so effortlessly for him during his time with Four Bears, but she had been gone for seven winters, and things were different.

He still saw her in his dreams, and each time he saw her he found himself not wanting to wake up. He wanted to stay with her, even if staying meant his own death in the physical world. Seeing her or talking with her sometimes made him cry, and when that happened he would release his emotions in a raw, uninhibited way that forced him from his dream, head pounding. In one dream, when he began to cry as Four Bears spoke about his mother, his teacher touched his arm and said, "We cry in our dreams when we are unable to cry in life."

Lying on his side in the wigwam, his head resting on his outstretched arm, he waited patiently to drift into sleep. The humidity that lingered behind a warm and rainy day slowly pulled beads of moisture from the base of his shaved skull before sending them on slow, tortuous journeys down his neck and across his shoulder. Reaching back periodically to wipe them away did little more than momentarily clear the skin so that more could take their place.

Sleep waited a few steps away, silently taunting him but never coming forth to envelope him. He breathed deeply, trying to go to it, but the space between them remained. Unable to dream about her, he let himself think about her, and his thoughts wandered to the time and place of her burial.

They had buried Four Bears in the shadow of the escarpment, not far from the small cluster of wigwams, when the sun had already begun its descent toward the top of the canopy. The place was well removed from the path, nestled in a small group of trees and not likely to be disturbed by anyone, even inadvertently. And it was close to the sacred forks, a location that would have pleased her.

Storyteller had tended to the body and a number of people, including His Spirit Watches, had prepared the grave. It was less than four feet deep, dug by His Spirit Watches with a solemnity and sense of purpose that touched Walks Alone deeply. He could not remember ever having seen anyone so beyond distraction. The women had helped by lining the grave with reeds and preparing a clay jar of food intended to nourish Four Bears on the long journey to the highest heaven.

They had placed her in the grave fully clothed, her linen shirt washed clean of the dried blood that had come forth to foretell the end of her life. She was buried like many of her ancestors— on her side, with arms folded against her chest and knees bent close to her torso—and without adornment. Only her medicine bundle, tucked under her left hand, had been placed in the grave with her.

A group of men and women had assembled at the grave, mixing with the surrounding trees in an elegant combination of people and nature, and all had waited respectfully for Walks Alone to speak.

Now, as he lay on his stomach in the gathering October night, the many things that he had felt then came rushing back to him in a wave of conflicting emotions.

He had been nervous, not wanting to say anything that would be out of alignment with the old ways, and even though he had spent hours thinking about what he wanted to say, the words had not come easily.

"Four Bears . . ." The words had lodged in his throat.

He was sad, tears welling in his eyes at the thought of losing his teacher to the black earth that was about to cover her.

"She . . ."

Even with so many people nearby, he felt utterly alone. It was in that place of isolation that he realized a hand was on his shoulder, and an instant later he understood that it was the hand of Storyteller.

"Your heart is good," she whispered. "That is why she wanted you to do this. Let your heart speak for you."

Walks Alone closed his eyes, taking a deep breath.

"It is good," he began, "that she will be here at Lechauwitank forever. From the highest heaven, she will look down with gratitude that we placed her here in this sacred ground.

"Soon she will travel the path marked in the sky by the stars of Ane, and everything she was to us will go with her." He paused for what felt to him like too long a time. "But everything she meant to us will remain here in our hearts."

With the last of the words, he felt the hand of Storyteller squeeze his shoulder gently in silent affirmation that the goodness of his heart had shown itself.

"This is my prayer," he added, "that the Great Spirit, who let his light shine through her and onto each of us, will allow it now to shine through us and onto all beings. And may each of us be worthy of that light."

Nothing else had been said. The body of Four Bears covered over, most of the people moved to the center of the small village of wigwams to sit and talk, to eat and tell stories. Only His Spirit Watches and Walks Alone remained by the grave, and by the time darkness had fallen the boy found himself alone. As he sat cross-legged, slowly sifting loose ground between his fingers, countless stars came to illuminate the summer night. He imagined Four Bears touching each of them as she made her journey to the highest heaven.

Walks Alone awoke with a start. He had drifted into sleep while thinking about the burial of Four Bears, but had only slept briefly. Now he thought that he might not be able to find sleep again, and he was discouraged by the prospect of facing the following day with little or no rest. He breathed deeply, trying to journey, trying to sleep, but willing to accept whatever the sticky darkness would allow.

Whether in journey or dream, he finally drifted off and went to a place that he had first seen seven winters earlier while alone in the early morning darkness of the wigwam of Talks For Us. He had returned to the place many times since, each time lost in the same dark confusion, each time hearing the discomforting words of the white buffalo: *Such is the path of the Lenape.*

As it had been each time, the path was confining, facing him toward the place where the sun sets and moving him that way as if he had no choice in the matter. The thicket of the forest floor pressed in on him from both sides, and the trees pushed down from above with a suffocating malice. He moved slowly, making his difficult way along the path, vines tripping him at nearly every step, thorns and bramble scratching his bare legs.

Then, as had happened in each of these visions, all was transformed as trees, brush, and rocks flew in every direction, as if swept aside by the hand of the Great Spirit himself, clearing a vast path to the west. He felt relief as the oppression lifted, and, for a moment, he stood silently, taking in a deep breath. But before he could take even a single step, the white horses thundered down on him from behind, as if driven by some unseen dark malevolence. Unable to get out of their way, he simply gave in to their fury, feeling them pound by and watching them disappear along the cleared path.

He didn't have to turn around to know that the white buffalo was standing behind him. It had been there every time before.

"What does it mean?" he asked without turning. "I know that 'such is the path of the Lenape,' but what does it mean?"

There was no response.

"But why would you come to me so many times . . .," he began, turning to face the beast. Then he stopped short, the question trailing into silence, as he looked not at the white buffalo, but at Four Bears. She smiled at him reassuringly, but said nothing.

"Why have you come, my teacher?" Even though the words had been said, the question remained, fixed in the pained look in his eyes. "Have you come to tell me the meaning of this message?"

Four Bears looked back at him with a deep compassion, but remained silent. Then she turned and walked away slowly in the direction from which the three horses had come.

"'Such is the path of the Lenape,'" Walks Alone called after her. "Please tell me what it means!"

But his teacher had disappeared. He tried to call out to her again, but when he opened his mouth nothing came out. His words were held back by the same dryness that lodged in his throat as he opened his eyes in the wigwam.

The sun was just above the horizon when he went to the wigwam of Talks for Us and Looks Back. He was only a few paces away when his uncle stepped from the entrance and into the refreshing coolness that had come with the new day. They exchanged greetings and then moved toward a large maple tree, beneath which they could sit and eat their morning meal while still keeping an eye on the path that led to the river.

As they ate, talking about the day that lay ahead, the village began to awaken around them. Activity was slow and isolated at first, but soon there were about a dozen people moving around in the light of the early morning. Walks Alone wanted to say something to his uncle about the dream and Four Bears, but he decided to wait until another time. Distracted by movement off to his right, he looked to see the massive form of His Spirit Watches walking toward them from the river. As was his way, the man had spent the night in solitude somewhere beyond the edge of the village. A thin smile curved his lips as he approached—a silent sign of affection for the boy with whom he had been through so much.

An hour later, they were walking to the place the white people called the Durham Iron Works. It was neither a long nor difficult journey, about half of which transpired on the well-worn path along the river.

It was mid-morning when they reached the large, noisy foundry by the river. The building and everything around it buzzed with activity that was familiar to the three men, if still somewhat mysterious. They moved confidently, having been invited along with other Lenape by the white man Logan, but ever aware that this was not their world. "It may be near Lenapewihittuk," Walks Alone thought to himself, "but the Lenape do not belong here."

The blast furnace had been built seven winters earlier, following the discovery of iron ore in the nearby Durham Hills. Walks Alone remembered the time well, as it was both the summer of his vigil and the summer in which Four Bears had died. Now well established, it produced a curious combination of things used by the whites—things like iron stoves on which they prepared food—and sent them by boat to Coaquannock and places even farther downriver.

As they moved toward the place where the meeting was to take place, Walks Alone noticed a group of men doing some work nearby. They were cutting wood, most likely to fuel the furnace, and they dripped with sweat in the gathering heat of the day. Walks Alone thought he recognized one of the men as the taller of the two who had threatened Four Bears and him on their way to Lechauwitank, but he couldn't say for sure. It had been a long time ago, and his only vivid memory of that moment was that of His Spirit Watches emerging from the woods.

The men stopped working to watch the three Lenape men pass. The tall man looked directly at Walks Alone, but didn't seem to recognize the young, muscular man of eighteen who had replaced a lithe boy of eleven. He did, however, recognize His Spirit Watches, and he began to move toward him angrily, axe in hand. Walks Alone could not imagine what would cause the man to challenge the massive Lenape, unless, he thought, the man had somehow been emboldened by alcohol, the presence of so many other whites, or both. His Spirit Watches looked at him cautiously but without fear, wisely unwilling to jeopardize anything that might happen in the meeting about to take place with the whites. He just watched the man approach.

Shouting words that Walks Alone did not understand, although he knew that they were profanity, the man had drawn to within five feet of His Spirit Watches when a voice shouted from the entrance to the iron works.

"You, there, with the axe! I don't know what the problem is, but I strongly suggest that you leave it be! Unless, of course, you would prefer to work somewhere else."

The man paused, and without looking toward the man who had shouted, called out, "Sorry, Mr. Logan. I thought he was someone else."

Walks Alone knew that it was a lie, and as he watched His Spirit Watches walk on, he knew that the man named Logan had unwittingly kept the tall man from being badly injured, if not killed.

On the other side of the building, near the river, a small group of Lenape had gathered for the meeting. In the center stood two sachems—Nutimus of the Munsee people in the north, and the aged Tishcohan, who lived in the village at Hockyondocquay and was easily recognizable because of his reluctance to wear tattoos. The group welcomed the three men warmly, and even though they had met Walks Alone before, the two chiefs now addressed him with an obvious reverence. Walks Alone acknowledged them humbly.

Within an hour, a meeting had convened on the bank of the river. Two white chiefs participated, including Thomas—one of the sons of William Penn—and James Logan, who was one of the owners of the iron works and the man who had prevented a confrontation between the tall man and His Spirit Watches. Near them sat an interpreter who had been hired to ensure that the two sides understood each other as clearly as possible.

Walks Alone knew that relations between the Lenape and the whites had been strained. The whites, under the leadership of Logan and the sons of Onas, had been granting rights to lands on which the Unami and Munsee still lived, and which had never been included in treaties. The Lenape had been making agreements directly with settlers without consulting with Logan and the Penns. Both sides were upset, and the meeting had been called to address their respective grievances.

At one point, Logan stood up and spoke of something that had happened many years earlier. Holding a piece of paper and addressing Nutimus and Tishcohan, he said, "Forty-eight winters ago, your fathers and the great Onas made an agreement—an agreement that lives in this deed between them. They agreed that Onas and his sons were entitled to Indian lands that stretch for as far as a man can walk in a day and a half. It is written here, and we ask that you honor this agreement on behalf of your fathers."

Looking at Nutimus and Tishcohan, the interpreter told them what James Logan had said.

"It must be," Nutimus responded, "that since most of the lands in the south have already been sold to you by our Iroquois brothers, this deed must concern lands in the north—the lands of my people."

"Yes," Logan answered immediately behind the translation into English. He then explained where it had been agreed that the walk would start.

Nutimus did not answer.

After a considerable pause, during which both the Indians and the whites held side conversations, Tishcohan said, "We know nothing of this agreement with Onas. It was many years ago and none of us know about it. Our fathers would have spoken about any such agreement with Onas, and a wampum belt would have been given to validate the agreement."

"But the deed is real," Logan protested. "I hold it here in my hand."

Nutimus and Tishcohan were unmoved. They did their best to be cordial, but it soon became evident that they would not acquiesce. There was more talking, there was eating and drinking, and there was smoking, but there was no agreement that Logan and the Penns were entitled to what they were claiming.

On their way back upriver to the village, the three men spoke of the events of the day. They talked about many outcomes, very few of which were favorable to the Unami people, and it now seemed as if the Munsee would be affected, as well.

"They will push this," Talks For Us noted calmly. "Logan and the sons of Onas do not have enough land to sell to the many whites who want it. They will push this."

* * *

Autumn had eased into Bucks County on late September days that tucked mild afternoons between cool mornings and evenings with an effortless grace. Even the rains seemed content to fall in the darkness of the pre-dawn mornings, as if unwilling to spoil even a single moment of the approaching days. As Jeff Phillips made the short climb from the creek to the upper meadow, small bits of grass stuck to the tops of his work boots, temporarily affixed by the residue of the light rain that had fallen earlier.

At the top of the hill, he looked in on the koi, not yet convinced they would do well in cooler weather, even though Dae and Jill had explained how the water plants they had added to the pond would create an ecosystem in which the fish would flourish year-round. They swam back and forth just below the surface of the water, their bright colors appearing and disappearing beneath the flat leaves of the water plants, seemingly oblivious to the cool October morning. "Let me know if it gets too cold in there," he said to a bright orange fish. "I've been up here in January and, believe me, it's no time for swimming." The fish continued on their endless back-and-forth journeys, apparently unconcerned about possible changes in the weather.

The gathering barn was beginning to take shape. The windows were in, and they admitted the morning light in grand splashes of yellow and gold, dappled by the shadows of the tall trees to the east. As he saw the incredible amount of light they allowed inside, Jeff was glad he had insisted on such large windows.

In the middle of the floor, the fire pit waited like a small, round swimming pool. Jeff was intrigued by the notion that it was a fire pit in which there had never been a fire. The concrete was clean and gray, without the slightest trace of the ash and black smears of soot that would soon mark it for the rest of its days. It was a curious thing to him—the way in which something never meant to be pristine had to be that way at first, as if only a blank canvas could be painted by destiny.

Strangely unwilling to keep the fire pit from its destiny for even one more minute, he went behind the stage to the area where firewood would eventually be stored. In addition to the handful of logs that had been piled there, he was surprised to find a box of synthetic logs, probably left behind by someone on the construction crew who wanted to confirm that the flue above the pit was drafting properly. A few seconds later, he had placed one of the logs in the middle of the pit and lit its brightly colored wrapper. Flames drew toward the emptiness of the aluminum flue, small harbingers of the greater fires to follow.

Jeff pulled a folding chair away from the nearby work table and, setting it directly in front of the burning log, sat down to enjoy the sight. The wrapper burned away quickly, leaving the first of many black marks on the floor of the fire pit. It was a minor thing, Jeff thought, but something that needed to be done—an initiation that was his to perform, and one that he felt compelled to do alone. He sat in the chair and stared at the small, slowly growing fire as the sun rose above the tops of the trees and cast its full, warming light on the meadow beyond the windows.

He opened his knees and began to tap on the edge of the chair, alternating hands in a primal beat—thud-thud; thud-thud; thud-thud. His wedding ring inadvertently struck the metal, adding a different sound that he integrated into the beat with a satisfied smile. Thud-thud-clink; thud-thud-clink. He thought about the powwow and the Indians in bright regalia dancing around the periphery of the circle, the slowly burning logs only a few feet away, and the thought was followed closely by regret that he hadn't danced with them when invited. Thud-thud-thud-clink; thud-thud-thud-clink; thud-thud-thud-clink. He raised his weight off of the chair and the sound transformed into something akin to that of rain striking a tin roof. Bing-bing-bing-clink; bing-bing-bing-clink. And, before long, he was integrating all of the sounds into a beat of his own creation. It rose into the early morning light—the tempo of a one-man powwow; the drumming of a single heart.

He continued his metal chair drumming as the synthetic log burned, and to anyone entering the gathering barn at that moment, it probably would have sounded like a poor substitute for something more authentic. But to Jeff it was authentic, because what he was feeling had nothing to do with a wedding ring striking a metal chair or rain hitting a tin roof. What he was feeling was the timeless resonance of the drums at the powwow, the same resonance that had risen in the air above the Delaware for thousands of years. He heard the drums; he felt the resonance. He heard the voices . . .

Jeff stopped drumming, certain that he had heard something not of his making. He had heard a male voice, chanting along with his silly drumming on a metal folding chair. It had come to join him as if somehow seduced by the beat, and with obvious forgiveness for his clumsy noisemaking and the fire of a fake log. He was sure of it.

He listened closely, but the only sound in the gathering barn came from an occasional crackle of the log. The voice was gone.

"Dad?" Jill's voice interrupted the moment from the doorway.

Jeff turned toward her, the sound of the unknown voice still echoing in his mind. "Good morning. Did you rest well, or is the baby waking you up these days?"

"She's pretty active. I keep telling her that she still has a ways to go, but I don't think she's listening."

"*She?*"

"Yeah, I'm pretty sure it's a girl. I tell the nurse at the doctor's office that I don't want to know what it is, mostly because I already know that it's a girl."

"So, what are you going to name my granddaughter?"

"Well," she offered, a thin smile curving her mouth, "after careful consideration, we've ruled out Gertrude."

"Good," Jeff played along. "It worked for Hamlet's mom, but it's not every woman who can pull that name off."

"Well then, until we come up with an alternative you'll just have to wait like everyone else. We still have six or seven weeks to settle on a name."

As they were talking, Dae came in, holding her trademark mug of morning coffee. "Hey, guys. Great morning isn't it?"

In response, Jeff asked, "What do you think of Gertrude?"

"As what?"

"As a name for the baby, of course. It's at the top of the list."

"Well, karma's a bitch," Dae said to Jill. "You may have a granddaughter of your own someday, and unless you like Temperance or Agnes you may want to re-think Gertrude."

"Geez, Dae," Jill laughed, "it was a joke, but I get the message. We'll go with something a little more *current*."

"And what's this?" Dae asked, pointing toward the fire pit. "Is it some kind of test?"

"It was just too new," Jeff offered, "and too clean. I thought I'd break it in."

Dae smiled cynically, even though his response hadn't surprised her at all. "The hood looks great," she said changing the subject. "William Bear really did a good job." She walked around the pit slowly, her gaze never leaving the images of animals hammered into the copper hood. Completing her review at the southernmost point, she smiled approvingly and said, "And this is the direction of Mr. Mouse."

"You're right," Jeff said, ignoring the mouse comment. "It's wonderful work."

"Well," Jill began, "we're taking Valeria to the airport to pick up her mom. Seeing Hope was all she could talk about last night. Do either of you need anything while we're down that way?"

"No, I think we're good," Dae answered.

Jill took a few steps toward the door before turning around, as if she had forgotten something. "I spoke with Ed Davies before he left yesterday afternoon, and he thinks the barn will be done in another two weeks. Most of the remaining work is in the apartment. Then they're going to focus on Hope's house. In fact,

they plan to go over some changes with Hope while she's here."
She turned again to leave.

"Wait up, Jill," Dae called after her. "I want to see that little
girl before you guys leave." She gave Jeff a quick kiss on the cheek
before saying, "Walt McNulty wants you to call him. He said he's
been trying to reach you." As she turned to follow Jill she added,
"I won't tell you what I said about you and your cell phone."

Alone by the fire pit once again, Jeff stared down at the
synthetic log. It had begun to break into pieces but was still
burning hotly. He smiled as he envisioned the black scar that it
would leave behind, satisfied with his small act of initiation. In
another two weeks, the barn would be a reality. In another few
months, Hope's house would be completed and he would have a
new grandchild. Through it all, he was quite sure that he would
be checking regularly to see if the koi were still alive. For a fleeting
moment, he was filled with contentment, a feeling that he neither
liked nor trusted regardless of how good it felt. He said a small
prayer of gratitude and then did his best to shake the feeling off.

He was leaving the gathering barn when he felt the pain in
his chest. It was severe and suffocating, and it suddenly occurred
to him that this might be something different than the pain of
an oncoming vision, that this might be a heart attack. But even
though the pain was different—stronger, intensified—the result
was exactly the same. He found himself in a different time.

He was still in the gathering barn, but the building was
crowded with people who were seated in neat rows facing the
stage. The synthetic log in the fire pit had been replaced with
a wood fire that was measured and inviting, like those in the
fireplace in the main house. The room was already warm from

the presence of so many people; too large a fire would have made it unbearable. As he watched with the others, a group of small children walked onto the stage, accompanied by Hope and a striking young girl who looked to be in her mid-teens. He knew immediately that it was Valeria.

The children looked like any elementary school class, and Jeff smiled warmly as Hope ensured that they were in their proper places on the stage. Valeria took a seat at the piano, adjusting the bench beneath her. Jeff was struck by how lovely she was. He wasn't surprised; he was just caught off guard by the commanding presence of the child he knew only as a gleeful four-year-old.

At Hope's signal, Valeria began to play and the children joined together in a song that Jeff had never heard before. Their singing was absolutely beautiful, and it drifted out across the floor of the gathering barn in waves of audible joy.

This vision was different from any that had preceded it. It was so peaceful, so completely filled with grace, that he looked for neither its message nor a reason for experiencing it. It was transcendence within transcendence, and he found himself praying that if there were even deeper levels he would experience them, as well.

Drifting into his reverie, he was aware of the additional beings who had gathered in the barn. They stood behind the people who were seated; they sat cross-legged on the floor immediately in front of the stage; and they stood outside, calmly watching through the huge windows, their presence sending a light as strong as that of the early morning sun. At first, they stood quietly, but they soon joined their own voices to those of the children, causing the entire building to vibrate with vocal beauty.

When the song was over, everyone applauded wildly, calling out their approval with complete abandon. Jeff had never seen anything like it.

At another signal from Hope, the children scurried to the sides of the stage and then returned to their places with strange items of all sorts. They brought back milk crates and empty plastic bottles; kitchen pots and small pieces of two-by-four; metal mixing bowls and empty paint cans. And they brought back things with which to bang on all of them.

Rising from the piano bench, Valeria retrieved a metal folding chair from the side of the stage and set it in front of the piano. She sat down and, dropping her hands to the edge of her seat, said, "Like most of these children I grew up with this, and like most of these children I grew up with it because someone taught me how to do it. For me, it was my grandfather." With that, she began to tap a beat on the edge of the chair, sometimes striking it with the rings on each of her hands. The children joined in with excited anticipation, following Valeria's beat and improvising beats to complement it.

What seemed to have no possible result other than discord gradually blended in an uplifting unison that brought everyone in the barn to their feet. They raised their voices with the beat in a euphoria that seemed capable of lifting the building from its foundation.

The makeshift drumming ended with Valeria banging the edge of her chair with crowning emphasis. Then, as the cheering erupted once again, she looked out across the throng of people and smiled at Jeff. It was in that moment that he found himself back in the solitude of the barn, the synthetic log all but burned to a small rectangle of ashes. It would be another hour before he left the building. He just stood there, transfixed, watching the side of the stage where he knew a piano would one day stand.

* * *

He sat in the sweat lodge watching the low glow of the single stone in the pit. It had put off enough steam to cause the child to sweat lightly, and he hoped that it was enough to keep his fever from rising. The child was four years old, less than half the age of Quiet Bird, and tending to him reminded Walks Alone that he was called upon to care for very few children these days. There seemed to be fewer and fewer of them with each passing winter. He had often listened to Looks Back as she ruminated about a time when infants were far more numerous. She had described the curious eyes with which they would look out on the sights of the village, secure in cradleboards on the backs of their mothers. Now cradleboards were rare and the future they once foretold was far more difficult to imagine.

He added some chestnut leaves to water that was heating in a small bowl in the pit, stirring them slowly into a brown tea. The brew began to bubble and he set it aside, wanting it to cool before he gave it to the child.

Many things had changed. Very few people remained in the village. Many Lenape had moved to the west, many as far as the next great river, but some to rivers even farther away. He wondered silently if they had found a home where they could live according to the old ways. He wondered if such a place even existed.

There were others like him, the children of mixed marriages, but nearly all of them lived in the white villages where their fathers lived. Intermarriage had forever changed the old way of remembering ancestors through the lines of the mothers, and the old way in which a man would go to live with the people of his wife. Villages had once grown accordingly; now, they weren't growing at all.

Even the role of a shaman had changed dramatically in his short lifetime. Under different circumstances, he would have had an opportunity to spend more time at the side of Four Bears, more time to learn about his responsibilities. Having instructed him in the use of herbs and plants, she had made something of a *nentpike* out of him, but he knew he had so much more to learn about the use of medicinal herbs. They had gathered many different plants in the forest, and he had come to understand their healing powers, as well as their dangers if used incorrectly, but there had been precious little time for the subtleties of herbalism—the subtleties that waited where science and spiritualism converged.

He also believed that more time with her would have made him a better *meteinu*, a spiritualist who knew how to treat a person's spirit as well as their body, a shaman who could ward off the effects of witchcraft and the presence of negative spirits. She had told him often that he had less to learn as a meteinu than he might think, and that the powers that were so evident in his journeys, visions, and dreams spoke to a spiritual maturation that was far beyond his physical age. He had been to the Place with No Words and he had journeyed there effortlessly, almost as if it were his right to do so, and she had been clear that such a thing was not to be taken lightly. In his heart, he knew that what she had told him was true, but since her death his abilities had become curiously restricted to helping others. The Place with No Words seemed beyond his reach, and his inability to do at eighteen what he had done at eleven stoked the fires of his self-doubt.

"Nentpikes and meteinus are old and wise," he said to the silence of the sweat lodge. "They are gray healers who have learned with both their heads and their hearts. If I were twice my age I might be ready to be one of them, but I am not twice my age." He paused, not wanting to appear ungrateful to the Great Spirit, but the words leaked out of his mouth with the negative emotion. "Perhaps I am not ready."

He reached down and placed a hand behind the child's head, gently raising it enough to allow him to drink some of the chestnut tea. The mere act of doing so resurrected the subconscious memory of having his teacher drip tea on his lips when he was fighting the rabies. The child coughed lightly but took in a good amount of the tea, and Walks Alone said a small prayer that the elixir would do its work well.

The covering on the entrance to the sweat lodge moved to the side and the face of Talks For Us appeared in the opening. He said nothing, waiting for a signal from his nephew. Walks Alone nodded slightly, silently inviting him into the sweat lodge.

"How is the child?"

"His fever is still high, but the tea is breaking its hold."

"You sat with him through the night. You must be tired."

"I will sleep when this is over. Tonight, perhaps."

Talks For Us sat quietly, emotionally walking a line between respect for a shaman and love for his nephew. He was there for support. Walks Alone knew it and he was grateful.

"Uncle," he began, breaking the silence, "please speak with me about my parents."

"I will speak with you about whatever you desire," Talks For Us answered, "but I don't know what I can say about your mother and father that I have not already said."

"Then perhaps that is what I need to hear. Perhaps if you say it often enough your words will fill this great void in my heart."

Talks For Us looked at the stone in the fire pit. Its glow was diminishing. His heart had ached many times for his nephew, but never so much as it had since Walks Alone had learned about his mother. It was inevitable that he would find out, and it was right that his teacher had been the one to tell him, but Talks For Us still found himself wishing that he could have been spared the great emptiness about which he now spoke.

Still staring into the fire pit, Talks For Us began to speak in soft, reverent tones, as if he were sitting in circle in the lodgehouse telling a story of ages past.

"Your mother's name was Margaretha, and she was very young when she and your father met—the age that you are now. Her people came from across the waters from a place called Germany, which is a different land than the land of Onas. They had very little, so when they came here they had to work for many winters to repay the people who owned the ship that brought them. They labored on a farm within sight of the mountain at the place we call Pocacuintink.

"The whites who owned the farm had a small child who became very ill. He was dying and his mother and father could not find anyone to help him." Talks For Us looked up at Walks Alone, who was now sitting with his eyes closed, as if seeing in his mind each of the things that Talks For Us was describing. "There are many powerful plants on that mountain, and the whites knew that Lenape women went there to gather them. One of the women was your teacher, Four Bears, and the whites had heard many things about her powers. They sent a man to our village, asking that she attend to their child. Your father walked back to the farm with Four Bears."

"And," Walks Alone interrupted softly, his eyes still closed, "my teacher saved the child's life using plants that few are aware of, plants that the whites sent my mother to gather, plants that Four Bears sent my father to find."

"Yes. The whites would not have known where to look."

The child began to stir and Walks Alone knew that the chestnut tea was working. "I must get another stone," he said, beginning to rise to his feet.

"I will do it," Talks For Us said, honored to help care for the child in any way. He transferred a stone from the low fire outside, carefully placing it in the fire pit. Walks Alone ladled just enough water onto it to elicit a quick hiss, like the warning of a snake before it turns to slither away.

Returning to his place, Talks For Us continued his familiar story. "Your mother's people were not pleased with the affections that she developed for Black Turtle, but the parents of the girl abided him because of the part he had played in saving their child's life. They did not object when he came to their farm, but in their hearts, I think, they always believed that their daughter would one day see the hopelessness of the situation.

"Your father and I spoke many times about the relationship, and as I have told you, I too questioned the wisdom of it out of love for my brother. But, even as I spoke, I could see what was in his eyes and sense what was in his heart, and I knew that my words were useless."

"Did my mother come here," Walks Alone asked, "to our village?"

"No," his uncle replied, "not often. When she did, she was treated warmly, as you would expect, yet everyone knew that it was not a good thing for her to do."

"Then they were married."

"Yes, they were married here, by Four Bears, and I knew from the look in their eyes that your mother was already with child. They tried foolishly to keep their union a secret from the whites, but within a few months it became impossible."

"And that is when the whites banished her?"

"Yes." Reluctant to continue the painful story, Talks For Us looked away, his sullen stare coming to rest on the glowing stones in the fire pit.

"And in the winter," Walks Alone began, telling the next part as if he had heard it many times and repeated it in his mind many times more, "my mother died giving birth to me."

"Yes," Talks For Us agreed, "there was nothing that could be done to save her."

"And my father? Tell me his story again."

"He lived the rest of his days with an empty heart. I am sure that he lived on only because of you, trying to set aside the pain of losing your mother. He became ill while you were still a small boy. Under different circumstances, he might have recovered, but his empty heart gave the sickness an advantage that could not be overcome . . ." He paused for what seemed like a long time, his final thought unwilling to be voiced to the humidity of the sweat lodge. ". . . not even by Four Bears."

Walks Alone raised the child's head to give him more tea. The boy swallowed more of it this time, which Walks Alone read as a sign that the illness was weakening. "He's getting better," he said, ladling a small amount of water onto the stone. "This is enough steam. I will remove the stone."

"I will do it," Talks For Us said, beginning to rise.

"No," Walks Alone responded. "I will do it." Using two stout sticks, he lifted the still-glowing stone from the pit and moved it outside. His movements were considered and deliberate, as if he had already moved beyond the conversation about his parents.

But Talks For Us knew that every detail was still with him, burdening his heart with more weight than that of five sweat lodge stones. He wanted to say something, but he thought better of it. He knew that his words would be wasted, much like the words he had said to Walks Alone's father years before when he had cautioned him about the relationship with Margaretha. He remembered the look on Black Turtle's face—a look that can only be worn by a young man in love—when his brother had turned to him and answered, "But, Brother—this is my destiny."

Remains To Be Interred After
Okay By County Coroner's Office

Grace Caufield, *Courier Times* Staff Writer

Human remains that were found in northeastern Bucks County nearly seven months ago will be formally interred tomorrow not far from where they were accidentally discovered. Permission to inter the bones was given by the Bucks County Coroner's

Office following a state-mandated search for direct descendants.

"We have been working closely with the sheriff's office," said Dr. Roy Cleveland, county coroner, "and we're both satisfied that a reasonable attempt to find living descendants has been made. With remains this old the odds of finding 'nearest blood relatives,' as they are referred to by state law, was very remote, but we still went through the required processes."

Sheriff Walter McNulty confirmed Dr. Cleveland's assessment, saying, "I'm satisfied that nothing more could have been done."

The remains, believed to be those of a male, possibly of mixed race, will be buried on the property of Jeffrey H. Phillips, R.R. 2, Riegelsville, about a half mile from where they were found. Mr. Phillips offered to provide a permanent site for the remains shortly after they were discovered, but the coroner's office was not willing to authorize interment until legal requirements were met.

Because some people believe that the remains are those of a person who was part Native American and part Caucasian, every precaution was taken to ensure that possible descendants were made aware of their discovery. According to Seth Williams of NAGPRA, "The Phillips family thought it was important to notify the descendants of the Native Americans who once lived in this area. They were known as the Lenape then, but are now referred to as the Delaware."

NAGPRA, or the Native American Graves and Repatriation Act, was established by Congress in 1990. Its authority extends only to situations in which remains are discovered on federal lands.

"Under the law," Mr. Williams continued, "the Phillips family has every right to do as they wish with the remains. We are grateful that they have chosen this course of action."

Mr. Williams explained that two different groups of Delaware people in Oklahoma were contacted about the discovery in Bucks County, one being in Bartlesville, the other in Anadarko. Both groups are federally recognized. A number of smaller groups were also contacted, including three in Canada, two in Wisconsin, one and Kansas, and a total of five in Pennsylvania and New Jersey. "About 16,000 people are represented," Mr. Williams added, "about 10,000 of whom are in Bartlesville."

"We feel better knowing that all of the groups were contacted," Mr. Phillips said, "and we're grateful for Mr. Williams's assistance in the process. Based on what he told us, most of the tribes he contacted thought it best that the man be laid to rest in the place where he lived and died."

When asked about the fact that the remains still haven't been conclusively identified as Lenape, Mr. Phillips added, "It appears that we'll never be one hundred percent certain. But you can be absolutely certain that both the remains and the grave site will be treated and cared for with complete respect."

"If the proposed site is any indication," Mr. Williams observed when advised of Mr. Phillips's comment, "we are very satisfied. It's a beautiful spot that faces the river and the rising sun."

* * *

If the horses in the main paddock were concerned about the group that had gathered for the ceremony, they didn't show it. Huddled in their own small group by the fence near the gathering barn, they grazed quietly on the lush green grass of October.

The ceremony was without ostentation. After everyone had assembled at the main house, they had simply crossed the footbridge, climbed the short hill to the upper meadow, and walked around the paddock to the gravesite.

Seth Williams stood reverently, the carved wooden box with the remains held in his hands. With him stood two people—a woman from one of the Delaware groups in New Jersey, and Raymond Last Elk Tully, the man whom Jeff and Dae had talked with at the powwow. Both had asked to be present.

Directly behind them, Jeff and Dae Phillips stood quietly with Valeria. The child held Dae's hand tightly, not afraid, but still unsure about what was happening. Hope stood to their right, as did Jill and Edward, and Roberto from the work crew. On their left, Grace Caufield, Robert Dawes, and Emily FitzRoy stood together. George Cameron was there as well, standing apart from the others at the edge of the woods.

"Whoever you are," Seth Williams began, "and whoever you were when you walked the earth, we honor your journey and we thank you for including us in it. Now we pray for another journey, confident that you have already made it—the journey to the highest heaven and the Great Spirit. May Ane—the same Milky Way that guided your path hundreds of years ago—continue to send its light to us, just as you have sent *your* light to us. Wanishi. Wanishi, our brother."

Williams set the box on the supports that were laid across the four-foot grave and turned to the others in the group. "Would any of you like to say anything? Please feel free to do so."

No one spoke at first, but Williams had been involved in too many similar ceremonies to rush the moment. He simply waited quietly.

"I think it's important," Emily FitzRoy finally said, "to honor everything this man may have been. To the native in him I wish *Shohola*. To the white in him I wish *Peace*. They mean the same thing and I wish it for every being that walks the earth."

Williams smiled warmly at her, nodding his head in gratitude. "Would anyone else like to speak?"

Robert Dawes took a small step forward. "My involvement here has been briefer than any of yours, but it's clear to me that this man has touched us all in a way that few of us can articulate. Whoever he was, he has inspired us to tell a story, and for me it is an honor to help tell it." He looked toward the wooden box and added, "Thank you."

"Last night," Dae began, "I read a wonderful quote by Kahlil Gibran. 'The light of stars that were extinguished ages ago still reaches us.' I know now what the words mean, and for that I also say thank you."

Another silence ensued, and Williams was again content to let it linger.

"We . . .," Roberto started, before stopping short. "My cousins and I, we are sorry for disturbing your sleep, and we are happy that you can rest now. *Vaya con Dios.*"

No one else said anything, and once comfortable that no one else would, Seth Williams looked at Jeff Phillips. Jeff shook his head slowly, silently indicating that he had nothing to add. Then, at Williams's direction, the man and woman who were with him lowered the carved wooden box into the ground. They mouthed prayers as it came to rest in the bottom of the grave. George Cameron also said a prayer from the end of the small semi-circle, his eyes closed, his head raised toward the sky. One by one, each person stepped forward to throw a shovelful of earth into the hole. When each had finished, the grave was still only partially filled.

"Please, Meester Phillips," Roberto began, "allow me to do this. It is only right."

Jeff nodded, and then invited the small group to return to the main house. "And Roberto," he added before leaving, "please join us when you are finished."

As they turned to go, Valeria let go of Dae's hand and ran toward the half-filled grave. Roberto stepped in front of her, concerned that she might fall into the hole.

"What's wrong, honey?" Dae asked. "Do you want to put some of the dirt into the hole? What is it?"

The child shook her head from side to side. Then she stared into the grave for a long, silent moment before turning to Dae and saying, "I just want to say that he's happy now."

And, with that, she raced ahead of the group, stopping only long enough to reach between fence rails and pat Bandit's face on her way to the main house.

Eighteen

They sat across from each other in the small breakfast nook at her house, eating the dinner that he had made an hour earlier. Long silences would pass but neither minded them. To the contrary, they each took comfort in the understanding that they could simply be with each other. There was little need to fill up every moment with conversation, and absolutely no need to fill up anything with idle chatter. In previous relationships, each of them had followed the conventional wisdom that exhorted things like, "Go slowly; take your time," but neither had experienced anything unique by following it. They were of the same mind that philosophical guidelines did little more than to make a relationship more work than it was ever intended to be. "If it's right," they had agreed, "it's right." And, for each of them, this was right.

"I like the wine," Grace said softly. "May I have a bit more?"

"It's an amusing little Tuesday-night wine, isn't it?" Robert deadpanned. "Oh, wait . . ." He drew the bottle away from her glass. ". . . today is Wednesday! Perhaps we should wait until next week to finish it."

Grace smiled but said nothing, reluctant to encourage him.

"Oh, alright," he said, "but just a touch."

"You know," she began, trying to change the flow, "I could get used to your vegetarian leanings. This is quite good."

"I'm glad you're enjoying it. It's all in the spices—*that* and not cooking everything within an inch of its life."

"Well, my refrigerator's in shock, but I'm definitely enjoying your meals."

They eased into another silence and it carried them through the end of dinner. She cleared the table, claiming that it was the least she could do, but they did the dishes together. They could have used the dishwasher, but there was something about the peaceful, relaxed cadence of washing, rinsing, and drying that appealed to both of them. Either may have found it an annoyance if working alone, but both reveled in it when working side by side. After the last dish was put safely away in the cupboard, they took the remainder of the Tuesday-night wine and adjourned to the living room.

Here, too, they found little use for what others considered normal. They sat in overstuffed easy chairs on opposite sides of a square coffee table, the wine in a clear glass chiller between them. Relaxing music flowed from the stereo speakers in opposing corners of the room. The television was in a little-used part of the house, and the fact that Grace found it unimportant was yet another thing that attracted him to her, another thing that encouraged him not to take his time.

"So," he started, "with everything else that's been going on, have you had time to work on an outline for your novel?"

"I already have a high-level outline," she answered. "There's still quite a bit of detail to fill in, of course, but it's a start."

"And you're going to focus on the same timeframe?"

"Uh-huh. William Penn goes back to England in 1701. The so-called Walking Purchase takes place in 1737. In between, the Lenape culture, in this area at least, is destroyed."

"Is that how you really feel about it?"

"What do you mean?"

"Do you really believe it was 'destroyed'? Is that the correct word?"

"It's a fair question, and I may change my mind as I go along here, but, yes, that's how I really feel about it. I still believe that the Lenape were victims of a numbers game. Whites were pressing into New Jersey and Pennsylvania at an alarming rate. They would have pushed the Lenape out anyway. But that doesn't excuse the way in which it was done."

"So where are you going to start?" Robert asked, reaching for the wine.

"At the end, I think," Grace answered, holding her glass out to him. After he filled it about halfway, she scooted back in her chair, extending her legs onto the coffee table in front of her.

Seeing her so completely at ease filled Robert with a warm peacefulness. He had not experienced the feeling often in his life, but he had learned how to recognize it when it did come along. It was an awareness that he didn't want to be anywhere other than where he was, or doing anything other than what he was doing. Confidence in the perfection of the moment was, for him at least, extremely rare.

Grace was still in dress clothes—a white, collared blouse and gray skirt—her outstretched legs covered in black stockings, her high heels lost to the space beneath the coffee table. She wore subdued earrings and a matching pendant that rested perfectly at her throat. To Robert, she had the look of a professional woman who spent too much time at her desk—not overweight, but only as fit as two nights and a Saturday morning at the gym would allow. Her highlighted brown hair was slightly mussed, and he decided that he liked it better that way than in the blown-dry state of perfection in which it usually met the workday. As she stared into her wine glass, thinking about the end of the story she was about to write, her blue eyes reflected the small bit of warm light that illuminated the living room. Robert found himself filled with gratitude that they had met in that secluded corner of the museum.

"In order to tell the story well," she continued, "I have to know where it ends, and to me it ends with the Walking Purchase. There's no question that there are still Lenape in the area after 1737—which is exactly why James Logan brought the Iroquois down to remove them forcibly—but the Walking Purchase is really where the story ends."

"So, is that where your research is focused?"

"For now, yes, but there's a lot to it. The whole thing was so carefully orchestrated over a period of years."

"Tell me about it."

"I have to get my notes," Grace said, beginning to rise from her chair.

"No," Robert insisted, "please don't get up. You look so comfortable and you're making me feel that way, so please stay where you are." Watching her move back into her chair, he added, "Just tell me what you remember."

Grace paused to take a sip of wine, thinking about the things that she had read recently. "It all started with that deed." She paused again. "There was a meeting at the Durham Iron Works in the summer of 1734. It was on the river, just below what is now Riegelsville.

"By the time the meeting took place, William Penn had been dead for sixteen years. The family interests had been turned over to his sons, but Thomas, the first of them to come to America, didn't show up until 1732. By the time he arrived, there had been no new treaties with the Indians in eighteen years and things were pretty much a mess.

"Responding to the overwhelming demand for land, Penn's representatives had sold it without regard for who was living on it, which of course included the Lenape. The Indians responded to the demand, as well. The Lenape cut deals directly with settlers, and the Iroquois made some deals of their own on behalf of the Lenape.

"Anyway, the meeting at the iron works was intended to straighten the whole mess out."

"Excuse me for a minute," Robert interrupted, "but I'm going to open some more wine." Starting for the kitchen, chiller in hand, he added, "Just give me a minute."

When he returned, he poured more wine in each of their glasses. "This will do it for me," he suggested, "I have to drive."

"You don't have to drive *anywhere*," Grace laughed.

"So, it's okay if I stay on a school night? I like that."

"What *I* like is that you ask, even when you know you don't have to."

"So," Grace continued, "we were talking—check that, *I* was talking—about the meeting in Durham. The Penn gang was trying to get control of a very unwieldy situation. They thought this deed they had would do the trick."

"What did the deed say?" Robert asked, taking a sip of wine.

"It was supposedly based on a 1686 agreement with William Penn. That's forty-eight years earlier! And it *claimed* that the Penn family had the right to as much land as a man could walk in a day and a half."

"Okay, I'm with you so far."

"There were two Lenape chiefs at the meeting. One was named Tishcohan, which I have seen spelled a number of different ways, and the other Nutimus. Emily FitzRoy laughed when I told her about Nutimus. She said that she used to go to a summer camp by that name when she was a kid. Anyway, Nutimus was a chief of the Munsee, the northernmost Lenape, and he was skeptical because his people lived on much of the land that would come into play. He would not agree."

"And that went over poorly, I assume."

"Very. The resistance of the Lenape was costing Logan and the Penns time they did not have. More whites were pouring into the area looking for land every day."

"What happened?"

"Nothing until the following year—at least as far as the Lenape were concerned. There was a subsequent meeting at Pennsbury in 1735, but the Penn representatives were already making plans for the walk, regardless of when it would be made."

"So, if the Walking Purchase occurred in 1737, this was a three-year process."

"Exactly."

"What happened at Pennsbury?" Robert asked.

"Well," Grace said, "*that's* where I am right now."

"To be continued, then?"

"Yes, to be continued, perhaps over a very hospitable Friday-evening-greet-the-weekend wine." She grinned widely.

"One of my favorite vintages," Robert answered. "One of my absolute favorites."

* * *

Jeff Phillips walked into the modest waiting room of the Wilson & Meyers Produce Company. It had been months since his last visit, and as he looked around he was struck by how little the place had changed. He was almost certain that the brown jacket that hung on a nearby coat rack had been there previously, and he had an uneasy feeling that the small pile of magazines that sat on the waiting room table hadn't moved at all.

There was no one at the desk behind the sliding glass partition, and that was very different. Jeff remembered the very pleasant white-haired woman who had been at the desk each of the handful of times he had visited the company, and he found himself hoping that she was well.

The door to the right of the glass partition swung open, just ahead of the squeaking of a dry hinge, and an elderly, but very fit, man entered the waiting room. "Hello, Mr. Phillips," he said, extending his right hand. "It's good to see you again."

"Mr. Meyers," Jeff nodded. "You're looking well. I hope life has been good to you."

"Can't complain. Well, I *can*, but I'm not going to." He turned and re-opened the door, holding it open for Jeff in a silent invitation to follow him. "I'm sorry there was no one here to meet you. Rosemary retired a few months ago and I haven't found anyone else that's willing to put up with me."

Somehow, Jeff doubted that, because the sound in the man's voice when he had said "Rosemary retired" suggested that he believed she couldn't be replaced.

Meyers' office hadn't changed much, either. It seemed like there were more photographs of his family on the bookcase shelves, and there was much less activity in the warehouse beyond the window, but everything else was almost exactly as Jeff remembered it.

Meyers invited Jeff to sit down and, after brushing aside some small, nearly invisible something from the top of his desk, began to speak. But the words caught in his throat.

Whatever Meyers had to say, Jeff knew it was serious. "It's okay, Fred. How can I help?"

Meyers looked back at him warmly, obviously appreciative of the offer. "You once told me—and I think it was one of the first times we met, back when you bought the Williams farm—that if I ever decided to sell this place, you would like it if I called you first."

"I remember."

"Well, Jeff, *this* is that call."

Jeff didn't know what to say. He had always been interested in the land that the produce company occupied, and he was grateful that Fred Meyers had honored his request, but he knew that this was much more than the buying and selling of land.

"How long have you been here?" he asked, well aware of the answer to the question, and equally aware of the man's need to talk about it.

"Everett Wilson and I started this place after we got back from the war. We were in the Navy together. We started out with seasonal things—strawberries, beans, corn, tomatoes. The orchards took a little longer, of course."

"So, sixty-four years?"

"Yes, almost." He paused for a long moment, staring at the wall behind Jeff. "I know it's been that long, but when I hear someone else say it, I can't believe it's been *that* long." He paused again. "If that makes any sense."

"It makes a lot of sense, Fred. It makes a lot of sense."

"Everett passed ten years ago. I've been doing this on my own since then. His son was involved for a while, but he wasn't much for the work. I bought him out after a few months. And neither of my girls stayed in the area, so they really haven't been involved."

"I understand, but . . ." Jeff was hesitant. He was very interested in the property, but he was more interested in what Fred Meyers was experiencing. He judged that the man was in emotional pain. "Are you sure you really want to sell? Are you sure that's the best thing?"

"I'm sure," Meyers answered. "I always kind of expected to die here on the grounds, but after Rosemary left I got to thinking about how long I've been here, and about how no one who started out with me is here anymore, and I decided that enough's enough."

"Again, I understand. Well, I'm still interested. Do you want me to propose something or do you want to put something together?"

"I have a number in mind, but it really depends on what you're going to use the land for."

"Why, for a produce company of course." Jeff smiled warmly, trying to reassure Meyers that he was completely serious. "In fact, I plan to ask you to help me run it for a year or two until I learn the business."

While obviously taken aback, Meyers had the clear sense that the man sitting across from him knew exactly what he was doing. "I didn't expect either of those things," he offered, "but it sounds like you have a plan."

"I would characterize it more as an idea," Jeff responded.

"Well," Meyers observed, "the county will be more receptive to your idea once they realize that you're planning to maintain the business. They're very focused on the preservation of large tracts of land."

"Yes, I'm well aware of it."

"As far as a price is concerned, I'm thinking eleven million for everything."

"And just to confirm, how many acres are we talking about?"

"Just under eight hundred, about a third of which can be cultivated."

"The price is fine with me, Fred, but I want to make sure that it's fair to you. Have you talked to real estate people about this? We're talking about more than land here. You have trucks, packing equipment, and . . ."

"I talked with my attorney and he thinks that I may be able to get more, but . . ."

"He may be right," Jeff interrupted, "it may be *worth* more."

Meyers looked straight into Jeff's eyes. "So, do we have a deal?"

"Only," Jeff answered, "if it's the right deal for both of us. You've worked hard for what you'll get for your business." He stopped short, surprised by the thought that his mind had conjured. "Harder than I've worked for what I'll buy it with."

Meyers smiled back at him. "Rosemary always said that there was something about you that she really liked. I think I see what she was talking about." He waited before adding, "That's my price and I'm offering it to you first, as promised. Do you accept?"

"Under one condition. I don't want anyone else to know about this right now. The lawyers have to know, of course, but other than that, I'd like to keep this very low key."

"That's okay with me. Other than my daughters, there's no one I have to tell."

"Then . . ." Jeff took a deep breath, not because of the money, but because of the way everything seemed to be falling into place. ". . . I accept."

* * *

Little more than a large closet, it wasn't the most inviting place to do research, but it was removed from the noise and activity of the newsroom, and as Grace Caufield read through information on various websites, she was grateful for the peace and quiet.

As she worked, she thought about the observation that Robert had made while they sat talking in her living room the previous evening. The Walking Purchase was much more than a calendar event. Even though it had taken place during two days in September of 1737, it had been preceded by three years of activity, some of it suspect, and it had been followed by nineteen years of Indian protests, all of which created a dynamic that took nearly a quarter of a century to play out.

She was trying to find information about the second of three meetings that preceded the Walking Purchase. None of the meetings was well documented, as evidenced by the fact that she had been able to find out almost nothing about them. There was some information about the first meeting, which was held at the

Durham Iron Works in October of 1734, but there was almost no information about the second, which was held at Pennsbury the following May.

As one website indicated, William Penn began work on Pennsbury Manor in 1682, shortly after his arrival in Pennsylvania. Modeled after country estates in England, it was situated between the Delaware River and Van Sciver Lake, near the present day town of Morrisville. In addition to the main house, it included a stable, a boathouse, a number of farm buildings, a bakery, and a brewery.

It was at Pennsbury that Thomas and Richard Penn, as well as James Logan, hoped to persuade the Indians to accept the 1686 deed that would validate their claim to lands that could be walked in a day and half. More Lenape were involved at Pennsbury than at the Durham Iron Works, including a chief named Lappawinsoe, but the outcome was the same—the Lenape were not moved to agree to the terms of the suspect deed.

But other things that happened in the same timeframe peaked Grace's interest.

On April 22, 1735, less than two weeks before the meeting with the Lenape at Pennsbury, a trial walk was made to determine how much ground could be covered in one and a half days. This trial walk was sanctioned by the Proprietary Council, but conducted without the knowledge of the Lenape.

The walk was arranged by Timothy Smith, sheriff of Bucks County, and a man named John Chapman. The extreme interest and focus of the Proprietary Council was evident in the letters of James Steel, receiver general under Thomas Penn. On April 25th, he sent a letter to Timothy Smith stating: "The Proprietaries are impatient to know what progress is made in traveling over the land that is to be settled in the ensuing treaty that is to be held with the Indians at Pennsbury, on the fifth day of the next month, and therefore I now desire thee, without delay, to send down an account of what has been done in that affair."

"This is," Grace said to herself, "more than two years before the walk actually took place. These guys really thought they were close to an agreement with the Indians."

Four days later, Steel sent a follow-up letter.

The Proprietaries are very much concerned that so much time hath been lost before you begin the work recommended so earnestly at your leaving Philadelphia, and it being so very short before the meeting at Pennsbury, the 5th of next month, that they now desire that upon the return of Joseph Doane, he, together with two other persons who can travel well, should be immediately sent on foot on the day and a half journey, and two others on horseback to carry necessary provisions for them, and to assist them in their return home. The time is now so far spent that not one moment is to be lost; and as soon as they have traveled the day and a half journey, the Proprietaries desire that a messenger may be sent to give them account without any delay, how far that day and a half traveling will reach up the county.

It was obvious to Grace that the trial walk had actually begun three days before the first of Steel's letters was sent from

Philadelphia. John Chapman accompanied the party as a surveyor, carefully noting the distances between designated points on the walk. Along the way, trees were marked so that the route would be obvious to walkers from the southeast. In some areas, trees and brush were cleared so that the path would be less obstructed. The trial walk took a total of nine days.

Grace's research revealed that at least two more trial walks would be made, one at the end of May, about three weeks after the failed meeting at Pennsbury, and another two years later in September of 1737, immediately prior to the actual walk. In both cases, careful attention was paid to any detail that would result in more land for the Penns and their representatives.

"They certainly knew what they wanted," she ruminated. "Or perhaps they knew what they needed."

Grace knew that the third and final meeting was held at Philadelphia on August 25, 1737, a little more than three weeks before what would eventually become known as the Walking Purchase. She could only imagine how impatient the Penns and James Logan would have been by then, since more than two years had passed since the meeting at Pennsbury.

"Everything was ready," Grace whispered to the small room. "All that was missing was the consent of the Lenape."

* * *

MAY 1735

"How do you make the pigment?"

"It is complicated, and it takes a long, long time."

"*What* is complicated? What must be done?"

"The rock must be ground to powder, which can take many days. Then the powder is washed many times over until the lightest parts have been removed. This, too, takes a very long time."

"And you did this for Four Bears?"

"I did. And she told me that I would one day do it for you."

Walks Alone sat erect, his legs folded in front of him, his back to the entrance to the wigwam. The process had settled into a predictable cadence. The fish bone would prick the skin between his shoulder blades, and then it would be drawn away; more pigment would be applied; Storyteller's hand would press against his back, signaling that the bone was about to prick his skin yet again. Only the occasional wiping away of blood interrupted the pattern.

"And you used charcoal for the black?" he asked.

"Yes," she answered. "I have always used charcoal."

He would get up to stretch from time to time, but for the most part he just sat there, his back to the light, while Storyteller cut a tattoo of the white buffalo into his back. With each cut, his bond with his teacher intensified, as he envisioned what it would be like to rise to his feet and leave the wigwam, marked for the rest of his life exactly as his teacher had been marked for hers. Each time the bone pierced his skin he was reminded of the countless things she had taught him, the many ways in which she had prepared him, and the formidable responsibilities she had left to him. And, when his blood was wiped away, he thought about how much he wanted to be like her. In his head, he doubted that he could ever be like her, and that doubt caused him to feel the sting of each cut, but in his heart he understood that he was already like her, and that understanding allowed him to easily embrace the discomfort of this rite of passage.

"Did you always know her? I mean, did you know her when she was young?"

"Yes. We lived in the same village as children."

"What was she like as a child?"

"She was like the rest of the children. We helped our mothers and sisters plant crops and prepare food. We fished in streams. We tanned hides. We did the same things that you see the women doing today, except that there are fewer women doing them now."

"Was she always different?" Walks Alone wasn't sure that he had asked the question in exactly the right way, but he knew that Storyteller would understand.

The woman paused in her work, the side of her hand still pressed against the back of Walks Alone. She smiled at the question, thinking about the young friend with whom she had grown up.

"She was like the rest of the children, except that she would sometimes become very quiet, as if a spell had come over her. When that happened, she would go away and be by herself. None of us would try to keep her from going, nor would we look for her after she had gone. Clouded Moon told us not to. He was her teacher just as she was yours." She touched the fish bone to his skin. "That is how it was with Touches A Deer."

"Touches A Deer? Is that how she was called?"

"Yes. She was called that because the animals were not afraid of her. Birds would eat from her hand. I saw this myself, more than once." She stopped talking long enough to dip the bone in more of the white pigment and press it beneath his skin. "It is said that once, as she sat in the grass, a deer grazed so close to her that she reached out and touched its face. It is said that the deer did not run away." She pierced his skin with the bone yet again. "But this I did not see."

"So," Walks Alone said, "she was always different."

"Yes. Her path was always clear. And she was always looked after by Clouded Moon. They were both great teachers . . ." She wiped blood away from the tiny cuts in his skin. ". . . and great healers, just as you are both teacher and healer."

"I have healed nothing but men with snakebites and children with fevers. I don't know what I would do if I had to heal something worse." He winced at the next cut into the tattoo and wondered why it would hurt when the ones before it had not. "And there is no one for me to teach." He winced again. "I do not believe that the picture of the white beast that you are cutting into my back will ever be worn by another Lenape along Lenapewihittuk. This will end with me." The next cut felt even sharper and it caused him to lurch forward.

"You are so sure?"

"What else am I to think?"

"Why do you ask me?"

"Who *should* I ask?"

"Ask Four Bears." She cut the pigment into his skin three more times before continuing. "Ask Clouded Moon. They will help you."

"I did not . . ." The next cut was so painful that he thought about asking her to stop. ". . . I did not know Clouded Moon."

"Did you know Four Bears?"

"Yes, of course, she was . . ."

"Then you know Clouded Moon through her, just as all people will know Four Bears through you."

He smiled at Storyteller's words. She was right. He had learned long ago that one always knows the teacher by the student, but he also knew that applying the lesson was seldom as easy as learning it, especially when it pertained to one's self. He heard the fish bone tap into the shell of pigment and he felt the pressure of Storyteller's hand, but he did not feel the cut.

"She would tell me . . ." He corrected himself, thinking about the teacher he had known through Four Bears. ". . . *They* would tell me to have faith that my path is true." He sat quietly, pondering the observation. He felt neither the need to get up and move about, nor the need to be finished with the tattooing. He was content to simply sit side by side with his notion of faith.

"Are you pleased with your work?" he finally asked Storyteller. When there was no reply, he turned to see only the bright sunlight beyond the entrance to the wigwam. A few moments later, Storyteller appeared there, holding a bucket.

Once again sitting behind him, she wiped the entire area between his shoulder blades with a wet, cool cloth. "It's unfortunate that you cannot see the tattoo," Storyteller began, "but I know that the animal is always with you."

"Yes," he agreed, smiling, "always."

Storyteller began to rub something on the tattoo in large circular motions. It felt cool and smooth to Walks Alone, but it bit into each of the tiny wounds with a ferocity that made its purpose unmistakable.

"What are you using?" he asked.

"A salve of sumac," she replied. "It will stop the bleeding and help the cuts heal quickly. It would be best if you returned in the morning."

"Wanishi, my friend, but we will be leaving too early." As he stood to leave, Walks Alone added, "Again, wanishi. I am in your debt."

"No!" Her tone was sharp and abrupt, and it spoke to the current of emotion that carried it to her lips. Then, as her mouth softened into a warm smile, she said, "It is I who owe you. It is I who must say wanishi."

"I do not understand," he said, as if asking for an explanation, but Storyteller said nothing.

It was late afternoon when Nutimus and his men of the stony country reached the escarpment. It had been six months since the meeting with the whites at the place they called Durham, and now a second meeting had been arranged at the home of Onas. It was much farther downriver than Durham, at least two day's walk away. For Nutimus and the other Munsee it was even farther, and they had come to Lechauwitank to rest for the night before going on with Walks Alone and His Spirit Watches. Others would meet them along the way, but, for now, they would eat and rest, and they would sit and talk about the approaching meeting with James Logan and the sons of Penn.

It was not yet dawn when the small band of men left the escarpment the following day. They headed downriver, making their way in single file along the well-worn path. They walked silently, as they always walked in the darkness, not wanting to alert anyone or anything to their presence. The woods were equally quiet, except for the mild movement of tree branches in the pre-dawn breezes of May. Off to the left, they could hear the flow of the swollen river as it rushed ahead of them toward their destination—the place the whites called Pennsbury.

As he walked in the line of Lenape, a few paces behind the dark hulking form of His Spirit Watches, the thoughts of Walks Alone wandered back to the previous night. Lying on his side, his head resting on an outstretched arm, he had drifted in and out of sleep. He had hoped to journey or dream, wanting to find Four Bears, or the white buffalo, or both. Being marked with the tattoo had made him feel closer to both of them, and he had been confident that they would come to him easily, but neither had.

He thought about his experience with Four Bears on the eve of the meeting with the whites at the Durham Iron Works. "*Such is the path of the Lenape.*" Many times he had experienced the opening of the oppressive woods, and many times he had turned to see the white horses bearing down on him in their relentless charge toward the setting sun. "*Such is the path of the Lenape.*" And the white buffalo had been there each time, bringing with him the same ominous message—each time except the last time.

Why had Four Bears not spoken to him? Why had she been unwilling to tell him what the message meant?

The first light of day edged onto the horizon beyond the river in the dull streaks of gray and silver that always preceded the sun. Walks Alone knew that they were tricksters, etching confusing shadows on everything, making each step more precarious than those made in darkness. They were tricksters indeed, and he moved cautiously, guarding against their deceptions.

"So, Young One," the familiar voice started, "you are now marked with the white buffalo. Are you pleased?"

Walks Alone imagined that Four Bears was walking beside him. It was easy to conjure her from the dark shadows in the faint morning light. "Why do you come to me like this," he asked, "when I cannot see you, when I can only imagine you?" He looked toward His Spirit Watches, certain that his words would cause his friend to turn around, but the massive man walked on in silence.

"I am pleased," Four Bears said without answering his question. "And I am pleased that we are once more walking along Lenapewihittuk, that we are finally making our way back to your village."

"You are not really here," he insisted. "I am imagining you."

"Of course you are," she agreed, "but does it matter?"

"What do you mean?"

"Messages swirl around us all the time, Young One, in things as obvious as the words of a wise man and in things as subtle as the wind in the trees. We recognize but a few of them. We ask the Great Spirit for signs and then we ignore the signs he gives us."

"So, have you come to tell me what the message means? 'Such is the path of the Lenape.' What does it mean?"

For a few moments, Four Bears said nothing. She simply walked by his side, just as she had walked there in life. It was as if nothing had changed. He even imagined that, had there been more light in the sky, she might stop to examine the leaves of some plant growing along the path.

"What," she finally asked, "do the horses mean to you?"

"They are powerful," he answered, "and cannot be stopped. They move through me as if I am not even there, as if I have never been there. And . . ."

"And what?"

". . . they are white."

"Such is the path of the Lenape," she said. "We flee ahead of the power of the white man, a power that moves past us as if we never even existed."

"But," Walks Alone began, "so many have already fled. There must be more to the message."

"Good, Young One. Good." As she spoke, the top edge of the sun appeared in the trees across Lenapewihittuk, but instead of illuminating Four Bears more clearly, it began to consume her.

"Please tell me!" he called after her, certain that His Spirit Watches and the others would hear. "What else is there to know?"

"The answer is in you," she said softly, disappearing into the dawn. "It has always been in you."

As he followed behind His Spirit Watches, Walks Alone wanted to ask him if he had heard the conversation with Four Bears, but he did not. He wanted to ask him if he had heard Four Bears talking, but he did not. He knew that it had all happened in his head and in his heart, but that what he had learned was just as true as if he had learned it in a more physical, more tangible way. *"Messages swirl around us,"* she had explained. *"They swirl around us all the time."*

It was not yet mid-morning when the group reached the inlet where Walks Alone and Talks For Us had once kept their weir, and as they passed by it the memory of the first time he had retrieved a fish from the trap came flooding back to him. He smiled at the thought. And it was still with him, cradled gently in the recesses of his heart, when he saw his uncle up ahead on the path, a rolled blanket tied across one shoulder.

"He," Talks For Us said as the group approached. "He."

As Walks Alone embraced his uncle, Nutimus asked about Tishcohan, who lived at Hockyondocquay, less than five miles away.

"They have gone on ahead," Talks For Us explained, "at least a day ago. It is more difficult for Tishcohan to make the journey now, so they left early to give him more time."

"As it should be," Nutimus said, nodding his head. "As it should be."

They walked for another two hours before being met on the path by another Lenape sachem, Lappawinsoe, and a small group of men from his village. Now a group of twenty, the men continued downriver.

Just before dark, they stopped at the Tohickon Creek, named "Deer Bone" because it had once been a valued hunting ground of their ancestors. It was just above an old path that led toward the setting sun, a path by which countless Lenape, including many from the other side of Lenapewihittuk, had left their native lands. For the men in the small band, the place represented both a storied history and an uncertain future.

Later that night, as they sat in circle, they talked again about meeting with the whites in Pennsbury.

"I do not trust their deed," said Nutimus. "If our fathers had made a promise to Onas, we would have known about it. There would have been a record. But there is nothing."

"I agree," said Lappawinsoe, "but there are many bad feelings between the Lenape and the whites. It would serve us well to give them something."

Waiting until he was certain that the sachems had finished, Talks For Us asked, "But what can we give them that they have not already taken? Many whites already live on these lands, and they live here without our agreement. The Penns want nothing more than to buy what they have already sold, and justify what they have already done."

"But if they come up Lenapewihittuk," Nutimus offered, "they will reach Munsee lands. They may even reach our hunting grounds in the mountains."

"In a day and a half?" someone questioned. "That is a long way to walk in a day and a half."

"I worry," said Lappawinsoe, "that our old ones do not know of this deed. And I worry that none of them are with us to listen to Thomas Penn and James Logan. And . . ." He paused briefly, considering some of the answers to the question he was about to ask. ". . . where are the other sachems? Where is Sassoonan?"

"All were not asked," Talks For us answered, "to meet with the whites."

Later, before he fell asleep, Walks Alone thought about the approaching meeting at the home of Onas, and about the things that had been talked about in circle. No one, not even Nutimus and Lappawinsoe, seemed to believe that the meeting would be fruitful for either side. An air of futility seemed to surround it. Some had even said as much, wondering aloud why they would walk for days for a meeting about which they had so many suspicions. It seemed to make no sense.

Walks Alone agreed that the meeting seemed to make little sense, yet something inside told him that there was much more to all of this than was apparent to Nutimus, or Lappawinsoe, or the aged Tishcohan. As Talks For Us had predicted six moons earlier, the whites were pushing, and Walks Alone was haunted by the thought that they were probably pushing harder than any of the sachems knew.

The Lenape walked for most of the following day before catching up with Tishcohan's group just below the great falls on Lenapewihittuk. They were at the place the whites called Trent Towne—the place where the fresh water of the river met the tidal waters of the bay far to the south. Walks Alone had never been this far downriver, and he was impressed by the falls, as well as by the number of whites in Trent Towne. As Talks For Us had explained to him, this was a great village for the whites, purchased by the English six winters before Onas came from England for the first time.

As they walked on, the presence of whites became more and more obvious, and as he became increasingly aware that he was now walking in a white world, he became equally aware that it bore very few signs of the Lenape who had once lived there.

The group moved more slowly for the next ten miles in consideration of the slower-walking Tishcohan, and it was mid-afternoon before they reached the place called Pennsbury.

On their way to the home of Onas, they passed through a bustling settlement, the focal point of which was a large square building that Lappawinsoe described as a lodgehouse for the whites—a place where they met to worship their god and sit in council.

The Lenape attracted attention as they walked toward the home of Onas, but to Walks Alone the whites seemed far less interested in his people than he was in them. They seemed to have so much to do, yet they were neither planting, nor preparing food, nor tanning hides. The other settlements he had been to were not this active, and he wondered if places like Coaquannock were like this, or even more so.

"They call this Pennsbury Manor," Talks For Us said to him as they neared the home of Onas.

"And this," Walks Alone asked, "is the home of one man?"

He was awestruck by what he was seeing. A huge building of red square stones rose high above the center of the property. It was obvious that people could live on each of its levels, and he wondered why so much space was necessary. He had seen windows before, in farmhouses and at places like the Durham Iron Works, but never so many. He imagined that one would not have to take more than a few steps in order to look outside.

There were other buildings nearby, including a number that were dedicated to farming. He had seen barns and outbuildings on smaller farms, but none of them approached these buildings in either size or decoration.

Lappawinsoe placed a hand on his shoulder, obviously aware of Walks Alone's shock at seeing this place for the first time. "That place there," he said, pointing to a smaller building by a lake, is only for boats, but they are not boats as you know them. They are much more than dugout canoes. And that house over there is just for the baking of bread, and the one near it is just for making the white man's alcohol."

"How many people live here?" Walks Alone asked.

"I do not know," the sachem replied, "but when this was the home of Onas, it was the home of one family."

Walks Alone thought about the wigwam in which he had once lived with Talks For Us, Looks Back, and Quiet Bird. He wondered if Onas had thought of this place in the same warm and endearing way.

But, even in its splendor, Walks Alone could see that something about the property was not right. The wood around the windows of the main house and on the sides of the smaller buildings looked weathered and warped, much of its color faded away. He saw at least two broken windows on the front of the house, and it was obvious to him that many of the gardens, especially the ones with flowers, were not being cared for. The plants that had died the previous autumn remained in the ground, now little more than withered stalks and leaves. They combined with emerging weeds and thistle in a garden of neglect, and the sight saddened him deeply.

"I do not understand," he said to Lappawinsoe, "why so grand a house would not be cared for."

"The sons of Onas do not see with their father's eyes," Lappawinsoe said. "He saw something in this land. He saw a place where his dream could live. His sons see something else, and they respect nothing that is beyond their vision. They do not respect us, but, what is worse, they do not respect the memory of their father."

"How can they not care for what they desire?"

"You see the neglect. They care only for that from which they can profit."

The night passed quietly. The Lenape stayed to themselves. They sat in their circle and talked, but spoke very little of the next day's meeting. Instead, they spoke of the time when the land on which they were sleeping was once the home of their ancestors. They spoke of the time when all the lands they had walked in the past two days were once the home of the Lenape—the lands to the south, to Coaquannock and beyond, and the lands to both the great ocean and the rising sun.

There were more people at the next day's meeting than there had been at the Durham Iron Works. Tishcohan, Nutimus, and Lappawinsoe sat in front of the semi-circle of Lenape men. Across from them sat four white chiefs—Thomas Penn, Richard Penn, James Logan, and William Allen.

"Who is the other man in front?" Walks Alone asked of Talks For Us.

"He speaks both their language and ours. He will help the chiefs understand each other, like the other man did at Durham."

Thomas Penn, the oldest son of Onas, spoke first.

"We welcome our Lenape brothers to the homes of Onas, the great friend of all Lenape. Here, in this place where he made his home, we meet with you to talk about promises that were made between Onas and your fathers—promises that we asked you to honor when we met at Durham six moons ago, promises that we will ask you to honor again today." He paused, waiting for the interpreter to catch up.

"As it was to Onas, it is important to his sons and all here who speak for him now that the Lenape and their white brothers live in peace. It is important that we sell only the lands included in treaties with the Lenape, and it is equally important that the Lenape strike no agreements with anyone who is not a representative of Onas." He paused again, waiting for the interpreter.

Like the rest of the Lenape, Walks Alone listened carefully, but he wondered to himself why the son of Onas would take so many words to repeat what had already been said at Durham.

"This is the deed," Thomas Penn said, holding the paper in the air, "by which your fathers agreed to give Onas the rights to all lands that a man can walk in a day and half. This was agreed to forty-nine winters ago, when the oldest among us were little more than children. The family of Onas has been very patient with its Lenape brothers, and we now ask that you honor the agreement and let the walk take place."

As the interpreter finished, the Lenape men spoke among themselves. Walks Alone said nothing, more interested in how the three sachems would respond. He watched as they spoke with each other, wondering which of them would speak for his people. Finally, Lappawinsoe rose to his feet.

"We have traveled far, and the Great Spirit has blessed us to be here at the home of Onas, who was the honored friend of our people. We come in peace, and in the hope that the people of Onas and the Lenape will always live together in peace.

"I was not with you at Durham, but Nutimus and Tishcohan tell me that everything you have said was also said there. They tell me that you still seek the rights to this walk, rights that you say were agreed to long ago in a time that lives in the memory of no man here."

The interpreter spoke in paraphrases, apparently not able to understand each of the words that Lappawinsoe had said.

"The promise you speak of," Lappawinsoe continued, "is so important that our old ones would remember hearing of it—their fathers and their grandfathers would have told them—but they are not here because the journey is too long for them."

As the interpreter caught up, an obvious agitation rose among the whites. They spoke to each other in hushed voices, some of them gesturing wildly.

"This is not happening as they had hoped," Talks For Us whispered to Walks Alone. "They are not pleased."

"And all of our people are not represented," Lappawinsoe added. "Some sachems are not here, including those who made the great treaty at Conestoga nineteen winters ago. Sassoonan was there, and he would have remembered a promise like the one you speak of, but he is not here now. Others who were there are not here now.

"We too desire to live in peace with the sons and friends of Onas, just as our fathers lived in peace with him, but we cannot agree that you have the rights of which you speak."

The interpreter finished, and with the last of his words, the anger of some of the whites was audible. It was clear to everyone that the meeting had been of no value to either side.

"And now?" Walks Alone inquired of Talks For Us. "What will happen now?"

"There may be more talking," his uncle answered, "but it will do little good. Some of the whites show their anger, even though their chiefs conceal their feelings well. They expected a different outcome."

"And us? What do we do now?"

"We walk home."

* * *

"Hello," the voice on the other end of the line said. "This is George."

"Hello, Mr. Cameron," she responded. "This is Emily FitzRoy at the University of Pennsylvania."

"Of course, Dr. FitzRoy. How are you?"

"I'm well, thank you, but I'm having a bit of a problem and I'm hoping you can help me with it."

"I will if I can. Would you like to tell me about it?"

"I have been trying to speak with the leaders of the Delaware tribes in Oklahoma, and I'm sorry to say that I've gotten the cold shoulder from the people in both Bartlesville and Anadarko."

"Do you mind if I ask why you want to talk with them?"

Not responding immediately, Emily FitzRoy found herself wondering how much of the story she should fill in.

"Are you still there, Dr. FitzRoy?"

She decided to start at the beginning. "Have you ever been to the Mercer Museum in Doylestown, Mr. Cameron?"

"No, I can't say that I have. And if you don't mind, I would rather that you called me George."

"Thank you, *George*. And please call me Emily. There's an exhibit at the Mercer, on one of the upper levels, and it concerns the Lenape in the Delaware River valley and their contact with Europeans."

"Please go on."

"Well," Emily continued, "the director of the museum is moving the exhibit down to the main floor and expanding it considerably. He wants to make it more accessible to everyone who visits the Mercer."

Cameron said nothing.

"Grace has been involved in the expansion, and I have been trying to help as well, primarily with the information about the present-day Delaware people in Oklahoma."

"And that's why you want to talk with the people in Bartlesville and Anadarko?"

"Yes, but I don't get the impression that they want to talk with me."

There was a long silence on the other end of the line. Emily sensed that George Cameron knew what he was going to say but wasn't quite sure about how to say it.

"Emily," he finally began, "when you work in other countries, how do the locals respond to you and your colleagues?"

"Truthfully, George," she answered, "they don't pay much attention to us. They're so used to having archaeologists and anthropologists around that we're just part of the scenery. I was in Peru this past summer and the people there are very used to tourists and scientists."

"I'm sorry. I'm not making myself clear." There was another silence on the line. "Were you around aboriginal people in Peru," Cameron finally continued, "people who follow the old ways?"

"A few . . ." Emily paused for a moment before adding, "I think I see where you're going with this. The people you're talking about are much more standoffish. They don't trust us completely."

"And why is that?"

"Their culture was destroyed, by disease and guns and people lusting after gold. And it's as if . . ." She stopped short.

"It's as if," Cameron continued, finishing her sentence for her, "they never got over it. Centuries have passed and they still haven't gotten over it."

"Yes, that's right. And you're saying that the Delaware still haven't gotten over it."

"Would you, Emily?"

"I'd like to think that I would say it happened a long time ago and . . ."

"They don't trust white people," he interrupted. "They may talk to you eventually, but it will take time and work to build a relationship with them."

"How do you build a relationship with someone who won't talk with you?"

Again, Cameron said nothing.

"Why wouldn't they want people to know where they're living today and what their life is like?"

"I'm not arguing that it might benefit them. I'm just saying that they'll have to trust you before they'll talk with you." When Emily did not respond, he added, "I know it's not what you want to hear. Is there anything else I can help with?"

"No, but thank you for taking the time to speak with me. You probably saved me a lot of time in the long run, not to mention the wear and tear of banging my head against the wall."

Cameron laughed. "Well, then . . ."

"Oh, there is one more thing. I know that Robert Dawes is planning to invite you to the opening of the new exhibit. I hope I'll see you there."

"We'll see. In the meantime, please take care of yourself."

Emily felt helpless as she ended the call on her cell phone, and helpless was not something she was used to feeling. She also felt frustrated. This was her contribution to the expanded exhibit. In some ways, it should have been the easiest portion to complete, and who better to complete it than an anthropologist? It should have been as simple as a trip, possibly two, to Bartlesville and Anadarko, meeting with tribal leaders and members of the tribes, getting information about their self-government, taking photographs of the people and their lives. It should have been a rare opportunity to talk with real, living people rather than sifting through the remains of what long-dead civilizations had left behind hundreds or thousands of years earlier. But it was to be none of those things. In fact, it was to be nothing at all.

Consumed by her frustration, Emily had no way of knowing that Robert Dawes would respond to her news by leaving an empty display case at the end of the exhibit—a display case that would remain empty until relationships had been developed; a display case that would wait patiently for trust to rise to the surface.

Nineteen

"Jeff..."

He heard his name in his dream but he didn't know who was saying it. He turned his head toward the sound, trying to hear the voice more clearly. His dream was light and peaceful, filled with the quiet understanding that everything was exactly as it should be, that everything was flowing toward its destiny as surely as the river in the distant darkness was flowing to the bay.

"Jeff..."

Who was calling his name? Was it someone in his dream or someone beyond? And why did they want to disturb something so beautiful, something that filled him in a way that few things could?

The autumn sky was a palette of a single color—a blue so cloudless, so translucent that it compelled him to stare straight into it as if searching for the face of God. He stood on the bridge above the creek bank, less than twenty feet from the place where the bones had been found, his eyes turned toward the welcoming sky. He slowly raised his arms to shoulder height and rose into the sky.

Completely unfettered, he rose like a child's balloon ascending above the grounds of a summer fair. He was completely free.

"Wake up, Babe. Jeff . . ."

The voice was Dae's, but where was she? Was she on the bridge below? Was she calling from the house? There was an urgency in the way she said his name, but he somehow understood that it was the urgency of something good, something that he would be very happy to attend to. She was okay—he was certain of it—so he allowed himself to float on for another breathless moment, not fully willing to be drawn away from such splendor.

Now above the trees, he looked down to see the length of the lower meadow that ran from the main house to the materials area beyond the bridge. The land on the far side of the house sparkled in a brilliant orange as the high autumn grass reached above a thin layer of mist and toward the blinding sun. Beyond the distant tree line, he could see the produce farm, its orchards little more than the abstractions of an impressionist painter.

Looking toward the upper meadow, he could see the roof of the gathering barn and the very tops of its high windows. The distant half of the main paddock was visible as well, the horses grazing not far from the burial site. Just beyond the paddock fence sat Hope's completed house, the front illuminated in sunshine, the back hiding in the shadows of trees.

He was suddenly aware of something directly beneath him, and he looked down to see animals grazing in the narrow portion of the upper meadow that ran above the creek. He squinted down at them, thinking they might be cows, but, as his eyes focused, he saw clearly that they were something else. They were buffalo, ten, perhaps twelve, of them, grazing calmly in that undisturbed portion of the upper meadow.

"I always wondered . . .," he said to himself, but before he could finish the thought a hand on his shoulder jarred him from his dream. He opened his eyes to see Dae's face looking down at him.

"Wow, were you sound asleep," she said softly. "I was worried there for a second. You're usually such a light sleeper."

"What time is it, Babe?"

"A little after three o'clock."

"So," he muttered, "getting back to the sleep part . . ." He stopped mid-thought, distracted by the huge smile on Dae's face.

"Edward just called. They're on their way to the hospital."

Adrenalin coursed across his shoulders and shot down his back, bringing him to an instant state of transcendence as complete as that of his flight above the upper meadow. He was wide awake.

"I'll get dressed," he said excitedly, pushing the blankets away from him. "No, wait, I need to shave first. He started toward the bathroom before turning around and asking, "Do you think I have time for a shower?"

"Yes," Dae laughed from the bed. "We both have time for a shower. You should know by now that first babies take their good, old time."

"But . . ."

"Why don't you jump in the shower? I'll make some coffee. I'm sure we'll get there in plenty of time." Dae headed for the kitchen, pushing her arms into a cotton robe.

Whatever else it held, Tuesday, November 10th wasn't off to a good start, weather-wise. It was cold and rainy, and just blustery enough to make one grateful to be in the warmth of the car. They drove along the new Route 611 until it merged with the original route not far from Easton. The yellow lights of the town came in and out of focus, clear when the windshield wipers had scraped the rain away, and blurred in each brief moment that the wipers were horizontal. Dae was calm, joyous about the impending birth of Jill's baby, but still aware enough of the hour to issue an occasional yawn. Jeff was nervous, and he couldn't have summoned a yawn if he had been awake for the previous three days.

As his eyes watched the winding road carefully, his thoughts drifted to Jill, and he allowed them to drift until Dae interrupted his reverie.

"What are you thinking about?" she asked. "Other than your new grandchild, I mean."

"Lots of stuff," he answered. "Mostly Jill, but lots of stuff."

"What about Jill?"

"We've talked about this before, so stop me if you don't want to hear the story again, but . . ."

"Okay, stop." After a long pause she added, "You know I'm just kidding. Of course I want to hear it."

"Jill started school early. She was a December baby in a school system that didn't want kids to start until they were six. Since she was only five when we thought she was ready to start; she had to be tested."

"And," Dae said softly, "the woman who did the testing for the school system lived next door."

"So, do you want me to go on?"

"Yes, I do. I think it's a beautiful story. I never get tired of hearing it."

"The test was on a Saturday, and I was out cutting the grass when Jill, all dressed up like she was going to school, walked next door to meet with Mrs. Sandley. She was over there for almost two hours.

"I was still working in the yard when she came bouncing across the grass, Jean Sandley waving to me from her driveway as she watched Jill safely home. It was bright and sunny, and Jill's nearly white hair seemed even lighter in the afternoon sun. She was wearing a white shirt and a plaid green jumper. I can see every detail now as clearly as I saw it then."

"I wish you had a photograph of it."

"I do, but it's one that only I can see—here, in my heart. And even with all the life that she and I have lived since—all the ups and downs and all the memories—when I think of Jill, I think about *that* little girl on *that* summer afternoon."

"What a great thing for you. What a *gift*."

"And now she's about to have a child of her own. My wish for her is that somewhere along the way she has a moment just like the one I had."

"I think your wish will come true," Dae said. "Knowing how much she's like you, I'd be surprised if it didn't."

They ascended the short hill that passed between the black railroad trestle and the Lehigh River and turned across the bridge into Easton. Off to their right the Lehigh dumped over the concrete falls and into the Delaware River.

Dae stared out into the cold blackness through the rain-splashed passenger window. "It really doesn't care," she said softly, "does it?"

"What doesn't care?" Jeff answered.

"The river. It just does its thing. It really doesn't care if it's bright and sunny or as yucky as it is right now. It doesn't care if this is the best day of our lives or the worst. It just does what rivers do, what nature does—it just bears witness to it all."

Jeff didn't say anything, mostly because he knew that anything he might say could only diminish Dae's observation.

A few minutes later, they reached Easton Hospital.

Once inside, they learned that Jill had been admitted and that Edward was with her.

"I guess this isn't a false alarm," Dae observed. "I think our family is going to expand today."

"And what a day for it to happen!" Jeff said gleefully.

"What do you mean?"

"November 10th is my mother's birthday. She would have been eighty-four today."

Dae just smiled. Her husband's emotional state seemed to have a physical presence. It was joy in its most raw, most primordial form.

Lillian Dae Martin was born at 6:01 p.m. As Dae would say the next day, and many times thereafter: "Everyone did fine— baby, mother, and father. Only Pop-Pop was a little shaky."

Jeff only agreed to make the drive home when it became obvious that both he and Dae were exhausted.

As they re-traced their route across Third Street, Jeff said that he wanted to make a brief stop. Dae knew where they were headed, and she also knew that the stop wouldn't be brief, but she was glad that they were making the journey to the cemetery.

On the other side of the bridge, they crossed under the railroad trestle, turned slightly to the right, and made the climb to the top of the escarpment. Once on top, they made their way along the wide road past blocks of old houses before emerging onto the wide flat area where Interstate 78 cut its imposing east-west path. On the other side of the highway the road began to gradually ascend as it neared the foot of Morgan's Hill. Then it zigzagged across the face of the mountain before straightening into a five-mile journey to the top.

As they drove, Jeff thought about the many times he had made this trip, and the many times he had looked out upon the splendor of the Lehigh River Valley from different points along the way. The mountain had once been the home to the deer and the bear, to the wolf and the bobcat, but now it was the domain of houses, schools, and the occasional gas station that sat hard by its undulating roads.

Just past an elementary school, two churches sat on opposite sides of the narrow road. Jeff turned left onto a road that was barely wide enough for the car, passing along the length of St. John's Lutheran Church and emerging in the old cemetery behind it.

It was well past dawn, but even though the rain had stopped earlier in the day, its chilly drear and oppressive grayness had remained behind. In the failing glow of a light behind the church, Jeff and Dae made their way across wet grass to a small plot, where two headstones bore the name Phillips.

"Well, folks," Jeff began as he swept leaves away from the front of the grave markers, "this has been quite a day. You must be ecstatic, Mom." He touched his hand to the name Lucia Anna, engraved above two dates: November 10, 1925 and February 5, 1986. "And, Dad, I know if she's happy, you're happy. Your great-granddaughter's name is Lillian Dae but . . ." He paused for a long moment. ". . . but you already know that."

As he drew back from the headstone, Jeff felt his hand ease into Dae's. A soft rain began to fall. Jeff paused at the other marker, where his great-grandparents were buried, and gently touched its cold, engraved surface.

"Lillian is five generations after them," he said. "Five generations."

"And how many before them," Dae answered, "that we know nothing about or will ever know anything about?"

As they walked toward the car, Jeff said, "My mother's funeral had to be postponed for three days because a snowstorm made the road up the mountain impassable."

"I know, Babe. You've told me many times."

"But the day she was buried was brilliant, crystal clear, and from the gravesite you could see the entire length of the river valley. All the trees were bare and it seemed as if you could see forever."

"It must have been breathtaking," Dae responded. "Absolutely breathtaking."

They drove back down the mountain in silence, raindrops gathering on the periphery of the windshield like vigilant spirits, guiding their path through the November morning.

* * *

When no one answered the door, Grace Caufield thought that she might have written down the appointment time incorrectly. "I'm sure he said two o'clock," she confirmed to herself. She rang the doorbell once more, and again there was no response.

"Miss Caufield," a voice called as Dr. Henry emerged from the side yard. "How nice to see you again."

"Oh . . .," she responded, obviously startled, ". . . Dr. Henry. For a moment there I thought I had the wrong time."

"No, no. You're right on time. I was just looking at some things over here on the side of the house." He surveyed a section of flowerbed by the front porch on his way to shake Grace's hand. "The gardens were one of my late wife's passions, but I'm afraid I don't do a very good job of keeping them up."

As she shook the man's hand, Grace suddenly saw the flowerbeds in a completely different way—what they had once been, rather than what they had become. She imagined a woman kneeling beside them, fawning over minute details in the sunshine while her bookish husband explored some obscure volume in the seclusion of his study. The image left her with a good feeling about both of them.

"I'm sure she appreciates whatever you do."

"It's kind of you to say that, Grace. It's rubbish, of course— she would scold me for letting her gardens run to riot, even though she wouldn't be surprised—but it's kind of you to say." Opening the front door, he added, "Please come in."

They stood in the kitchen, which seemed as gracefully congested as the other rooms Grace had seen, as Dr. Henry heated water for tea. A few minutes later, teacups in hand, they adjourned to the comfort of the leather chairs in his office.

"So," Henry began, "your book ends with the Walking Purchase?"

"For all intents and purposes, yes. I may include a little about the following four or five years, when James Logan hired the Iroquois to forcibly remove the remaining Lenape from the Walking Purchase lands, but yes, that's basically where it will end."

"And, if I remember our telephone conversation, you're fairly comfortable with the events surrounding the meetings at Durham and Pennsbury."

"I think so. There's just not that much information about them." She paused briefly. "To me, the more interesting thing is the trial walk prior to the meeting at Pennsbury."

"Oh, yes."

"Would it be too strong to say that the Walking Purchase was meant to be a knockout punch?"

Dr. Henry smiled at her use of the term. "I think you could say that. The Lenape were certainly reeling, if I may continue your metaphor, and regardless of the intent, the Walking Purchase clearly did them in."

Grace listened to him carefully, watching his face as he spoke, and it was clear to her that he had absolutely no question about the intent. "Dr. Henry," she began, "you know much more about these events than I do, but almost every source I've checked confirms that this was a set-up from the beginning. It was . . ." She paused, searching for the appropriate word.

"Heinous?" Henry offered. "Does that come close to what you're looking for?"

"Heinous enough," Grace agreed, "to cause the Lenape to later lash out and kill whites. A number of sources claim that there's no record of a Lenape killing a white person between the arrival of William Penn and the Walking Purchase. But they killed a number of them as a result of the Walking Purchase and the subsequent alienation from the British. They had to be pretty upset."

Henry looked at her expectantly but said nothing.

"What happened in Philadelphia in August of 1737? I mean, that's when the Lenape acquiesced to the walk. *Something* must have changed."

Dr. Henry took a sip of tea, looking into the cup as he returned it to the saucer, as if he expected to find the answer to Grace's question there. "I'm not sure," he answered, "that anything had changed. I think things had *intensified*. It had been well over two years since the meeting at Pennsbury, and the pressures that Thomas Penn was feeling then had only increased. People continued to pour into the area looking for land. There was plenty to be had, but the Lenape were in the way."

"So why, in your opinion, did the Lenape finally give in?"

"I think there were a number of things." He shifted into the corner of the leather easy chair. "The first was that the Lenape were feeling quite a bit of pressure of their own. Relations with the Penns and Logan had become increasingly strained, and that did not serve the Lenape well. They just couldn't afford hostilities.

"Another is that the Lenape believed the walk would be made along the Delaware River, and that was worrisome enough for them."

"You mean because of the possible intrusion into their hunting grounds to the north?"

"Exactly. They couldn't imagine a worse outcome, even though the actual outcome was *much* worse. That's where the map came in."

"The map?" Grace moved forward in her chair. "I'm not sure I know what you're referring to."

"At the Philadelphia meeting," Henry said, "Thomas Penn showed a map to the four Lenape sachems. Apparently, it was a rough, hand-drawn thing. It showed the general contour of the Delaware River to the northwest above Philadelphia, and then back to the northeast at Easton. Along the northwest leg, Penn had drawn a line, indicating the direction of the walk."

"But it wasn't," Grace interrupted, "the line of the actual walk."

"No," he agreed. "The actual walk was considerably more to the west."

"And what about the walk off after the walk? Isn't that where Benjamin Eastburn comes in?"

Henry smiled again. "You've obviously been doing some reading. Yes, Eastburn was the surveyor general, and he was the one who changed the rules. Or," he qualified, "the one who executed the plan of the people who wanted them changed. He created a line from the end of the walk, near the present-day town of Jim Thorpe, northeast to the Delaware River, making the area of the walk twice what the Lenape expected."

After making some notes regarding Thomas Penn's map of the walk, Grace said, "I have to go back to what I said when we first started. This *was* an intentional knockout punch. The more I learn about it, the more obvious that becomes."

"There are some other things," Henry offered, "but they won't change your opinion."

"It would take a lot to change it," she responded. "Please go on."

"Well, two things come to mind. The last major treaty between the Proprietary Council and the Indians had been made in 1718. The treaty was really with the Iroquois, who were pretty much running things in the entire area by that time. Of the sachems who signed that treaty, three were still alive at the time of the meetings in Pennsbury and Philadelphia—Sassoonan, Shickalimy, and Civility. None of them were invited to participate in the meetings that led up to the Walking Purchase because . . ."

"Because," Grace interrupted, "if Thomas Penn's 1686 deed was legitimate, it would have at least been mentioned in the 1718 meetings."

"Yes, of course."

"Forgive me for interrupting, Dr. Henry. And you're right, my opinion is not changing."

"The other thing is this: the Lenape sachems who were at Pennsbury and Philadelphia asked that, if they agreed to the walk, their people would be allowed to live unmolested on whatever lands changed hands. Although agreed to by the Penns, the promise was later broken when the Lenape were run off the land."

They sat quietly for a minute or two, Grace taking some additional notes and Henry studying the imaginary tea leaves in the bottom of his cup.

"Would you like more tea?"

"Yes, if it's not too much trouble. That would be nice."

Grace stood up to stretch, while her host was in the kitchen heating water for tea. As she looked around the office, she was once again struck by the orderly chaos that had been so apparent to her on her first visit. There were books and papers everywhere, each seeming to lie exactly where it had last been used. She was absolutely certain that Dr. Henry could find anything, even a single sheet of lined notepaper, within a second or two of needing it. She sensed very strongly that in seeing his study she was looking directly into his mind.

The view from the other side of the large desk provided even greater insight into the complexity of both the office and the man. Books occupied every space that would accommodate them, and there were entire shelves of binders and journals. On one wall, a square, framed parchment map occupied a large area between bookshelves. The zigzag line of the Delaware River was immediately recognizable, but there wasn't a single word on the map to identify anything else. There were drawings, most of them quite rudimentary, that indicated villages, hunting grounds, and fishing areas, but there were no words.

Grace's attention was drawn to a black and white photograph on Dr. Henry's desk. A couple smiled back at her. The man, who was much too young to be Leonard R. Henry, Ph.D. and Professor Emeritus at Princeton, bore a striking resemblance to the man making tea in the kitchen. The woman who sat beside him, the side of her face pressed against his, a small tuft of white flowers in her hair, looked out from the photograph with a compelling vitality that left Grace nearly breathless. She wasn't merely living, she was alive, and it was in that moment that Grace embraced the distinction for the first time. It was easy to imagine the woman in the flowerbeds outside, bringing as much joy to the day as the sun above her and the flowers at her feet.

"I see," a voice said from the doorway, "that you and Julia have met."

Grace looked up, startled for the second time in one afternoon, to see Dr. Henry doing his best to balance two cups of tea. "I'm so sorry," she offered. "I didn't mean to pry."

"Not at all," the man answered. "And besides, how does one pry in a place like this?" His face broke into a wide smile that spoke to his own inner vitality.

"This is a wonderful photograph, Dr. Henry. She is absolutely lovely."

"It doesn't do her justice. Believe me when I say it doesn't do her justice."

As she reached for the cup of tea, Grace's fantasies about their life were as wild and far reaching as the plants in the gardens of the front yard. She wondered if a photograph of Robert Dawes and her would ever sit on a desk or hang on the wall of a study, and the notion made her smile.

"If you don't mind," Grace said, easing back into the leather chair with her tea, "I would like to talk about the Walking Purchase, itself. Just in my own modest research I have found many inconsistencies."

"Such as?"

"Well, some people confuse the Walking Purchase with the trial walk that took place before the meeting at Pennsbury, even though they occurred more than two years apart."

"Yes, it's an excellent example."

"And there's considerable disagreement about what actually happened, including in the accounts of supposed eyewitnesses."

"Which makes sense when you think about it, especially if the eyewitness in question had any conscience whatsoever."

"What are your views, Dr. Henry?" Grace turned to a clean page of her lined tablet.

"The four Lenape sachems," he began, "finally acquiesced to the walk during the meeting in Philadelphia, which the Lenape called Coaquannock, on August 25, 1737. The actual walk took place a little more than three weeks later on September 19th and 20th. In between, as we have already discussed, yet another trial walk was made.

"The official walk included quite a contingent of people, at least at the beginning. It was overseen by Timothy Smith, the sheriff of Bucks County, and Benjamin Eastburn, the surveyor general. Two of Smith's deputies were involved—John Chapman and Nicholas Scull—as was James Steel, Jr., the nephew and clerk of the receiver general."

"I'm aware of his uncle's involvement," Grace interjected. "I read about a letter from him to Timothy Smith asking about the status of the trial walks."

"Exactly. Then, of course," Henry continued, "there were the actual walkers—Edward Marshall, James Yates, and Solomon Jennings. There were others, although very little has been written about who they were or why they were involved." He paused for a moment, as if mentally confirming the names of the participants. "Oh, I almost forgot. A man named Joseph Knowles, who was a nephew of Timothy Smith's, was sent on ahead of the walkers with horses carrying provisions."

"And the Lenape, Dr. Henry? I know they were at least involved on the first day."

"Yes. John Combush was one, and Joe Tuneam was another. His Lenape name was Neepaheilomon, and he supposedly spoke English very well. There was a third man, named Tom, who was Tuneam's brother-in-law.

"The walk began in Wrightstown, here in Bucks County, about ten miles southeast of where we are right now, but the location differs from account to account. Most of them agree, however, that it was started by the sheriff at 6:00 a.m. on the 19th.

"It followed a generally northwestern route, along the Durham Road at first, and then along existing Indian paths and through wooded areas that had been re-cleared following the August 25th meeting. The trail was very easy to follow, which inspired the immediate objections of the Lenape, who were concerned about both the pre-arranged trail marks and the direction of the walk. They were adamant that the walk was to be made closer to the Delaware River.

"The walkers stopped for lunch at noon, and then walked until 6:15 p.m., the additional fifteen minutes being allowed to make up for the lunch break."

"So," Grace asked, "the Indians were vocal about what was going on?"

"Yes. They even complained that their moccasins were not suitable for the terrain they were walking, since they had expected to be walking closer to the river."

"That night," Henry continued, "they slept near the town of Hockyondocquay, which is where Lappawinsoe lived."

"One of the four sachems who agreed to the deed in Philadelphia, right?" Grace confirmed.

"Yes, the same man. The second day did not get off to a good start. The weather was cold and rainy, and some of the party's horses had run off during the night. It took some time to find replacements. To make matters worse, the Indians, angered by the events of the first day, didn't show up for the walk. Timothy Smith responded by sending word to Lappawinsoe, asking for men to take their place. Lappawinsoe, who had obviously been told about the direction of the walk and the clearing of sections of the trail, told Smith's messenger that he would send no men, saying something like, 'They got all the best land and they can go to the devil for the bad.' Nonetheless, John Combush did return with two other Indians, but they ended up walking less than ten miles before turning back in the rain.

"With all the delays, the second day didn't begin until eight o'clock. Solomon Jennings was the first walker to quit, leaving between 11:00 a.m. and noon. James Yates gave up about thirty minutes before the walk ended, apparently 'lame and tired,' but there are accounts that . . ."

Grace completed the statement. ". . . that he had been drinking too much and fell into the river."

"Precisely. Edward Marshall completed the walk at 2:00 p.m. near Pocono Mountain, where the town of Jim Thorpe is located today. As the winner, so to speak, he was entitled to both money and lands from Thomas Penn. He eventually received a little money and no land, a betrayal that may have caused him to later admit that the Lenape had been deceived."

Grace finished writing a note about Edward Marshall and then underlined something higher on the page. "So it was Benjamin Eastburn who drew the northeasterly line to the river?"

"Yes. The Lenape were outraged that the walk had covered more than sixty-five miles, especially Lappawinsoe, who had spoken so eloquently at the meeting at Pennsbury. And they became angrier still when Eastburn drew a right angle as the northern border of the walk. So, instead of drawing a line due east to the Delaware River, he drew it to the northeast, resulting in a loss to the Lenape of nearly twelve hundred square miles."

"And things," Grace added, "were *never* the same after that."

"To use your term," Henry agreed, "it was a knockout punch."

"One thing bothers me . . .," Grace began. "Well, actually a number of things bother me, but one thing *really* bothers me— how did the Lenape not see this coming?"

"I understand," he said, "but the deception was quite thorough. In 1718, the Proprietary Council used the Iroquois to its advantage, having them make agreements on behalf of the Lenape. In fact, Shickalimy, who had been appointed by the Iroquois to represent the Lenape in the 1718 meetings, was only half Lenape. And the same sachems who were involved in 1718, and who could have spoken more reasonably to the legitimacy of the suspicious 1686 deed, were intentionally excluded from the meetings leading up to the Walking Purchase."

"You referred to them before," Grace said, looking at her notes. "Sassoonan, Civility, and Shickalimy?"

"Yes, precisely." Henry paused long enough to put his empty teacup on a nearby end table. "So, now that I know where your book ends, may I ask where it begins?"

"In 1701, when William Penn departs from Pennsylvania for the last time. It's just amazing to me that a culture so long established could be brought down in just thirty-six years."

"There was certainly more both before and after, but you are quite correct that the real damage was done in those years." For a moment he didn't say anything, lost in thought about the timeframe Grace was focused on. "Yes," he finally added, "it was a sin."

Grace thought about the title she was considering for her book and smiled pensively.

* * *

She stood at the back of the top deck of the ferry, her gloved hands resting on the railing. It wasn't a good day to be standing outside—she would have been more comfortable on one of the lower decks—but Emily FitzRoy couldn't imagine making this short trip in anything but the open air.

Across the harbor, the business district of New York City shivered in the morning drear, embarrassingly naked without its trademark insignia. The landscape was still imposing, a cluttered kingdom of concrete and steel, but the absence of the World Trade Center made it less formidable, more vulnerable, as if its king had died in battle.

The ferry began its slow withdrawal from the dock, easing into the harbor and then turning to the port side and toward Ellis Island. The soft rain continued to fall, but it felt amplified out on the water and she pulled up the collar of her coat to meet the edge of her knit cap. She thought about going downstairs, but the thought passed as quickly as it had come. This was a trip that had to be made outside.

Isn't that how it's supposed to be? she thought. *The millions of people who came here from other countries—did they first see America while drinking a latte on the café deck? Hardly. They were outside, full-faced to the elements, squinting at the Statue of Liberty— terrified of what would happen in the ensuing hours; excited about what might happen in the days that followed; hopeful that the future held more than the past.*

Her own ancestors had settled in Jamestown long before people immigrated through Ellis Island, but it was easy for her to empathize with those who had arrived in New York at the turn of the century—castoffs from just about every country in the world—and as the wet wind blew against her face, she felt as if they were standing at the railing with her. She could feel their strength and their resolve; she could sense the ether of anticipation that subdued their fear.

"Isn't that how it's supposed to be?" she said quietly, with no one but the harbor to hear.

Fifteen minutes later, she was walking toward the front doors of the Immigration Museum. As she climbed the steps, a group of elementary school children gathered hastily in the rain for a class picture. "They couldn't have picked a worse day," she said to herself as she watched the photographer, a round woman in a purple jacket, wipe water from the lens of her digital camera.

Emily had come to Ellis Island to see an exhibit pertaining to to the Lenape, its earliest inhabitants. She had seen the exhibit at the Mercer, and she was more than familiar with the exhibit at the university, but she had read that this exhibit included information about the current-day Delaware people who lived in parts of Oklahoma—the people with whom she most wanted to talk.

"Excuse me," she said to a young man at the information desk, "can you tell me where the new Lenape exhibit is?"

"Of course," he answered, rising to his feet with a broad smile.

Rather than returning the smile, Emily stared back at him with a look that said, *Please just tell me; please don't offer to show me.* She was used to the way men reacted to her, and she had long ago learned to control moments like this. When she wanted the attention, she allowed herself to be flattered. When she didn't want it, she turned it away as quickly and as directly as possible.

"It's upstairs," the young man answered. "I'll be happy to show you if you'd like."

"I appreciate it," she said, "but I think I'll be okay."

She walked across the sprawling main lobby, which had once been the baggage room, to the elevator in the far corner. A few seconds later, she emerged on the third floor. The entrance to the exhibit was to her right—"Lenape: Ellis Island's First Inhabitants."

The seriousness of the exhibit seemed augmented by the austerity of the location in which it was housed. It had obviously not been constructed for someone who preferred to be hit in the face with information; any person who came here had to be willing to seek it out. A series of old, but very well maintained rooms extended away from the entrance and toward a distant back wall. Floors of hexagonal white tiles ended at brick tile walls, which rose up in turn to high, plaster ceilings. Steam radiators kept watch in each room, connected to distant boilers by exposed pipes that ran along walls to find them. There were no high-tech maps or displays, no dioramas, nothing to walk around for a multi-dimensional perspective. Most of the rooms had what appeared to be closets which had been converted into informal display cases—in the first, the gigantic tusk of a mammoth rested on end, silently testifying to the age of the Lenape culture.

The exhibit was laid out chronologically in an order that had become increasingly familiar to Emily—the Paleo-Indian Period, the Archaic Period, the Woodland Period. Visible and extremely well-written placards described Lenape life in each of the timeframes. As she expected, most of the information was cultural, including descriptions of Lenape life during the time of William Penn, but the information about the years that followed openly described the deceit and betrayal endured by the Lenape. The litany was disturbingly consistent.

Emily found some things peculiar about the overall exhibit. Nothing was displayed on the floor except a dugout canoe that would have been nearly impossible to include in any other way.

At the same time, the handful of display cases, most of which held books, papers, or small artifacts, were very poorly lit. At first, Emily thought it was an oversight, but as she moved through the exhibit she found herself leaning toward the notion that the lighting was by design—a not-so-subtle metaphor for a culture that had been lost in the darkness.

She was surprised by what she found in the last room. It was dedicated to the descendants of the Lenape who now lived in other states, including the Delaware in Oklahoma. There were photographs and quotes from the people, cases that displayed the crafts of their artists, and large placards with wonderful quotes from their elders. It was obvious to Emily that someone had developed enough of a relationship with these people to gain this much insight, and she wondered who that was and how it was done. But even though it went far beyond what she had been able to find out, the information in the room felt like little more than a carefully crafted veneer. She was left with the haunting sense that much more waited on the other side of the wall, in an imaginary room that had been excluded from the exhibit.

As she made her way back toward the entrance, she thought about the exhibits at the university and the Mercer Museum, and this one at Ellis Island, and she found herself hoping that something of an enlightenment might be occurring— an enlightenment that would make the history and plight of the Lenape culture more accessible to anyone who wanted to understand it.

Before she left, she stopped to re-read a placard that was mounted high on the wall of a room near the front of the exhibit. She had glanced at it quickly before, but now she took the time to examine its words more carefully. She drew them to her as if pulling them down to the floor, where she could move around them from every perspective.

> *Their Government is by Kings, which they call*
> *Sachema . . . Every King hath his council, and that*
> *consists of all the Old and Wise men in his Nation,*
> *which perhaps is two hundred People: nothing of*
> *Moment is undertaken, be it War, Peace, Selling*
> *of Land or Traffick, without advising with them;*
> *and which is more, with the Young Men too. 'Tis*
> *admirable to consider, how Powerful the Kings are,*
> *and yet they move by the Breath of their People.*

According to the information, these were the words of William Penn, written in 1683, when he had been in the province of Pennsylvania for less than a year.

The ferry trip back wasn't direct. It made a stop at the Statue of Liberty, before returning to its original departure point. It was raining a little harder now than it had been earlier, and Emily found herself nearly alone on the top deck. She stood by the railing on the starboard side as the boat circled in front of the great copper lady.

Emily had made the trip a number of times before, and each time had experienced a similar response to the statue. "It doesn't look that big," she said to herself, and even framed by a gray sky it really didn't look that big. But then she saw the few people brave enough to be out in the elements, moving past the statue's pedestal like insects in the rain, and she understood clearly both its mass and the massive ideal it represents.

On the trip home, Emily played William Penn's quote over and over in her mind. *They move by the breath of their people,* she thought to herself before saying the words aloud. "They move by the breath of their people."

She found Penn's words to be beautiful, a tribute to the relationship between Lenape leaders and the people they led. "But who is moving now?" she asked the solitude of the car. "These people have clearly moved Jeff Phillips, and they moved George Cameron long ago. Have they moved Grace and Robert?" The windshield wipers swept back and forth against the glare of headlights in the northbound lanes, moving her to an undeniable conclusion. "And they're obviously moving me."

She imagined the small island before the Statue of Liberty had been placed there. What she saw was raw and primitive, rich with tall trees and green undergrowth. At the water's edge, bronzed natives cast fishing nets into the water while their children explored on the nearby sand. Somewhere far away, great canvas sails filled with wind and rushed to the west. On the decks below, people watched with emotions as far flung as the very sea on which they were sailing toward liberty. The sails would not stop filling for hundreds of years, and Emily wondered what the Lenape, the original inhabitants of Ellis Island, must have thought when they first saw their billowed magnificence on the eastern horizon.

* * *

AUGUST 1737

The deathwatch was nearly over and they were both at peace with it. Time and circumstance had brought them together—a

Nanticoke man, an elder of a people that had once been feared as witches and sorcerers; and a young Lenape shaman, a man forced to grow into the role before his time.

As the relentless torrent of white people had washed from the ocean to Lenapewihittuk and beyond, people of different tribes had been pushed to the west and the north. Very few Indians remained on the east side of the river or on the lands to the south of the great bay into which it emptied. When it became difficult to move farther west because of the intrusion of the Iroquois there, those who had lived to the east and south for generations were forced to move north to the stretches of the river above Coaquannock and Trent Towne, and toward the lands of the Munsee. Among them were the remnants of the Nanticoke, the feared people from whom His Spirit Watches was descended.

The man with whom Walks Alone now waited was one of them, weakened by a journey he was too old to make, overcome by sickness from prolonged exposure to the heat and rain, and resigned to be chased no farther from his home. His earthly journey would end soon, and as he lay on the reed mats in front of the young Lenape, he mouthed barely audible prayers to the Great Spirit.

The man was completely alone. The people who had traveled with him had moved on, leaving him to the care and compassion of the young shaman. There was little that Walks Alone could do except pray for and with the man. It would have been better, he thought to himself, if His Spirit Watches were with them. Then the man would at least have spent his last hours comforted by the compassion of one of his own people. Or it would have been better if Four Bears were with them. Then he would have passed peacefully into the life beyond, gracefully guided by her seemingly limitless wisdom. But the thoughts passed quickly as Walks Alone resolved to be whatever the man needed, whether it was compassionate, wise, or something else. He resolved that this stranger would know Four Bears and His Sprit Watches through him, their friend and pupil.

As Walks Alone held his hand, the man slowly opened his eyes and turned his head to look at him. "It is good," the man said, "that I have come here to die with you. Perhaps now . . ." He coughed from the mere exertion of speaking. ". . . perhaps now I can stop running from a deceitful enemy—an enemy who smiles as he takes my home."

Looking directly into his eyes, Walks Alone pressed the man's hand into his.

The man took a few labored breaths before even trying to continue. "The enemy who waits for me now stands straight, talks straight. He will win, but he does not make me angry or ashamed."

"Then," Walks Alone answered, "perhaps he is not your enemy. Perhaps he is your friend."

A thin smile crossed the man's face as he repeated, "It is good that I have come here to die with you." He began to inhale, but the air never made it to his lungs.

"Wanishi, my old friend. Wanishi for allowing me to wait here with you. Your spirit guide waits with you now. May he show you the way across Ane."

Walks Alone closed his eyes and took in the deep breath that had evaded the dying man. He drew it deep into his abdomen, forcing his entire midsection out in a round ball. He held it there for as long as he could before blowing it back into the air of the wigwam. He drew in another breath, and then another, exhaling each in turn until he drifted into a vision. A male wolf waited there, its dark eyes looking out at him from a face that had gone white with age. They silently assured him that there was a place farther upriver—a peaceful place to which one could not be followed; a bright place that the shadow of deceit could not overtake. The wolf turned and followed the path along the water, walking steadily, as if certain that nothing could catch it now. Walks Alone smiled as he opened his eyes. "Yes," he said to the lifeless form of the old Nanticoke, "it is good that you have come here to die."

He sat quietly with the body of the old man for a long time, softly inhaling the smoke of the cedar that burned in a nearby bowl. He didn't know how much of the day had passed, and he might not have known were it not for the commotion that rose beyond the covered entrance to the wigwam. Rising to his feet, he moved out into the early summer evening as the last of the long shadows shinnied up the trees on the escarpment across the river.

In the growing darkness outside the wigwam, His Spirit Watches stood with Nutimus and a small group of Munsee men.

"The Nanticoke man," Nutimus began, "does he still live?"

"No," Walks Alone said softly. "His journey has begun." It was clear to Walks Alone that there was news of the meeting from which the men had returned, but equally clear that none of them, not even Nutimus, would say anything to distract from the solemnity of death. "Tell me," he said, breaking the silence for them, "what happened in Coaquannock."

"We have agreed to the walk," Nutimus answered. "Four of us made our marks—Lappawinsoe, Tishcohan, Monockyhickon, me. We signed the paper of Thomas Penn and James Logan."

"What of Sassoonan," Walks Alone asked, "and what of Civility? What of Shickalimy?"

"None were there," Nutimus answered. "The white men asked none of them to be with us."

Walks Alone stood pensively, looking straight into the eyes of Nutimus, but obviously reluctant to ask his question.

"You may speak," Nutimus offered. "You have proven yourself more than worthy to speak."

"Why did you agree? Nothing has changed in the past two winters." He paused before adding, "If there has been any change, it has been for the worse."

"Your words are true. Things have worsened. And that is why we agreed—to keep a peace with the many whites who pour onto these lands."

"It is a hard path," His Spirit Watches offered, "but a wise one. It was made a little easier by the map that Penn showed Nutimus and the other sachems."

"Map?" Walks Alone asked.

"Yes," Nutimus interjected. "Penn's map showed that the walk will take place not far from the river. Our hunting lands will not be lost. It is not what we want, but if our fathers agreed, as the white men insist, it is the best that can be hoped for."

"When is the walk to take place?"

"Soon," His Spirit Watches answered. "Within a moon."

"And Talks For Us? What did my uncle say?"

"He is angry," Nutimus said. "He does not trust one word that comes from the mouth of Penn."

"Wanishi," Walks Alone said softly, "and I give thanks to the Great Spirit for the leadership of sachems like Nutimus. May the grandchildren of our grandchildren say his name with reverence."

Nutimus nodded but said nothing. Then the small group of men walked away to sit in circle, eat, and talk about the meeting in Coaquannock and the impending walk of Lenape lands.

* * *

New Lenape Exhibit To Be Dedicated at Mercer Museum

Grace Caufield, *Courier Times* Staff Writer

A new exhibit pertaining to the Lenape Indians who once inhabited Bucks County and the Delaware River valley will be dedicated at the Mercer Museum in Doylestown on Friday, December 11th.

The museum, which was built by Henry Chapman Mercer, renowned Bucks County historian and archaeologist, is the home of more than 15,000 artifacts collected by Mercer during his lifetime. Most of them are the tools of different trades and crafts, but there are exceptions. For many years, the museum has also housed an exhibit about the Lenape Indians and the period following their initial contact with Europeans in the early seventeenth century.

According to Robert Dawes, director of the museum, the original exhibit has been dramatically expanded and moved to a more convenient location on the museum's main floor. "The new location is just off of the central court," Dawes noted, "and easily accessible by any visitor to the museum."

The new exhibit includes greatly expanded information about the 11,000-year history of the Lenape culture in this area. The information is complemented by many rare artifacts, some of which were in the original exhibit, but many of which were donated or loaned following a public request by the Mercer. "We're delighted," Dawes added, "that many private citizens have provided us with some very unique pieces, and institutions like the Smithsonian have been far more generous than we ever expected."

Even though the formal dedication will not take place until December 11th, the new exhibit will open to the public on Thanksgiving. "We think it's a symbolic time to open the exhibit," Dawes observed, "and we look forward to having many visitors with us during the long holiday weekend."

When asked about empty display cases at the far end of the exhibit, Dawes said, "That space is being held for what we hope will be the rest of the Lenape story, including information about the 16,000 Lenape, or Delaware, Indians who still live in different parts of the United States and Canada. We believe that they are the descendants of an extraordinary culture, and that they celebrate a rich and timeless tradition. We look forward to the day that their story will be told here."

"More and more information about the Lenape people seems to be entering the mainstream," he observed. "We're extremely pleased to be a part of it."

* * *

SEPTEMBER 1737

In the darkness of the familiar wigwam on the edge of the village, Walks Alone stirred restlessly. The small fire in the center of the wigwam had burned down completely, leaving behind nothing but gray ashes and the faintest smell of burned wood. When he was jolted into wakefulness, that smell was the first thing to greet him; when he managed to return to sleep, it was the last thing to send him on his way. But neither sleep nor wakefulness lasted very long.

He was certain that something was terribly wrong. An agitation lodged somewhere deep within him like an invisible splinter, its presence impossible to verify, its painfulness even more impossible to ignore. Like the smell of the burned-out fire, it would not go away, taunting him mercilessly about how long it might choose to remain concealed in darkness.

It was still well before dawn, long before the chirping of birds that announced the return of the sun, when sleep finally listened to his silent pleas and drew its veil across his eyes. He welcomed it with a gentle gratitude that he somehow managed to conjure from the dark ether between consciousness and deep sleep. And, on the heels of his thankfulness, came his final journey to the place in the woods where he had first seen the white buffalo.

Everything was much as it had been on each of his previous journeys. The path that faced the setting sun was tight and restricting, inhibiting even the simple act of turning around. Old undergrowth crowded in on him from both sides, tangled vines threatening to trip him at each step. The thick forest canopy pressed down on him relentlessly, preventing even the smallest rays of light from reaching the path where he stood. Then, as they had been each time before, the brush and the vines and the density of the canopy were blown away as if by the hand of the Great Spirit himself. Everything was cleared, instantly replaced by open space for previously restricted limbs and fresh air for laboring lungs.

Then the horses came—the three massive, white horses, hot determination glowing in their fiery eyes, irresistible energy blasting from their nostrils. Pounding by him effortlessly, as if they didn't even see him, they consumed the path beneath their powerful hooves in huge, unimaginable chunks. Walks Alone watched breathlessly as they disappeared toward the horizon.

Sensing a presence behind him, he whirled around, expecting to find the white buffalo, Four Bears, or both. Instead, he was shocked to see a wave of his people moving toward him on the path. Thousands strong, they moved slowly past him—men, women, children; elders being helped or guided, babies bound securely to cradleboards; the young and the vital, the dying and the infirm. They followed the cleared path together without looking back, their eyes focused on whatever lay ahead.

As he watched, he knew that he was seeing more than the last of the Lenape who lived on Lenapewihittuk; he was seeing *all* of the Lenape who had *ever* lived there. The spirits of the dead walked with the living, waiting patiently, compassionately for those who were not strong enough to complete the journey. They passed for what seemed like hours to him—*his* people leaving *their* land. He watched until every one of them had disappeared at the point where the path touched the distant horizon.

He began to follow after them, but he had only taken a few steps when the vines to his left and right slithered toward his feet like snakes, entwining his lower legs and climbing up his body until they had bound him completely. He struggled frantically to free himself but his efforts were useless. He was immobile, hopelessly entrapped.

"Such is the path of the Lenape."

He tried to turn to the right, but the vines were too constricting. He was forced to wait until the familiar figure of his teacher walked past him and into his view.

"Can you free me from this?" he asked Four Bears.

"Perhaps," she answered, "but it doesn't matter. You will be awake soon. And besides, the vines are not real; they are only a message."

"But they feel real."

"Only as real as the message, so you are clearly hearing it."

"What has happened here? If the horses are the white people, why do our people follow them?"

"The whites cleared the path of the day-and-a-half walk. They marked the trees so their runners could make the best times. They did this after you went to Pennsbury with Nutimus. And they did it again before the walk."

"But," Walks Alone exclaimed, "the walk was to be made along the river, not toward the setting sun."

"Lappawinsoe, Nutimus, and the others were deceived," Four Bears replied. "The walk was not along the river, and soon the deceit of Penn and Logan will be even greater."

"Why do our people leave?"

"They look for new homes and new lives. It is a white path, but the Lenape, like all native peoples, will follow it. Some will follow behind the whites, but most will flee before them."

"And me, when will I go?" Even before the words had left his mouth, Walks Alone knew the answer. The constrictions of the vines felt even tighter as he added, "I will not go. I am to remain behind."

"Yes, Young One," she said compassionately, "*that* is the message." She reached out and touched the side of his face, running the tips of her fingers from his brow to his chin. "I must leave with the others."

"But . . ." He choked on the thought and his words were held back with it. "But . . ."

"Will you see me again?"

"Yes. That is what I want to know—will I see you again?"

"That is for the Great Spirit to say. He is always with you, even when it is too dark to see one step ahead on the path. And . . .," she continued, nodding to a point behind them on the path, ". . . *he* will wait with you. As he said at the beginning, he will wait with you."

With that, the vines loosened their grip and Walks Alone turned to see the white buffalo standing on the path. He stood peacefully, as if unaffected by all that had happened, as if concerned only with the fate of the young shaman.

"But . . ." He turned back toward Four Bears but she was gone. He tried to follow after her, but, in the next instant, the path was blocked as completely as it had been at the beginning of his journey. The brush and branches, vines and leaves grew so quickly that the path was lost instantly behind their dark obstruction. He turned around to see the path behind, the buffalo, and the rising sun. Filled with fear, but content that this was indeed his destiny, he forced himself to take the first step to the east.

Then he awoke.

He threw back the skin that covered the entrance to the wigwam and stepped into the rainy September morning. It was much too late to be waking up, yet his head was still filled with sleep and the residue of his troubling dream. He could see each of its images—the white horses, the Lenape, Four Bears, and the white buffalo; he could hear the words of his teacher. He carried all of it out into the gray day, its great burden made heavier by the fear that he might have seen Four Bears for the last time.

There was no activity in the village. He knew that most of the people who still lived there had already left for a day's work on the farms of the whites, but he guessed that others were engaged with chores that allowed them to be inside, out of the dreary autumn rain. He called out in greeting as he approached the wigwam of Talks For Us and Looks Back. When the voice of Looks Back responded, he entered the wigwam to find her sitting by a small fire with Quiet Bird, carefully shaping a round clay pot.

"The morning is already old," Looks Back noted, "and you are just greeting it." She smiled warmly without looking away from her work. "I think you may have already grown soft."

Walks Alone smiled, grateful that Looks Back was still his mother and would always be his mother, and equally grateful for the teasing that distracted him from his dream, if only momentarily.

Quiet Bird rose to her feet and hugged Walks Alone enthusiastically. They had spent a great deal of time together on the previous day, after he had first arrived at the village, yet she greeted him on this dismal morning as if they hadn't seen each other for many winters. And the joy of her embrace brought with it the awareness that the events of the last ten winters had forced them to be apart much too often. No one, not even Looks Back or Talks For Us, would ever criticize him for it. In that time, he had evolved into a person of great importance and responsibility, even though the span of his life was only nineteen winters, and he could not be expected to do what others did. Even so, in his heart he quietly criticized himself for it, knowing that any day not spent near his family—and there had been many of them—was a day that would never dawn again.

Now fourteen, Quiet Bird was evolving into a young woman—tall and as fit as each of her parents—and Walks Alone had noticed the look in his uncle's eyes when other men looked at her. Not all of them were Lenape—some were from other tribes, some were white, and some were a combination of white and native—and his uncle's resistance to the new ways became even more strident where his daughter was concerned. As she left his embrace, Walks Alone said a silent prayer that the Great Spirit would send someone, or something, to guide her journey.

"It is a good day for this work," Walks Alone offered, nodding at the newly shaped pot. He sat with them, the details of his dream once again haunting his morning.

As he watched, Quiet Bird took a piece of knotted rope and carefully wound it around the pot just a few inches from the mouth. Once satisfied that it was exactly where she wanted it, she gently pressed the rope into the clay. She smiled softly, obviously pleased with her work, and then pulled it away, leaving the indentation of the rope and its spaced knots in the surface of the pot.

"It's beautiful," Walks Alone said. "Very beautiful."

He sat pensively, watching them work but saying very little. Every so often, one of them would make an observation or ask a question and he would respond, but for the most part he watched them work and tried to avoid being preoccupied with his dream.

"Why is my son troubled?" Looks Back finally asked. She looked away from her work and directly into his eyes.

Even with Quiet Bird sitting nearby, he didn't hesitate to tell Looks Back about his dream.

"Somewhere in the night this came to me . . .," he said, and he repeated the details of his encounter with the three white horses in the woods. Both Looks Back and Talks For Us had heard him tell the story before, and they knew that he had experienced it in both journey and dream, but to them it had never been more than a dark vision, something that they did not want to become real.

"This morning," he continued, "Four Bears came to me, as she has before, and she told me what it all means."

Looks Back stopped working, her clay-spotted hands drawing back from a conical pot. She looked up at him, grim anticipation in her eyes.

"We are deceived," he said in response to the look in her eyes. "The whites will not walk along the river as the sachems were led to believe by Thomas Penn and his map. They will walk more to the northwest. And they will walk much farther than the sachems think they will, their path having already been cleared and the way having already been marked."

"How much land?" Looks Back asked.

"And then we . . ."

"How much land?" she insisted.

Unable to look into her eyes as he answered, Walks Alone stared at the clay pot. "All of it. They will take all of it. After the walk they will make an unfair boundary and . . ." He once again raised his eyes to meet hers. ". . . they will have it all."

A tear made its way down the cheek of Looks Back, a tear that did not go unnoticed by her daughter. Quiet Bird rose and went to sit next to her.

"There is more," he said.

"What more can there be?" Looks Back's words crawled into the air on audible fear.

"I saw our people—all who have lived and all who live now— following the path of the horses toward the setting sun. The others went but . . ." He paused, silently regretting what he was about to tell her. ". . . but I did not."

The face of Looks Back filled with dark emotion as she gave voice to things that she would never say to a shaman but had to say to her son. "But it is only a dream." Even before she was finished saying them, she knew that the words were nothing but raw hope. She knew that it was *his* dream, *his* journey, and it had come to him many times over the course of many winters. Yet she wanted it not to be true. "It is only a dream," she repeated.

"My teacher came to me . . .," he said in solemn response, ". . . again."

Looks Back jumped to her feet and left the wigwam. Walks Alone did not follow her immediately, wanting to give her time to be with her thoughts. He tried to comfort Quiet Bird, but she was now crying as well, upset by the reactions of her mother. Assuring her that he would return quickly, he went to find Looks Back, but as he turned toward the entrance, she walked back through it, followed by Talks For Us. His uncle looked sad and forlorn, as if lost to utter resignation.

Over the next hour, Talks For Us spoke about what had happened. He talked about being at Hockyondocquay with Lappawinsoe and Tishcohan when Joe Tuneam and the others appeared there unexpectedly. He recounted what they had said about the walk not taking place along the river, and confirmed that the white men making the walk had indeed walked more to the northwest, stopping for the night not far from Hockyondocquay itself. He talked of the disgust of Tuneam and the others, and of their refusal to continue on the walk that morning, and he spoke of the sheriff's request for more Indians and of Lappawinsoe's reply that they could go to hell.

And he spoke of his own disgust. "They cleared the path in advance, maybe more than once, and they marked the trees so the walkers would keep a steady line to the northwest."

As her husband said the words, Looks Back looked at Walks Alone. She knew that it was *his* dream.

"It was all planned," Talks For Us exclaimed, "long before the meeting at Coaquannock, maybe before the meeting at Pennsbury!"

It was *his* journey.

"I said they would push this," Talks For Us said, his anger fading into the affirmation of what he had always known to be true, "and they have pushed it until it can be pushed no more."

"It can," Looks Back said sadly, "be pushed more."

"What do you mean?" Talks For Us asked. "How is that possible?"

She looked at Walks Alone solemnly, and this time she understood that she was only seeing the shaman. Her son had disappeared somewhere in the haze of a distant past.

* * *

It was the Friday after Thanksgiving and, as Robert Dawes had hoped, the museum was crowded. As he watched a steady stream of people file in and out of the Lenape exhibit, he knew that the decision to open on Thanksgiving weekend had been a good one. People had extra time to take in an exhibit that lent a new vitality to the staid Mercer, and, besides, Thanksgiving was the one time of year when the joined history of the red man and the white flowed with a mythic grace.

Content that things were running smoothly, Dawes retreated back across the central court and toward his office. As he passed more people in the court, he smiled once again at their obvious attraction to the new exhibit.

Reggie McCarthy didn't notice the regal Dawes as he passed by just a few feet away. He was too busy trying to keep his brother Darwin under control. Darwin was awestruck by the central court, pointing gleefully to the covered wagon suspended from the ceiling four floors above. "Calm down!" he said to Darwin in a strong, but controlled, whisper. "It's just a fuckin' wagon."

But Darwin had never seen a real Conestoga wagon before, and he certainly had never seen one hanging from the ceiling of a castle. He jumped excitedly, as if he could somehow fly up to touch it.

Darwin was nearly a foot taller and much stronger than his brother, and Reggie was having trouble controlling his frenzied gestures toward the wagon. They were attracting way too much attention. Doubtful that Darwin's excitement would subside any time soon, Reggie resigned himself to a temporary delay in his plan. "Okay, *imbusel*," he said to Darwin, leaning close to his brother's ear, "we'll do it *your* way."

"We'll do it your way!" Darwin repeated. He hadn't raised his voice, but the natural acoustics of the surrounding concrete carried it to people yards away. A few of them turned to look at the two men.

"Okay, okay," Reggie said to his brother, "just keep your . . ." He caught the expletive mid-throat, not willing to have it repeated to the people in the central court. "Just keep your voice down."

As they made their way up the steps to the higher levels, Darwin took every opportunity to look down into the central court from the nearest railing. By the time they reached the sixth level, he was beside himself with the view of the court and the improbable things suspended in the air only a few feet away. A longboat stretched out immediately in front of them, but now they were looking at it from above, and Darwin delighted in seeing the oars once used to propel it. The wagon hung in the air across the court, and it looked even larger when viewed from the same level. Darwin bounced his open palm on Reggie's shoulder, barely able to contain his glee.

It took some time, but Reggie was eventually able to calm Darwin enough to return to the floor of the central court. As they resumed their walk, Darwin's eyes gazed upward, darting back and forth between the things he had looked out at from each of the higher levels. Reggie had to guide him so that he wouldn't walk into people, but at least he was being quiet. They had already been there for forty-five minutes, much longer than Reggie had planned. He had told the lady at the reception desk that they would be less than ten minutes, and she hadn't charged them the regular admission fees, and Reggie knew that staying too long would only attract attention he did not want.

"Excuse me," he said to a woman who was standing off to the side with a young boy, "is this where the new Indian exhibit is?"

"Yes," she answered, "that's it there in the corner, under that sign." The sign read "Across the Millennia—The Lenape on the Delaware and Beyond," and the woman wasn't quite sure how the man could have missed it, but she was too preoccupied with a fussy child to pay too much attention.

Reggie led Darwin into the exhibit and began to look around. The strange assortment of artifacts, some emphasized by special lighting, assaulted both his senses and his sensibilities. There was a wooden mask, half red and half black; things that looked like small belts of purple and white beads; clay pots, some with markings that made no sense to him at all; spear points, arrowheads, and knives; and a number of pictures of Indian men with ponytails and tattoos on their faces. *Fuckin' heathens*, he thought to himself, making sure not to utter anything that might be repeated by Darwin.

A young woman in a blue blazer stood near the center of the exhibit, a plastic nametag identifying her as someone who worked for the Mercer.

"Uh . . .," Reggie said as he and Darwin approached. The woman was pretty and dressed in nice clothes, and she inspired an instant insecurity in Reggie. He didn't know if she was smart, but she looked back at him with a confidence that implied she could answer any question he might have, and the mere thought made him feel as if he were coming apart inside.

"Uh, i . . . i . . . is thi . . . this . . ." His stuttering waited for moments like this—moments that made him feel hopelessly insecure—and he wanted to give in to the crushing compulsion to grab Darwin and leave. But he stayed, somehow buoyed by his disgust that *fuckin' injuns who don't even live around here no more* were drawing this much attention. " . . . where th . . . th . . . the . . . ded . . . ded . . ."

"The dedication?" the woman asked. "Yes, sir, this is where the dedication is going to be. On the eleventh, two weeks from tomorrow."

It seemed to Reggie that everything they had done since entering the museum had attracted attention, and he began to believe that this wasn't such a good idea. He drew in a deep breath, trying to summon the strength to complete the task at hand. "Do you think . . ." He paused to take in another breath. "Do you think there'll b . . . b . . . be a lot of p . . . people here?"

"Oh, yes," the woman answered quickly. "And, of course, the director of the museum, Mr. Dawes, will be here, as will Dr. FitzRoy from the University of Pennsylvania and Miss Caufield from the newspaper. This is all the result of their work."

Reggie didn't hear the last part. He had found out what he wanted to know, when she had said "and Miss Caufield from the newspaper."

Reggie thanked the woman, trying to ignore her perpetual smile, and pointed Darwin toward the entrance. He stopped once or twice on the way out of the exhibit, feigning interest in artifacts in display cases and making mental notes about things like the three steps that led back up to the main floor. As he crossed the central court, Darwin shuffling along at his side, Reggie's confidence began to return. By the time they reached the parking lot he had regained his composure, far away from the threat of nice-looking, smart women, the kind of women who look down on real men—real men who really understand what's going on in the world; real men who don't . . . "Take no shit from nobody," he said out loud.

"No shit from nobody," came the predictable echo. "Take no shit from nobody."

* * *

Talks For Us walked upriver along the path, a heavy burden in his heart. He tried to walk quickly, but he found himself stopping at places like the inlet where he and Walks Alone had kept the weir—places where they had hunted and fished; places where they had sat and talked about Black Turtle and Margaretha; places where they had discussed the impossible tasks of sachems like Tishcohan and Lappawinsoe; places where they had shared their feelings about the destiny of their people. He would have had trouble walking by them on any ordinary day, but on this day he found it impossible.

He walked out of the shadow of the hillside and into a bright clearing of high, dying grass. It bowed gracefully in reverence to the coming winter. He knew the place well. Walks Alone had told him many times of his encounter with the two white men there, and the way in which His Spirit Watches had driven off the danger. Now, as he thought about Four Bears and her boy pupil, face to face with two armed men who could see no further than the evil at hand, his always-smoldering gratitude to His Spirit Watches once again burst into flame.

Halfway across the clearing, he saw a form coming at him from the other direction. At first, it was little more than a dark movement in the shadows, but as it neared the clearing it crystallized into the form of his nephew. He smiled as he watched Walks Alone draw closer, proud of what the boy had become, and awestruck that such a gift to his people should have come from an ill-fated love. *But, Brother—* The words rushed forth from the crevices of his memory. *This is my destiny.*

"I was on my way to see you," he said to Walks Alone.

"I know," his nephew replied. "I saw you walking in a dream."

"What did I say to you in my dream?"

"Nothing. You just looked at me, tears in your eyes."

"I will walk back with you."

"No, Uncle, I think it would be best if I walked back with *you.*"

They walked downriver, and silence walked with them for a long time. Walks Alone knew what his uncle had come to tell him, and that his silence hung on his reluctance to let the words pass between them. "I know that you must leave," he said softly.

"And I know," Talks For Us answered, "that you cannot go with us. I know that you want to, but you cannot."

Walks Alone stopped and turned to face his uncle. "Thank you for knowing. Wanishi." He paused for a moment, staring directly at Talks For Us, before adding, "Do Looks Back and Quiet Bird know?"

"Looks Back has always known. She is sad, but she has always known. And we have told Quiet Bird."

"When will you go?"

"Tomorrow, or the day after, perhaps. Winter will be here soon."

They turned to resume their walk, the cool September morning lighting their way with a profusion of color. Orange and yellow leaves moved slowly above them against a crystalline blue sky, melting in the shadows of the next hillside and then reappearing farther down the path.

They talked of many things—things that stretched back to Walks Alone's last memories of his father and earliest memories of his adoptive parents; things that one of them might have forgotten; things that neither of them would ever forget. Each of them knew that this would not be their last conversation, but each understood clearly that it would be the last conversation like this—just the two of them on one last journey along the river. And as they walked in and out of the shadows along the path, they moved in and out of the sunless understanding that they were going home to say good-bye.

Twenty

It was the perfect time to tell them, and Jeff had been looking forward to the moment with excited anticipation. Hope and Scott were both there for the long Thanksgiving weekend. Harry was home from school, but only for three nights. Everyone was together, and if his plan made as much sense as he thought it did, each of them would play an important part. But what he was about to propose would not be easy, and it would change all of their lives for many years to come.

He had asked everyone to come up to the gathering barn after dinner, and while everyone else stayed behind to talk, clean up, and take turns looking after seventeen-day-old Lillian, he and Harry went on ahead to set up for the family meeting.

"What do you have up your sleeve?" Harry asked as they entered the barn. "What wild dream are you going to follow?" Then he stopped in the middle of the floor, turned to his father and added, "Or are you already following it?"

Jeff smiled. "You'll just have to be patient."

With his son's help, Jeff piled logs in the fire pit. They placed them on end, leaning against each other, a pile of kindling in the space beneath them.

"That should do it," Jeff observed. "Light the kindling and we'll see what this looks like with something other than an artificial log." He already knew what it would look like, having seen it in more than one of his visions, but he still felt a wave of excitement as Harry lit the smaller pieces of dried wood. At first, the fire was little more than a random series of small flickers, burning like the fire in the middle of a log tepee, but it grew quickly, rising steadily through the weathered logs.

"Looks good to me," Harry said. "It's quite a fireplace."

"I'm sorry you can't stay longer," Jeff said without acknowledging his son's comment. "These visits always go so quickly."

"I know, but I have to get back. Finals will be here before I know it, and then I have to get ready to leave for England. I can't wait to spend the semester over there, but there's a lot to do before I go."

"Maybe Dae and I can come over to see you in the spring."

"That would be great. I know you've seen a lot of places over there. Maybe we can visit them together."

Jeff grew quiet, seemingly interested in the growth of the fire, but Harry knew what was on his mind. "She's doing well, Dad."

Without looking away from the flames, Jeff answered, "I'm sure she is. I never had any doubt that she would have a great life, but I still regret that I'm not in it. At first I thought her anger would pass, but she hasn't talked to me in three years."

"I think it's tough for both of you, tougher than either of you let on, but I still think it will pass."

"I used to think that. I used to think that things would change as she got older, as she began to see things as an adult, but that hasn't happened yet."

Harry hesitated, knowing that it would be hard to find anything that would be more difficult for his father to hear. "She just needs more time."

Jeff heard the words but he had trouble taking them in. He knew that *more time* undoubtedly meant different things to different people, but to him the words required a difficult verbal math. He had never been able to do the calculation. And when it pertained to a daughter who refused to speak to him, its incalculability was heightened beyond reason.

"Harry . . ."

"Of course, Dad," Harry interrupted. "I'll tell her you asked about her."

The fire had begun to burn brightly by the time everyone had convened in the barn. Jeff and Harry had arranged chairs around the periphery of the fire pit, but there were only eight of them, far too few to fill up the circle. And the distance between them was even more pronounced because the chairs of each of the couples were placed close together. Jeff hadn't planned where people would sit, but when everyone was seated, Hope and Scott were on the north point of the circle and Jill and Edward were on the south, the baby sleeping in her father's arms. Jeff and Dae sat on the west point, directly below the brown bear, and Harry sat to the east, Valeria trying to sit still on the chair next to him. No one believed that she would stay there for long.

"I know this is a little strange," Jeff started, "but I wanted to do this here. I wanted to know what it feels like to be gathered in this barn and around this fire pit."

"It's not a problem, Dad." Jill began, "but could you speak a little louder?"

He smiled at her joke, but, in his mind, he could see his visions of gatherings around the fire pit and he was grateful that this was the first of them.

"A few weeks ago," he began, watching the flames jump toward the copper hood, "I bought the produce farm across the road." He looked at Dae, knowing full well that this was one of the few things he had ever done without talking to her first. She looked back at him with a soft smile that assured him that she was neither upset nor surprised.

Everyone was thinking *why?*, but no one asked.

Jeff continued to look at Dae as he added, "I'm going to give it to the Lenape people."

The circle was so still that the sound of Valeria moving about on her chair was as pronounced as the sound of hammers on the roof had been only weeks earlier. It was the profound silence that always precedes the coalescence of questions in the surprised mind.

"You mean," Dae finally said, "as a place to live? Like a reservation?"

"Yes, as a place to live, but not as a reservation. That's a government thing."

"Who exactly are you talking about," Hope followed, "when you say *the Lenape people?*"

"The ancestors of the people who once lived in this area. Most of them are in Oklahoma, but there are others in Canada and Wisconsin, and there are some here in the east."

"Have you talked to any of them about this?" Hope asked.

"No."

"Then how do you know any of them will want to live here?"

Jeff had expected that Hope would ask these exact questions. Her experience with indigenous peoples in places like Honduras had made her particularly sensitive to the ways in which they see things.

"They may not. But even if we end up with eight hundred acres of farm and woods, I think this is the right thing to do."

The comment drew a line in the sand that assured everyone that this was not a debate about the pros and cons of such a gesture. *The right thing to do* did not speak to the *if*; it spoke to the *how*.

Dae was willing to sit and listen and participate in whatever way made sense, but she was also well aware of the direction in which the conversation was heading. "You've obviously been thinking about this for a while. What's your plan?"

"I know that sentimentality and reason seldom keep company," he answered, "but this is the true home of the Lenape. They should have a place, even if it's just a few acres. Hope is right, no one may want to live here, and if that's the way it turns out it'll be okay, but I still want to try."

No one said anything. They all knew that his sentimentality was indeed showing, and they also knew that it was an extremely powerful part of his makeup. Reason applied only to people who were willing to accept its limitations, and Jeff Phillips was not one of them.

"So," Scott asked, "you're going to let them use the farm for houses?'

"I'm glad that *you* asked that question, Scott. No, not exactly. The produce farm is a viable business and it can be self-sustaining for them—a way for them to prosper. Yes, they'll need houses, but there's more than enough land for them to be integrated into the farm."

"And," Scott added, already knowing the answer, "you'll set up a trust to complement the farm business."

"No, *you'll* set it up—all of it. I know it's a lot to ask, but I would like you to consider giving up your job to run it."

Scott sat back in his chair, for the first time overwhelmed by the gravity of the discussion.

"I don't want anyone who accepts our invitation to have to rely on anyone other than themselves. We'll create a school. Hope, you have a ton of experience in that area so that will be your part in this. Jill and Edward, you'll be responsible for the entire physical site." He paused before adding, "And Roberto is going to need a lot more cousins."

Hundreds of thoughts rushed forward in a rapid series of questions, observations, and answers.

"None of us knows anything about running a produce company."

"Fred Meyers has agreed to work with us for two years. He'll probably spend the winters with his daughters in Florida, but he'll be up here between Easter and Thanksgiving."

"How many people do you think that property will accommodate?"

"A few hundred, maybe, if we're smart about where we build houses."

"What if more than that want to come?"

"We'll expand. There's more than enough land on the north side of this property, right across the road from the farm. We can use it if we need to."

"What if it goes beyond that?"

"Then perhaps we will have done something truly meaningful, and we'll just have to figure it out at the time."

"Is the farm zoned for residential?" "What about water and sewage?" "Did you buy all of the business or just the land?" "Will the road accommodate the traffic?" "Have you talked with the county executives about this?"

Jeff answered the questions one by one, clearly detailing what he knew to be true, and candidly addressing what still needed to be worked on. Even though there were blanks to be filled in, he was confident that any potential deal breaker had been resolved. There was only one possible pitfall.

Dae extended a mental thumb and put it squarely on the issue. "Jeff," she began, "will politics get in the way here?"

There were few things that Jeff had thought about more. Even though he thought this was indeed the right thing to do, it was possible that the different ancestral groups of the Lenape might think otherwise. Some might embrace the idea; others might reject it completely. And some might insist that only their group was truly entitled to the land.

"If there's anything that will keep this from working, it's the Delaware themselves. I don't know enough about their internal workings to predict what will happen. Even Emily FitzRoy was stonewalled when she tried to speak with the people in Oklahoma.

"But this is their land." He stopped short, fully aware of what he had said. It would have been more accurate to say this *was* their land, but that's not how it had come out, and he was satisfied with the mistake. "They have a right to decide whether or not they want to live on it.

"Regardless of what you may think, I'm not being naïve here. I know that there will be race issues. There are people in this area who won't be able to accept this. I know that there will be resistance from some areas of government. Anything that smacks of restoring lands to Native Americans opens ugly cans of worms for them. And I know that even the people we are trying to help may not trust us completely. Some of them will think that this gesture is inspired by the white man's guilt. We'll probably have to deal with all of that."

Jeff looked into the blazing fire, his passion burning equally hot. He drew in a deep breath, trying to calm down.

"I keep thinking about something that William Penn said. I think Grace Caufield told me about it, or maybe it was Emily FitzRoy. Penn said something to the effect that he would not abuse God's love or be unworthy of divine guidance by defiling what came to him so easily. *"What came to me clean"*—that's the exact way he expressed it. So much of what I have—so much of what *we* have—came to us clean. One minute, I was just trying to do my best; the next minute, six Ping-Pong balls slid into a tube and I supposedly became something else. The hopelessly wealthy me was supposed to be different than the struggling me. Well, if that's what the Great Spirit had in mind . . ." He stopped, saying nothing for a few seconds. Valeria scrambled onto her mother's lap; white smoke trailed into the waiting flue. "If that's what he had in mind, he picked the wrong guy to give money to in such a *clean* way.

"I don't pretend to have all the answers, here, but maybe, just maybe, we have an opportunity to do a little bit of what William Penn intended when he came over here. When I die I don't want to explain to God that I had this idea but didn't have the courage to act on it."

Obviously restless, Valeria climbed down from Hope's lap and walked over to Jeff. "Pop-Pop," she said, tugging on his sleeve.

"Valeria," Scott called to her, "Pop-Pop's talking right now."

"Pop-Pop," the child insisted.

"What is it, Kiddo?"

"Will you make me a peanut butter and jelly sandwich?"

Gentle smiles curved every face in the circle. No one could say for certain if Jeff's plan would work, but everyone knew that it was going to be tried.

"There's stuff in the refrigerator in the apartment," Harry said softly.

"Okay," Jeff said, rising from his chair. "Valeria and I are going to make a sandwich, and then I want to tell you all about a dream I had—a dream about buffalo."

As he took Valeria's hand and headed for the apartment at the end of the gathering barn, Jeff felt an unusual sense of completion. There was a very long list of things that had to be done, and he wasn't sure which of them would be at the top of the list on Saturday morning, but for a brief moment things felt complete. Something had come full circle.

* * *

APRIL 1738

Walks Alone could not shake off his sadness. Wherever he went and whatever he did, it lurked in a shadowy background, ready to rush into the smallest crack between thoughts or words. No distraction was enough to prevent it from coming forward.

He had gone to the woods thinking that solitude would help. There he could sit quietly and think about his teacher, his aunt and uncle, a father he could barely remember, and a mother he had never known. And maybe, he fantasized, he would walk out of the woods to find Talks For Us retrieving fish from the weir with his bare hands, or Four Bears sitting quietly near the fire pit in the lodgehouse. Maybe he would emerge from the forest and find that all of this had been little more than a very bad dream.

His Spirit Watches had insisted on going with him, concerned that nearly everything that lay beyond the escarpment was too unpredictable, too volatile to face alone. But Walks Alone had been just as insistent about going by himself, and he had managed to dissuade his friend through uncharacteristic stridence. As Walks Alone moved through the woods, it was painfully easy to remember the worried look on the man's face when he told him, "I will be back in a few days."

The journey had been spontaneous and rambling, as he moved from place to place with no other plan than to try to re-capture something, although he didn't know what that something was. He had climbed the mountain beyond the escarpment to once again stand high above the river, watching almost breathlessly as early spring began to fill in everything in the sweeping valley below. He had returned to the rock overhang where he had spent the first night of his vigil, sitting there for hours thinking about the bobcat and the deer.

He had made his way back to Lenapewihittuk, at a point more than a mile downriver from the escarpment, before deciding to move back up the hillside and toward a different destination. He had walked all the way to the place called Pocacuintink, the mountain where his mother and father had once gone to find plants at the request of Four Bears. He had spent a night there, lying by a small fire, wondering about his parents on the mountain on that long-ago day. Did Black Turtle's hand brush hers as they searched for plants in the undergrowth? Did Margaretha smile at him as they walked?

The terrain was much more rugged away from the river, and he had been restricted to the slow, interrupted pace that the forest would allow. At one point, he came upon a large chestnut tree that had been marked with white paint on its southeast side. Standing beside it and squinting into the distance, he could see at least two more trees that were marked similarly. He knew that the walkers had come this way more than six moons earlier, following a trail that stretched all the way to a time when his people would no longer live along Lenapewihittuk.

After that, he had wandered in the woods almost aimlessly, consumed by thoughts of the autumn betrayal and the smiling faces of Thomas Penn and James Logan at Durham and Pennsbury. He thought about what had happened since. The discontent of the Lenape had grown as more and more white people pressed onto the land after the walk, and the relationships between his people and the whites, and even his people and the Iroquois, had become severely strained. It was difficult for him to believe that heated confrontations hadn't boiled over into something worse. Life was tenuous and foreboding, a nearly constant sky of dark clouds on the front edge of a thunderstorm.

When the sun was directly overhead on the second day, he watched from the cover of trees as a handful of white men worked on a half-built barn in a nearby clearing. They were so focused on their work that they paid little attention to the ground around them. They probably didn't notice that new grass was filling in a circle where the wigwam of Talks For Us and Looks Back had once stood. They probably didn't see the last remnants of the black circle that had once been his family's fire. Surrounded by the scent of newly felled logs, they could not have known that the air around them had once danced with the smells of roasting venison and dried strawberries. They might have known that the ground had once been a Lenape village, but the generation following them would not, and the generations after that would neither know nor care.

Unnoticed by the white men, he drew back into the trees and turned toward Lechauwitank. Even walking along the tree line above the river, rather than on the easier but more dangerous path below, he knew that he could be back at the escarpment before nightfall. As he made his way home, he would occasionally see the path below and be reminded instantly of walking there with Talks For Us, with Four Bears, with His Spirit Watches, and with Nutimus and his men from upriver.

He came upon a stream that rushed over the top of the hillside, churning in small clouds of white and silver as it dropped toward the river below. He could have made his way across, but he decided instead to follow it for a while, satisfied that he had plenty of time to get back to the escarpment, and more than happy for the company of the sounds of the swollen stream.

The stream bent away from the river for a short distance before turning back on a path almost parallel to it. As he continued through the trees, the ground began to rise gradually, eventually cresting in a gentle ridge above the creek. He stopped at a place that was about a half mile from the point where the creek tumbled over the crest of the hill. It was peaceful and welcoming, and he sat down to take in the warm feelings that it inspired in him—feelings that had evaded him for a long time.

His decision to spend the night there made little sense. The sun had only dropped halfway to the horizon, and the day still held more than enough light to see him home, but he was all too content to stay, in part because he was reluctant to go back to the escarpment. Being there would only put him with people that he would eventually lose, just as he had lost everyone else in his life. It felt better to be alone. He had been named for his reluctance to be led by the hand by anyone other than his father, and once Black Turtle had died, he had insisted on walking unattended. Even the affection of Looks Back and concern of Talks For Us had not been enough to make him grasp an extended hand. And now, through the events of his life, he had grown into his name with a completeness that few could have predicted.

Sitting quietly above the creek, he watched the small world below as it changed in the afternoon light, small animals and birds passing through it like characters in a timeless story. Everything they did—each movement in the air or along the ground—had been done countless times before, yet he experienced them now as if seeing them for the first time. He felt fully alive; his senses peaked, as if he had been in a sweat lodge for hours.

He had already examined the things that his uncle had given him many times, but now he looked at them in a different way. He knew that his grandfather had traded with a European for the amulet, and that he had then passed it to Talks For Us, but he wondered about the place where it had been made and the person who had crafted it. He wondered if the artisan had ever thought about how far it would travel or where its journey would end. Touching each bead in the wampum belt, he smiled with the awareness that it told the story of the parents of Black Turtle and Talks For Us. His uncle had told him the story many times, always tracing his index finger along each of the rows as he spoke, and now Walks Alone whispered a small prayer that a time would come when he himself would tell the story to others.

Walks Alone built a small fire not far from where he had sat for hours, and as he lay watching its orange flames, he asked the Great Spirit to give him a message in journey, vision, or dream—a message, should it be according to the Great Spirit's will, that would be for him rather than someone else. "This one time," he said to the fire, "I ask that you tell me what you want for me."

Somewhere in the blackness of the night, long after the fire had burned down to nothing, he felt himself rising gently into the air. As he looked down, the ground below slowly transformed into something he did not recognize. The creek had been reduced to a gentle trickle of water, nearly narrow enough that a grown man could stand with a foot on each side of it. Beyond it sat a great dwelling that reminded Walks Alone of the house of Onas at Pennsbury. Immediately below him sat another large building. It looked like a barn, but it had large windows that spoke to a different use. There were other buildings as well, smaller but with the same peaceful quality about them, and there were fenced-in areas where the figures of animals stood quietly in the darkness. He strained his eyes, trying to see everything more clearly as he rose higher and higher into the air, but before long all of it was obscured by thin gray clouds that moved across his field of vision like weakening puffs of smoke.

The buildings were now far below and no longer discernible. In one direction, Lenapewihittuk made its never-ending journey to the south; in the other, the forested hills stretched into the night as far as he could see. He was certain that it was impossible to ascend high enough to see where they ended.

Then, as an answer to his prayer, the Place with No Words appeared in the sky in front of him. It was massive and imposing, filled with countless dwellings, any one of which was countless times larger than the house of Onas. It seemed to be big enough for every person, and the family of every person, who ever lived, and even big enough for all of their ancestors and all of their descendants. He was still far from it, and yet it was immense. He could only wonder in amazement what it would look like if he were standing at its doors.

The vast mountains behind it were covered with snow so bright that Walks Alone could only look at them momentarily before averting his eyes. Beyond the mountains, arcs of lightning coursed in great horizontal flashes that seemed to illuminate the face of heaven itself. True to the name by which Four Bears had called it, it conveyed its message in silence: *That which lies beyond is more powerful than anything that can be imagined. In it, there is only being.*

As Walks Alone began to float back toward the ground, the thought of leaving the Place with No Words—and a message that had finally come for *him*—filled him with profound regret. He wanted to stay. Northing that might happen below could ever compare to what he had experienced there. But, as if his wants were of little matter, he eased further and further down, and deeper and deeper into a dreamless sleep.

He awoke with the sun, the images of the Place with No Words inextricably lodged in his memory. He went to the stream to splash water on his face, trying to fully rejoin the physical world, but even the cold water was not enough to shock away the emotional remnants of his journey. They walked with him as he went to find food. He hoped to find berries or an edible plant, or if he was lucky, an unaware fish. Leaving his blanket behind, he walked upstream.

The morning was bright and blue, the nearly perfect beginning of a spring day. He moved quickly through the cool air of the woods as the sun began to peek above the tall trees that overlooked the river to the east. Where the woods were open, the light fell gently through the canopy, brushing his shoulders with the first of its warming rays. He felt exhilarated, even hopeful, for the first time in days.

Walks Alone was foraging in an area of undergrowth when he heard the voices. They were not close, but they were definitely moving toward him. He moved into the brush where he could observe without being seen by anyone who might pass by.

The voices grew closer, and, within a few minutes, three Iroquois men appeared a few hundred feet away. They were moving quickly and confidently, talking in normal voices, obviously not concerned that they would be seen or heard by anyone—white, red, or otherwise. He wasn't sure what they were doing, but he knew that they weren't hunting, since they would have frightened off any animal long before coming into contact with it. At first, he was concerned that they might find his blanket and the remains of his fire, but he quickly determined that if they stayed the same distance from the creek, they would pass by both.

When he was satisfied that they were well downstream, he left the cover of the brush and headed back along the edge of the hill to his small campsite. Once there, he quickly retrieved his blanket and re-traced his steps through the trees. Before long, the ground sloped down to where it was almost level with the creek. The trees were not as heavy and there was almost no undergrowth, so he was able to move quickly. Suddenly nothing seemed as important as getting back to the escarpment. He stopped briefly to drink from the stream, kneeling down to draw the cold water to his lips in cupped hands. When he stood up, he saw a young Iroquois standing by himself only yards away.

Walks Alone could see that he was probably just a few winters younger than himself, and afraid. He didn't know what the Iroquois was doing there, but Walks Alone could sense that he was concerned about being alone. Perhaps he had become separated from the other three men; perhaps he was trying to find them. Walks Alone knew that there was no reason for this to become anything more than a chance encounter. Recent events, including the contentious walk of the three white men the previous autumn, had made a problematic triad of the Lenape, the Iroquois, and the whites, but things still balanced on a precarious edge, not yet beyond control. Even the festering discontent of the Lenape had not turned into anything other than heated arguments and occasional shouting matches. There was no reason for this to get out of hand.

But, in the moment that Walks Alone saw the man's brow furrow into a purposeful scowl, he knew that the situation had already gone beyond reason. Drawing his knife, the young Iroquois ran directly at him. Walks Alone extended his right arm straight out, hoping with the last of his hope that his offering of peace would alter this unwanted outcome. He waited as long as he could, but then he felt his hand move instinctively toward the bone-handled knife of His Spirit Watches. He had never killed a man with it, but it settled into his grip as surely as if he had used it to slay a hundred enemies. Rushing forward, one, three, five steps, he crushed into the torso of the Iroquois. He felt the man's knife plunge into his lower abdomen as his right hand thrust outward and upward, the entire length of his knife's blade burying in the man's left lung. Drawing away from Walks Alone, a hideous gasp whistling from his mouth, the Iroquois staggered two steps and collapsed onto his back, his head thudding sharply against the ground. Blood spurted from the middle of his torso for a brief moment and then stopped.

Walks Alone lurched backward, dropping his knife on the ground beside him. As he pressed his hand against his own abdomen, the warmth of his blood rushed out between his fingers. He tried to remain standing but could not. He dropped first to one knee and then the other, unable to do anything but give in to the lightheadedness and pain. He wanted to pull himself to a standing position, but instead of rising he fell even farther, collapsing awkwardly onto his backside.

The consequence of passing out was death, and he pressed against the wound in his abdomen trying to somehow fend it off. He tried to focus on the clouds drifting above the canopy, but the fluid in his eyes reduced them to little more than blurs of white. Wincing against the unbearable pain, he forced himself onto his elbows, turned his eyes toward the forest canopy, and spoke to the ambiguous patches of white that floated above it.

"Who will remember me?" he asked aloud. "Who will remember . . ."

* * *

Seated on the edge of the bed, Darwin watched his brother's poses in front of the full-length mirror on the back of the closet door. Reggie had a serious, almost mean, look on his face when he said, "Bitches like you." Then he adjusted his look, furrowing his brow just a little more, and repeated, "Bitches like you."

"Bitches like you," Darwin repeated automatically.

The front of Reggie's jacket was unzipped to the middle of his chest, open just enough to expose the handle of the official collector's replica of the Beretta M9 that was tucked in his belt. He watched it carefully, checking to make sure that it remained visible as he extended his arm and pointed at the mirror. His plan was that the plastic replica would be seen, but that it would never leave his jacket. He didn't want to hurt anybody or get hurt, himself. He just wanted to "Scare the livin' shit out of that bitch."

"Livin' shit . . .," Darwin said from the bed, unable to take his eyes off of his brother who had said the last piece aloud without realizing it.

Reggie stood there for the better part of an hour, rehearsing the final moment of the plan. If he had to take Darwin with him—and he was certain that his mother would insist on it—he would leave him in the car when he went into the museum. He would walk past the front desk to the back of the ground floor, and then up the steps to the second level. He would avoid walking through the central court, staying between the pillars and display rooms until he reached the corner where the new exhibit was housed. As he descended the three steps into the exhibit, he would look for someone from the museum staff—hopefully not the woman he had met before—whom he could ask about Grace Caufield. Then it would simply be a matter of unzipping his jacket, walking up to her, saying what he had to say, and escaping to the car.

"Ya can't write letters to bitches like this," he said to the mirror. "Ya can't even call them on the phone. Ya gotta get in their face."

Darwin didn't know who he was talking about. He hadn't understood from the beginning. He knew that Reggie was angry, but he didn't know why—or at whom. To him, the entire thing was a complete mystery—a mystery that had started with Reggie jumping up and down on the newspaper in the middle of the living room floor, and had gone as far as this pretend fight in front of the mirror. In between, there had been a confusing trip to that castle in the middle of town, but it had been more fun than he had expected, mostly because of the covered wagon in the air. "In their face . . .," he repeated back to Reggie, ". . . Gotta get in their face."

Reggie's anger had assumed a different form since that visit to the museum. It had transformed from violent outbursts about people in the media taking the side of Indians, and about college professors uncovering information about biracial relationships that occurred hundreds of years ago, into something more uniform and insidious. It had slipped into the mainstream of his hate, moving effortlessly in his bile like a dark, undefined swimmer.

When he allowed himself to think about it, usually as he lay in bed in the dark, Reggie felt invisible. Just as he couldn't be seen in the blackness of his bedroom, he felt as if he wasn't seen in the clear light of day. He hated his job at the gas station. He hated the women who talked on their cell phones as they handed him their credit cards, not even looking at his face. He hated the blacks with those ridiculous wheels on their cars, wondering if something that expensive could be paid for with food stamps. No one even knew he was alive, and other than a mother he despised, and a brother he had to drag with him wherever he went, he doubted that anyone ever would. In the dark, he shrank beneath the overwhelming burden of his hate, but out in the world he was content to hide behind its armor. What he wanted from Grace Caufield—the *Injun lovin' liberal media bitch*—was a look of fear, a look that said, "Yes, I see you, Reggie, and I am scared to death."

Reggie pointed at the mirror one last time and then left the room. "I have to go to work," he said to Darwin as he left. "Try to stay out of trouble while I'm gone."

"Stay out of trouble."

Five minutes after Reggie left, Darwin shuffled into the hall, past his mother's bedroom, and down the steps. When he reached the first floor, he kept shuffling, past the small dining room and to the cellar door. The open risers of the steps frightened him, inspiring images of boney fingers with long, bloodied fingernails reaching through to grab his ankles, and he descended the steps as quickly as he could. The dank smell of the cellar filled his nostrils as he moved across the uneven dirt floor and toward a wooden slat door on the far wall. He opened it cautiously. The string that turned on the single light bulb was in the center of the room, in the center of the blackness. The room had terrified him when he was younger, and it was only because he had gone into it so many times with Reggie that he could summon the courage to enter it now. Reaching into the darkness, he found the string, and a moment later the room was filled with a low, gray light. He knew exactly what he was looking for—the box that his father had shown him when he was a young boy; the box that had eventually become off limits at the insistence of his mother; the box that time had covered with a heavy layer of white grit; the box that contained the gun.

* * *

The three Iroquois men were sitting near the stream, talking and waiting for their young friend. He had drunk too much the night before, and had been in no particular hurry to move into the new day. Joking about his over-indulgence, they had left the campsite without him while he was off in the trees. Now, not wanting to descend the hill to the river without him, they waited impatiently, watching for some sign of him.

As they talked, one of them stopped mid-sentence, raising a finger and pointing toward the water. A body was floating toward them, face down in the stream. One of them jumped into the water, interrupting the body's measured journey toward the edge of the hill that overlooked the river. As he turned the body over, exposing the purple gouge in its abdomen, his fear that it was their friend dissipated in the immediate recognition that the man was Lenape. He looked back upstream, his mind racing with thoughts about what might have happened.

One of the men standing on the bank motioned to the other. "Go to find him," he said stoically, understanding fully that most of the possible outcomes were not good. Watching as his friend took off at a half run, he turned to the man in the water and said, "I have seen this man before. He is one of their medicine people."

The man in the water jerked away from the body instinctively, visibly concerned by what he had heard, but he held onto it with one hand, understanding that they were in a bad situation. "This is not good," he said without taking his eyes off of the body. "The Lenape will not like this, and the whites will pretend not to like it. It will be a difficult thing for our sachems."

"We must hide the body," the man on the creek bank said. "We cannot leave it where it will be found."

"But who will bury it?" the man in the water asked, implying that it would not be him. His friend understood both his question and his fear. Being disrespectful of another native or the ways of his people was very serious business; being disrespectful of a shaman was ground that neither of them wanted to walk. The man in the river looked around excitedly, hoping that a solution would present itself. A rock overhang a few yards downstream gave him an idea. "We will hide him under the rock," he said. "If anyone finds him, it will be a long time from now."

Guiding the body carefully, he let it float to a point below the rock and then pushed it into a narrow cavity that had been created by the spring waters. "Help me," he said to his friend, causing the man to join him in the water. Working together, they retrieved rocks from the bottom of the rushing stream and piled them against the body so that it would remain hidden for as long as possible.

"These will not keep the body here long, especially if the spring is wet and the waters are high, but they will keep it here for a few days. Then someone else will find him in the water."

As they piled the last of the rocks, they looked upstream to see both of the men they were looking for, one draped across the blood-smeared shoulder of the other. The two men got out of the water and the three Iroquois headed for the river with the body of their friend.

For a number of moons following, the three men would talk about the incident. They would speak of the regret they felt each time they saw the mother of their young friend; they would speak of what might have happened if they had not jokingly deserted him as he squatted in the woods; and they would speak of the fact that it had turned out to be an unusually dry spring, and that the body had most likely not been swept back into the stream for someone else to find.

* * *

Jeff Phillips had discussed with a number of people his plan to give the produce farm to the Lenape, and, as he had expected, had heard reactions ranging from "unbelievably magnanimous gesture" to "incredibly bad idea." He was particularly interested in the perspective of Seth Williams, the NAGPRA representative, and had waited to broach the subject with him until he was on the East Coast for the dedication at the Mercer.

Now, as they walked along the low ridge that followed the creek between the gathering barn and the bridge where the remains had been found, he laid out his plan for Williams, at least to the extent that it had been developed. Williams didn't respond at first, seemingly wanting to ponder every possible outcome before commenting on any one of them, and Jeff was content to let the walk pass in silence.

"This is a beautiful place," Williams finally said. "You're a very fortunate man."

"Very fortunate," Jeff agreed. "You may be interested to know that I've decided to keep buffalo—up here, along this ridge. Just a few of them."

"What prompted that decision?"

"I dream about them. I see them in . . . well, I see them in visions."

"You're even more fortunate than I thought. Visions are a profound blessing—the gift of the Great Spirit."

"Profound is a good word. Yes, I think I would agree with *profound*."

"And how long have you been having these dreams and visions?"

"It's difficult to say, but for a very long time. I came to understand in retrospect that milder versions of them—milder than what they are now, I mean—started a long time ago."

"What does that mean?" Williams asked, stopping to look at Jeff. "Are they more vivid now?"

"*That*," Jeff answered, "and they announce themselves in a more forceful way."

Williams said nothing. He resumed walking, his eyes surveying the ground in front of each step.

"I get this feeling in my chest," Jeff continued, "as if a hand is reaching into me from behind and pulling me inside out. I can't catch my breath."

"And then?"

"And then I lapse into vision. I may find myself in a completely different place . . ."

"Or time?"

"Yes, or time. Does that mean something to you?"

"Perhaps."

Jeff could sense instantly that Williams was hedging and he couldn't understand why. He was revealing something deeply personal to this man—his usually well-honed instincts had assured him that it was alright to do so—and now Williams was holding back, not saying what was on his mind.

"If you knew me better," Jeff began, "you wouldn't be hesitating right now. Please tell me what you're thinking."

Williams started to speak but then stopped, the words sticking in his throat. He started again. "I'm not proud of what I'm thinking, Jeff. It's bigoted and small minded, and it hurts to know that I am not above it."

Jeff knew that Seth Williams did not expect him to respond to so serious a prelude.

"In the traditions of my people, and of all aboriginal people, those who have such intense experiences are regarded as shamans. They are great healers, great seers. And . . .," he hesitated again, ". . . and they are poor, at least as far as material possessions are concerned. They are consumed by their spiritual nature. The outside world is of almost no importance.

"You are a rich white man. Whatever you want is no more than a moment away. One minute you decide to keep buffalo, and the next minute they are grazing on your property. I have been taught to believe that . . ."

"That it's not right?"

"Yes, that it's not right."

Now Jeff suppressed the desire to say what *he* was thinking, opting to walk with it for a while.

"Do you think I'm a bigot?" Williams asked, finally breaking the silence.

"No," Jeff responded, "I think you're human. What you're saying makes sense to me. I don't know what to do with it, but it makes sense to me." The words he had held back now came forth more easily. "I didn't ask for any of this. I didn't ask to be wealthy, and I didn't ask to have visions." He hesitated, struck by what he was about to say. "And I certainly didn't ask to feel the way I do about your people. Everything just happened."

"Nothing just happens," Williams observed solemnly, knowing full well that the answers to his own questions were wrapped in those same three words.

Jeff knew it as well, and he let the realization pass as easily as the water in the creek below.

"I'm not keeping buffalo, I didn't build the gathering barn, and I'm not offering the produce farm to your people because I'm making up ways to spend my money. Something is driving me to do it!" The inflection of his voice had risen with each word, and he was surprised by where it ended up. "Something is driving me to do it," he repeated more calmly.

Williams pulled in a deep breath and then exhaled it into the chilly December day. "You want to know how my people will respond to your offer?" he asked softly, bringing the conversation full circle. "You will walk uphill with this, uphill and into the wind. You will not be trusted; your motives will be questioned at every turn; and you will want to give up many times."

"But?"

"But I can tell that your heart is good, and when you say 'something is driving me to do it,' I can only answer by asking what I can do to help. So . . . What can I do to help?"

They walked past the bridge from which a truck had once dangled precariously, dumping its load of rocks into the creek below and exposing to the light of day something that had waited in the darkness for nearly three centuries. They walked all the way to the place where the creek eased over the edge of the hill in search of the river. *Uphill and into the wind.* Jeff thought to himself. *Nothing just happens.*

* * *

The formal dedication of the new Lenape exhibit was an unusual combination of enthusiasm and grace. There was an understandable excitement about it, especially on the parts of Grace Caufield, Robert Dawes, and Emily FitzRoy, but the excitement was tempered by a palpable respect for the subject matter.

A crowd of nearly two hundred people had gathered in the central court, its gray austerity softened by floor lamps that had been brought in for the occasion. Those in attendance stood in small groups, drinking champagne and eating hors d'oeuvres, some of them feigning worry about the over-indulgences of the holiday season.

Robert Dawes acted as master of ceremonies, standing on an inconspicuous podium to acknowledge the work of Grace Caufield and Emily FitzRoy, as well as the contributions of Dr. Leonard Henry, George Cameron, and others. He introduced the sitting president of the Bucks County Historical Society, who spoke briefly about the original exhibit on the sixth level and how it had been transformed into "Across the Millennia—The Lenape on the Delaware and Beyond." He also asked Seth Williams to say a few words, not as an official representative of the Lenape people, but as a man of Lenape heritage. And, in closing, he acknowledged both the amount of respect and lack of pretense with which the event had been planned.

There was a ceremonial ribbon cutting, after which people were invited to visit the exhibit at their leisure throughout the evening. Individuals, couples, and small groups socialized quietly, some in the central court, others in the exhibit itself.

The parking lot at the foot of the hill was almost full, so Reggie McCarthy was forced to park in a space near the end of the very last row. Parking so far from the building had not been a part of his plan, but it was not enough to deter him. He backed into the space, turned off the engine, and then turned the ignition key just enough to keep the radio and heater on.

"Now look," he said to Darwin. "I have to go in here for a few minutes. I want you to stay here and listen to the radio."

"Listen to the radio."

"I'll be right back."

"Right back."

Retrieving the plastic replica of the Beretta from the back seat and pushing the barrel under his belt, he zipped his jacket and repeated, "I'll be right back, Darwin. Wait here for me."

Darwin watched his brother walk between cars and up the hill to the museum. The entrance to the hulking building was brightly lit, making it appear to Darwin like the entrance to a cave in the side of a great mountain.

"Right back," he said to the windshield. "Wait here."

A song played on the radio, but the volume was turned down so low that Darwin could only hear the music. The words were lost to him. He started thinking about Reggie and wondering how long he would really be. Just how long was "right back"? Had "right back" already passed? If he was really going to be "right back," wouldn't he be back already?

"And," he muttered to himself, "the covered wagon is in that building. In the middle of that building. Hanging from the ceiling." He began to move his knees up and down, gently at first and then more vigorously as his agitation increased. "Right back," he said to the radio.

Darwin stared up at the brightly lit entrance. He thought about Reggie; he thought about "right back;" and he thought about the wagon in the sky above the central court. Without touching the ignition key, he left the car and headed up the hill.

Inside the museum, Reggie McCarthy moved along the corridor behind massive concrete pillars. He passed a room full of things that looked like they belonged in a kitchen, and then smaller rooms containing pottery and things made out of what looked like tortoise shell. At other times—and to other people—the artifacts in these rooms might have been of interest, but to Reggie in this moment they were all but invisible. At the end of the corridor, he stopped by a room full of printing artifacts, taking a deep breath as he unzipped his jacket part way. Then he turned and walked into the Lenape exhibit and descended the three steps.

There were only ten or fifteen people in the room, less of a crowd than he expected. Most of the others were socializing in the central court. A young man stood in the middle of the room, dressed in a blue blazer like the one the woman had worn when Reggie was in the museum at Thanksgiving. Relieved that he would not have to talk to her again, he headed straight for the man in the blue blazer.

Jeff and Dae were standing not far from the docent, talking with Seth Williams.

"Excuse me for a moment," Jeff said, "I want to speak with Emily about something."

Reggie was only a few feet from the docent when someone said something to him. He turned his head to see a woman smiling at him, her hand extended. "Welcome to the exhibit," she said. "My name is Emily FitzRoy."

Dumbstruck, Reggie stared at the woman's face. She was beautiful—tall and slender, with the presence of the supermodels he had seen on television—but there was something different about her, something that Reggie could not put into words. And she was looking directly at him. She wasn't talking on her cell phone like the girls who handed him their credit cards when he pumped their gas; she was looking squarely into his face.

Purpose draining out of him in a torrent, Reggie tried to speak, but all that came out was his mortifying stammer. "Gr . . . Gr . . . Gra . . ." He tried again, every aspect of his being shrinking with each movement of his lips. "Gr . . . Gra . . . Grace . . ."

"Grace Caufield?" the woman asked. "Are you looking for Grace Caufield?"

Through the mist of his abject embarrassment, Reggie watched the woman's eyes grow wide with fear. Confused and disoriented, he thought he could make out the form of a man arriving at the woman's side, but the man was not the reason for the woman's fear. That was being caused by something to his right—the tightly gripped gun that was rising into the air. He jerked his head instinctively, partly out of panic, partly out of fear, and saw Darwin standing beside him.

"Bitches like you . . .," his brother's voice droned.

"No!" Reggie shouted, grabbing his brother's arm as the sound of gunfire split the tranquility of the room.

Jeff Phillips staggered backward, the pain in his chest more amplified than ever before. The same hand tried to pull him inside out, drawing every ounce of air from his lungs. Only one thing was different. This time there was no vision.

THE BEGINNING

"Give thanks for unknown blessings already on their way."

— Native American saying

Epilogue

THANKSGIVING 2010

The baby awoke with a start and began to cry.

"I thought she might sleep through," Jill said, raising her daughter to her shoulder. "I'll get her a bottle."

"No," Harry said from across the circle, already heading for the kitchen in the apartment. "I'll get it."

"You've been up and down all night," Jill called after Harry. "First the firewood, now a baby bottle."

Dae looked over at Jill, silently hoping that she needed help with Lillian. "He likes it," she said, "and besides, he's not good at sitting still. He comes by it naturally."

Jill saw the look in Dae's eyes, the result of the comparison to Jeff, and handed Lillian to her.

"Dae," Hope began, "you haven't said much tonight. You're part Italian and part Irish. You must have dozens of family legends."

Dae smiled at the comment, gently rubbing the baby's back. "Not really," she answered, "at least that I'm aware of, but I guess I do have some things to add.

"The best thing about my family is that we all stayed in the same place. My brothers and sisters—there are seven of us—all grew up and stayed in the same place, at least while my parents were alive. I always thought that most families were like that, but I have come to learn that very few are.

"My dad was from a big family too, and they all lived in the same area where I grew up. Maybe it just runs in the family."

"Where are you from?" the woman to Dae's left asked.

"Not far from here—southern New Jersey. Jeff and I lived there when we were first married. That seems like a long time ago now." She turned her attention to Lillian, trying to distract herself. "My dad and all of his brothers lived there, and my mom's family was from the same area. They met after the war . . ." Interrupting herself, she added, ". . . well, their story was very much like others we've heard tonight."

"I remember when you and Dad first met," Hope said to Dae. "He was always talking about holiday gatherings with your family. He used to tell me that everyone came to them, and that they were crowded and noisy and sometimes chaotic—and that he loved them. I think part of him wished that his own family had been like that."

"I often felt the same way," Chick offered. "We all pretty much went our separate ways. When we saw each other at holidays, it was usually after one of our families had spent ten hours in the car or traveling through crowded airports. We always had a good time, but someone always had to go to a lot of trouble to be there."

Harry reappeared with the bottle, handing it to Dae.

"It was never that way with us," she said, offering the bottle to the baby. "We all just got together. Everyone brought food;

everyone brought beer or wine; and we just had a good time. And when it was over, we all got in our cars and drove home. At the time, I doubt that any of us ever thought much about it."

"That's so unusual," Scott said. "I don't think I know a single family that's like that today."

"We were fortunate," Dae answered, "and now, on those occasions when we don't see each other at Thanksgiving or Christmas, I think we miss it. At least I do."

"Perhaps," the woman to Dae's left started, "your husband saw this property as a place where he could bring his family together."

"I don't think there's any question about it. It was extremely important to him."

"And," the woman added, "that same desire may have been at the core of his decision to give the land across the road to our people."

"It was part of it. Jeff was driven by a number of things, including a sense of place. He always talked about a refuge—a place that would always be there for his family. He never had the resources to create it, often because of his own decisions, until we won all that money. That opened the door for him—the door to his refuge. And once he began to create it, he never really stopped."

"And why," the woman said, "do you believe he decided to give the land to us?"

"I don't know if it was a decision, if there was a moment in time when he thought, 'I'm going to do this.' I think it evolved. He knew very little about the Lenape—or any other tribe for that matter. In his entire library he had exactly two books about Native Americans." Remembering her husband's jokes about the two books, she pulled in a deep breath.

"Finding the remains in the creek bank changed all of that. It brought people into our lives—people who investigated the possibilities with us. As we learned more about the history of your people, something began to grow in all of us, and it just kept growing. Jeff was very caught up in it. In many ways, I would have been more surprised if he *hadn't* done something like this."

"But," the woman interjected, "it has never been proven conclusively that the remains are Lenape, or even that they're *half* Lenape."

"I know." She paused, raising Lillian to her shoulder and patting her back. "Once, after Jeff told us that he was buying the produce farm, he and I were talking about his decision. We talked about the remains and the possibility that they might not be Lenape. He looked right at me and said, 'If we end up at the right place, does it really make any difference?' I think, for him, it was a leap of faith."

Watching Dae's face, watching her tend to the baby as she spoke, and listening carefully to her words, the woman sighed audibly at the phrase. "I can only say," she answered, "that some of us are extremely grateful that the Great Spirit saw fit to help your husband—and all of you—make such a leap."

A hushed silence moved around the circle, each of them sitting with the words, many of them thinking about their part in the "leap of faith."

"And what about you?" Dae asked the woman. "The two of you have been so attentive, so quiet. You're great listeners."

"We have been taught to be great listeners. It's part of our culture. Sitting in circle, listening to stories, listening to what the old ones say—it's all very important to us.

"You all know my name—Winifred Rowe Carlson. My Delaware name is Waits By The Water, but the young ones in Bartlesville call me Dr. Winnie. I think I like Dr. Winnie best.

"I am descended from the Lenape who lived here many generations ago. My ancestors refused to be anything but Lenape—they refused to inter-marry with the Europeans—so they had to follow the Trail of Tears. The stories of my family go all the way back to the Muskingum River valley in Ohio, many years ago, but I must admit that many of them are just that— stories, some of which have become what you call family legends."

"And I," the man sitting next to her said, "am John Carlson. To my people I am Cannot Stay On The Ground, which is difficult to say in the old language. My ancestors, you see," a wide smile stretched across his face, "did not know about pilot's licenses. I have heard some old ones try to say my Delaware name, but it always comes out awkwardly."

"It was a difficult decision for us to leave Bartlesville," Winnie offered, "and perhaps one day we will return—but when we heard about the possibility of living here, on the storied river of our people, we were drawn to the opportunity. We believe that it is the will of the Great Spirit that we are here."

"We are gratified," Scott began, "that you have decided to come. Nineteen people have accepted our invitation. We look forward to having them with us as soon as the initial tract of houses is finished."

"And the business?" John asked. "How is that going?"

"We took the opportunity to make some improvements while we were planning for the houses. And Mr. Meyers has been very helpful. We'll make a small profit this year, and I think the company will do even better when it's operated by young, energetic people with a direct stake in its success."

"Mr. Phillips was very wise in making the business a part of this opportunity," John suggested. "It is often difficult for our people to find work. Being a part of a self-sustaining business is something many of them have only dreamed about. I expect it to be very successful."

"I know that some of the people are from Bartlesville and Anadarko," Winnie observed, "and I have heard that there are some from Wisconsin."

"Yes," Jill answered. "The family from Wisconsin has a son who has been diagnosed with Asperger's. They're hoping that his needs will be better served here in this setting."

"I hope that I can be of some help to the boy," Winnie replied, "and I'm sure that being here will help once he adjusts to the change. I think it will help all of us once we've adjusted."

"When will you be moving?" Hope asked the couple.

"As soon as housing is available," John answered. "As soon as we can move in." He stared into the fire as he added, "We owe all of you a great deal."

"You don't owe us anything," Jill responded. "Dad's vision was to create an opportunity. He provided the place, but each person who comes here will be making his or her own way. They'll be buying their own houses, participating in their own business, and sending their children to their own school. My father was adamant that the government not be involved. He didn't envision an Indian reservation; he envisioned a home for the Lenape." She hesitated, thinking that she may have said something inappropriate. "I mean, for the Delaware."

"It's okay," Winnie added. "In fact, it's more than okay."

"While we're speaking of Jeff," Dae said, "I want to share something with you. I found it a few days after he was . . ." She drew in a deep breath. ". . . a few days after he died. I don't know when he wrote it, and I'm not even sure I understand it completely, but I'd like to read it to you."

After carefully handing Lillian back to her mother, Dae drew a folded piece of paper from the pocket of her jacket. "This is what he wrote:

We strive impatient on the circle's edge
To find the path that is our destiny;
Insisting that the way be iron sure,
And arrow-straight in its trajectory.

At the center the Great Spirit watches
As we move back and forth between each choice,
Walking in both foolishness and wisdom,
And waiting for the guidance of its voice.

Tangled up in ropes of hesitation
And willing not to take faith by the hand,
We pass by the road intended for us
To walk again the circle's endless strand.

Nothing's found behind the door unopened,
And nothing waits along the road untrod;
Life may wander out along the circle,
But paths of destiny lead straight to God.

"I thought you would enjoy hearing it." Dae re-folded the paper and returned it to her pocket.

"It sounds to me," Winnie said softly, "as if he's describing the medicine wheel."

"That's exactly what he called it: 'Medicine Wheel.'"

Winnie rose to her feet, clapping her palms loudly. "So," she said, looking at the children, "who would like to hear a story?" They responded gleefully, only too happy for an activity intended just for them. "Who can find the picture of the turtle above the fire?" It was between the places where Harry and Hope were sitting, and it didn't take the kids long to locate it. "Well," she continued, pointing at the image that had been pounded into relief in the copper, "I want to tell you a story—a story about a time when the earth was completely covered with water. There was not even a single place where a person could stand . . ."

* * *

APRIL 2011

Dae Phillips awoke from a sound sleep around five-thirty. At first, in the months following Jeff's death, the silence of the main house had been comforting to her, but over time it had become something else—something too massive to comprehend, something without an outer boundary. When she lay in bed at this hour of the morning and listened carefully, she was certain that she could hear the gentle cascade of water on the water wall at the foot of the steps. She had slept enough, but it was too early to get up. Nothing else, and no one else, on the property would be stirring for at least another hour. She lay on her back, staring at the soft shadows on the ceiling and thinking about Jeff.

It had been more than a year since the shooting at the Mercer Museum, and she had only dreamt about him a handful of times. A series of nightmares had haunted the nights of that December, as she was forced to relive the senseless death of her husband on the night of the dedication. He had died for absolutely no reason. His death had been absurd and seemingly without purpose. Hatred had stepped forward to be his executioner, but it had refused to show its own face. It had hidden behind the tortured innocence of a man-child who existed only in the troubled shadow of his brother. And hatred had even refused to kill her husband straight on, looking directly into his face. It had chosen instead to strike an accidental blow—a cruel, maddening turn of happenstance.

She took in a deep breath and released it to the room, allowing herself to drift into meditation. She turned away each thought that tried to enter her consciousness, preferring to seek the solace of emptiness. Perhaps, if she were empty enough, she thought, something else would rush in to fill the void. It was in that emptiness that she fell back into sleep.

In her dream, she was a bystander—the unobserved witness to the movement of a single figure on the path along the river. She squinted into the sunlight, trying to see who it was, but the glare was too bright for her to make out anything other than the dark figure of a man. Drawn to it by a primal urge, yet disturbingly reluctant to get too close, she tried to awaken, but the dream held her, as if steeled by its purpose.

The figure walked below the face of a steep hill, down which a rocky stream fell to the river. But instead of dipping under the road at the bottom of the hill and dissolving into the canal, the stream made its relentless churning way directly to the river. In the shadow of the hillside she could see the figure clearly—the figure of her husband.

His gait was quick and measured, as if he was traveling somewhere, but he carried nothing to indicate that. He was just walking.

As she watched, she saw another figure, this one walking toward Jeff from a distance, moving out of the shadow of the trees. Each of them entered the bright sunlight, becoming nearly invisible in its glare. She squinted so intently that it made her face hurt, so intently that she feared she would have to abandon the figures to the light. Then, as if an unsaid prayer was answered just as silently, she was standing on the path, watching each of the men approach. Jeff continued at his steady pace. From the other direction, a young Indian walked with equal resolve. He was tall and muscular, his head shaved clean except for the black scalplock that hung halfway to his neck. He wore an amulet, a striking half moon of bronze that framed him in majestic portrait. At the waist of his leather leggings, a bone-handled knife shone brightly in the sun.

As the two men stopped to face each other, Dae stood in awe of the scene. They could not have been more different. One was an anachronism, the other out of place, but she wasn't sure which was which. One was contemporary but older, the other was younger but from a long-ago time. One was red, the other, white, yet they seemed to be exactly the same—brothers defined by the color of a common destiny.

The young Indian listened intently as Jeff began to speak. It seemed that he recognized English, but not what Jeff was saying. He said something in response, but neither the language nor the words made any sense to Jeff. They resorted to a crude sign language, trying to make themselves understood through simple gestures of their hands, but their efforts quickly proved futile. They stopped trying simultaneously, as if finally content to be nothing more than travelers on the same path.

As they moved away in opposite directions, the Indian suddenly turned and said something to attract Jeff's attention. Then, as Jeff turned around to face him, he added, "Wanishi."

Jeff recognized the word immediately. So did Dae.

"Wanishi," the man repeated once more before turning and breaking into a half run to the south.

The two men had not looked at her. She was certain that they had not even seen her. She was there to receive a message, a message that something had been passed to her. For the rest of her life she would define it as purpose, as destiny, as a connected cause; and regardless of which of those things it was, she would embrace it completely. And as she awoke to the dawn of another promised spring, she could feel its heart beat in unison with hers.

* * *

Jill Martin stepped out of her house and into the April day. A slight chill hung in the air, but she knew that it would dissipate quickly once the sun crested above the trees. As she neared the fence of the main paddock, she pulled pieces of apples and carrots from the pocket of her windbreaker, watching the horses move toward her from their favorite spot by the fountain. "Morning,

Bandit," she said, patting the horse's neck. A wisp of dust rose in the air above her hand. "You need to be brushed. Maybe when I get back from the produce farm." She passed out the apples and carrots, ensuring that each of the horses got its share.

She headed for the barn, taking what had become her usual route around the paddock, toward Hope's house, and past the forsythia. There she paused, as she always did, at the two graves. Modest stone markers stood in the early morning shadows, quietly anticipating the arrival of the morning sun. One was etched with the initials JHP, the other with a picture of a turtle. "Good morning," she said quietly.

It was impossible for Jill to stand there without remembering the service for her father. It had been appropriately brief, little more than the burial of his ashes in the presence of his family and a few friends. At Dae's request, the ashes had been placed in a small wooden box that was exactly like the one in which the remains of the man in the creek bank had been interred. Robert Dawes had guided the ceremony, also at Dae's request, and he had done his very best to ensure that it was as informal and welcoming as possible. "People always say 'he would have wanted it that way,'" Dawes had observed, "and in this case it's quite true. Jeff would have been uncomfortable with anything else."

"Good morning," a voice called from behind, and Jill turned to see Dae walking along the fence, her coffee mug clutched in her hands.

"Hi, Dae. Did you sleep well?"

"Uh-huh. And you?"

"I'm having some strange dreams, but none of them are about Dad. I fall asleep every night hoping he'll come to me in a dream, but he never does."

"He will. Believe me, he will." She took a sip of coffee before adding, "And how are you feeling? Any sign of morning sickness?"

"No, I'm fine," Jill answered. "I really don't have time to be anything but fine. There's so much work to do."

"If it gets to be too much, you have to say so." Even as she said the words, Dae knew that Jill would never say so. It just wasn't in her makeup.

"I have to get going," Jill said. "I'll talk with you later."

"You know," Dae responded, "I've been thinking. The main house is too big for me. I just rattle around in there. Maybe you and Edward should move up there, or Hope and Scott. One of your houses would be more than enough for me. Heck, for that matter, the Creek House . . ."

"Dae," Jill interrupted, "you belong in the main house. Edward and I wouldn't feel right moving up there, and I doubt that Hope and Scott would either."

"It just seems like such a waste."

"I'm sure it will all work itself out in time. It hasn't been all that long since . . ." She stopped mid-thought, taking a last look at the grave markers as she walked away.

Dae knew that she was just being brave. It had seemed like a very long time to all of them.

Jill walked to the horse barn where she kept the strange-looking vehicle that had been fashioned from a refurbished golf cart. As she pulled out of the barn, she reminded herself that it would probably be a good idea to make another one. Movement to and from the produce farm had increased dramatically.

She followed the service road along the crest of the ridge, stopping briefly by the area that had been fenced off for the buffalo. They grazed quietly, including the cow that was waiting to give birth. She stood by herself at the far end of the pasture, and Jill knew that if buffalo were anything like horses, it wouldn't be long before her calf was born. Continuing along the ridge, she passed above the bridge where the accident had occurred. It seemed so long ago, she thought as she drove, that Roberto's cousins had made the errant turn onto the bridge, setting the events of the past two years in motion. She could still see them standing in the creek bed, motioning wildly; she could still see the look on Roberto's face when he first saw the skull.

Two hours later, she was talking with John Carlson and Fred Meyers in the loading area of the produce farm. Meyers had only been back from Florida for a few days, but he was already fully re-engaged in the farm's day-to-day activity. Carlson had taken a particular interest in the operation of the farm and had been spending quite a bit of time working with Meyers. Watching the two men work together, Jill suspected that they might become good friends.

A truck pulled up to the loading dock outside and Roberto jumped out of the cab, gesturing wildly. "Mees Jill, you have to come quickly! Eet is very exciting!"

"What's very exciting?" she asked. "Is everything okay?"

"Yes, eets fine! The buffalo, she has given birth!"

Jill rode back with Roberto, followed in a car by Carlson and Meyers. As they approached the fence above the ridge, she could see that Dae, Hope, and Valeria were already there.

The calf was less than thirty minutes old, but it already stood nursing in the bright day.

"Should we call the vet?" Jill asked, as they all stood transfixed by the new arrival.

"I'm not sure why," Dae said stoically. "There were buffalo long before there were veterinarians. I'm sure they both know what to do."

It was clear that she was quite correct.

"So," Dae began, bending down to talk with Valeria. "Do you like the baby buffalo?"

Valeria shook her head from side to side, clear in her response.

"Why not, Honey? It's so cute. Why don't you like it?"

The child looked through the wire fence, focusing on the calf in the distance.

"It's not like the one in my dreams."

Dae was surprised. She had never heard the child speak about her dreams, let alone her dreams about buffalo. "Why?" she asked. "What's different about it?'

"It's not white."

Appendix

The titles of the following books are mentioned in this novel:

Son of the Morning Star by Evan S. Connell

Bury My Heart at Wounded Knee: An Indian History of the American West by Dee Brown

Handbook of the Delaware Indian Language by Scott Hayes Wenning

Excerpts from the following books are included in this novel as part of the historical record:

Indians in Pennsylvania by Paul A. W. Wallace, copyright Commonwealth of Pennsylvania, Pennsylvania Historical and Museum Commission, Harrisburg, Pennsylvania

David Zeisberger's History of the Northern American Indians (1910), which is the property of the Ohio State Archaeological and Historical Society, Columbus, Ohio

Excerpts from *A Collection of Papers Read Before the Bucks County Historical Society*, printed for the society by B.F. Frackenthal, Jr., of Riegelsville, Pennsylvania, are included in this novel as part of the historical record. They are housed at the Easton, Pennsylvania Public Library and include:

Our Stone Age by John S. Bailey of Buckingham, Pennsylvania, read at Pennsbury on July 18, 1882

Prehistoric Man in Bucks County by Charles Laubach of Durham, Pennsylvania, read at Pipersville on July 19, 1892

Lenape Stone by Rev. Dr. John F. Lundy of Philadelphia, Pennsylvania, read at Neshaminy-Warwick Presbyterian Church on July 27, 1886

Exhibits pertaining to the Lenape, or Delaware, people are located at, or were at one time located at:

The Mercer Museum in Doylestown, Pennsylvania

The University of Pennsylvania Museum of Archaeology and Anthropology, Philadelphia, Pennsylvania

The Museum of Indian Culture in Allentown, Pennsylvania

The Ellis Island Immigration Museum in New York, New York

In some instances, quotes from these exhibits are included in the narrative of this novel as indicated.